Willow

Sam Bateson

Willow | Sam Bateson

Copyright

Self-published by Sam Bateson in 2020

Published on Kindle by Sam Bateson on Amazon Kindle Platform in 2020
Published by Sam Bateson, printed by Amazon in 2020

Copyright © 2020, Sam Bateson

Sam Bateson has asserted his right to be identified as the author of this Work and may use this Work in accordance with the Copyright, Designs and Patents Act 1988.

This novel is a work of fiction. Names and Characters are the products of the author's imagination, and any similarity and resemblance of any persons, living or dead, is entirely coincidental.

All rights reserved. No part of this publication may be reproduced, stored in a retrieval system, or transmitted in any form or by any means, electronic, mechanical, photocopying, recording, or otherwise, in any form currently or hereafter developed, without the prior permission of the copyright owner

www.sambateson.wixsite.com/sambateson

Willow | Sam Bateson

Copyright 2
Willow 8
  -1- Missing Person 10
  -2- Next of Kin 16
  -3- The Spider's Web 25
  -4- Person of Interest 31
  -5- The Blue Stitch 41
  -6- Character Witness 47
  -7- Fallen Angel 55
  -8- Embargo 58
  -9- Remains 65
  -10- The Ninth Year 73
  -11- Outlived 77
  -12- Suspicious Activity 80
  -13- Identity 83
  -14- Mummy and the Strange Man 89
  -15- Vigil 95
  -16- The Ghost 103
  -17- The Seven Bells 107
  -18- Cause of Death 111
  -19- Bloody Knuckles 116
  -20- The Rendezvous 121
  -21- Muddied Waters 125
  -22- The Night Owls 132
  -23- Circumstantial Evidence 137
  -24- Forgive Me, Father 145
  -25- The Rumour Mill 150
  -26- Reviewing the Evidence 153
  -27- Broken 159
  -28- The Tin Man 166
  -29- The New Headmaster 169
  -30- Cracking the Bottle 172
  -31- Love Thy Neighbour 181
  -32- The Second Service 187
  -33- Into Her Own Hands 194
  -34- Incriminated 199
  -35- The Confession Tape 205
  -36- He Had a Heart 211
  -37- The Devil Among Us 220
  -38- Scaling Back 223

-39- The Smoking Gun...	229
-40- ...and the Hand That Holds It	235
-41- The Victim	245
-42- Open Wounds	249
-43- Bravery in the Field	261
-44- No Going Back	264
-45- The Other Half	268
-46- Case Closed	272
Need Help?	**281**
More from Sam Bateson	**282**

Willow | Sam Bateson

For Charlie,
who helped me to be better.

Thanks to Katrina Gill, for her superb artistry on the cover art for this book.

Thanks to Chris Hayton, for his scanning services.

Willow | Sam Bateson

Willow

Willow | Sam Bateson

-1-
Missing Person

The day was becoming night, steadily, slowly. The crisp, orange glow of that sunset was becoming the sort of inky black that signalled midnight during the summer months, and as that night time came, the problems of the day vanished, ebbing away as those serious thoughts of the residents of little Heathestone morphed into something new, something pleasant, as some dreams tend to be.

A few bucolic houses scattered here and there were the only sign of some form of civilisation; and between those relaxed semi-detached dwellings lay some vague hint of the green carpet of grassy fields that stretched far and away beyond towards the city.

So far away, though, was that great, bustling metropolis of Liverpool, that its own occupants had no idea that the small town of Heathestone even existed, let alone had a free and bustling life of its own; so insignificant was it, that the place seldom had anything noteworthy occur in any of its history. It was a most unremarkable place, though one as vivid and bustling as any town you can think of.

All but some of the residents of that little town had gone soundly to sleep; assuredly resting their weary bones, cleaning their minds of the junk that the previous day had clogged them with. These were the lucky ones; those whose minds could rest at but a moment's notice. But others were not so fortuitous; some were still hard at work, unable to distract themselves from the activities that had bled over from the earlier hours of the day, like the toilsome work-doers at the small, seldom used Heathestone Police Department. Where others had gone to bed, certain members of the public service there were still busying themselves, almost autonomously; filing paperwork, manning the cells – as superfluous an activity as that was to do – and making the ever-helpful pots of tea and coffee for the few remaining stragglers of the service.

Coffee was not, however, on the mind of a particularly tireless resident of that quietened station; Phillips was more concerned with filling out the day's reports. The professional life of the Detective Chief Inspector was something of a minimal affair, and so this work was what he lived for. So preoccupied was his mind with it, that he rarely considered anything beyond those duties to which his career was directed.

Nothing much distracted him from that work of his; it required minimal effort, however, so infrequent was it that any difficulty arose that required the intervention of the police. But no matter how engrossed he was in his work, he was always welcoming of a friendly visitor to his office; it was around a quarter past midnight when Fiona appeared in his doorway – she was ready for home, and assumed that Phillips was too; she did not think that too much work had come to him that he should have to stay so late, but the duties of a Detective Inspector such as herself were much less administrative than his own.

She knocked upon the door of his office twice, such was her custom, and pushed the door gently aside; a feeble glow from the office beyond spilled gently into the dimly lit room that constituted the Criminal Investigation Department. Her desk was cleared for the day, and her desk lamp was the only source of dim illumination. Framed in the doorway, she paused for a moment, waiting for Phillips to look up from his work. With a single word, he regarded her with a cool assurance;

"Enter." He said; and she did.

"Don't you ever stop? We've only had three arrests today. I can't believe it's taken you hours to do the forms." She replied, walking into the office towards him. He looked up from his papers and glanced at her for little more than a moment. He chuckled and then reverted his attention to the forms.

"They do if you intentionally write in mistakes just as an excuse to start again." He waved a hand at a nearby cluster of recycling bins; within, she espied the remains of about two dozen documents, all near-identical. She paused, staring in amazement;

"You're meant to save paper, you know?" She said, almost sarcastically.

"That's why they're in a recycle bin and not the rubbish." He glanced at her again and smiled a subtle grin. She chuckled by way of response and moved to sit opposite him at his desk. For a moment, she surveyed him with a silent appreciation; he continued to write in silence, the sound of his pen scratching on the paper the only disturbance. She scoffed, though this did not distract him.

"How do you do it?" She began, ponderous. He looked up and made an inquisitive noise. "I mean, everyone else went home an hour ago. Most have gone to the pub, but you? You, I just don't get." He set his pen down on the desk and regarded her.

"Do you want to know the best part of having my own office?" He began; she tilted her head inquisitively. He patted his hands rhythmically on the papers, then got up from his chair, which moved across the carpet with a dull sliding sound, and moved across the room to a nearby bookcase. It was made of three shelves, with a set of small double doors at the very bottom. The top two shelves were adorned with books of varying topics, from official police documentation to fictional novels and biographies, each of his own choosing. The lowest shelf was stacked as normal, though each spine was tilted at an angle, such that there was a large space at one end. She had never noticed this before, but as he approached the bookshelf, she espied it at once. She was about to ask him about this space, but her question was answered before she had chance. From the dim gap, he produced a bulbous and grand-looking carafe, with a glass stopper in the narrow spout. The liquid within was brown and filled it by about a half. He swished the carafe in her direction. "I've got my own little pub right here." He smiled, and with his free hand he removed the stopper. Placing it down, he used his once more available hand to fish out two short glasses from the same shelf before moving back to the desk. Fiona chuckled, and watched as he placed the glasses down on the desk.

"You know, that's against code?" She said.

"But I clocked out an hour ago, with everyone else, so I'm on my own time." He retorted, filling one of the glasses before moving on to the other.

"A mere technicality." She chuckled. "So, you've got the drink, now all you need is the people, you'll have a buzzing little local in here." She said, leaning across the desk, which was now apparently functioning as a bar of sorts, to take one of the generously portioned glasses of whiskey.

"It's the people I can't stand." He said, chuckling as he poured out the second measure. "No offence." He added, seeing her expression, one of faux indignation.

"None taken, I think. You're a miserable bastard, you know that? No offence." She replied.

"None taken." He laughed. Then he held his own glass aloft and tilted it towards her, throwing himself down into the chair as he did; it reclined only slightly as he relaxed into it. "Here's to miserable bastards, even on their birthday." He said. Fiona started, nearly dropping her glass back onto the desk.

"Birthday?" She coughed, having already half swallowed a dose of the drink. He nodded. "Oh Christ, I'm so sorry, I forgot." She said, shaking her head into her free hand.

"Don't worry about it." He replied, waving a hand. "You know I hate birthdays anyway. Or did you forget that too?" He chuckled, by way of lightening the mood. She smirked, and raised her own glass towards his, which was still half in the air. The two glasses came together with a resounding ringing sound and the liquid within sloshed carelessly. The two then brought the drinks to their lips.

"This round is on me, then." Fiona chuckled, swallowing the swig she had taken. Phillips laughed too, nearly casting his drink onto the floor.

Fiona finished her shot with remarkable speed, even with most of it having already been drunk before the toast; as she finished, she brought the glass down onto the table. A few drops of liquid still remained inside, but these were near invisible against the dark of the office. She raised herself to her feet, pushing the chair across the carpet as she went, and moved for the door.

"Please get finished up in here. Life's too short to waste on filling out paperwork." She warned, before turning back.

"Someone has got to do it, though." He replied.

"Yes, but you've already filled out the same form a dozen times." She said, pointing to the recycling bin containing his evening's work. He merely glanced at it before turning back to his drink, which was now almost completely consumed.

"Go home, Anthony." She said, commandingly.

"I will, I will." He replied. "I promise I'll just finish this up and get gone. See you tomorrow." He said, finally finishing his drink and returning his attention to the form he had been filling previously. She moved through the door, but was stopped by his voice again; "Oh and Fiona?" She turned to him. "Never call me by my first name again." He said, almost jokingly. She chuckled, turned again, and closed the door as she left.

Phillips was alone again.

His mind returned to the form; the drink had energised him, and he vowed to finish the document quickly so as to leave the place forthwith. But little did he realise, his night was only just beginning.

It was about a quarter of an hour after Fiona had left that his phone began to ring; across the room, the thing began to chime on its pedestal. Highly unusual, was it, for it to be calling out to him at such an early hour; by now it was about half past midnight.

Somewhat surprised at this sudden interruption, he started and looked over to it; he regarded the thing for a moment, half thinking that he had imagined it; but then it cried out again, then a third time. In an instant, he was to his feet; he was somewhat reluctant to answer the call, for he knew that it could only be being made because of an emergency. That was not something he wanted to deal with at that time in the morning.

He picked up the phone in his right hand and raised it to his ear. He did not think to speak first, but upon hearing no voice at the other end of the line, he decided to engage in conversation first.

"DCI Phillips, Heathestone CID."

"Phillips, it's Theresa. Sorry to call you so early." Came the reply. Phillips recognised the voice before she said the name; it was Dispatches, across the hall. It would have been easier for her to have come to him directly.

"Morning, Theresa, what's the story?" He replied, his mind now alert. "More to the point, what are you still doing at work? I thought the out-of-hours workers were coming in?" He said, glancing at his wristwatch.

"Yes, I *am* the out-of-hours for the week. Listen. Got a job for you. Could be an all-nighter." She sighed. Phillips returned with a similar exasperated noise of his own. "Call in from a Mrs Sarah Greene, she and her husband have come home from a dinner and their daughter is missing and unreachable. Mis-Per is Willow Greene, seventeen. Sarah is worried." She said, concisely. Phillips pondered for a moment.

"Any details; last known location, witnesses?" He asked.

"So far nothing. She says she's been around the streets for most of the day and nobody has seen her, neighbours and the like." She continued. Phillips furrowed his brow and rubbed his forehead with a lean finger.

"What's the address?" He asked, and she told him; it was one familiar to him. "Right. I'm on my way, thanks Theresa." He said, somewhat frustratedly. With that, he hung up the phone and set it back down into its pedestal. It chimed as it resumed charging.

Phillips paused for a moment, contemplating his next move. He had it in a moment, and he took up the phone once again; dialling the local police code, and keying in 124, he was through to Fiona in a moment. She did not pick up immediately, as the continual, rhythmic sound of the ringing tone met his ears before finally, a dense rustling sound and the sound of an engine.

"What is it, Phillips? Don't tell me, you ran out of paper for your forms?" She chuckled, her voice but a barely audible sound above the gentle thrum of the engine indicating that she was on speakerphone and driving.

"This is a work call, not pleasure. Got a missing person report, seventeen-year-old female. It can't wait, I'm afraid I'm gonna have to ask you to come back in." He said. Suddenly her voice took up a more serious and alert tone;

"Shit. Okay, I'll be there. What's the address?" She asked, and he told her; as to him, it was familiar to her. "I'll be there in fifteen. Does Grisham know?" She asked.

"No, he's next on my list. We'll probably be on a skeleton crew tonight, so brace yourself. Could be a long one." He warned. At that point, he ended the call and held it level in front of him for a moment, whispering something to himself. He knew Superintendent Grisham would not appreciate a call at that time of night, but he had no choice. He dialled the home number he knew Grisham would be reachable at and lifted the phone to his ear once more. Somehow, he thought that night was going to be the start of something he would not enjoy.

-2-
Next of Kin

It was a little after one o'clock when Fiona and Phillips arrived at the Greene household; an unassuming place it was, scarcely any more ornamental than the other houses it shared the little street with. So quaint in appearance was it that one could consider it quite desirable, with little window boxes brimming with colourful blooms. All curtains were drawn, but a solitary window, evidently the sitting room, was illuminated by a strong light from within.

"Grisham is already here, I see." Fiona said as Phillips drew up along the pavement. She pointed a finger towards another car adorned with *POLICE* decals. Phillips drew the handbrake tight and switched off the engine, pulling out the key as he did.

"We don't even know if the girl is missing yet, it's early days." He said, fishing out a pen and notepad from the glove compartment on the passenger side; Fiona sat out of the way. "I want you to have a snoop when we get in there, see if there's a sign of anything." He resumed, inking down the date in particularly neat handwriting on a fresh page of the notepad.

"Sign?"

"Yep. We need to start ruling things out as soon as we can; if she's run away, there will be clues. If we find nothing, well. We'll start looking at other scenarios." He withdrew his seatbelt and forced open the door. Fiona followed him, pausing as she closed the door to allow Phillips time to come around the car. Directly he arrived, she followed him up the garden path to the front door.

Phillips cleared his throat, and seeing that there was no doorbell, rapped on the glass of the door three times. There was the sound of movement from within.

After a few brief moments, the glass became illuminated, backlit by a warm lamp that had been switched on beyond it. A shadow danced about on the glass, like a hologram, moving and distorting as the figure moved towards the door; it paused at the glass for a moment. Then, the sound of a latch being pulled, and the door swung slowly inwards. It was a female who stood before them, gaunt and with red, puffy eyes; the half-cleared remnants of tears glimmered in the leaking streetlamp-light.

"Sarah Green?" Phillips asked. She sniffled and nodded.

"Good morning, I'm DCI Anthony Phillips of the Heathestone CID. This is Detective Inspector Fiona. May we come in?"

"Is there any sign of her yet?" Sarah gasped through a sob. Phillips turned to Fiona, who by now was close to his side.

"We'd like to ask you some questions first, if we may come in? We'd like to help." He said with a friendly tone. Sarah looked from the tall Phillips to Fiona; she did not say a word, but stood aside at last to let the pair through. They stepped past her, and at that moment another figure appeared at the far end of the hallway; it could have been none other than Gary, Sarah's husband. Phillips assumed as much and turned to him for a moment; everyone's faces were concealed by sharp, harsh shadows from the lamp that stood on a squat table nearby. Sarah had now closed the front door. Behind Gary was the kitchen, and to his left was a set of stairs with a short bannister, the lip of which Gary was gripping; he swayed, as if dazed.

"Good morning, you must be Gary?" Phillips said, regarding him for a moment; Gary nodded his head deliberately. Sarah inadvertently pushed Phillips aside in a bid to return to the sitting room. Gary swayed an arm in the air, indicating for the others to follow, and they did.

The sitting room was tastefully adorned; family photographs cluttered the mantlepiece of the fireplace, and the coffee table was littered with floral decorations and magazines; it seemed like a cross between a lounge and a waiting room, but that was evidently their preference.

Grisham was sat on a spacious, plush sofa along the wall beside the door. He was glancing at the magazines on the table, though none of them took his interest. At sight of his cohorts, his mood altered; suddenly he was alert and to his feet.

"Phillips. Fiona, good to see you." He said, gesturing them with an outstretched hand. They nodded by way of acknowledging him, then glanced to the door as Gary swayed through it towards them.

"Please, have a seat." Gary said, waving towards the sofa. Neither Fiona nor Phillips sat. "Would either of you like a drink?" He continued. Phillips replied in the positive, requesting a strong coffee with no sugar. Fiona shook her head. Gary then slipped through the door and headed for the kitchen.

"Gary and Fiona are here just to go over the situation, get an idea of what has happened so far. In these kinds of situations, it's always best to have multiple eyes looking at the same information." The Superintendent began, turning back to Sarah and sitting on the sofa once more.

"May I call you Sarah?" Phillips said, gently. "Or would you prefer Mrs Greene?"

"No, Sarah is fine." She muttered, not looking back at him.

"I can wait for your husband to return?" Phillips continued. Sarah shook her head. "Would you mind if my colleague had a look around the house? Purely investigatory, you understand, I'll stay here and ask some questions." He continued, turning to Grisham. At that, she glanced up for a moment. Phillips was unsure if she understood him, or if she would reply; evidently, she was traumatised. Eventually, she nodded.

"Yes, please, feel free." She said, speaking at last and, for the first time, clearly. Phillips turned to Fiona and nodded knowingly. She walked from the room. Now at last, Phillips took seat, and produced his notebook and pen from his pocket.

"Now Sarah, when did you last see Willow?" He asked. She paused for a long moment, and brought a hand to her face, wiping a solitary tear from her face. She sniffed once and then sighed an answer;

"It was yesterday morning, probably eight forty-five, nine o'clock. Somewhere in that time." She said; Phillips scribbled down her answer in clearly legible handwriting.

"So she's been missing for over twenty-four hours? You didn't think to contact us sooner?" Phillips said, confused; Gary mumbled something.

"We wanted to see if she would come home. When it got to this afternoon, we thought it was unusual that she hadn't yet." Sarah said.

"Where did you last see her, this property?" Phillips continued. He would pick up on that detail later. She nodded. "Where did she say she was going?"

"She was going to school. It's five minutes down the road." She said, quietly. As Phillips wrote down her answer, Gary appeared in the door behind him.

"She would never go anywhere without telling us where first. She was good like that; this is very unlike her." He said, loudly; he entered the room as Phillips swung around to see him; his voice was louder and somehow more grating than his soft appearance would have conveyed. Phillips took the steaming mug of tea from his outstretched hand.

"Could she be out with friends, would she have been in

touch with them? Phillips replied, taking his first sip of the drink. He started, slightly, for he had asked for coffee; the taste was vastly different, and it took him by surprise. Gary sighed, and threw himself down onto the sofa beside Phillips, who did not raise the discrepancy.

"We know her friends really well. Nobody who we've spoken to have heard from her since they finished school." Sarah continued, forcing Phillips to swing around again. His neck began to ache.

Fiona, by now, was familiar with the layout of the Greene household, so thoroughly had she inspected it – at the head of the stairs was a small bathroom, tastefully decorated with black and white tiles; directly next door was a master bedroom with a large double bed against a far wall. Lamplight spilled in through the window above the headboard; it was evidently the master bedroom. Opposite the bathroom, at the far end of the narrow landing space, was a spare bedroom, which was nothing but a clutter of old pieces of furniture and discarded clothes. She dared not dig her way through that quagmire for fear of injuring herself on some unseen danger. That left the final room, next door to the spare bedroom; having found nothing in the other rooms, she figured that her last chance would be in here.

She gently pushed the door open – it was already ajar – and took in the room, as much as the dim light would allow. She could just make out the outline of a single bed, the sheets of which had been made up hurriedly that morning and undisturbed since. Beside it, a desk stood with one leg somewhat shorter than the other three, kept steady by the use of a number of discarded notebooks beneath the foot. A few items were scattered on the desk, a collection of items one would expect to find on one belonging to a teenager: a variety of charging cables, pens and so forth. In the middle, with the lid half closed, was a slender MacBook, tethered to the wall by a white cable. Fiona only saw these things once she had turned on the light.

More details leapt out at her now that she could see clearer; the carpet was plush, with a circular, white rug protruding from under the bed. She filed into the room, careful not to disturb any of the books collected on floating shelves hanging from the wall; doubtless they had been flung off before.

She strode through the still air of the room, and espied a silver, articulated lamp on the desk; evidently it could swivel from whatever was on the desk to over the bed. Other than these small trivialities, the room was scarcely adorned; it certainly was not what Fiona had anticipated. She approached the desk, hoping that the notebooks stacked on it would yield some results; she packed these into a wide, slender leather bag she had the gumption to fetch along with her. Then she moved to the MacBook, which was sat slightly askew; it was then that she noticed that there was no phone set down anywhere; it certainly was not to be found plugged into the charging cable that was stretched across the desk to the right of the lamp. Highly unusual, she thought, if a little stereotypically.

She unplugged the MacBook from its charging lead – for she knew there were countless spares stored at the station – and slid it into her messenger bag.

"And you're certain Willow said nothing about where she could be after school, anything at all?" Grisham implored to the ever more secretive Sarah; she merely shook her head and began to weep again.

"I already told you, I'd have remembered." She sobbed.

"Yes, she never went anywhere without telling us first. We remembered every time. Well, *she* usually remembered." Gary continued, pointing a finger to his wife. Phillips continued to write into his notebook, in part to keep up the illusion of investigation; in the last ten minutes, he did not ascertain any useful information.

"What about on the phone, have you tried calling her?" Phillips asked, delicately.

"Well of course we fuckin' have!" Gary snapped at last. Phillips started; Sarah merely sighed a wretched annoyance before continuing to cry. "It's the first thing we did." Gary continued, calmer now.

"Where have you both been tonight?" Grisham interrupted in an attempt to realign the conversation. Sarah turned her head, sharply.

"What are you trying to say?" Gary hissed, suspiciously.

"I'm trying to say; 'I want you to tell me where you've been tonight', it's simple enough. Only I suspect you're inebriated." Grisham continued, calmly so as not to exacerbate the situation. For a time, neither Gary nor Sarah said anything; they did not look at one another, simply into empty space.

The sound of footsteps on stairs floated in through the open door. Fiona followed them at last.

"Thank you for letting me look around your home." She began. "It's nice." She resumed, smiling a reassuring grin. Gary merely scoffed, forcing himself up from his chair; he stalked past her and vanished into the dark kitchen. All eyes besides Sarah's followed him; Phillips settled his back upon Fiona, who merely stood in some combined state of amazement and annoyance. She turned back into the room.

"Well, is there anything else you'd care to mention?" Phillips asked, realising they were not going to get a straight answer to his previous question. "Anything at all? It's important." Phillips continued; he faced her directly now and had closed his notebook. Fiona approached, almost in silence. Sarah shook her head. "Any idea of her whereabouts?" Phillips resumed. Gary stormed back into the room.

"You want to figure out her whereabouts? You talk to Harry. Harry Baines, the little scum." He hissed, annoyed. Sarah sighed, audibly again.

"Harry Baines?" Fiona asked, confusedly.

"That's the guy." Gary seemed to harbour such a discontent for the person that even as he spoke, he began to turn a shade of red that was alien to both Fiona and Phillips, even though both of them were accustomed to enraged individuals. "He's *very good* at the whereabouts of women. You want to talk to him." Phillips flipped open his notebook and jotted down the name. The scratch of his pen was louder than a pin-drop, but that was simply because it was the only sound in the entire house.

"What makes you think Harry is involved, what would he have done that would cause your daughter to go missing?" Grisham asked.

"Kidnap, harassment, there's nothing I wouldn't put past that kid." Gary slurred. Grisham sighed and turned to Phillips, who at last flipped the cover back over the pad. He tapped the cover with the tip of his pen.

"Well thank you very much, you've been very helpful and given us plenty to go on." He said at last, with a courteous smile. He glanced from Sarah to Gary, each as aloof as the other. He continued; "I understand how difficult this must be for you, you've been very cooperative." He resumed, once again looking from one parent to the other; still, they did not respond.

"Well, thank you both. Leave it with us, we'll be in touch." Fiona said, with a similar smile. "And thank you Gary, we'll check in with Harry." She assured him; he scoffed again, slightly and rose to his feet once more.

"I'll show you out." He said, with a more relaxed tone than

he had been using before; evidently, he had calmed down. Phillips regarded him with a cool thoughtfulness, before looking past him and into the kitchen; something unusual had caught his eye;

"Just a minute," he said, raising a hand and standing. Gary looked alert. "your back door, it's latched?" He continued. Gary swung around.

"Eh?" He muttered, moving into the kitchen; Phillips was past him in a moment. The back door was wooden, and painted blue on the inside; outside was white.

"Get the light." Fiona said as she, Phillips, Grisham and Gary moved into the kitchen, almost at once, somewhat clumsily.

"What's up, what are you on about?" Gary hissed, almost upon Phillips. He brushed him aside and set his eyes upon the latch; it was damaged.

"Get that light on!" Phillips hissed. In the gloom, he could just make out the outline of the latch, broken open. The stationary component was torn from its mounting, and one screw lay somewhere unknown; a splintered screw hole was all that indicated a previously attached component. Phillips tried to turn the latch but found he could not; it was locked. More to the point, he established that it had been broken from the outside. "Gary, I'm afraid your house has been broken into." Phillips said, calmly and almost to himself. His fingers probed a large split in the wood, which ran in a long, jagged line from halfway up the door to the very bottom. Gary sighed, knitted his brow, and forced his fingers onto his forehead. "Fiona, the light, dammit!" Phillips continued, startling Gary, who looked up in alarm; Fiona was stood by the opposing door and was clicking the switch on and off; but no illumination filled the room. The light was broken.

"I wondered why it wasn't working." Gary said; evidently, he had tried it already, but no light was afforded to him.

"No wonder," Sarah began, jolting the group with her suddenness; "the bulb has gone." She continued, pointing at the light. Sure enough, there was no lightbulb in the fixture; just an empty, purple lightshade.

Gary looked alarmed.

Phillips looked bemused.

"You haven't had a visit from an electrician today?" Fiona asked at last, entirely seriously. Sarah shook her head.

"There's no reason why that thing should be missing." She hissed. She glanced at Gary, who offered no explanation.

"Well it isn't our biggest issue right now." Phillips began, moving from the kitchen at last. "We have enough to be moving forward with. We'll be sending our forensic team in the morning. For now, I recommend you don't touch anything in the kitchen." Phillips continued.

"Wait, forensics? Why?" Sarah spluttered.

"Because a barged down door adds a wrinkle to this situation, we need to get to the bottom of it." With that, he swept past the parents; the others followed him from the kitchen and into the hallway, for it was accessible both from the lounge and the kitchen and headed for the front door. "We'll be in touch." Phillips resumed, turning in the doorway, causing his little following to stop abruptly in front of him.

"Thank you for your help, officers." Gary muttered, as Grisham swept past him, followed by Fiona; before she was through the door, she turned to Gary.

"Sorry, I meant to give you this." She said, handing Gary a small piece of white card; several black letters and numbers were printed on it. "If you hear anything or have any questions, call that number. That's your point of contact with us. Gary took the card and regarded it closely; by the time he was done, Phillips was at the end of the path, gesturing with his hands as he spoke to Grisham. Fiona was heading out, so he closed the door with a soft click.

"What do you make of that then?" Phillips said, fishing out his notepad again.

"In my professional opinion? Very strange." Grisham replied.

"In mine, too." Fiona concurred. Phillips turned to her, quizzically but in a manner she recognised as being tested. "Well for one thing, I don't believe a man can spend that much time in the kitchen and one, not notice that the door latch was busted, and two, that he didn't find it strange that he had absolutely no light source." Phillips raised his eyebrow. "I don't know if they are, but it's like they're hiding something." She continued.

"Yes, they didn't seem keen to tell us where they've been tonight." Grisham agreed, scratching his head.

"You're good at finding things though," Phillips said to Fiona; "what did you come up with?" Fiona hoisted the messenger bag aloft.

"Notebooks, probably diaries. And a MacBook. Could be a motherlode." She said, with an officious tone. Phillips nodded approvingly. "What do we know about Harry Baines?"

"Not much. Just his name. But, it's a lead, something for us to go on. I'll run his name through our database, see if we have anything on him. Tomorrow, I want you to go through that laptop to see if there's any clues." Phillips said, closing his notebook and gesturing to her with it.

"Keep me informed. I'll be on mobile if you need me." Grisham said, glancing at the pair of them with rhythmic perfection. With a nod made in unison, the trio set about their business.

-3-
The Spider's Web

Phillips burst into the office and found it a hive of activity; far different now than when he left it that morning. The criminal investigation department team had moved in for the day, and Inspectors were busying themselves with their assigned cases; phones rang, voices chattered, and the smell of coffee filled the air.

He swept through, making sure to avoid the piles of paper which sat over the edge of desks in surprising abundance. There was the occasional 'hello' called his way, and he returned them when he heard them; he was polite that way.

Fiona sat at her desk; it was closer to his office than the others. The MacBook sat in front of her, the screen alive with windows and apps. Her eyes scanned one window, upon which blue and grey text bubbles were scattered; she was reading messages sent between Willow and a friend. She did not notice that Phillips had entered, so overpowering was the sound of activity around her.

"Fiona!" Phillips cried by way of catching her attention. She looked up in an instant. "What have you got, and don't say 'nothing'." He said. Fiona started, and beckoned him over.

"Phillips, glad you're here. Come and see this." She said. He complied, and rushed over, suddenly energised by the good news that a search had yielded results. He was by her side in an instant, and in another, he had drawn a chair over from the adjacent desk; it was unoccupied, so he supposed the owner would not mind the absence of the chair. He peered over her shoulder, glancing at the screen.

"Okay, what have you got for me?" He asked, breathlessly.

"Take a look. Willow has a huge group of friends, one thousand, three hundred and two to be precise. At least, that's Facebook friends. But she only seemed to talk to about a dozen or so." As she explained, she pulled up the relevant messages with relative ease and speed. 'Lookie here." She pulled a particular group chat Willow had been a part of; it contained three recipients, Timmy, Gemma and Stacey. Willow too. "Listen to this." She cleared her throat, then pointed to the screen.

She began to transcribe the messages:

07/03/18
3.43pm

Gemma:
So, that creep followed me home again.

Willow
What, again?

Gemma
Yeah, him and Mustafa. They followed me all the way back, I've had dad looking to see if he's still there.

3.44pm

Timmy
And is he?

3.45pm

Gemma
No, I think he's gone. I'm sure I keep seeing that camera peeping through the bushes at the house, though.

Stacey
Sleep with the curtains shut tonight, lol

Gemma
This isn't funny, Stacey, I'm really fckn scared of him.

Timmy
Tell Mr Shaw?

Stacey
Sorry, jesus xoxo

Willow
Mr Shaw won't do anything. He's too scared of Harry

Gemma
That makes two of us…

"Well, it seems Harry has form." Phillips said, sighing. He dropped the collection of papers he had been clutching down onto the desk in front of her. "Harry Baines. Known to the police. So 'known', in fact, that it's a surprise we don't invite him to the Christmas parties." Phillips said as Fiona rifled through the sheets.

"So how come none of us have heard of him?" She asked, confused. Phillips chuckled.

"Because most of Harry's offences are minor, petty crimes and the like." He replied. He drew the papers towards them and fished out a sheet marked with a yellow tab that protruded from the top of the stack. "I thought the name was familiar, though, I'd heard about his little problem with this Gemma already, here." He handed the sheet to her; in the top corner, a mugshot of the boy; unkempt hair, chiselled face; his appearance did not surprise her.

"*Charged with harassment, lewd behaviour and invasion of privacy*. He seems like a wonderful boy." She said, glancing at the charge sheet.

"That's not all. I talked to Mr Worth, the Headmaster at the school Willow and Harry both go to. He tells me Harry's father left him several years ago, before he was Headmaster. I think I'm gonna go and talk to Mr Worth in person today, see if I can find anything else out."

"What do you want me to do?" Fiona asked, folding her arms and leaning onto the desk.

"Unfortunately, this is nothing I didn't know already; Harry is a bit of a misogynist." Phillips said, pointing at the screen. "What else you got?"

"Take a look at this." Fiona replied, swiping across the trackpad with ease; in a few taps, she had brought a new set of messages to the fore; this time, there were no replies. "These were sent about three months after that last chat."

Phillips read the messages aloud, and at speed.

12/06/18
00.48am

Willow:
I miss you, when are you coming home?

09:45am
Willow
…?

Willow
Why are you ignoring me still?

13/07/18

Willow
How are you, I haven't seen you for ages? Come home, it's not the same without you :'(If you won't come home, I'm going to join you, please don't make me do that.

These messages continued over the course of another month. Phillips, realising that to read all of them would take the better part of a day, turned back to Fiona.
"What do you think to that?" Phillips hissed, so as not to be heard by the others in the office. Fiona responded in a similarly hushed tone.
"I think she was in a bit of denial."
"How so?"
"Look." She scrolled the chat screen back a number of weeks, then pointed at the screen; it was the last message Stacey had sent;

04/06/18
3.56pm

Stacey
Sorry Willow. I'm so sorry to do this to you. But I'm going away, and I don't think I'll ever see you again. I love you. But here isn't where I want to be anymore xxx

"When I've compared it to her other messages, it seems different. Somehow, it's more eloquent, more well-thought out. That's not all, look at the next message." Said Fiona, pointing at the screen; he read it out loud.
"'I can't believe you'd do this to me. I thought what we had was special. Why would you go away? I'm so sorry that you feel like you have to, but I would never want you to go. Remember what we said, 'you go, I go'?' What does that mean?" Phillips quizzed, turning to Fiona, his arms out in front of him.
'Well I think I know what it *could* mean, but it was two years

ago. She can't have gone through with it." She said, cryptically.

"You think Stacey took her own life?" Phillips said.

"I did a bit of digging. Stacey's body was found in a ditch out of town. Death ruled as a suicide." Fiona whispered. Phillips raised himself to his feet.

"Right, well let's not jump the gun, we're connecting things that aren't connectable yet. She's only 'missing'." Phillips said. He turned to leave, but Fiona stopped him.

"Wait, there's something else." She said, extending an arm; Phillips swung around. She tapped open a web browser, which had been minimised for her convenience; a long list of web addresses sprang to his eyes; all different kinds of sites; Facebook, Twitter; but more interestingly…

"What's that one?" Phillips asked, pointing at a string of letters; "*Peace of Mind Paternity*? Whatever was she doing getting a paternity test?" He asked, standing upright and rubbing his chin with two fingers.

"I'm not sure. This isn't the only one, either. Look." Fiona swiped up on the trackpad with two fingertips, sliding the addresses up and off of the screen. More results were rendered, innumerable clever names for paternity tests that were far more cheerful than they had any right to be. "She was clearly on a roll with the paternity tests. Might be worth asking Sarah or Gary if they knew anything about it?" She continued, pausing.

"Maybe. Right now, it can wait. You keep snooping, see if there's anything else you can find. I've got an appointment with Harry Baines." At that, Fiona started.

"You found an address?" She asked, closing the laptop lid. She positioned herself in an inquisitive manner and looked up to him.

"Mr Worth was graceful enough to give me his address and a bit of a character profile. I'll need all the help I can get." He said ominously, turning slowly. "In the meantime, I want you to go to the Greene's, see what Forensics has got to say. Grisham is already en-route." He said; she nodded.

"Is Harry a person of interest then?" Fiona asked.

"Everyone we speak to is, Fiona. I don't trust anyone." He then stepped towards his office, far more convincingly this time;

"That a skill?" She called after him.

"Damn right." He shouted in reply, much to the surprise of the other bodies in the room.

-4-
Person of Interest

The Sun was rising even as Phillips left the police station. With Harry's information in hand – what limited amount of it there was; there seemed no record of him anywhere, he did not seem to have an online presence, bank accounts or anything of that sort of thing.

Hopping into a spare police car, he glanced once more at the address; it was somewhere on the outskirts of town. He was not looking forward to meeting this boy; he did not expect a confrontation, but he had to be careful not to become incensed, as was so easily achieved when meeting the kind of person Harry sounded like.

The house was somewhat tricky to find; though he knew the streets supremely well, he had apparently not heard of the little alcove of land the address was found on. When he eventually found it, perhaps an hour or so after leaving though having travelled no more than a mile or so as the crow flies from the station, Phillips was at once amazed at the isolated dwelling; it was accessible only by a long driveway, with a deep woodland surrounding it; it was not a grand house, nor was it destitute. It was merely a small bungalow with a muddy white façade; all of the windows had blinds that were lowered; even at a distance, Phillips could tell that a great number were snapped and bent into total disrepair. Even the driveway was damaged, with great potholes that virtually swallowed up the vehicle's wheels as it went. He drove around the driveway as it arched in a circle in front of the house; all around, tall hedges stood as pawns before the tall trees beyond.

The yellow door was chipped and stained where the paint had seen better days, though the frosted glass that formed the top half of the door was surprisingly well-maintained and in relatively good condition. Phillips approached on foot, unsteadily traversing the rickety wooden steps to the porch, before approaching the door; he hardly dared to touch the door for fear that it harboured untold years' worth of germs. With some reluctance, he balled his fist and rapped against the door with his knuckles; the knock rang out in a hollow fashion, as though the door itself was paper thin.

There came no noise from within; for a few moments, he believed that nobody was within, such was the gulf of time between his knocking and his repeating the gesture to hopefully get some attention. Peering through the glass, he became aware of some faint music coming from within; he had the vague idea that that was why nobody was answering, and so he knocked a third time, louder now. Still no reply.

He finally took it upon himself to enter, though he realised that with a lack of a warrant, he had very little right to. He felt that if he could explain to whomever was within why he had done so, then they would understand. So, he gripped the doorknob, which was loose and chipped in places, and turned it; the door fell open in an instant, for it was either unlocked or incapable of being locked. Judging by the rough exterior of the rest of the house, Phillips favoured the latter explanation.

The inside of the house was very unusual; the walls and floor were clad with wooden planks, polished to such a shine that nearly blinded him. Some unusual notion befell him as he looked about; had he accidentally wandered into a house in a small American town? Had he somehow stepped back to the eighties? For a moment, he was disoriented, for the place was nothing like he had ever seen in Heathestone before.

A long, tattered rug stretched from the porch, in which were tossed half a dozen shoes or so, all the way along the hallway, passing four doors on its way to the kitchen at the far end. He followed it, as if the rug was a one-way direction stretching out in front of him. He gripped his messenger bag close to him to prevent it striking several delicate-looking items that were positioned atop a lengthy sideboard.

"Hello? Is anybody home?" He called over the sound of some light pop song playing in the distance. No reply came to him; he moved through the hall and noticed a number of photographs hanging in clean frames upon the wall. They were of two parents and a small child. He moved his face close to see in the dim light that was quite inadequate to see with. He took in the features of the mother in the photograph; she had smooth skin and was dressed in a tasteful, soft pink jumpsuit, though the colour could have been a result of the exposure to light.

"Hello, can I help you?" Came a voice, somewhat irate; Phillips turned around and faced the sound; framed in the kitchen door, he saw the same woman, though she was drastically different. No longer was she smooth and supple, but instead she had become haggard and aged. The photograph must be very old, he thought. The lady was obviously leaning back to see through the door. Her frown was just visible between the soft, short hair that dangled in front of her eyes.

"Good morning, I'm sorry to intrude. I'm DCI Anthony Phillips of Heathestone CID, I'm here in relation to a missing person case." He said gently, smiling reassuringly. Her scowl did not vanish, even as she straightened her posture and continued whatever it was she was doing on the worktop.

"Who's reported him missing? It's quite rare for him to stay the night here." She said, to his confusion.

"'Him'?" Phillips stepped through to the kitchen and found she was cooking a hearty breakfast of bacon and eggs; the toaster hummed away to itself on the counter. Phillips stomach immediately began to growl like a dog.

"My son, Harry?" She said, turning back to her cooking. "He's very rarely in this house. But he always comes home for his breakfast." She said, smiling and raising the frying pan slightly from the hob.

"And where is Harry now?" Phillips asked, turning to her.

"Just out. He goes from time to time. Who reported him missing?" She said, virtually in one breath.

"Oh, nobody, he isn't the one missing. It's, uh, Willow Greene, she hasn't been seen some time." He explained, keeping details just vague enough.

"And what does this have to do with my son?" She asked, turning the temperature beneath the frying pan down.

"We believe he may help our enquiries." He said. Before she had a chance to reply, he spoke again; "I wonder, do you know when Harry will be home? I'd like to ask him some questions."

"I think any minute. He has a long-range nose." She said, smiling.

"Excuse me?"

"He can smell his mother's cooking. He'll be home soon enough." She said, whimsically. Phillips contorted his face into a frown.

"Yes, well until then, I wonder if I could have a look around, does Harry live here, or otherwise have some personal space? A bedroom?" Phillips asked. He moved over to her as she fished the bacon from the frying pan.

"He doesn't spend that much time here anymore. A couple

of times a week, he'll sleep here, in his room. It's down the hall, first on your right. Please feel free to have a look. I'm Louise, by the way." She said, reassuringly and turning to him. She offered to him a slim strip of bacon, but he refused with a smile, despite the protests from his stomach. She plucked it from her fingers with her teeth and chewed on it in an eccentric manner. He smiled nervously, and then swung about, leaving the kitchen once more.

He walked curiously down the dark hallway and took in the smell of cooking, though he realised it would do his mind some good to try and ignore it.

Harry's door was as inconspicuous as the rest; a simple, wooden surface with the same sort of knob as he found on the front door. He gripped the bronze knob and turned it; it was cool beneath his fingers, evidently unused for some time. He pushed the door and it fell away from him with a minimum of effort. The room beyond was dim, though sheets of golden light filled the air, illuminating a mist of tiny dust particles that swayed and hovered in the turbulent tumult his opening the door had created.

He found the place to be in remarkably good order; the bed was made with fresh sheets, and a pile of ironed clothes lay on top of the duvet. The carpet, however, was old and worn; a path from the bed to the door was faded into the fibres. There were few furnishings to speak of, save for the bed; a tall cupboard stood obstructing the window, the curtains for which were undrawn and half-ripped.

There was no desk or chair; not even a lamp. A light on the roof was draped in cobwebs, and he scarcely imagined that it was functional.

He opened the cupboard door and saw only a handful of clothes; perhaps three or four different shirts and several pairs of trousers, all of which were muddy and torn. At the bottom of the cupboard were two small drawers; he opened one and found it full of socks and underwear, all of which were unpaired and almost thrown in, such was the jumble of them. The other yielded more positive results; it contained a tangle of cables, perhaps for a mobile phone or other such accessory, and a few small, flimsy cardboard boxes with discarded silver foil in them which Phillips dared not to touch.

Beneath all of this was a hardcover book of sorts, thick

bound and soft. Phillips carefully scraped all of the refuse aside and slid the book from its hiding place. It was torn and broken in places, but it was otherwise clean; a few loose photographs poked out with bent corners here and there, indicating to Phillips that he had discovered a photograph album of sorts, albeit a shoddily assembled one; he tried to pull open the cover, and with it came several pages, all stuck together; his stomach turned somewhat, as he saw that barely any of the pages were as flexible as paper should be. In spite of his repulsion, he allowed the first available page to fall open. On both leaves were pasted three photographs, all looking as though they were hastily taken, with blurry artifacts in the foreground suggesting they had been taken from a place of concealment. Phillips thumbed through the pages, provided they could be opened, and noticed that the subjects of the photos were all the same; females, all his own age with some exceptions. Most were in school uniform, though others were in more casual attire; it suddenly struck Phillips that they must be his schoolmates.

Then a noise; a faint laughter and some shouting. It seemed to be coming from the driveway. Phillips looked up and filed the photo book into his messenger bag. He stepped aside and peered through the small sliver of the window that was not concealed behind the cupboard and looked around. He saw, approaching the house with a swaggering walk that was ill-constructed, a young man, perhaps seventeen or eighteen, with long, dirty blonde hair that looked as though it had not been adequately cut or washed for some time. At the far end of the driveway, just visible between the walls of the hedges, stood a gaggle of boys, perhaps three or four of them, all evidently friends of his, laughing and jumping in jovial fashion walking away. They were soon out of his view.

Phillips moved silently across the room, quietly closing the cupboard after ensuring he had not left anything noticeably out of place that would arouse suspicion. By the time he was in the hallway, Harry was already in the house.

"Harry Baines?" Phillips asked, his hand still on the doorknob. Harry paused in the front door, having not yet closed it behind him. He did not say a word.

"Oh Harry, you're home." Louise called, appearing behind Phillips. "I've tidied your room up, made your bed and put some fresh clothes in there for you." She continued; Phillips turned and raised a hand to stop her.

"Did you take out my used clothes?" Harry asked, his voice a gravelly, thick one. Phillips sighed frustratedly and tried once more to interrupt, but Louise was faster.

"No, I haven't had the time yet, sweetheart." She said, wincing.

"So what the fuck have you spent today doing?" Harry growled, prompting Phillips to intervene.

"Steady, son, you think you're big and clever..." He began.

"Don't call me son, creep." Harry interrupted; Louise continued;

"Sweetheart, this is..." Phillips raised his voice;

"DCI Phillips, and I'd like to ask you..."

"Yeah, I don't care." Harry hissed, stepping past the pair with the same cocky swagger. "Louise, breakfast ready?" He called out, gruffly. Louise stammered, but nonetheless directed him into the kitchen.

"Wait a minute, Harry." Phillips called, swinging around to follow him. "I'd like to ask you some questions about a missing person." With that, Harry paused and turned slightly.

"Who?" He said, softly.

"Willow Greene." Harry started at the name and turned back fully.

"What about her? Why you asking me?" He said, moving towards Phillips; it was not in the DCI's nature to recoil, but he felt the urge to, one he supressed as much as possible before answering.

"We're following lines of enquiry, which involves you just answering a few questions for me." He replied. Harry trembled, though only just perceptibly.

"What line of enquiry?" Harry asked, with a menacing tone. When he was not replied to, he said much louder "What fucking line of enquiry?"

"What matters is what you can tell us. When did you last see her?" Phillips replied, sternly. When Harry did not answer, he asked again, standing up as straight as he could to tower over the boy, who did the same though to a much less impressive degree.

"I saw her walk home from school on Wednesday. She

went to her house, around the back, that's it. I didn't see anything else." Harry enunciated every word, his eyes forming a frown as he spoke. Then he turned, suddenly, and went into the kitchen. Phillips sighed and followed him.

"So, you didn't actually see her going into the house?"

"Did I fucking stutter? She went around the back and I left." He said loudly, throwing himself into the chair at the kitchen table his mother had prepared for him; he began to wolf down his breakfast. Phillips turned to Louise, who merely smiled an uncomfortable smile; it was almost a grimace. Phillips turned back.

"You haven't seen her since? Not at school yesterday?" Phillips asked, realising any more would be clutching at straws.

"What makes you think I was at school yesterday? Come on, I'm not at school now." Harry replied through revolting chews that were virtually animalistic. Phillips smiled, sweetly.

"Because I doubt you're the kind to admit to being truant in front of a police officer." He replied, with faux sincerity. Harry scoffed, spraying half-chewed food across the table.

"If you think I'm gonna piss my pants over being truant, you clearly don't know me, copper." Harry responded, taking up another forkful of food. *Copper* was a term he had not been called in a while; perhaps he *had* stepped into old-time America.

"Well thank you, Harry, you've been very..." And he trailed off. He paused. "I can see myself out." He turned to Louise, who smiled, and raised an arm.

"Allow me." She said, turning to Harry and stroking his hair. Harry shook his head, and sat patiently, waiting for her to stop. Eventually she did, and with that he resumed his breakfast, somewhat annoyed. Louise led Phillips through the door and down the hallway; their footsteps were softened by the rug on the floor. She pulled open the door and allowed Phillips to pass through it into the open air.

"He hasn't been the same since his Dad left." She said, suddenly, and with an unsure smile and a chuckle. Phillips drew an uncomfortable breath but did not exhale it as words; then, he noticed her eyes were glazed and quivering, for they were brimming with tears. "I hope you find the girl." She continued, wiping her eyes dry.

"We will" Phillips assured her; behind her, he espied Harry

moving through the hallway and into his room, with the plate in his hand. He slammed the door behind him. "Thanks for the help." Phillips continued. He nodded his head and smiled, then turned out of the door and stepped towards his car.

Louise smiled as she watched him leave and as he pulled away towards the main road, she closed the door. At that moment, Harry's door flung open with a slam; Louise started, and turned about; Harry was stood in the doorway, tense somehow. He had removed his trousers and was now stood in his underwear.

"Harry dear, how's breakfast?" She smiled.

"Where is it?" He asked, menacingly. She could barely make out his words.

"Sorry, honey?" She replied, the smile faltering now.

"*Honey* my ass. Where is it? My book?" He hissed, moving towards her. She recoiled slightly, though he merely filled the gap by encroaching upon her even more until his face was pressed merely a few centimetres from hers; his rancid breath, reeking of tobacco and other substances, filled her nose; her eyes began to water. *Don't tremble* she thought, with futility; her body was a mass of shivers.

"You fuckin' scared, huh? So, tell me where it is?" He said, softly. She barely mouthed the words;

"I don't know."

"What?" He growled, moving his ear close to her face.

"I said I don't know!" She cried, tears running down her face. Harry scoffed, then again, stepping away from her. For a moment, her fear dissipated as he began to chuckle as he turned to face the opposite direction. He rubbed his nose delicately and paused. It was an indescribably painful moment of silence, solitude and peace, before suddenly, with his hand balled into a fist, he landed a heavy blow to her face which floored her in an instant. She was not knocked unconscious, but she knew almost immediately that he had broken her nose, so sudden and overwhelming was the jarring pain that came over her. She yelped as she crashed to the floor, drawing her hands to her face in a futile attempt to grasp and grab at the pain. It was some miracle when, shortly after, her face became numb.

She felt a longing hope that Phillips was just on the other side of the door to help her; perhaps he had heard her cry of pain and would come barging through to rescue her; but it was a futile hope. The more she waited, the less her hope reassured her.

In the next instant, Harry was upon her, fists flying, landing horrible blows and cracks that echoed throughout the bungalow; soon nothing could be heard but the rising and falling of his cruel hands, balled into the most brutal of weapons, intermittently joined for a moment by her imploring outcries, begging for respite, only to be silenced in the next by another strike, indistinguishable from the previous or the next. Her arms flailed for a time, in some effort to fight back, but she was being laid out; she barely had the energy to squirm. Nothing she could do would prevent his attach; he was a man possessed. But deep in her heart, she knew better; possessed though he may be, he was no man.

His blows began to slow, and finally, he seemed to think she had been punished enough, for he landed one final strike on her chest, one which she sincerely believed had broken a rib; even if that were the case, Harry was not concerned. In his mind, the lesson had been taught. She lay beneath him, her clothes torn and frayed, and her face sweating and smothered in a swirling foam of blood and bruise. She sobbed and inhaled a deep breath that continued even as her lungs became full; she desperately wanted to exhale, but she knew that to do so would bear her yet more pain, and she did not think she could cope with that. Eventually, she relented and forced a ragged breath from her painful lungs. A sickening mix of saliva and blood spilled from her mouth, dribbling in great globules onto the wooden floor.

Harry pressed his cheek to hers, covering himself in crimson fluid. He sniffed her hair, then pushed himself up from the ground, breathing heavily. He wiped the stain from his cheek and licked his finger before heading back to his room, slamming the door behind him.

He re-emerged a few moments later, pulling on a change of clothes; not the ones his mother had ironed for him, but some that were already in his cupboard. He paused in the hallway for a moment, watching his squirming mother. She called his name indistinctly, but he merely stepped through the hallway and into the kitchen. She cried his name a final time as he threw open the back door, slipped through it and into the open air.

Louise spent much of the next hour lying on the floor as her body became more and more stiff and unpleasant a vessel to be living in. In fact, it was late afternoon when she finally found the strength to bring herself to her feet and head into the kitchen. By that time, Harry had still not returned home.

-5-
The Blue Stitch

When Fiona arrived at the Greene residence, it was a little after two o'clock. The sun was beating down upon the town like a scorching hot blanket of light, and many residents were out in force, taking advantage of the fact that their children were in school to enjoy the sunshine and top up their currently non-existent tans. But Fiona was out for business, not for pleasure.

In the daylight, the Greene household was completely different; no longer was it a foreboding, looming spectre in the dark, ominous and menacing; now, it was a completely normal, inviting home. It did not seem in any way disturbing or threatening. That fallacy had gone with the night. For the moment, the house looked as it should; unassuming, innocuous. Save for the plethora of police vehicles and the large, white van parked alongside the pavement, one would be forgiven for thinking it was merely a clone of the other houses it shared the street with.

Fiona drew up alongside the kerb some distance from the house, so vast was the number of other cars she was fighting for space with. She could not have been more than twenty or thirty yards from the end of the garden path, but it was enough time to roll up her sleeves and adorn her face with a tasteful pair of sunglasses that dimmed the blinding sunlight down to a more comfortable level. She approached the garden gate, swung it open, then allowed it to close behind her; in truth, had she held it any longer it would have burned her hand.

The front door was open; now she could see what made the place so unique amongst her neighbours; a bustling cacophony of activity occurred within; officers were busying themselves, moving hither and thither between rooms, going up and down stairs, such that many spent much of their time dancing about in order to get by another. It was barely organised chaos, corralled with half-hearted commands from a flustered-looking Superintendent Grisham from the garden. He espied Fiona approaching, then sighed with something of a combination of relief and exasperation.

"It's like herding flies." He said, lifting his hand to his brow to wipe away a sheet of sweat. "What are you supposed to be, something out of Miami Vice?" He asked, noting her sunglasses and casually rolled-up sleeves.

"It's hot. What's going on?" She dismissed his question, moving past him and through the door. It was somehow hotter inside; "Can we get some air in here?" She hissed, removing her sunglasses, and fanning herself ineffectively with them. Grisham pointed through the space, though she could not see this for her eyes were still not adjusted to the relatively dark interior.

"We've got all of the windows and doors open. Other than that, not much we can do." Grisham said loudly so as to be heard over the chorus of voices from around him.

"Any chance we could get an ice cream van over here?" Cried one male voice, sarcastically.

"I'm with him." Fiona chuckled.

"What?" Grisham had not heard anything by virtue of a loud thud of the door closing behind him.

"What's going on, sir?" Fiona asked, dismissing him again. She began to move towards the living room door.

"Oh, well, Sarah's sister is in town from the city, so they've all gone out together, they left when we arrived. Gary didn't seem so happy about it." Grisham said, following Fiona.

"That figures. He doesn't seem the type to be happy about anything." Fiona replied, deciding that Gary's belligerence upon her first meeting him was not an anomaly.

"I've noticed." Replied Grisham; the pair of them filed into the lounge, which was alive with activity; here, officers mingled with white-clad figures, unidentifiable by virtue of their masks and hoods to the point that any casual observer would regard them as faceless androids. Fiona had a knack for knowing who was who due to her uncanny knowledge of gaits and mannerisms, a skill she had picked up through the time she had spent getting to know them. These figures were busy with various forensic activities, which Fiona thought was quite premature; the girl had only been missing for three days.

"Seems excessive, don't you think?" She asked, by way of saying so. Grisham shook his head.

"Not really. The busted door alone is reason enough to treat this place as a crime scene, even if it's unrelated to Willow." He explained, pointing towards the kitchen. Fiona tilted her head.

"I suppose so; besides, I suppose anything that comes up here could be useful." She conceded. "Talking of which, have we found anything?" She asked, introducing her reason for being there. Grisham turned about suddenly, startling her.

"Well, we haven't found much, which tells us a lot." He said, moving towards the kitchen. Fiona followed closely behind.

"Like what, what have you looked for and not found?" She quizzed, confusing even herself. She suddenly became aware of a figure moving towards them; dressed all in white like the others, the figure was tall, more so than both Fiona and Grisham, and she commanded the room as soon as she entered. Fiona recognised her immediately.

"No fingerprints from anybody who does not live in the house. We've matched unidentified prints with those found on the notebooks you brought in, which we know Willow has touched, so we can say with near certainty that they are hers. No damage to any other doors but the rear, which tells us that whatever happened to it was not part of a long search to get into the house." Jacqueline said; her knowledge of forensic signs was unrivalled in the Heathestone CID.

"So, nothing out of the ordinary?" Grisham asked, stopping when he was close to Jacqueline, who was also now stationary.

"That's just the things that *don't* tell us anything. Follow me." She said, ominously; she gestured to a white receptacle that had been placed on the coffee table, within which could be found a selection of plastic gloves, face masks and plastic goggles. Fiona and Grisham collected one of each, dressed themselves with them, and moved back towards the kitchen door, beyond which they found an even more clinical operation in progress.

The back door was open, and two figures were examining the wooden surface with cylindrical magnifying glasses, whilst another lifted a tray full of plastic tubes from the ground. Someone else was dusting every visible surface with a fine powder that seemed to reveal a dense collection of prints, whilst yet another was marking points on a wall with small, yellow stickers. A photographer milled about with a camera, photographing everything that had already been marked out. Fiona observed the whole affair, curious.

"We'll start here." Jacqueline said stopping in the middle of the room, gesturing to the ground; Fiona did not immediately recognise anything unusual, but her eye was not as attuned, it would appear, to see the minutiae that Jacqueline's could identify. "When rubber slides across a surface like these floor tiles, it leaves smudges. These smudges," she began, pointing out the marks with her little finger, being careful not to disturb the pattern. She continued; "were caused by the soles of a shoe. You can see the sweeping mark, but if you look closely, there is a collection of square marks arranged into a semi-circular shape. That's where a shoe slid across the floor followed by the heel of the shoe touched the ground, stopping the sweep."

"I'll be honest, Jacqueline, you've got a great eye." That was Fiona; Jacqueline smiled, though the face mask prevented anyone from seeing it. "What does it mean?"

"This isn't the only one; if you look carefully, you can see where the same pattern repeats itself." She made a circular gesture with her hand, highlighting the wide area of smudges Fiona and Grisham had not noticed before. "It's consistent with rapidly moving feet and tends to indicate a scuffle or a fight. We did consider it could be caused by dancing, but it's too random to simply be dancing, which tends to be more ordered."

"I see." Said Grisham, nodding. "Any chance of identifying these prints?"

"Not really; they're not formed well enough to have retained their shape. We can't use walking prints, left when the person was walking, because footsteps are lighter in that situation, so don't leave traces that are as obvious. There may be some, but we haven't found any yet." She explained, drawing herself erect. "That's not all, though. Over here," she began, moving a few feet away. She gestured at a small cluster of numbered stickers on the floor, the significance of which was once again lost on Fiona. "We found small droplets of blood. All largely the same size and shape. The droplets are all loosely circular in form, which tends to mean they are as a result of falling straight down as opposed to spatter, which would result in long streaks."

"Have you found any trace of glass? Anything like fine, powdery glass, from a lightbulb say?" Fiona asked, furrowing her brow and rubbing two fingers together; Grisham frowned too, confused. Jacqueline's face remained unmoved.

"Nothing like that, no. Any reason?"

"No, no reason. Just a hunch, is all." Fiona said, cryptically; she did not go into detail so as to avoid coming to unreasonable conclusions.

"We did manage to find some interesting things on the door, however." Jacqueline then directed their collective attention to the kitchen table, upon which had been placed the tray full of evidence tubes. She gestured to them. "We pulled these fibres from the splinters in the wood. Now, we obviously assume these were transferred when the person who broke the door down made contact with the surface." She said; Fiona picked up one of the cylinders between her thumb and forefinger and peered within; the cloudy plastic made it difficult to see with clarity what was within, but she could just make out a thin fibre, maybe three or four millimetres long, with frayed tips. The fibre was a very deep blue, virtually black, though Fiona could see even through the translucent tube that it was not quite dark enough.

"So, whoever that fibre belongs to…" Began Grisham

"Is our intruder." Concluded Fiona, placing the evidence tube back into the tray. "Any clue where it would have come from?" Fiona asked, diverting her attention back to Jacqueline, who was shaking her head even before the question had fully been asked.

"We'd have to run fibre matches on every item of clothing in the house. The issue is, the fibres are so generic, they could really have come from anywhere."

"Dammit."

"And the blood?" Asked Grisham, hopefully.

"We haven't been able to run a positive identification yet. Once we get these samples back to the lab, we'll be able to see if it matches anyone in our system." Jacqueline replied, much to Grisham's approval. He nodded gently.

"Fiona, follow me." He said, lifting the mask from his face. He turned and moved swiftly to the door, and Fiona obeyed the command to follow. The pair of them removed their protective equipment almost simultaneously.

"What do you make of it?" She asked as they walked through the lounge, past yet more forensic analyses in progress.

"It's curious. The investigation is still in its infancy, so let's not draw any conclusions just yet. I see where you're going with the lightbulb, though." He conceded, nodding to her. "But until we know what happened here, let's assume they're unrelated." He concluded.

"Got it." She agreed.

"Great, I'm going to go back to the station, they seem to have things in hand here." He then glanced at his watch with a theatrical flourish. "I'm going to grab some lunch, you fancy something?" He asked, changing the subject altogether.

"Well, I've come in a car, we'd have to go separately." She said, by way of turning down his offer.

"I was driven here, but they're staying here, so I could really do with a lift." He admitted, much to her amusement.

"I see. Come on, I'll drive you." She said, fishing her car keys from her left pocket. "I'll report to Phillips on the way."

"Good idea. Where is he, by the way?"

-6-
Character Witness

Phillips swatted the air with a frustrated air as he drew into the car park of Heathestone's secondary school. Kids of all ages, races and genders were swarming his car, excited that their day had been interrupted by the arrival of a member of the police. His desire not to mow any of them down forced him to creep towards a free space at such a pace that he was barely moving. None of this was unusual to Phillips, of course; he was used to being something of a strange presence to most people, so underused and undervalued was the police force of the town. His being there meant bad things.

It was lunchtime, and all of the pupils of the school were mingling around the yard, flitting in and out from narrow crevices between stone buildings. They laughed and japed, not fully aware of the seriousness of Phillips' visit.

Phillips drew into his space and was finally free of the gaggle of children who had inconvenienced him. He sighed frustratedly, rubbed his forehead, then applied the handbrake to prevent the car from rolling away.

As he hastened to remove his seatbelt, his mobile phone began to ring with the same default ringtone it had been using since the moment he bought it. Jumping in his seat, he turned his head to the phone screen, and sighed as he realised what was going on. He shook his head, frustrated at his highly-strung reaction, then jabbed the screen to accept the call.

"Fiona, what's up?" He asked, turning his attention to his notebook.

"Apart from the temperature?" Came the half-jumbled reply from the phone's speaker. Phillips chuckled, writing the date onto a fresh page in his book.

"Yes, apart from the weather."

"I've got a quick update on the Greene household; forensics has turned up good again." She replied, her voice cutting out every now and again. Phillips closed his notebook with interest.

"Ooh, excellent. Go ahead." He requested; and with that, she regaled him with the report attained from the forensic analysis of the place. He listened with interest, frowning at some of the more unusual details; *blood*? *Blue stitches*?

Once she had concluded her recollection, he furrowed his brow and rubbed his chin with a quiet, contemplative regard. "Curious." He said.

"That's what I thought." Came the fuzzy reply. "What do you make of it?"

"Well, if we were looking at a murder inquiry, I would say we have a pretty good idea what happened. But we don't know enough to draw any conclusions just yet." He said, sufficiently loudly for her to hear.

"My thoughts entirely." Came Grisham's distant voice.

"Grisham?"

"Yep?"

"I didn't know you were there!" Phillips was surprised; in the full five minutes they had been conversing, never once did he interrupt; at least, until now.

"Me and Fiona just grabbed a bit of lunch on the way to the station." Grisham explained, his voice louder now.

"Lunch!" Phillips spluttered. "Thanks for the invite, gits." He scoffed. Grisham chuckled.

"Where are you now?" Fiona interrupted. Phillips considered for a moment, returning himself to the present.

"Um, I'm at Heathestone Secondary, I'm just gonna have a chat with the headmaster, see if he knows anything about Willow's movements." He explained.

"Well, have fun. I might go back for seconds." Grisham said.

"Where are you again?" Phillips quizzed, indignant.

"Doesn't matter. We'll see you back at the station." Grisham dismissed. With that, Phillips jabbed the screen once more and terminated the call. He scoffed light-heartedly, then plucked the device from the holder and slid it gently into his pocket.

With his wits gathered, he popped the door open, then slipped through the narrow gap, being careful not to damage the red car beside him. By now, the gaggle of students had somewhat dissipated, but those who remained now had their interest renewed by Phillips' new movements. He wrestled through them, being careful not to injure anyone as he battled through the crowd.

He seized the attention of a nearby teacher, on her way around the school to check for any misdemeanours in progress. He accosted her to solicit help, but it would appear she was expecting him;

"Hi, you must be Phillips? We've been told to expect you." She said, much to Phillips' surprise; it was the first time he did not have to introduce himself to anyone. He bowed his head into a nod and smiled.

"That's right, I'm here to see..." He began, but he was cut off.

"Mr Worth, yes, he's waiting for you. If you'd like to follow me?" She said, stepping back and directing him to the door. He nodded and conceded to follow her. She led him through the large wooden doors of the main entrance; a sign on the door read; *Students, please use side entrances*. He felt privileged to be one of the few allowed to go through those main doors, so strode through them with the kind of auspicious decorum he deemed appropriate.

The inside of the school was drastically more modern than the outside; old stone masonry had given way to anaemic white painted walls and clinical light fixtures; all of the students wore dark blue blazers atop white shirts. Blue was a theme in that place, with Blue doors and accents; it was evidently the colour of the school. Even the crest was a combination of blue and red, emblazoned with a caricatured lion and eagle facing each other, almost in a battle pose. Phillips did not dare to think he had any hope of translating the Latin motto.

He was lead through the hospital-like hallways of the main building – from outside, he could make out four blocks, but there could have been more concealed behind them; in fact, he was unsure if they were even separate buildings, as the deeper into the labyrinthine corridors he descended, the more he believed the buildings were connected. He did wonder, almost aloud, why the headmaster did not favour a more prominent location for his office.

All the while, he followed his accomplice, who had either worked there for, or she was a fast learner; not once did she have to backtrack or apologise for making a mistake; she walked with an assurance of her goal.

Eventually, and after much walking and taking in the building, Phillips was directed to a door marked;

MR. H. WORTH
HEADMASTER

With a word of thanks to his guide, he tipped his head and moved towards the door. When he looked back again, she had gone, presumably back to her duties. He rapped on the door, waited and after hearing a vague 'come in' from within, he gripped the handle, depressed it, and pushed open the door.

The office beyond was much the same as the rest of the school, yet evidently it combined both the old and the new; old stone upper walls grew out of white, painted cement lower ones. The ceiling was one of a fine, well-maintained oak. The floor, too, was grand; highly polished veneers of wood lay in perfect rows, directing Phillips nicely towards the centre of the room, where he found the headmaster sat at a fine, heavy desk. Papers were stacked into neat piles, and a slim laptop almost concealed the man from him. Two leather seats sat before the desk; Phillips did not sit in one until he was invited to do so.

At the sound of the door closing, Mr Worth looked up from his rapid typing, softened by his gloved fingers, and regarded Phillips for a moment; the lines on his bald head wrinkled as his eyes pointed towards the policeman, though the head itself barely moved. In an instant, he was to his feet;

"Ah, you must be Sergeant Phillips?" He said, cheerfully. Phillips corrected him;

"Yes, DCI, actually. But yes, I'm Phillips, a pleasure to meet you." He held out a hand, expecting the man to shake it, but rather, he almost recoiled;

"Oh, I'm sorry. I don't." He said, somewhat more dejectedly than he had been when greeting him initially. Phillips frowned and lowered his hands. "I'm a germophobe you see. I have been all my life. I'm very sorry, I hope you won't think ill of me. That's not to say I'm assuming you're ridden with germs, but it's a point of principle. And what headmaster would I be if I instil principles into my students and then not respect my own?" He said, elaborately. Phillips understood. "My sincere apologies." He continued. Phillips bowed his head;

"No apology necessary, everyone has their ways." He said, reassuring him.

"And everyone has their reasons. What are yours, to what do I owe this visit?" Mr Worth asked, sitting down again. He directed Phillips to sit down in one of the chairs; he obeyed in a moment.

"An unfortunate reason, I'm afraid. I'm here in regard to Willow Greene, who has gone missing." He said, gravely. Mr Worth's smile faded, dissolving into a face of panic; then to one of concern.

"Oh, erm, Willow? Oh yes, I'd noticed she was absent from many of her classes, I thought it a little unusual." He said, unsurely, prodding the laptop trackpad, bringing up a spreadsheet of class registers to check for her absences.

"I was wondering if you could tell me a little about her, from a faculty standpoint?" Phillips asked; he imagined whatever Howard Worth would tell him would be more impartial than her parents.

"Erm, yes. Of course, Willow. What can one say?" He chuckled. "Such a lovely girl, and popular too. She was on our hockey team, had a very promising career." Mr Worth said, reclining back into his chair. "Her mother called this morning, she explained to me in the briefest of conversations what had happened. I'm afraid she was light on details, and I pressed her for none. It's an unfortunate thing to lose a child." Mr Worth stood up and moved to a cabinet of the finest oak that rested beside a large bay window, through which was a superb view of the playing field. From it he produced a wide carafe with a slender neck; it had a brown liquid within. He held it dramatically in his hands and turned to Phillips, inviting him to partake in some.

"No thank you, not whilst I'm on duty." Phillips said, somewhat hypocritically, waving a hand. Mr Worth placed the carafe back down and produced a glass. "Sorry, what did you mean a moment ago, 'to lose a child'?" Phillips asked, perplexed; what had he been told?

"Well," Howard stammered. "I would assume she hasn't been found yet? So, she is missing. She is lost." He explained, in a somewhat roundabout manner. Before Philips could go on, he poured himself a generous measure of the liquid, which Phillips smelled, even at that distance, as a fine scotch. "Do you think that's a good idea, whilst you're working?" Phillips asked.

"Normally I wouldn't. But one has to have his treats, especially when we have visitors. So, Phillips. What is it *I* can do for you?" Mr Worth asked.

"Well," Phillips paused. "May I call you Howard?"

"Certainly, but not in front of the students. Principle." Howard said, sternly.

"Principle." Phillips muttered in unison with the headmaster. "Howard, I wonder if I could ask about some of Willow's friends." He continued.

"Oh?"

"Yes, I was wondering if you knew if Willow had a

particularly large friend group?" He asked.

"Well naturally I have a great many students to keep track of, you understand." Howard answered. Phillips nodded knowingly. "But Willow was one of my favourites; we got on very well, she and I. I believe she found me to be an inadequate help with certain matters, however. She would rarely come to me if she had a problem, I noticed; she would favour going to a person of lesser authority. People are like that, they would prefer to discuss issues with family, friends, than go straight to the police." He said; Phillips pondered on this for a moment and found his summary to be correct. "All of this to say I paid particular attention to her. She was popular, yes, but only to a small number within her circle. She rarely spent time with anyone beyond four or five individuals." He continued, finally answering the original question.

"Well I'd like their names and addresses if possible. I'd like to discuss Willow with them. Perhaps they had some contact with her before she went missing." Philips said, almost speaking the truth; in his mind, he pictured a number of his investigators doing such tasks on his behalf.

"Of course. Here are the names." And with that, Howard began writing down the identities of a number of students with a fountain pen. The blue ink dried almost immediately upon contact with the paper. "Please take this to the reception desk. They will see to it that you get whatever contact information you require." He continued, handing the note across the desk to him. Phillips took it from him with two fingers, folded it neatly and placed it delicately into one of his pockets. Howard retracted his hand with such a swiftness that he nearly tore the paper. "Will that be all?"

"No, I'd like to ask you about a student here, Harry Baines?" Phillips asked; he noticed a certain decline in the headmaster's shoulders, yet at the same time the faint hint of a smile flickered and vanished.

"Yes, Harry Baines. An unfortunate boy, really. Many a time he has been in this office, normally at the receiving end of some horrible accusation. The terrible truth is, most of them turn out to be accurate. I refuse to send him away from this place, as it is our duty as a school to enlighten him and supress this behaviour." He said, theatrically. Phillips frowned with confusion. "Are you linking him to this investigation?" Howard quizzed with a high inflection.

"It's too early to say at this time. We are in the investigative stage at the moment."

"Well I may say that he has had a problem with women,

particularly these last few years since his father moved to the city." Howard nodded, knowingly. Then Phillips remembered the photo album; he would have asked for the identities of those photographed had he believed it would be so easy. He immediately decided to dismiss this idea, as he did not wish to give any indication about suspects yet.

"Well thank you, Howard. You've been very cooperative; I'll make a note of that in my report." Phillips said, rising to his feet. He was about to hold his hand out, but then he remembered his host's phobia. He thought better of it. "If I could ask one more thing of you?" He said.

"Of course?" Howard replied, standing to join him.

"I want to get as broad an appeal for information out as possible; I think if we can link our interests, ours and the school's, we'll be able to reach a wider audience; students, parents, guardians and the like. I wonder if we could hold an appeal meeting in your dining hall this evening?" He continued, gesturing with his hands. Howard looked uncertain.

"I see little reason why not; however, it would be quite an inconvenience, we should have to keep the caretaker to open up for you, have cleaners work late and so on." He said, almost desperate for an excuse. It was the particular mention of cleaners that led Phillips to surmise that he did not want any alien contaminants in his school, which would doubtless be brought by a large number of the press and police.

"Any staff who are required to stay and do their duties late will be compensated. It would be a great help if you could oblige. We want to find Willow." Phillips countered, furrowing his brow. Howard sighed.

"Is there no other place it could be held?" Howard replied defensively.

"We could use the town hall, but it's tricky. Local policy, you see, we have to give at least three days' notice, but we can't afford to wait that long. We would really appreciate your help here." He pressed. Howard sighed again.

"Alright, I'll put a general notice around, perhaps I can rally around some volunteers. Will I be required for the evening?" He said, dejectedly; it was as though it was a major inconvenience; a view Phillips could not quite understand.

"Thank you, that's much appreciated. And if you wouldn't mind, it would be valuable to have a representative of the school present. Thanks again." Phillips said, continuing; "Unless you hear from us, we will start the appeal at around half past eight tonight."

"I shall make a note of it and see you there." Howard replied, hoisting his fountain pen into the air; he wrote the time down with a flourish. Then, without looking up from his task, he continued; "Goodbye, DCI Phillips." He said animatedly. With that, Phillips took his leave and closed the door behind him; it was a good thing he had taken in the details of the school, for now he had to find his way out alone. As he went, he wondered how he had never noticed how eccentric the residents of Heathestone were, such was the scarcity with which he had interacted with them.

-7-
Fallen Angel

Were it not for the golden sunset striking the sky to fire at the horizon, Reverend Daryll would have been blind; he brushed his way through the thick undergrowth, his trousers snagging on low thorns and the tangle of twigs beneath his feet. It was approaching a quarter past eight and the sun was low. All about him the trees loomed high and foreboding, their canopy a rainbow of Autumnal colours. It did not occur to him that the trees about him were those of despair, their seasonal change bringing them towards a naked death. He saw them more as a testament to the beauty that comes from all of the negativity; he knew that in a number of months' time, those leaves would be their lurid green once more. Out of death, new life would emerge.

He scanned the undergrowth, glancing here and there, until he found his target; an errant, brightly coloured crisp packet. It amazed him, as he fished it from beneath the fallen leaves, that he could detest something so vivid and colourful; but it was artificial, something hideous and unnatural. It had no place there. He flourished it in the air, and raised the black bin liner to his side, discarding the wretched packet with a motion of his hand that eloquent of disgust. It landed in a pile, joining the other pieces of refuse and detritus he was dedicating his time to locating.

He sighed a despairing note, then moved on through the woods. He had been at this task for some time, so that his feet and hands were tired. He swept a veil of sweat from his firm forehead, and in doing so discovered that his ginger fringe was wet with the stuff, slicked down and pressed against his skin. He craved for water, which would be reward enough for his hard work.

A fine stream of light, like a spotlight, came upon him; he had arrived at the break in the trees and stepped towards it. Beyond, a beautiful vista of clouds that appeared as great collections of cotton shapes, almost lit from within by the creaking embers of a great fire; he stepped into the clearing and stood near the edge of a great precipice; far below him, a shallow lake met the base of the cliff with soft ripples that disturbed the illusion of a great mirror below him. At the other side, he watched a couple walking away by the sandy path that ran along the water's edge;

their black Labrador bounding and fussing at their side; he shouted a hello to them and bid them a pleasant evening; they returned his salutation. He noticed, as he watched, that their dog seemed to stop and stare out across the water; Daryll fancied that it may be about to leap into the lake for an aquatic playtime, but it never did; rather, it paused, staring out, growling and yelping. It never raised its voice into a bark, but the owners could see it was distressed by something; they ordered it along with a push on its head and it complied, though Daryll was not sure if it was happy to do so. He watched as they became smaller by the distance and soon, they vanished through the gate to the west and over the crest of the hill beyond.

He turned his head around and took in the church. It was nestled between two small hillocks, and with the sun behind it, its shadow was long. Birds sang in the still evening air, and all about him the world glowed orange; then, a sound.

He was unsure what to make of it at first; a garbled squawking, as if some bird or other such creature was in pain somehow. He swung about, expecting to see some small animal that had found its way up the hill and was now lost in the woods. He saw nothing; so close was the noise that he expected he would be able to espy it; its sound could not have carried through such a thick wall of vegetation. Thinking he must have imagined it, he turned back around and saw a grey bird, its identity hidden by its swift, blurring movement, streak by in front of him, flying almost vertically; he cried out in alarm, equally startling the bird, which swung around and flew off in the opposite direction. Daryll collapsed in a heap, casting the bin liner into the air. It soared high, became snared by the wind, and was carried out of his reach. With the wind within it, its contents were kept packed to the bottom, so they did not spill out.

Daryll, steadying his stance, looked about for the flying bag; finally laying eyes on it, he watched in dismay as it arched in the air, down and away from him. Finally, it landed in the water below; it was disturbed by the rippling the bird had left behind in its flight. He sighed, dusted himself down, then resigned himself to recover what was now his own litter.

He moved swiftly through the woodland, for he knew that with each passing moment, more of the rubbish would find its way out of the bag and into the water. He headed down the incline and the trees became scarcer, thinner and less enveloping until he arrived at the gated fence that surrounded the base of the hill.

Bolting the gate behind him, he strode around the lake, wondering how he was to get the waste back; perhaps, by chance, it would drift back to him; but down at the base, the wind was still, and the water was unmoving. The rippling had ceased.

Failing to find a solution, he resolved to go about things the easiest, yet also the least convenient, way. He rolled up the loose hems of his trousers, slipped off his shoes and socks, leaving them at the landward end of the short pier that jutted out into the water, and stepped in. It was colder than he had anticipated, but he was reassured by knowing that it was only a shallow pool. However, as he drew nearer to the bag, he realised he had wildly misjudged the depth; it had been so long since he had been in those waters – he only realised then that it must have been when he was but a very young man – that he had quite forgotten what a height the water came to on a person; soon, his trousers were submerged, despite them being rolled tight about his knees, and eventually, when he was no further than a few yards from the litter, he was waist deep to the stuff. At least now he had become accustomed to the temperature.

He reached out a slender arm to fish out the bag, and eventually his fingers gripped the upper edge of the rim. Grunting, but nonetheless pleased with himself, he drew the bag towards him, being careful to keep all of his collection within the flooded interior. It was heavier now; at first, he considered this to be because of the dense water weighing it down. But it became so difficult to pull the bag that he assumed it must have been snagged on something submerged, perhaps a heavy branch or log from above. Desperate to keep the bag from being torn, he plunged his hand into the bag and under the water; it was too murky to see what was beneath the surface. His grip did not fall upon anything, so he probed further.

Finally, he gripped something; something slender and soft. Thinking he had grabbed a fish in error, he withdrew his hand in alarm; he looked down in an instant and the bag floated away as the obstacle moved itself, slowly. Only then did he realise that it was not his reflection, but another face staring back at him from under the water.

-8-
Embargo

The evening was cold and dim. The sun had set now beyond the horizon, and the stars were emerging, bullet holes in the sky through which their light was shining. The moon was bright now, and the only trace of the day was the tiniest sliver of orange glow softening into the dark. Normally, by this time, the school was concealed, invisible against the twilight backdrop. But now, it was an unusually active hive of activity; cars flooded the car park, and a gaggle of parents and other locals swarming to get inside. The interior was similarly awash with visitors, flowing through the corridors like blood cells swimming along veins in as orderly a fashion as they could.

Present in the building was Phillips, of course; he had been there for some time already, organising the affair with Superintendent Grisham. All the while, a watchful Mr Worth oversaw proceedings. Fiona, on the other hand, was just arriving. Much of her energy was expended on her battling through the swelling crowd as it threatened to drown her in a suffocating mass of people. Even as she neared her destination, she found a thronging gathering of people, an inconvenient crowd assembled outside the dining hall. With all of her will, she pushed onwards, bursting clear of the crowd and through into the dining hall. The crowd was held back by two other officers; even they feared for their safety as the mass became threatening.

Gathering herself, Fiona took in the new space; the room was dim; save for the warm ceiling lights that cast a bright, dusk-like glow about the room, the place was reliant on the rapidly fading light from outside that was only just visible through the window for illumination. The floor was clear of detritus; five long, wooden tables had been cleared away, packed neatly to the side of the room, three stacked on one side, the remaining two opposite. It must have been the effort of no less than half a dozen volunteers, who she could see busying themselves with the unfolding and distribution of chairs. No doubt Mr Worth had commandeered their services, but their work was one of the most overlooked; few people were concerned with such trivialities.

The room was completely devoid of people, save for half a

dozen or so figures milling about at the far end of the room; some were stood atop a low proscenium, beyond which a red curtain was draped, itself emblazoned with the school coat-of-arms, which Fiona was seeing for the first time. Along this stage was sat three small tables positioned end-to-end, with a white sheet on top; on the left – as she looked at the ensemble – stood an easel with a large, colour photograph of Willow, the first time Fiona, and indeed many of the members of the police force, had seen her. Her beaming face stared out at the non-existent crowd, her brown hair falling in curves about her face. Her blue eyes were piercing and icy, but gentle and friendly.

Fiona approached the group, eventually getting close enough to identify Phillips, who she could see was talking, gesticulating wildly, to a man she did not recognise, but Phillips knew as Howard, and another woman. She glanced to the other end of the stage, and spotted Sarah and Gary, whose presence did not surprise her. Sarah sat in one of the chairs set at the table already, whilst Gary was off to the side of the stage, fidgeting with his phone; this did not surprise Fiona.

By now, Phillips had espied Fiona approach, and as she drew nearer, he smiled gently, then extended a hand, with which he aided her in ascending the platform to stand with that small group of insiders.

"Fiona, thank goodness you're here." Phillips said, patting her on the shoulder.

"No worries, I came as soon as I could." She replied, straightening her blazer.

"Howard, this is my Detective Inspector, Fiona, Fiona, this is Howard, headmaster here at the school." Phillips said, standing aside, gesturing to the man; immediately, she put out a hand. Howard approached; he did not take her hand for a reason she did not know. "He doesn't." Phillips whispered, just out of Howard's earshot. Smiling, she lowered her hand to her side.

"A pleasure to meet you, madam. I look forward to working with you." Howard said politely, bowing his head. Fiona smiled a cautious grin.

"Well, I wish we were working together under different circumstances." She admitted. Howard, curiously, smiled again.

"Of course. Oh, may I introduce my wife? This is Sandy." Howard continued, turning to the other person Phillips had been talking to; she was dressed in a floral blue blouse and grey leggings; her blonde hair fell upon her forehead gently, and it flowed and moved with the slightest movement of her head. Her glasses were half-rimmed and delicate, her smile honest.

"A pleasure." Fiona said, shaking her naked hand.

"Likewise." Sandy replied, her voice little more than a squeak. With that, Fiona espied Phillips moving around the long desk to shuffle some papers. Then, to her right, a booming voice.

"Fiona, great to see you." She swung about; moving towards her was Grisham. His walk was sturdy and confident, his stern face giving way to a smile as her eyes caught his own.

"Superintendent, good evening." She said. They did not shake hands; such was their familiarity.

"Grisham, I'm the Superintendent." Grisham said, introducing himself to Howard, who merely nodded his head; he found the great number of people he was being introduced to something of a hardship and so his confusion manifested itself as a silence. "Well, now that we're all here, I think we ought to get started. We appear to be ten minutes behind already." Grisham said as he glanced at his watch, his authority instantly commanding those within earshot; almost immediately, the stage was to action, as the group moved around the desk to their seats; Phillips sat with Grisham to his left and Fiona to his right. Howard sat at the right-hand end of the desk, whilst Sarah and Gary, who up until now had been silent and reclusive to the group, sat on the opposite end.

At the sound of chairs moving and the discussion on the stage coming to the end, the officers, who up until now had been holding back the throng, parted, allowing the crowd in. For a moment, there was scarcely organised chaos, as the group made their way into the space, identified the seats, and connected the object with intention; *there are chairs, so we shall sit*. Phillips watched as the group found their seats, though there was little reasoning to their organisation; some were methodical in finding an optimum position, others were careless and simply sat at the first chair they came upon.

Soon, however, the hall became quiet, and the few stragglers who had not yet found a space moved into some position as they found would best afford them a vantage point. It took a moment for silence to fall completely, but when it did, Grisham spoke first;

"Good evening everyone, I'd like to thank you all for coming at such short notice tonight. I am Superintendent Grisham with the Heathestone CID. To my right is Detective Chief Inspector Phillips,

Detective Inspector Fiona, and Howard Worth, the headmaster here at the school. To my left are Sarah and Gary Greene, the parents of Willow Greene." His voice, amplified dramatically by the microphone array before him, echoed through the room, almost to distraction; so commanding was his tone, though, that it inconvenienced no one. "I'd like to pass over, if I may, to DCI Phillips, who will explain the situation." He continued. Phillips nodded and he leaned forward into a microphone. As he spoke, reporters began transcribing his speech.

"Thank you, good evening. At approximately three thirty-four on Wednesday afternoon, Willow Greene was seen returning home from school by schoolmates. Her parents were out for the evening, and upon their return found Willow missing. They reported this at approximately quarter to one this morning. Enquiries are ongoing, and at this early stage, we cannot comment on leads or any speculation. All I can say is we have reason to believe Willow could be in danger. We are concerned for her safety, and we urge Willow to contact either her parents, or us at the police station so that we can evaluate the situation. If anyone has any information regarding her whereabouts, we ask them to please give us that information so that we may act swiftly." Phillips said, his authority more prominent than he anticipated; he considered it unusual to be regarding the mystery so seriously at this early stage; somewhere in his mind, he was aware that these were unusual circumstances, and they called for swift, early action. "I would now like to invite Mr and Mrs Greene to say a few words." He continued, turning to the aforementioned couple. He turned back, and almost immediately caught sight of a blonde-haired boy in the audience; he recognised the unfortunate smell almost at the same instant. *What is Harry doing here?*, he wondered.

He had no time to consider this conundrum, for as soon as the thought entered his mind, Sarah began to speak, her voice scarcely more than a whisper.

"Hello, thank you all for being here. Erm, our beloved daughter Willow…" She began.

"Louder!" Came a voice from the audience; a murmur filled the room, but it was silenced after a moment.

"Sorry. Our beloved daughter Willow," She continued, louder yet still barely audible, "was a wonderful girl. We love her so much, and we just want her to come home."

"*Was?*" Fiona whispered, turning to Phillips. He dismissed her with a wave of a hand.

"Sorry." He whispered, seeing the annoyance on her face. "I want to hear what she says, or more *how* she says things." He said, quickly, so as to hear whatever Sarah was going to say next.

"She is loving, kind and caring. Popular, friendly and she is missed. Willow, please come back to us." She said, her voice breaking. Gary sighed, somewhat noticeably; all eyes came to him.

"Yes. Anyone with information about her whereabouts, particularly people who may have followed her anywhere," Gary resumed, loudly, brashly, glancing in Harry's direction, noticeable only to the boy he looked towards, "please let the police know." He finished. At that, Harry became uneasy, and he mouthed unpleasantries at the parents. Phillips espied this in a moment, and he drew the microphone towards his face.

"We would like to reiterate; at this stage our investigation is ongoing. We cannot comment on individual lines of enquiry, but we are pursuing any avenue that comes to us." He said, despite his knowing that there were few leads to begin with. "We are not treating her disappearance as suspicious, and we urge all citizens to be vigilant." He resumed, casting an eye over the hall. He leaned back and turned to Grisham.

"Yes, that's an important note. Now, as we understand it, Willow was last seen wearing a pair of black trousers, white shirt beneath a blue blazer and white and blue striped tie. We understand this to be her school uniform. She is described as white with brown, shoulder length hair. Her height is between five-foot-three and five-foot-five with a slim build. Now, if anyone becomes aware of any information that may help us, kindly telephone the helpline in the publicity packs available on the desk here, quoting case number 24062019/019. That number is also in the publicity pack. You may also contact Howard Worth at the school, also by referencing the crime number. He has kindly volunteered to aid us in the investigation and will report to us. Thank you for your time this evening, we will not take questions at this early stage." Grisham said, as though rehearsed. At that instant, he pushed his chair back and came to his feet. The crowd clamoured and approached the stage, but by that time, those gathered upon it were almost through the stage door, itself concealed by the red curtain. A volunteer took to the stage to distribute the packs, each sealed within a paper envelope.

Gary walked ahead of Sarah, who was still visibly upset; Fiona took her arm and offered such comforting words as she knew would work. Meanwhile, Grisham approached Gary with a stern strut; he hissed as quietly as he could;

"Gary, a word." With that, he used his presence to urge Gary through the door, beyond which was a large room; it was dim with only a single orb light upon the low ceiling; what function this room served was impossible to say, as it was devoid of any feature or furnishing. Gary sighed, having predicted what Grisham was about to say.

"Alright, I'm sorry for blaming the kid. But I know I'm right." He said, quietly.

"That's as may be, but we don't even know what the situation is yet." Phillips hissed, joining the conversation, quite to the surprise of Grisham, who stepped aside. "Now listen, Gary, trust me when I say, 'we're on your side'. I know you're not particularly keen on the lad, but you can't let personal feelings get in the way of the investigation. I didn't lie; we're not treating this as suspicious yet." He said.

"But the busted lock? You're telling me she did that?" Gary said, louder.

"We can't explain that now, forensics found no evidence against any one person. It's all circumstantial." Fiona interrupted, leaving Sarah for a moment. At that moment, Fiona's radio crackled, with a voice speaking vaguely from the other end. She gripped the receiver and stepped back out of the room so she did not interrupt the conversation.

"Our priority is finding Willow, not blaming anyone when we don't even know why or how she's missing. In any case, if she *has* been kidnapped, which I find highly unlikely, you're going to want the public on your side. You can't go about blaming innocent people, no matter how vaguely; because if the guilty party sees that, they're going to think we're not onto them. That's not what we want." Phillips finished. He placed a hand on Gary's shoulder. Sarah stared after her. "Let us do our job. We'll find her." Phillips continued.

"She's been missing for too long already. Something had better come up soon." Gary hissed with irritation. Behind him, the stage door cracked open again; Fiona appeared, though she did not enter; with all eyes upon her, she gestured.

"Sorry, Phillips, Superintendent, a word?" She asked, somewhat nervously. She seemed uneasy; with a frown each nearly disfiguring their appearances, the two men approached her; she ushered them through and closed the dor. She directed them from the stage, and they obliged to step down the stairs and found themselves concealed behind a stack of foldable chairs.

"What is it?" Grisham asked, his face urging her; then he caught sight of her pale face and wide eyes. "What is it?" He asked again, with more seriousness than the first time.

"I'm afraid we may have a body. It's unconfirmed, but the man who found it, Reverend Daryll, he recognises it. It's Willow." She said, quietly so as not to alert the journalists mere yards from them. Phillips gasped; Grisham frowned sadly; Fiona simply stood in the stunned silence all three of them had been left in.

-9-
Remains

Bright floodlights sliced through the still night air. The once tranquil lake was awash with the presence of some dozens of people; their shadows long with the anaemic glow of those lights. Four or five officers were floating in a pair of rafts on the still surface of the water. At the landward edge of the pier, three officers were constructing a white tent; they were currently erecting the metal skeleton. Ever and again, faint beams of torchlight scanned the night sky from the cliffs opposite the church, as forensic activities unfolded there.

A hum of chatter filled the air; police jargon was exchanged, and the occasional reporting was told to superiors; it was a subdued atmosphere, but one of great tension and nervousness.

The arrival of the Superintendent did nothing to calm matters; a convoy of two cars brought he, Fiona and Phillips to the scene; Fiona drove with the latter, for he was tired and did not want to risk being at the wheel of a car. Grisham led the way in his officer-driven vehicle. He drew along the path, which was not normally accessible to vehicles. He flashed his badge at the sentinel at the gate, who lifted the police tape barricade to allow the car through. Phillips followed suit and the guarding policeman tipped his hat as he passed. Their proceeding through that barrier led them to clearer paths; they had nearly knocked down a number of people in the crowd that had gathered to take in the goings-on.

In the bright light, Grisham just about made out the figure of a person; it was surreal to see, but her outline was as though it had been drawn by a child in white marker; long, flowing lines, simplified yet human in form. He deduced that it was someone from forensics, dressed in a full-body suit, a hood that enshrined their face and hair, and blue booties on her feet. Grisham raised his radio to his mouth and spoke into it;

"Jacqueline is here." He said; Phillips replied in an instant.

"Let's hope they've got something." He said, waking suddenly.

"They were on their way when I got the call." Fiona said, drawing up beside Grisham's now stationary vehicle. He was already getting out of the car by the time she switched off the engine – alighting the car, he collected his things and moved into the scene, taking in the situation with an eye that was keen, yet attuned to subtleties. As Phillips stepped out of his own vehicle, Fiona a moment later, he could just make out the Superintendent making his introductions. When they were all done, he began making enquiries.

Phillips regarded the scene with a quiet curiosity; he made particular note of the little rafts out near the base of the cliff; within, rowers were scanning the waters with high-powered torches in between keeping control of their craft. Evidently the mysterious face that had been observing Daryll had become lost once more. There was something remarkably calm about the entire affair; save for that obscure chattering that kept the air alive, all was seemingly as normal. Phillips was unaware of the status quo, however – he had never been to this part of the town before. Now he was beginning to wish he had become familiar with it prior to this unfortunate meeting.

"What do we have, Jacqueline, and don't say 'nothing'." Grisham began, holding his hand to his chin. Jacqueline turned to him and cleared the mask from her chin, for it had sprung back over her face.

"Well the Reverend over there" she answered, gesturing the aforementioned, "says he got a pretty good look at the face; brown hair, female, generally matching Willow's description. We've been scanning the water for her, but she must have sunk, as we've lost her again." She resumed. Grisham interrupted.

"These waters aren't very deep. A couple of meters, if that. Get those men in the water if they have to." He said, turning out and pointing at the water-bound crew.

"There's something else, sir." Jacqueline interjected.

"Oh?"

"Yes. Follow me, I'll show you." With that, she gestured with an outstretched hand; her body suit squeaked and rubbed as she moved; she had become accustomed to it, though it annoyed Grisham. He, Fiona and Phillip followed her as she made her way around the lake via a dusty path that could lead to the fields beyond or proceed further to meet the base of a gentle incline that led to the top of the cliffs; for a few moments, they were out of the reach of the vast floodlights opposite them and were led through darkness by Jacqueline, a guide who was evidently used to the route.

She led them to the gate at the bottom of the hill, and it was pushed open by another officer standing there. Phillips recognised him but did not acknowledge the man. They scrambled up to the crest of the hill, narrow streams of light filtering through the vegetation; it was very eerie to be there in the darkness. Bright spots of light sat on the ground in places, whilst the breeze caught and blew leaves about in a manner that caused the bright patches to flicker; disoriented, Phillips believed he was walking on a reflection of the delicately blinking starlight above him.

Save for Grisham getting his sleeves snared by snagging thorns, they came upon the crest with relative ease; there, they found more floodlights illuminating the clearing at the cliff edge. A multitude of forensics staff mingled in amongst little orange flags sticking like needles into the ground. Suddenly, a bright flash, as one of the assembled workers photographed some detail they had been examining. The sound of a rattling generator hummed in the night, though was so unobtrusive, it barely inconvenienced any conversation.

Jacqueline stepped over to a container containing protective equipment; it was identical to the one in the Greene household, so Fiona recognised it immediately. Jacqueline opened it and fished out three masks, latex gloves and hairnets. She handed these to the trio, who donned them forthwith. With all of the precautions as were necessary, they stepped into the crime scene.

"What are we looking at here?" Phillips asked, his voice muffled by the mask and nasally by virtue of the nose clip. He eyed the flags and expected to find evidence at their landings, but so far as he could make out, none were immediately noticeable.

"Blood, and a lot of it." She said, gesturing at one of the flags; she squatted down beside it as Grisham approached. In the light, he could just about make out the crimson hue he had at first assumed was just a colour change in the leaf; but upon closer inspection, he recognised the smooth surface of the fluid. It was unmistakable. Phillips and Fiona explored a patch on their own; it was barely noticeable. "We're lucky it's been such a warm Summer, no rain." Jacqueline pointed out.

"I'd never have spotted that, not in this darkness." He said, nearly stumbling as he tried to find his balance. Jacqueline looked up.

"That's why I'm in forensics, Phillips, and you're not." She said; he threw her a cautionary glance, but he thought nothing of the comment.

"Anything else? Hair, skin flakes, saliva?" Grisham said, rising to his feet; so tall was he, that he would have gone lightheaded as he rose. Fortunately, he was so accustomed to it that it did not affect him anymore.

"We're still looking, but I doubt we'll find much else. We need to figure out who this blood belongs to, that should get the ball rolling. If we can match it to the blood in the house, we'll have a clearer picture." She answered, rising to her feet, and stepping towards the cliff edge. She knew, as well as the others, that if the blood did indeed belong to whoever was in the lake, it actually proved very little. "If someone else is mixed in with that blood, then we're on to something." She continued. She turned about to face the group. "Sniffer dogs picked up a scent and followed it that way," she said, pointing with a flat hand over the fields behind the church. "The trail led straight to the Greene household."

"So she was brought from the house, over the fields, to here?" Fiona quizzed.

"That's the theory. I'm sorry I don't have more for you, but these aren't the best conditions for this; we need broad daylight." She said; Phillips stepped past her and took to the edge of the precipice; how fortunate, he was, that he did not have a feeling of vertigo. "What we really need is a body, then we can start running comparisons." She continued. Phillips turned around.

"I think they've got something for you." He said; almost immediately, the other three were upon him; he felt a rush of horror as he feared he should be cast over the edge by them, but they ceased beside him and peered over the lip; far below, there was a man in the water, perhaps up to his shoulders; he bore, in his arms, the half-submerged form of a girl, her face one of terror. Her clothing was torn and frayed, and water poured from her open mouth and nose. Those grim details were obvious and sharp even at that distance.

In an instant, the four were to action, as they stepped back from the edge, turned about and rushed towards the edge of the perimeter; Phillips and Fiona discarded the gloves, masks and helmets atop the container. Then, they struck out through the undergrowth once more and once again, they passed the sentinel at the gate who did not hear them approach. They now became aware of the distant wailing of sirens, the approach of an ambulance.

Into open air once more, they moved quickly around the fringes of the lake, its waves delicately lapping at their feet; they were unconcerned with such trivialities, for now the body was being unloaded from the raft it had been sailing aboard; the drenched officer was forthwith wrapped in a warm towel. The group watched as the body was carefully carried by gloved handlers; Grisham recognised them as a part of the Coroner's team. They were moving it into the tent, which by now was completely constructed. Once it was within, the drape across the entrance was drawn so as to completely conceal the interior. The group arrived at the entrance to the tent, and after a conversation with the officer on guard at the seal, they were allowed to enter; once more, they were forced to adorn protective clothing.

The interior was bright, though only lit with a small number of electric lamps; the white canopy was enough to reflect a bright glow into the space. It was small, but not cramped; in the middle of the tent, a stretcher was erected, and the body had been lain upon it. The coroner, a middle-aged man with a thin veil of grey hair, was busying himself with investigations.

Now within close enough proximity, the group observed the body for the first time; she was pale and still, her mouth and eyes open wide, as though forced open. Her hair was a tangle of dirt and water, and a red stain began oozing, not flowing, from the extreme ends of her locks. The coroner was already aware of this, and promptly began busying himself with locating what he presumed was an injury. He pushed her hair aside, almost like a curtain, and peered at her scalp; a tear in her skin was immediately obvious, and around it he recognised short, rough strands.

"Blunt force trauma. This individual was struck on the back of the head. Probable fracturing of the *parietal* bone." He moved her scalp and found it moved more than he anticipated. "Separation of the *coronal suture*. The *parietal* and frontal bones are disconnected." He explained, grimly. Fiona inhaled a terrified breath.

"Is it possible that she hit her head once she hit the water?" Phillips asked. The coroner turned to him with a perplexed face.

"Unlikely. An impact with water is not enough to cause this kind of damage. Not from the height we're talking about. This was caused by a strong hit from behind, probably from a club or a rock, something like that." He explained. The coroner spoke in low, calm tones.

"What about impact with the lakebed?" That was Fiona.

"So, she falls, lands in the water and splits her head open on the lakebed. It's possible, but I don't think at all probable." He said; for a moment, Phillips believed he was going to entertain his idea.

"Why is that?" He asked.

"Because if she splits her head open in the water, then that isn't her blood on the cliff. Which means it was either someone else's and is unrelated, or she got that injury before she went over the edge." Jacqueline interjected. Phillips realised that she was right.

"That's why it's 'pure speculation'." He pointed out, turning back to the body.

"Anyway, that water is as deep as a person is tall. That's still quite deep, so she would have had to have been weighted down to have her head strike the bed." She pointed out. But Fiona believed she had the answer to that point.

"Hence the rocks." She said; all eyes fell on her, so she explained; "Check out her pockets." She pointed to them. As the eyes of the group met her pockets, they noticed that her baggy trousers were bulging with sharp points and solid shapes; they did not look like enough to sink a person, despite the great quantity evidently hidden within the deep pockets of her trousers.

"Speculation. Where is the person who found the body, Daryll?" Grisham asked, naming the man.

"He's outside talking to an officer." A policeman standing across the tent said. He gestured out of the entrance.

"I'd like to speak to him. Phillips, Fiona, I know this isn't up to you, but I want you to go to visit the Greene's in the morning. Someone needs to make a formal identification. You're dismissed for the night, thank you for your help." He said, turning back to the girl. Fiona stopped him;

"Phillips, wait." She called. Phillips turned around, swinging his arms; he moved back over to her. She moved her mouth closer to his ears and whispered. "Is it just me, or is there not really a family resemblance?"

"How do you mean?"

"She's unlike both of her parents. It's strange." She said, a little louder. Phillips shrugged.

"Get back on her laptop as soon as you can, see if she made any orders from those Paternity Test sites. We'll speak with Gary and Sarah about it." He continued; she nodded, then turned, and vanished into the gloom of the night. Phillips pondered for a moment; "Tricky." Then, he turned fully and moved back to the table. "Such a tragedy." He muttered. At that moment, the coroner pronounced her dead, having been checking, with futility, for a pulse or any sign of life.

Finally, Phillips turned again; he swept through the short tunnel of the entrance and pushed aside the curtain. Grisham, who ducked as he passed through the exit, followed quickly.

By now the scene outside was calmer; in the time they had been in the tent, the group had missed the rafts being packed away and the officer numbers being halved.

As Phillips moved out away from the scene, he realised at once that the car he had arrived in was not where it had been left. *Dammit*, he thought, *why did I send Fiona out without me*? He gritted his teeth in frustration. He turned about and spotted Grisham, once again staring into the distance, stoic and curious. Grisham espied the forensics group busying themselves atop the cliff, their lights flickering through the black night. Then he spotted a civilian-looking man by the floodlights; he was discussing something with another officer, who made notes as he talked. Grisham recognised him in a moment and stepped towards the conversation.

The officer saw him approach first, and he paused his scribbling for a moment to greet him. With those out of the way, Grisham spoke;

"I'll take over from here, thank you." He said; and with that, the officer handed him the notes he had been taking; they were almost entirely illegible, perhaps to everyone save for the person who had written them. Seeing the futility of trying to understand them, Grisham dismissed the officer with the wave of a hand. Daryll watched him go, and then smiled to Grisham. It was not a revelling smile, it was one bittersweet; still polite enough to greet the Superintendent.

"Good evening Daryll, I'm very sorry to keep you so late, so I'll make this brief." In the background, Grisham heard an engine fire up; Phillips had commandeered a fellow officer to take him home.

"It is no problem at all, I would rather see this resolved than sleep." He said, quietly. Grisham struggled to hear him. He lowered his own voice to allow his ears to become accustomed to the quiet, a trick he had learned in his younger years.

"Thanks again. What were you doing when you found the body?" Grisham said, somewhat suddenly and sharply. Daryll leaned back in a quiet alarm.

"I was clearing litter from the woods at the top of the cliff. It was such a beautiful evening, and my mind was in turmoil." Daryll said, shaking his head.

"Why is that?" Grisham asked, his interest piqued. Daryll paused.

"Personal. The litter, it represents a disregard. The lack of caring. It has affected me in ways it would not affect others. My congregation is changing." He continued. Grisham wrote this down, then a thought struck him.

"Where is the litter you collected?" He asked.

"Well, normally I sort through it, recycle what I can then throw away the rest. I haven't done that yet, though. The bag is just inside the narthex." He continued, pointing to the entrance of the church.

"I'm afraid you won't be sorting it; there may be evidence to go through." Grisham said. He made a note to have it collected. "Do you know anything about Willow, did you ever come across her?"

"Oh yes, I knew her alright, Delightful child, so friendly. I would often see her at Sunday service with her family, they are all delightful. But somehow," He paused. ", I don't know. She seemed to have fallen in with the wrong crowd."

"How do you mean?"

"I like her friends; I think her friends are lovely people. But she started to become popular, and that drew some unpleasant characters. It broke my heart to see that." He said, crossing his arms and shaking his head.

"What kind of unpleasant characters?" Grisham urged, closing the book; he leaned forward with a subtle forcefulness.

Had it been daytime, or there been more floodlights around the perimeter of the crime scene, Grisham would have noticed; he would have seen a blonde-haired boy who was standing at the outskirts and staring in, having been refused entry to the interior, his fists balled and bruised.

-10-
The Ninth Year

Gary awoke with a start, though it was not an abrupt one; apparently the young girl jumping up and down on his chest had been doing so for some time, as Sarah was already rubbing her bleary eyes into clarity. The room was still dark, save for a kaleidoscope of colour growing through the tiny crack in the curtains at the far side of the room. In between thudding impacts of Willow's excitable jumps upon him, he stole a glance of the alarm clock; why had it not woken him up sooner, he thought – why was his morning starting like this?

It was because the eight in the morning alarm he had set the night before was not due to go off for another two hours or so. She was early.

"Christ, get her to go back to bed!" He hissed with annoyance; he managed to free a weary arm from beneath the duvet and rolled Willow off of him into the space currently occupied by his wife. Willow laughed excitedly.

"It's too early yet, baby. You promised no earlier than eight o'clock, remember?" Sarah said, pushing Willow clear of her part of the bed.

"Yes, but Daddy promised he would pick me up from school yesterday, and he didn't keep his promise." She replied, innocently. Gary groaned into his hand.

"Yes, sweetheart, you've got a point there." Sarah replied, jabbing an elbow into Gary's side. He let out a poorly concealed yelp. "In that case, six o'clock it is. Come on honey, up you get." She continued, aiming her playful yet demanding order at her husband, who let out another groan. Willow screamed with excitement, then jumped clear from the bed; in an instant, she was through the door. Sarah followed her with her eyes, then turned to face Gary who was almost snoring again.

"Harrumph." He moaned.

"She's got a point. What's the point in my trying to get her to be good when she has you as a role model?" Sarah hissed. She could hear Willow in the next room changing from her pyjamas into a dressing-gown.

"She's old enough now to walk home on her own, it's only

five minutes down the street." He replied angrily.

"She's nine, Gary. Mrs. Stebbing next door doesn't let her son walk home alone, and he's three months older." She retorted, but Gary merely scoffed.

"All I'm saying is I really don't think me not walking her home to teach her a bit of responsibility is reason enough for me to be woken up at six in the morning. It's even less of a reason to be performing bad CPR on me just because she wants to go downstairs and unwrap some teddy bears or some shit. She's not six anymore, Sarah." He said, pulling the duvet up over his face.

"Fine, you stay in bed." She replied, pulling the duvet down past her ankles. She flipped her legs over and planted her feet on the ground. "I'll go and be the parent, seeing as that's clearly a chore for you." She continued, untangling the dressing-gown from itself.

"Sarah, come on, don't be like that." He implored – Sarah saw through his feigned remorse and shot him a look.

"It's just another birthday you're not interested in seeing, isn't it? I don't know why she bothers trying to convince you anymore." She replied, trying the fabric belt around her waist. "Besides, you know she hates teddy bears and all that stuff. She never has, I don't know why you keep *forgetting* that." Gary rolled over with his back to her, and sighed; within seconds, he was snoring again.

Sarah looked at him and sighed loudly; she knew that he was barely sober. Another hungover birthday for Willow to look forward to. With that, she turned and moved for the door; she heard Willow barrel past from her room. Sarah's eyes scanned the landing as she left the room; it was still in semi darkness. Down the stairs, she could hear her daughter bouncing on the bottom step; she may have been excited, but she was as patient as she was enthusiastic, despite the apparent urgency to awaken her family.

"Where's Daddy?" She almost screamed, before being hushed by her mother.

"He's got a headache, so he'll be down soon, sweetheart." She said; she expected Willow to sigh or make some other dejected noise, but her enthusiasm was undiminished. She continued bouncing until she could feel her mother's hands on her shoulder blades; with that, she hopped from the step and rounded the rail. The living room door was closed, to conceal the mountain of presents within. Willow made for the handle, but was stopped;

"Uh, wait!" Sarah said, raising a finger. With that, Willow paused, and stopped at the door, her hand still twitching as though it was clutched around the handle. Her mother smiled, then moved to the door, pulling the handle and pushing the door – a paradox, she thought. She had tried to explain to Willow what a paradox was once; it only served to worry her that someone would go back in time to pay her grandparents a visit.

Through the tiny crack in the door her mother had opened, Willow could now see a pile of presents; she nearly forced the door off of its hinges, her impatience to get in somewhat firmer than her mother's efforts to stop her. She bounded into the room and pounced on the presents; there were boxes and bundles wrapped in flowery patterns, whilst others were of a much more reserved yet still colourful design; she recognised her parents presents straightaway; they were concealed in a big sack near the radiator; she would open those last.

"What do you think, then?" Sarah said with a gushing inflection. Willow crawled about on the floor, picking up errant boxes that were disturbed by her arrival; all the while, her eyes flitted from box to box, and her mouth moved silently.

"Fourteen!" She said, putting one of the presents back.

"What's that, sweetie?" Sarah responded.

"There's fourteen this year." She sounded almost upset. She had more last year; it was a concept Sarah had dreaded bringing up so many years before, but Willow was not a baby anymore.

"Well honey, you're getting older now." Sarah began, moving into the room and sitting on the armchair. A sickly-looking cat purred on the arm, though it did not look up as she sat; it merely stretched with nonchalant annoyance and settled again. "You're not always going to get piles of presents. Fourteen is still a lot, though, sweetie!" She said, watching for her face to drop ever further – but as she watched, she espied a little innocent, yet mischievous, face dawn upon her.

"That's okay, Mummy, really. I'm sure I'll love them all the same." Willow squeaked; a half smile curled across her face, and once again, she drove into the pile of presents. Sarah smiled too; as her daughter tore into a box, she settled down and ran her fingernails through the cat's fur. It made an appreciative sound.

Soon after, Willow emerged from her rapidly diminishing pile; already, she had uncovered several stacks of books, stationary and soft toys, which were forming part of a mound rapidly springing up in the middle of the room. Her favourite was a book on the space race her grandfather had got for her.

"Look Mummy," she cried eventually, "this one's from Daddy!" She simpered, holding the crudely wrapped parcel aloft; Sarah looked at it, surprised; she wondered why it was not in the sack, with the rest of their presents for her.

"Ooh, right, well go on, you open it; I wonder what it is?" She said, softly. Willow did not need telling twice, as before her Sarah had finished her sentence, she was already tearing into the wrapping; within, a soft tuft of white and green fuzz emerged from the tears. It looked vaguely like a stuffed toy, but one that was crudely put together – or falling apart. Sarah realised almost immediately that it was the infamous stuffed dinosaur that Gary had seen in a charity shop three weeks before and taken a liking to. He was keen to buy it, despite her insistence that Willow had gone past her dinosaur obsession the previous year. As a matter of fact, Sarah did wonder why he had snuck out the week before; now she knew.

Willow held the thing in her hand – it was a four-legged herbivore. She rolled it about in her hands and contemplated why her father had bought it for her.

"It's a dinosaur?" She said trying with feigned effort to sound thrilled; Sarah saw through it almost immediately.

"But you like dinosaurs." Sarah said, unconvincingly.

"I did, but that was las year. I'm nine now!" Willow replied, putting the thing down; with one of the four legs shorter than the others, it toppled over immediately. "I'll leave it out. Do you think he'll mind if I don't play with it?" She said, turning to her mother. Sarah continued to prod the cat affectionately; it coughed gently.

"No honey, somehow I don't think he will."

-11-
Outlived

"I'm so sorry to be here under these circumstances." Phillips said, leaning in towards Sarah. He could not see her face, for it was buried in her hands. Gary stood over her with his hand upon her shoulder; he almost looked fed up, even as he heard her weep.

"Where is she?" She said between sniffles and sobs.

"She's on her way to the mortuary at Heathestone General. But we can't be certain it's her just yet, so you'll need to come and identify her for us." He continued. Fiona, who was sat across the room from him, twisting her radio in her hands, looked into his face with a solemnity she could not hide. "Do you think you can do that for us?" He continued. Sarah did not respond; she swept a few stray hairs from her face. Gary yawned. Phillips sighed silently to himself and spoke again; "Look, I understand how difficult this must be for you," he began. He was always trained to say '*both of you*', but only one of the two seemed distressed. "If you'd rather not see her, you could provide a saliva sample, and we can do a DNA identification?" He suggested. Before he had a chance to finish the sentence, Sarah unexpectedly spoke;

"No, no!" She cried, lifting her face up to the amazement of the officers; she had not been so drastic in front of them thus far. "I want to see her. I want one more hug." She said. Phillips raised the corners of his mouth into something resembling a half-smile, sympathetic. Gary did not respond; instead, he simply pushed himself out of his chair and left the room towards the kitchen. Before he left, Fiona espied his nonchalance, and regarded him with a concern at his indifference; Phillips had noticed it too.

"I'm sorry to have to ask you this, but I'm afraid I have to, Sarah." Phillips asked as he heard the rear door open, then after a pause, close again; Gary had gone out. "We found some very strange things in Willow's browsing history, and we need to ask you about them."

"She can do whatever she likes on the internet. I'm not here to police her or anything." Sarah snapped, surprising Phillips, who sat upright.

"We have reason to believe Willow was trying to get access

to a DNA test. Is this something she ever discussed with you?" He asked; her eyes, unflinching, kept on him, wide and angry. For about half a minute, there was silence, in which Phillips reasoned that he was not going to get an answer from her; Sarah merely sat.

Abruptly, the kitchen door flew open. Phillips started, gripping the armchair with startled hands. He saw Gary swing through the door, clutching a brown bottle in his left hand, the beer within frothing gently. With as much of a conversation, Phillips rose to his feet. He nodded to Fiona, who similarly bounced to her feet.

"We'll send a car in the morning. Try and get some rest." He said to Sarah, calmly. She did not look at him as she nodded. "We'll see ourselves out." Phillips tipped his head to Gary, in a manner which he imagined would engage him; he merely nodded in response. With that, Fiona came to Phillips' side and they began to leave. They were stopped by Sarah, who gripped Fiona's trouser leg suddenly. Gary rolled his eyes.

"Who found her?' She asked, with a confidence the officers had not seen in her yet. Phillips turned to Fiona.

"Daryll, at the church." She responded. Sarah chuckled a pleased laugh.

"Was she alone?" She continued. Phillips frowned, and Fiona looked at him, unsure. "When she died, was she alone?" She clarified. Phillips answered for Fiona.

"We can't say right now, I'm sorry. I promise you; we *will* find out what happened to your daughter." He said, resting a hand on her shoulder. Once more, however, she did not reply. He rubbed her arm slightly in as comforting a fashion as possible and turned about again. The pair left the living room and headed out towards the door; they could see the light of the coming sunrise beckoning them towards the Saturday that was on its way shining through the frosted glass of the door.

Leaving the house, they closed the front door behind them; now Phillips saw the blood red sky of a day that threatened to downpour; still, the air was cool and fresh; Fiona breathed in the cold and in a moment, her lungs were refreshed. She sighed loudly.

"That never gets any easier." She said as they approached the car, clearing the garden path.

"No. Someone's got to do it. I'd just rather it was someone else but me." He said, somewhat selfishly; Fiona understood. "I'll see about organising that car for them." He continued. He unlocked the car door and opened the driver's side. He stepped in with his feet first. Fiona followed suit on the passenger side.

"I'm not convinced Gary will be going; is it just me, or does he seem a bit aloof?" She admitted.

"No, I know what you mean. I know grief affects people in different ways, but he hasn't shed a tear once. It's like his daughter dying is an inconvenience for him." He considered. Fiona nodded.

"In any case, I'm not sure we need them to make an identification." She continued as the pair fastened their seatbelts. Phillips fired the ignition and the car roared into life.

"Oh? Why's that?" He asked.

"Because I recognise her. Even in that twisted face, there was a vestige of the Willow I've seen."

"On her laptop?"

"No. In Harry's scrapbook."

-12-
Suspicious Activity

The kitchen window was open, and through it came the sound of a chorus of birds twittering and tweeting; it was loud, but hardly annoying. The sky was alive with rippling clouds that bounced upon the red veil of haze of sunrise, the coming of which was not visible on that side of the house.

Inside, the smell of cooking wafted through the hallway and permeated each room, regardless of whether or not the door to it was closed. Sizzling bacon and thick sausages lay in pools of their own fat inside the pan. Ever and again they were moved by the tip of a wooden spatula that was stained and cracked in places by constant use. Liquid spat and foamed, but Louise did not mind; it was another scar to add to her already battered body.

She stood humming a tune – normally she would listen to the radio, but Harry had destroyed it in a fit of rage the previous week. As she probed the food, ensuring it was cooked to the perfection her son so desired, she contemplated; thinking of Willow, for she knew Harry would not do so with any degree of solemnity, she wondered over what had happened to her. Of course, she had heard the gossip that a body had been found, but did not want to put the two anomalies together; certainly, Willow had vanished, but it could not be her body; Halloween was in a couple of months, so perhaps a fake body intended for decoration had become entangled in the investigation? This thought lingered in her head for no more than a few moments, for she realised at once how ridiculous such a notion was.

Her mind turned to a truth she was only now deciding to accept; that things were as straightforward as they seemed; that it *was* Willow, and that she was dead. It seemed so incredible, so indescribable a horror, that she could not bear to think what was afoot. Who had murdered her, if she had been murdered at all? Could Harry be capable of such a thing? It worried her to consider that he could be. After all, she thought, how he behaved with his own mother! Such a cowardly act, masked by his own belief that she was the one in the wrong. It turned her stomach to think what he could have done to Willow.

Yet, as despairing as she found herself when considering

all of this, she still did not believe he was capable of something as heinous as *murder*. She feared him, fretting over what he was able to do, yet at the same time sought to protect him. How, why? Her mind was a jumble; how could her son be the way he is? Why was she in such contempt of him, yet harbour a love for him that only a mother knows?

She realised that she had stopped humming, and the food was becoming overcooked; she fretted that she had been daydreaming, and so ripped the frying pan from the hob, only to have the fat spill up the shallow ides and onto her hand; she held herself well, yet let out a cry. With a whimper, she twisted around and slammed the pan down on the table, immediately burning the wooden surface. She threw her hands into the air in frustration and dashed for the sink. Something to cool her hands!

She allowed cool water to flow over her fingers, yet she could see beneath the clear liquid that her hand was turning red. For a moment she did not consider that Harry would be annoyed at her over this discrepancy – as he was wont to do. But he had heard the commotion, the clatter of pan on wood, and had come to investigate.

He was fully dressed, surprising for that time of the morning, and was relatively clean. He came into the kitchen whilst still pulling his shirt down over his torso. He paused in the door and scoffed as his eyes passed from the ruined food to Louise, who turned the tap off as she became aware that he was there. She turned to him and smiled a nervous smile.

"Oh, Harry, I didn't expect you up so early. Sorry about the noise, I've done your breakfast." She said cautiously; she moved over to the table and fished amongst the meat with the charred spatula. "It's a little overdone, but I think it will be fine once I scrape off the burnt bits." She smiled, nervously. She was aware of him moving towards her, and a sensation of dread came over her. She began to shake, though not visibly. Harry placed a dry hand on her far cheek and turned her face towards his own. Her grip loosened on the spatula, and it dropped into the still bubbling fat. His hold was firm, but somehow not threatening; she thought that she could easily escape from him, but she did not dare to try.

Now that she faced him, she could see a scowl on his face that seemed seared into his features; it was more or less a permanent visage, he used it so much. Then, he slid his hand under her chin, placing his thumb firmly on her right cheek, such that he could squeeze her chin firmly. She gasped as he gripped her and let out a sob – how she wished she was stronger, she would act. But she did not try, as he was so far not erupting. He drew his face close to hers, his rancid breath falling onto her nose. He then pressed his face onto hers, squashing her nose into his. He closed his eyes and let out a tear that streamed down his cheek – a tear! He was capable of emotion!

 This display lasted for little more than a second, for he released his grip on her face; she gasped and inhaled deeply, as he moved past her, thumping his shoulder into hers as he went. She stood, panting for a moment, as he moved for the back door.

 "Don't you want your breakfast, then?" She said, turning; he either did not hear her or he was ignoring her as he drew the bolt back on the door and swung it violently open into the lower cupboards – he had smashed the door window before now – and made to go. She stepped forward after him; "Harry?" She called. Finally, he paused; *had she just tried to stop him*? He thought; *was she trying to be forceful with him*? It had worked, and he turned around, staring with an expectant face. "Harry, please. You have to tell me. This Willow girl, what do know about what happened to her?" She asked. Suddenly, his demeanour changed; abruptly, his shoulders drooped, and his eyes popped; Louise moved ever closer to him, yet he recoiled at every step. He shivered as she quizzed him, his spine tingling. She put out an arm to try to rub his shoulder, but he tore himself clear of her reach. She started backwards, and he winced. Then, he turned about, cleared the door, and slammed it behind him. She jumped as the slam resounded around the house, shaking the windows as it went.

 Louise was alone again; only her thoughts to keep her busy. His attitude unsettled her; she had always considered him strange, but now there was a new context to his eccentricities – but he was gone now. The police would discover what was going on; so she turned, fished a sausage from the pan and put it across her teeth; it was not as overcooked as she thought. Then she resumed humming as she moved through the room and into the hallway.

-13-
Identity

"One o'clock, they should be here any minute." Fiona said, glancing at her watch. Phillips sat beside her, thumbing through several pages of reports that were stapled together. She glanced at him, then to the papers. "Anything interesting?" She asked, nodding.

"Nothing." He sighed by way of response and flipping back to the cover sheet. "No personal effects on her person. No phone, purse, nothing. Did you find anything like that in her room?" He quizzed, spinning his head to eye her.

"Just her laptop. To be honest, I didn't look all that thoroughly." She sighed, staring ahead once more. Phillips perused the documents once more.

"Well, we've got divers searching the lake-bed. If these are down there, we'll find them." He sighed, flipped close the pack again, then clasped it between his hands. At that moment, a nurse moved past the pair; Phillips looked up at her as she went before she vanished into a side room. Phillips, ignoring this distraction, turned back to Fiona, who, he could see, had not reacted. "You're tense."

"Is it any wonder?" She hissed, loudly. Then, she turned to face him directly; "Don't you start detecting on me, Phillips." She pointed with an irritated finger.

"Relax." As soon as he said that, he thought how much of an effort that would be. "They'll be here soon." That was that for a while; all about them, phones rang, alarms beeped and the general hum of a hospital in smooth operation filled the air. "God, I hate this bit." He continued; Fiona looked to him as he gestured the window in front of them, overlooking another room. Willow was laid within.

"It's not a favourite of mine, either." She replied. Philips lifted the sheets aloft and gestured to them with a spare hand;

"Have you had a chance to read the statements yet?" He said; Fiona looked over again and nodded nonchalantly. "What did you think to the Reverend? Darryl?" He said, glancing through his, admittedly thorough, statement. Fiona sighed and spoke almost at the last part of her breath.

"He seems okay, nice enough I mean." She said. She folded her arms and furrowed her brow. "I still think it's a bit suspicious though;".

"Oh yes?" Phillips prompted.

"It just seems very coincidental that he was 'clearing away litter'," she gestured with her fingers, "at that time of night; *and* in the area of a crime scene. I just can't really credit it." She mused. Phillips soaked up her analysis and considered it too.

"So, you think he's a suspect?" He asked; of course, he knew that everyone was considered a suspect at that time, but he wanted her opinion, and she was happy to give it.

"Well it's just his word, isn't it? No witnesses, nobody to back up his alibi. Well, I say *alibi*, it's hardly the most convincing story ever told." She leaned over to the statement and flipped through the pages, pointing out what he had said; "*...wind caught the bag full of litter and carried it into the lake below. I went to recover it...*' etc, it's all a bit contrived if you ask me." She continued, sitting back into her chair. In the distance, a door opened and closed again; the sound of feet rapped on the sanitised floor.

"It's too early to speculate yet, of course, but I'm inclined to agree." Phillips said. "Let's see where we get... aah!" He stopped abruptly; Fiona started. Phillips folded the statements into his bag and hoisted it onto his back as he rose to his feet; Fiona turned to face the direction he was looking in, and in doing so espied a somewhat dejected looking Sarah and Gary ambling through the corridor in the accompaniment of a male nurse and another police officer. Phillips smiled a wary smile. "Sarah, Gary, thanks for coming down. I can't begin to imagine how difficult this is for you." Sarah looked up; her eyes were red and bloodshot, as though she had been crying all day – Phillips supposed that she had. Gary, on the other hand, did not have such a look in his eyes. Fiona noticed it before Phillips did. The male nurse manoeuvred himself around the group and moved to the door beside the window.

"If you'd like to come in." The nurse said; Sarah and Gary turned to look at him; for a few moments, nobody moved; it was as though time had stopped. Sarah seemed frozen in place, though Gary made to push her, though it did not work. She appeared rooted to the floor, staring into empty space with eyes of glass. Fiona tilted her head.

"Sarah?" She said, gently. At the sound of her name, she started, looked around, as though she was lost. Finally, and with some reluctance, she eventually moved for the door. Phillips was surprised by Gary, who for a moment actually hesitated too; he drew a shivering breath and then followed Sarah. Fiona espied it too, though neither of them mentioned it. Rather, they followed the two parents into the room; it was cold and clinical; bright white lights filled the room with a sanitary glow. The refrigeration was in full effect, and perhaps unsurprisingly, the five people developed a chill as they passed through the thick doors.

It took Sarah a few moments to espy her daughter; she glanced around the room, taking in the plethora of medical instruments and bits of equipment scattered with great precision around; she understood the function only a select few of them.

Finally, though, her eyes settled upon the table in the middle of the room; it was a stark, metal thing with legs that were screwed into the floor. About it was draped a blue sheet, with a human shaped form beneath it; the vague form of a face was at the furthest end of the table from the group; the nurse approached, removing a pair of blue gloves from a receptacle by the door. He invited the others to do the same. Sarah reluctantly did so, but Gary merely ignored the instruction; back to normal, Phillips thought.

The nurse moved to the head of the table and gestured for the group to come closer; the two officers remained where they were; this was not something they needed to be close to. Sarah and Gary approached, both somewhat tentatively. Soon, everything would become real for them. Gary gently touched the side of the table; he did not expect it to be as cold as it was. Sarah stood closer to the head of the table, but at a distance. The nurse cleared his throat, then spoke with a gentle, purring voice.

"I will remove the sheet, exposing her face and shoulders. If you need to see any other part of her body in order to make the identification, please tell me. I should warn you; she may not look as she did in life. Take all the time you need." The nurse gripped the sheet in the top corners and made to lift, but Sarah stopped him by gripping his wrist firmly. Immediately, all eyes were upon her; Gary sighed and rolled his eyes. She sniffled and blinked away a tear that was forming coldly in her eye, then nodded.

Releasing the nurses wrist, leaving an imprint on his skin, the nurse nodded then returned his gaze to the sheet, which he lifted and rolled down her face, moving the top over itself and bringing it down doubled over at her chest; her head and shoulders fully uncovered. A shiver overcame the parents, who both drew a breath that shook and rattled in the cold air. They took in her pale face, observing every feature; they knew immediately that the girl upon the table was their daughter.

Her face had become even more withdrawn and cold; now her lips were blue, and her eyes were wide and deep in her face. The thin wisps of her hair had been delicately, but not ornately, drawn back behind her head, such that the vicious damage done to the strands was rendered near invisible. Sarah believed it was all a lie; she was convinced that she had espied, ever and again, Willow's chest rising and falling with rhythmic recurrence, but the anomaly of the girl being the only figure from whom great plumes of thin fog did not emerge quickly waylaid this illusion; her breath did not exist, and eventually, Sarah had to resign herself to the knowledge that the girl was not about to jump from the table and shout 'boo'.

For an almost indeterminate amount of time, silence filled the room; even the ambient sounds of the hospital had softened into a melody that was actually quite peaceful and ambient.

"In your own time." The nurse said, at last. He pushed himself away from the table and moved to stand with the two officers positioned near the door. With a gloved hand, Sarah gently probed the girl's face; she wasn't sure why, and Gary made to stop her, but she threw him a terse look; he recoiled in an instant.

"Gary, I have to know she's real." She said; within a moment, he understood; it was almost a delirium of denial that she had to require any more proof that the body before them was not a mere effigy, but the real, truest form of their daughter. She turned back to the table and gripped the figure's head by the ears; another tear fell down her face. In her mind, however, she was not her daughter – at least, not as she remembered her; brimming with life.

At last, she turned her head towards the nurse – she was unsure who to tell – and spoke in a soft, raspy voice.

"Yes. It's Willow." She said; Gary gripped her shoulder, his arm around her; his face was one of contorted horror; suddenly, it seemed apparent that he was moved. Phillips could not decide if it was because her death was becoming real to him; or perhaps it was a realisation of what he had done that was concerning him. Either way, he would discover the truth, in any case.

Fiona nodded at her admittance and, at first, muttered her response;

"Thank you, Sarah, Gary. You've been very helpful." By the end of the sentence, she had raised her voice to a legible level; for her to begin her sentence at that level would have startled the lot of them. "We'll need you to fill out some paperwork. When you're ready, of course." She added, after seeing the look Gary had thrown her; it was one of annoyance. Back to form, Phillips thought once again.

"The grief councillor you spoke to before coming in here will be available to you for as long as you need." The nurse said; Phillips was somewhat surprised that the councillor had not come into the room with them; it was highly unusual. Sarah just nodded in response. She resumed prodding Willow's face, feeling every bump of her skin and kneading her soft cheeks. Perhaps she envisioned Willow would become annoyed and leap from the table to have her stop; but she didn't. She remained there, as cold and as lifeless as she had been when they entered. She was now resigned; Sarah could do nothing. She moved her face to within mere inches from Willow's and whispered something softly into her ear. Gary could not intercept the message, save for a few words that did not form coherence when assembled. She then stroked the lifeless hair of her daughter and then drew herself erect again. That was as close to a hug as she could get for now.

Gary placed a hand gently onto her back and pressed her to move. She reluctantly complied, and then, hanging her head, she stepped quietly away from the table. The nurse returned to the head of the table and gently lifted the blue sheet back over Willow's face. Gary spent a moment looking back, but quickly turned back, no longer contemplating his daughter beneath; she was gone. Phillips stepped towards them;

"If you'd like to follow Officer Daniels, she'll escort you to fill out the release forms. Thanks again for your help." He said, gesturing Daniels; she was the officer who had led them in. Sarah didn't even react this time; no nod, smile or anything of that sort. She simply exhaled again and allowed her tears to fall upon the floor. Phillips stepped aside, nodded at Gary and allowed them to pass. Daniels, who had now entered the room, held out an arm and gestured for them to follow – the three of them moved through the room and out of the door.

Phillips paused and turned back to the table; he could just about make out the outline of her form and lamented to himself at the pointlessness of her death; she was too young.

"Let's get her to Forensics." Fiona said, distracting him from his stupor. He turned about to face her, and said;

"Yes, you're right. I'll send for Mark, he'll arrange it."

"You alright?" Fiona replied, sensing that he was not.

"Yeah. Fine. This type of thing doesn't happen enough. I guess that's a good thing, but it can't prepare you." He said. Fiona understood and nodded in agreement.

"No matter how hard we try, we'll never get used to this." She said, complimenting his thoughts with her own. The nurse approached and smiled to them.

"I'll escort you out." He said, gesturing the door. Phillips paused and looked back to the table for a moment, then turned back to the door. He was followed by Fiona, then by the nurse, who closed the door once they were all clear and into the warm corridor. The light switched off at the closing, plunging the lone girl into darkness.

-14-
Mummy and the Strange Man

Willow could not sleep. It was half past the tenth hour at night, but for some reason she could not ascertain, her eleven-year-old mind was alive with concerns only an eleven-year-old could dream up. *Timmy was mean to me yesterday – Stacey isn't friends with Sam anymore – Mum and Dad were arguing again when I got home.* That last thought probably was not one shared with Timmy, or Stacey, or Sam. There again, maybe it was; they never mentioned the negative aspects of their home life. It certainly would not cross their minds to mention it. A child's world is their own.

Willow had not stayed around long enough to listen to what her parents were bickering about today; they were loud enough that she could hear them perfectly well from her bedroom. It had been the second day they had been at one another's throats; last night, Mum had found Dad's stash of cider behind the old vinyl records in the garage. Today, she merely heard one parent screaming a string of abuses at the other, often at the same time. Even from outside, for they had not closed the window, the voices reached her ears. So, she did not even stop to talk to them on her way through. She would not be heard, even if she had peeped through the door.

She dropped her bag at the foot of the stairs – then thought better of it and picked it up again – and hurried up the steps to her bedroom where she spent the remainder of the evening. She used most of this free time by switching on her computer – a hand me down with a CRT monitor, which she nicknamed 'Fat Back' - and getting online. It was a new experience for her; mum and dad had been reluctant to let her use the internet, despite her maturity. She blamed her teachers as they were the ones who had described the internet as though it was some sort of cesspool of vile things. In saying that, she knew it was only her mother was concerned. Dad barely said a word on the subject, other than to grumble at the expense of the new computer he was forced into replacing his old one with.

It was Stacey who had convinced Willow to try out this *internet* thing. She was one of the first in their class to try it out, by virtue of her parents encouraging her to try it out for herself. She knew that the teachers were wrong; used properly, the internet was a valuable tool for the modern student.

Get yourself on Myspace Stacey had said. *It's the go-to place*, she insisted; Willow had never used it before, but she was keen to try; *you can talk to anyone in the world! I'm talking to someone who's into reading, like me. Maybe you can find someone who is interested in sports, like you?* That gave Willow the incentive. Nobody she knew was as interested in sports as she was; especially the girls, who thought the games she liked were 'for boys only'.

Willow did not imagine her mum and dad would be terribly pleased about their daughter online – the horror! There again, she had realised by now that she would hardly be under any scrutiny. They would hardly care.

Stacey was her first friend on Myspace. Willow had chosen the username *W1ll0w* (because, oddly enough, every other variation of her name was taken). Stacey, or *Stace7991*, recognised it immediately, and added her forthwith, immediately beginning to communicate. Their conversation was largely concerned with explaining how the site worked though more of their time was dedicated to gossip. But Willow did not care about the mundanity of their time online; but it was *exciting*. Finally, she was in the online world, with such an engrossing attachment that by her third hour, she had already lost the sound of her parents from her ears.

It was about nine o'clock in the evening when she decided she had had enough. By then, Stacey had gone, and Willow had been talking to someone from her school, somebody by the name of *HM4st*. She did not recognise that name; she could not decipher it no matter how hard she looked at it. It must have been a sixth-form student, she thought, because he was very mature in his verbiage. She did not think of it like that, of course, but she could not understand some of the words he was using. But that conversation had been curbed when *HM4st* had gone offline some forty minutes ago. With nobody left to talk to, she logged off for the night, switched off her computer and clambered weakly into bed. It was only in the silence she was surrounded with now that she realised her parents had stopped fighting. The silence was bliss, though for her, it was strangely isolating; the silence pressed on her as though it was manifesting itself as a humidity that thickened the air and kept her from sleeping.

So she simply laid there, trying her best to nod off; her eyes were scrunched shut and she was in the comfiest position she could think of; she slept with two pillows and a thin duvet; she could not stand being bundled up and compressed. Perhaps that was why the silence bothered her so much?

By half past ten, all she could think about was the problems of that day – poor Stacey, not talking to Sam anymore. Worse, was Mum and Dad.

She decided that she was not likely to go to sleep any time soon; she was now acutely aware that all noises had ceased from downstairs; it was so quiet, that she was disturbed. The still, silent air was like a vacuum around her. Why were they quiet? Perhaps one or more of them had gone to bed? That must be it. Dad always goes to sleep immediately after an argument. Or leaves the house; in any case, he would not be downstairs.

There came a point sometime in the next fifteen minutes where she decided that she would maybe be more tired if she were to go downstairs and get herself a glass of water – some years ago, she would have had to call down for Mum to bring her one. But now she was allowed to go downstairs for her own drinks; she was a big girl now. She threw what little duvet still covered her off, dove clear of the bed and scurried across the carpet quietly; if Dad was in bed, she did not want to wake him.

The door came open with little more than a click, and with that she was into the hallway. It was dark; she could not see further than a few feet in front of her eyes, but even as she explored the gloom, her eyes became accustomed to it more and more; the streetlamp light through the window in her bedroom had prevented her from doing so earlier. She moved to the end of the landing, past her parents' bedroom. She pressed an ear gently upon the wooden door to listen for the sounds of snoring, or something else that might signify that her Dad was within; no noise came. *He must have gone out*, she thought, sighing with the knowledge that he would eventually return and start the screaming match over again.

So, realising that to tread in silence would be a waste of time, she skipped to the head of the stairs, gripped the bannister rail, then walked down the stairs. She had always been taught to be careful on stairs.

She jumped from the last step and spun around to face towards the kitchen; passing the living room door, she saw a faint light emanating from underneath; the low profile brought the fibres of the carpet up to a frightening height in their shadows. What startled Willow most was the quiet hum of *laughter* following the dim light. Laughter! She had not heard mirth from her parents in months now. It was a female laugh; her mother was amused by something, it seemed.

A rush of thrill came over the girl, who was overcome with joy; her Mum was laughing again, with Dad no less! It brought her such happiness to her, so much so that she wanted to see what was bringing her such amusement. Without hesitation, she gripped the doorknob, turned it and pushed the door open.

"Mum, Dad, what's so funny?" She said, a beaming grin stretching across her face. As she rounded the armchair, the laughter stopped and there was an attempt made by a near invisible arm to slam the door shut again. When Sarah realised that her daughter was already through it, she dove for the single lamp that was on and switched it off, plunging the room into a penetrating darkness.

There was a figure sat on the sofa beside Sarah – or at least, it had been, but she was to her feet before Willow had a chance to see who it was. It was not Dad, though.

"Willow!" Sarah shouted, clouting her daughter on the shoulder with a well-aimed hand. Willow bounced, mostly with fear; she had never been struck before. The figure on the sofa had, by now, made efforts to disguise himself by feigning an interest in something on the floor to his right such that his face was now away from her.

With a yelp, Willow made her discomfort known and she made to run from the room. Once in the corridor, she tried to escape up the stairs, but her mother was faster. She gripped

Willow by her wiry arm and dragged her back towards her, making sure to close the door behind her. "Willow, I want you to listen to me!" Sarah said in as calm a voice as she could muster in her annoyance. Willow just cried.

"No! Let me *go*!" She screamed, trying to wrench her arm free. Her mother gripped her shoulder with a free hand and brought herself down to Willow's level.

"No, *listen*!" She shook her daughter by the shoulders. "Me and your Dad have had a falling out. Now, your Dad was going to help me move the sofa," that part was a lie, "but he's gone. So, this nice man has come to help me move it." She said, feigning some form of sincerity.

"Who is he?" Willow muttered through the tears.

"It doesn't matter. What does matter is that you don't tell Dad about this, understand?" Sarah retorted in a moment. Before Willow could ask why, Sarah spoke again. "Dad would be very upset if he found out that somebody helped me move the sofa without him. So, if he asks you who helped me, I want you to tell him that you did a little heavy lifting for mummy, alright?" She said with the vaguest presence of a smile finally appearing on her face. Willow had stopped trying to break free but was still crying. "Do you understand? Tell me you do, Willow." Sarah said again when no reply came to her. She shook Willow again to get a reaction, and finally she nodded reluctantly, such that Sarah was not sure that she meant it. It would have to do. "Good. Now get yourself up to bed and stay there." She concluded before releasing her daughter and urging her with the other hand to go towards the stairs.

Willow, still shaken, made a half-hearted effort to climb the steps, but she stopped herself upon the third or fourth to ask her mother something.

"Mum?" She called; Sarah was halfway through the door, but she stopped and turned in silence. Even in the darkness, Willow could sense an annoyed stare. "Could I have a glass of water?"

It was then that Sarah realised that there was all this fuss over a drink. She could not believe it. She scoffed, then let out something resembling a genuine laugh.

"Sure, Honey. I'll bring one up for you in a minute. You get yourself up to bed and I'll see you soon."

With that, Willow climbed the rest of the stairs quietly and solemnly. She could sense her mother watching her from the door, making sure she made it into her room before returning to the lounge.

When she was back in bed, poor Willow could not even think about sleep. Not anymore. The fact that she did not sleep at all that night was exacerbated when she realised, at about three o'clock in the morning, that her Mum had not even brought that the glass of water up to her yet.

She never did, all night.

-15-
Vigil

It was a very strange day; one of remembrance; one of forgetting. One to celebrate; one of mourning. The entire town had come together in unison to forget the tragic circumstances of her death and celebrate her life. It had come as one to remember her existence, and all the joy that she brought to the community, and to mourn her tragic passing.

It was the usual sombre affair – the school remained open, despite it being the first day of the weekend. Howard had taken it upon himself to prepare a memorial vigil for Willow with the good grace of her family, despite the fact that they would not be in attendance; all of her classmates and their parents were invited.

It was in the moments proceeding the vigil that the headmaster contemplated what had happened seriously, for the first time; suddenly, her death had struck him in a profound fashion that brought him memories of his time with her. He peered out of his window, overlooking the sports field, clutching a round tin, perhaps three or four inches deep. An old, rusted thing with a dented lid. He rotated it in his hands, and reflected, quietly to himself, remembering vividly something from barely a year before;

"Mr Worth?" Came her voice, a glimmering hum of excitement from behind him; he distracted himself from the rugby match currently underway and turned about. Willow was stood there, gently closing the door behind her.

"I thought I couldn't see you on that field. Aren't you meant to be in PE?" He asked, gently probing his student file to check her timetable; he was right. But he expected her to have an excuse, such was her nature.

"Sprained my ankle, sir." She said, confirming his thought.

"You don't seem to be limping?" He replied.

"I'm trying not to; I want people to think it's fine."

"Why, just let it heal!" He protested, moving towards her.

"But sir, the sooner Mrs Stone thinks it's better, the sooner she'll let me do PE again!" She retorted. Howard sighed.

"You're like me, Willow, keen and feverish. I don't know where you get that from, I've never noticed it in your parents." He chuckled; she replied in kind, so he was assured that he had not crossed a line. "You must rest it," he resumed, sliding her into a chair by his desk; "it'll get better on its own, but you must let it rest." He repeated, knowing full well that he was not getting through to her.

"It'll be fine. Anyway, I needed to ask you something." She said, changing the subject in an instant.

"Of course, sweetheart, anything." *An odd choice of word*, she thought. But she didn't pause for a second longer on that;

"Can you swap my geography lessons on a Wednesday week A and Thursday week B for a place in the sixth form PE lessons." She said, sitting forward; she winced as her leg twinged; Howard noticed.

"I don't think that's such a good idea." He said, nodding to her leg. He sat down at his desk.

"Oh please, sir! You know as well as I do that there's sixth formers who skip PE."

"Yes, but they use it as a study period for their exams." He retorted almost immediately.

"Oh please, sir! I'm really not good at geography anyway." She protested.

"It's a core subject, it'd be irresponsible and unfair if I let you swap lessons." He said, his smile vanishing.

"But if someone isn't good at art or something, they don't have to do art lessons. But if artsy people aren't good at geography, they still have to do it. How's that fair?" She resumed. Howard sighed again. "Anyway, what use do I have for geography? I'd understand if I wanted to do something geographical, but I don't; I want to do sports studies. If you want to prepare me for life, let me be prepared for the life *I* want!" She protested. He always did admire her spirit.

"Well, you've got me there. I'll see what I can do, but I can't promise anything." He responded. She smiled meekly, sitting back in her chair. "Was there anything else?"

"No sir" She responded instantly. "That's all there is." And with that, she rose perhaps unsteadily to her feet and turned to go.

"You know, Willow?" He said, stopping her in her unsteady tracks. She turned back to face him. "You know you can talk to me about anything. Is something bothering you?" He said, almost as a whisper; she paused and mumbled something before talking directly at him.

"No sir, nothing. Just parent stuff, nothing I can't handle." She smiled. He replied with his own, and then gestured for the door.

She nodded and made to move out of the door; she bent over to collect her bag. Howard immediately noticed that her shirt had come untucked; he could not have his students being scruffy.

"Tuck your shirt in, you little scruff!" He said with faux anger; she jumped up at his words, half turned and laughed. Nonetheless, she obliged, and pushed the hem of her shirt into her trousers. "Much better." He said with a smile. She slung her bag over her shoulders and once more moved for the door. He watched as she vanished through it.

The door swung open again; in came the deputy headmistress. Her tightly knotted bun of hair bumped against the frame as she slid her head into view; Howard was stirred from his stupor, so he turned about.

"Sorry, Howard, we're ready for you." She said. It took him a moment to register what she meant, but then he remembered; he sprang up from his chair, almost forgetting how he had got there, only remembering after a moment that he had largely re-enacted his memory. With that, he swapped the round tin and with his now free hands, grasped a collection of papers upon which was typed an eloquent speech he had prepared.

"Certainly, I'm on the way." He muttered, moving across the room. With that, the deputy headmistress abandoned the door and fled into the corridor. Howard followed close behind, readying himself for the hundred or so people he expected in the main hall. His nervousness was not evident in his stride as he struck out through the labyrinth. He glanced once again at his notes, wondering if the 'thoughts and prayers' he would implore the town's population to give would be enough to satiate the stricken family.

All through the town, residents were united in mourning - they had all somehow been touched by Willow's life, whether through mere familiarity or direct knowledge, the tragedy was a striking and callous reminder that mortality was slave to no-one.

Chief amongst the memorials was a sermon led by Reverend Daryll at the church. It was a relatively subdued affair; the church was barely big enough to contain two dozen people, but the turnout was immense. Daryll stood aloft in the pulpit, surveying the packed nave with his gaze. His hands lay flanking a wiry microphone that cast his voice around the room with a powerful resonance.

"In planning today's sermon, I found that guidance was

necessary; a trust in the Lord and His wisdom to allow me to find the courage and the words with which to address you today. It is important, in times of crisis that we find the strength to confide in the Lord, to trust Him with our grief and to rely on him to cleanse us of it." As the Reverend spoke, Sarah shuddered at his advice; she had never been particularly religious, but her knowledge that Willow found a reliance on the Church gave her the strength to set aside her prejudice and do what Willow would have wanted.

"When we have a cold, imagine in Winter, we seek medication. Evil and sin are a cold, a virus; like any virus, we must cleanse ourselves of it when we find we are sick with it.

"Willow was one of those children of the Lord, a presence that lit up the room and brought a smile to those who surrounded her; her friends were many and she was beloved by her family. It is difficult to fathom her loss and even more so to come to terms with it. With the combined efforts of this community, I believe we can unite against the evil that has found its way within our lives. Now, let us all join in a moment of reflective prayer." He concluded, his powerful voice drawing to silence; nobody was surprised when he lowered his head, as though in a bow, and closed his eyes; the congregation followed suit.

Sarah did nothing but wish for her body to awaken from the apparent slumber she was slave to; she must be in the throes of a terrible nightmare that would end in a moment. She wished, and prayed, that it was not true – that Willow would be asleep in the next bedroom. Until she opened her eyes again, at the end of her prayer, it was possible. Once the prayer was concluded, it would be real. She could not tell what Gary was thinking, his stoic form mimicking her own – he was always reserved. Only he knew his own mind.

The rest of the room was as silent. Nobody shared a thought, yet the communal peace that had befallen them was palpable, another presence that formed a gravity. Not a bad thought passed through their minds; not a moment of ill belief was brought upon any one of them. The world was quiet, each individual existing within their own mind; thinking their thoughts, praying their prayers.

After a few moments of reflection, Daryll rose his head once again, and instinctively the rest of the crowd followed suit. Sarah's eyes came open wearily, hoping for her wish to be true; but as she awoke from her prayer, she realised that she was not in her bed, leaving a nightmare behind; she had awakened into it.

"Now, I invite Sarah, Willow's Mother, to say a few words." He gestured to her with a commanding hand, his gaze struggling to find her in the congregation; when he did, she rose as their eyes locked. Gary shuffled his feet to let her pass and she moved down the aisle to bottom of the steps. By now, Daryll had left the pulpit and had descended to allow her to take his place. She moved to the head of the steps and fished a folded piece of paper from her trouser pocket, moving the hem of her blue blouse from out of the way.

"Hello," she began, nervously. "I'd like to thank you all for being here on this very difficult day." Her voice faltered at every word, but her intonation was surprisingly confident; her voice was carried into the rafters like a flock of birds. "Gary and I would like to thank everyone for their support, we need all the help we can. We're lucky that we have a community to give that help." With that she paused; she read the remainder of her speech to herself;

Willow meant many things to many people. To us, she was a wonderful daughter. To her schoolmates, she was a dear friend. To anyone else, she was a bright, intelligent and helpful young lady. She was valued by so many and loved everyone. Her passing has affected us all, but we must all unite and remember her life. We must not be sad that her life has ended but rejoice that she lived. She was a positive young person, so we must dedicate her memory to maintaining positivity and light.

Thank you all again. Your support means so much to us in these difficult times.

She decided, however, to insert a small amendment – thus, lowering the note so that nobody could see it, she began to improvise; ever and again, she would pass her eyes over her words as though she was reading them. "Willow's death is a tragedy beyond mention. It was the result of a campaign by a sadistic individual who wanted little more than to bring misery to myself, my husband, and this town. Whoever this person is, they will be brought to justice." She looked up briefly and scanned the crowd. Save for a few astonished faces, few people were struck by what she was saying. "We must rely on the Police and any information you have to give to solve this heinous crime.

"Willow meant many things to many people." With that, she continued reciting the speech as it was written on her piece of paper, which she found was nearly torn from the strain frustration in her hands had rendered upon it.

Eventually, her conclusion was punctuated with her immediate leaving of the pulpit. She strode down the stairs in stoic silence and took her seat once again, not caring about the looks following her as she went. Gary gently rubbed her knee, but she moved it free of his grip in annoyance; he could see the tears in her eyes.

The remainder of the sermon was scattered with references to unity and solidarity – much of the same for the duration. The congregation joined in a hymn and further prayer until the hour was over. Sarah was surprisingly keen to leave the church; perhaps the uncomfortable feeling that was winding knots in her stomach was stronger here because of her non-churchgoing nature. She did not know why, but she felt an unease.

Upon leaving the church, Sarah stopped at the gate to converse with well-wishers. Daryll stood like an iron golem beside her, strong and monolithic, particularly in stark contrast to her relative sombre stance. Many people told her the usual; their thoughts and prayers were with her and her family. *What remained of it*, she thought. She was surprised, however, when she espied that Louise was coming towards her. She was keen to avoid conversation with her, but she was left with little choice.

"Sarah, my condolences." Louise began, taking Sarah by the hand.

"Thank you, yes." With that, she tried to move to the next well-wisher, but was dragged back by Louise.

"I'm very sorry about Willow. Harry sends his regards, too." She continued.

"Does he?"

"Yes, he does."

"You'll forgive me for not being entirely convinced."

"I'm sorry?"

"It doesn't matter." Sarah hissed, turning to see where Gary had gotten to. "I've got other things to think about right now, Louise." She continued, finally spying Gary a distance away near the edge of the small lake. He was looking out over the waters. With that, she pushed her aside; Daryll, aware of the tension, distracted Louise with more light-hearted conversation.

Half a dozen or so people tried to stop Sarah to offer their own condolences as she moved towards her husband, but she made efforts to either avoid or ignore them. As they watched, most were aware of her heading for her husband, and let her be. Others assumed she wanted to be alone and let her, not knowing where she was going. Soon, she fell to her husband's side. He barely acknowledged her arrival.

She looked at his face, then followed his gaze to the cliff at the opposing end of the water.

"That's where it happened." He said, breaking his apparently self-imposed silence; she exhaled and nodded.

"Gary, we'll get through this. We'll have to." She said to reassure him. He grunted, his gaze still latched onto the rocky face. "Nothing we can do can bring her back. We *need* to get through this." She rubbed his arm.

"Sarah, let's not pretend that things will all be fine and dandy when this is all over." He sighed, annoyedly. Sarah turned to him, her brows almost meeting in the middle of her face.

"Excuse me?"

"*Ahem.*" Came a rough sound behind them. Somebody was clearing their throat, perhaps to attract their attention; they both turned with surprise. There, at the head of the beach, stood a tall, elderly man; his shirt was grubby and untucked in places. A thin veil of hair partially obscured his shiny scalp. Sarah's heart sank.

"What's he doing here?" She whispered. Gary screwed his face up with annoyance.

"I've come to offer my apologies." He hissed, his voice coarse. "I loved Willow, and I'm sorry that she's gone." He continued. Sarah moved towards him.

"I bet you loved her, you dirty bastard." Sarah replied with a stern voice. His piercing blue eyes never left hers; he did not reply.

"Sarah, not here." Gary protested, his face still one of hatred. It did nothing to deter her, and she continued.

"You have no right to be here, you pervert. How dare you?" By now she was upon him, her face mere millimetres from his own. Even his breath was putrid, she thought – like the man himself. "Come near me or my family again and I'm calling the police." By now, Daryll was aware of the altercation; he bolted over, almost clearing the fence as he went. His Stole flapped in the breeze and his soft vestments caught the air in all sorts of billowing ways. In a moment, flowing across the ground like a ghost, he was between them.

"Come now, the pair of you." He said softly; he was wary of exacerbation. "Let us not bear any ill will today. This is a day of peace and respect." He said, almost sternly, as he turned to the elderly man.

"If *he* had any respect, he wouldn't be here now. He wouldn't be in this *town* anymore." Sarah retorted, pointing an irritable finger. By now, Gary was behind her. He moved her away by pushing her at the shoulders. She took a wide berth around the man, never allowing her eyes to leave his. "They should never have let you back here. Not after what you did." She hissed. Gary continued to move her.

"Come on." He urged.

"I'm sorry." The man said, turning as they passed him. Gary and Sarah stopped and turned, surprised. "I'll stay away." He finished, softly. A smile crept onto his face. It was a calm grin; Sarah took it as cocky. With that, Gary turned her about again and moved her gently up the beach towards the Church. A group of onlookers had gathered, but as the pair approached, they dispersed. Sarah espied Louise to her left driving away. Casting a cautionary look back, Gary spotted Daryll following them as the old man stood contemplatively at the water's edge.

-16-
The Ghost

"Yes, I understand that, Sarah, but you must remember..." Phillips began, fingering the spoon in his mug. He held the phone to his ear with his spare hand. Fiona sat across from him. She could hear Sarah's voice interrupt him; that is why he stopped. "Of course, that makes sense, but please listen to me." He paused; Fiona did not hear any protests from the other end of the line. "With any investigation, every suspect is innocent until proven guilty. It's called the presumption of innocence, and it's up to us, through the investigation, to challenge that of a suspect. So, I appreciate that you're keen for us to follow every lead, and we are. I can't say too much, but we're on top of possible suspects so there's no need for you to worry." He said, almost expertly; one would think he was reading from a script. The sound of a voice faintly fizzed from the speaker. "Yes. Yes, we will." He sat back in his chair. "I'll speak to you soon, Sarah. Goodbye." He concluded; he moved the receiver from his ear, hung it above the cradle for a moment, lest she continue talking. When it became apparent that she would not, he dropped it into the charging slot. He rubbed his face with a weary hand and sighed. Fiona leaned forward, gazing across his desk towards him.

"What did she want? Has she got new information?" She quizzed.

"Possibly. A lead. She wants us to look into a guy called Sebastian." He replied.

"Sebastian? Can't say I know who you mean." She responded, thinking hard.

"I've heard of him. I've read the file we have on him, too." He said. Fiona donned a frown.

"He has a file in our system?"

"Yep. I first read it about a year ago. Terrible case, really. He used to be the headmaster at Heathestone Secondary, years ago. He seemed like an okay guy at first. Then there was the incident with that young girl." He continued, mysteriously. Fiona slithered up in her chair, in something of an amazed manner.

"You're scaring me now, what happened?" She asked, her face now one of horror. Phillips sighed, then after a moment, he stood up from his chair. It creaked as he moved. He stepped towards his bookcase and removed the concealed bottle from it. This time, he did not ask Fiona if she would like a glass; he poured the pair of them one each and slid hers across the desk towards her.

"You'll need that." He whispered. "I can't recall her name, now." He said, louder now. He rubbed his eye with a finger and sat back in his chair. "Bright young lady, as they often are. Popular with her friends and a big family. You won't find any of them here anymore, they left after the accident." Fiona's face screwed up with confusion further, so Phillips continued; "She was a very *sensitive* girl, as I can gather. Didn't suffer fools though. One afternoon, she goes to the headmaster's office."

"Sebastian?"

"You got it. He was the last person to see her, alive. She had a problem with being bullied, you know, the usual thing." He said. Fiona nodded and made a noise as if to agree. "She thought she could confide in him. Her friends could recall her going into the office, the next thing they knew, she's hysterical. Accused Sebastian of touching her inappropriately whilst she was distraught. She alerted the police, but she was found less than twenty-four hours later in a ditch with lungs full of fire extinguisher foam." He winced.

"Oh my God!" Fiona hissed, bringing a hand to her mouth.

"They found the extinguisher in a bush nearby. A later inspection found it to be registered to the school, specifically Sebastian's office."

"What happened?"

"He denied everything, of course. There was no physical evidence incriminating him, but a psychiatric report deemed Sebastian the likely culprit. He was never charged, though because of there being no evidence, it was all circumstantial. By then, the damage was done, the story was enough to ruin him, so he resigned from his post. I think threats from the family convinced him to go." He resumed. He took a swig from his drink, finishing it in a moment.

"So why is he still in the town?" Fiona asked.

"He, to this day, insists he did nothing wrong. And because he was never charged and there was a lack of evidence, he still maintains it was somebody else."

"He was replaced by Howard, I'm guessing?" Fiona responded. Phillips nodded and pointed a finger at her, confirming her suspicions.

"Correct. He was deputy-head at the time. He was promoted straightaway." He confirmed.

For a moment, Fiona contemplated; something was about to dawn on her, but she could not fathom what it was; not only did something seem to add up, there was something else that conflicted within her.

"Why haven't we questioned him?" She asked at last, the other thought still concerning her.

"He wasn't on our radar. After his wife died last year, he's largely gone to ground. I didn't even know he was still alive. Sarah was right to bring him up, we need to bring him in and have a word." He reasoned at last. When Fiona did not reply, he tilted his head. "Something is troubling you, isn't it?" He said, sensing her discontent. She looked to him with a frown.

"Well, it's... I don't know. This girl, what was her name?" She asked.

"Stacey, I think. Why?"

"What about that message we saw on Willow's laptop? They were to someone called Stacey, right?" She continued. Phillips pondered for a moment, casting his mind back;

"What are you saying?"

"Stacey sent her that message saying; 'I'm going somewhere and I'm not coming back'. Then Willow said, 'If you don't come back, I'm going to join you'."

"You think Stacey wasn't murdered? You think she took her own life, is that what you're thinking?" Phillips scoffed.

"As I said, it's a hunch. But if Sebastian *was* innocent, and there's no other explanation, then it must be possible. Then, Willow was talking about how much she missed Stacey and how much she wanted to join her. What if..." Fiona began.

"You don't think she was suicidal?" Phillips concluded.

"I think we need to check on it. That's all. No harm in looking into the possibility."

"You're right. I think one of us should go and have a word with Sarah about Willow's mental health." Phillips fished out his notebook and opened it to the next available page; he began scribbling something down. "Will you be alright to go and see Sebastian whilst I'm doing that?" He asked; he knew it was a big ask. If Sebastian was what was being said of him, then Fiona would doubtless be uncomfortable.

"Of course. I can handle myself." She replied, assuredly;

Phillips knew she would be fine.

"Good. I'll schedule the time in for both meetings." At that moment, his phone began to ring; he jumped up to answer it, slamming his glass down onto the desk. "Just as soon as we've been to see Mark." He continued.

"When's he doing the autopsy?" Fiona quizzed.

"Within the hour." He replied. He picked up the phone. "DCI Phillips." He said. He paused as a hysterical voice screamed a reply. "Woah, woah, calm down, Sarah, what's happened?" He asked, calmly. Fiona sighed slightly at hearing she was back on his case. "What do you mean, 'he needs to go to hospital'?" He quizzed; Fiona jumped up from her chair in amazement, then listened for any clue; she could not hear the response other than as a hurried, illegible hiss. "We'll be over as quick as we can. Stay with him until we arrive, don't talk to anyone." Phillips said, urgently. He slammed the phone into the cradle once more, then took up the bottle of brandy again, taking a small swig from it. Fiona looked to him with a perplexed expression. "Gary has been attacked." He sighed.

"What?" She replied, loudly. "Who by?"

"Fucking *Harry*."

-17-
The Seven Bells

"The rat-faced little bastard." Sarah hissed, peering through the window at her husband; he was lying on a gently reclined bed that kept his head above his feet; blood poured from a deep gash on his lower jaw, whilst a nurse tending to him gently dabbed the wound with a wet sponge. Phillips leaned against the window by its frame, looking through it. Fiona stood behind them, her head in her hands; she was tired.

"What happened?" Phillips asked. Sarah sighed and began talking.

No two people are alike. That is what Sarah believed; in some instances, she thought, it would be nice to have two similar people; those who do good are in short supply. Meanwhile, there is an abundance of evil doers and characters of disrepute – like Sebastian.

Gary distracted her by tapping her shoulder with the bottom of a short glass; a clear liquid sloshed inside it. She looked to him first, then at it and took it from him.

"Thank you." She whispered, her voice hoarse. Gary rubbed her hair with his now free hand and moved across the room. He sat opposite her, placing his own glass down on the little table beside his chair. He looked at her with a pensive gaze. "What?"

"Nothing." He said, instantly. "You really think Sebastian could have done this?" He whispered; Sarah barely heard him.

"I'm sorry?"

"I said, do you think this could have been Sebastian?" He repeated, louder, more confident. Sarah sighed.

"I'm not answering that question." She hissed, wiping her nose with her wrist.

"Why not, you were keen to accuse him before?" He quizzed.

"What is this, you wearing a wire or something?"

"Of course not, I just want to know what you really think." He answered.

"I was angry because he was there, alright? He took me by surprise, of course I flew off the handle." She confessed.

"So you *don't* think it was him?"

"No! Well, yeah. Maybe." She sighed. Gary scoffed. "Look, it isn't up to me to accuse anyone or do the Police's job, that's up to them. Does it seem like he *could* have done, yes. But do I think he's capable of busting down a door and restraining an athletic girl, now I have doubts." She continued. All the while, Gary observed her closely.

"So if not Sebastian, who?"

"The more you're drilling into me about this, the more I'm beginning to think it was *you*." She said, pointing at him with the glass in her hand. She took a long swig.

"That's not funny."

"No, I know it's not. That's why I said it."

"You accusing me, now?"

"No. I just want you off my case." She stared at him, sternly. He stared back the same.

A knock. It came from the front door.

Gary and Sarah looked in the direction of the sound almost at the same instant. Then she looked to him and eventually he to her. He rose to his feet, put down his glass, and moved to the hallway. Sarah watched him as he left. He placed a firm hand on her shoulder, paused, then vanished through the lounge door.

He was gone for a short while; after a suspicious amount of time, finally the door clicked open. No sooner had that happened, than a sudden thud echoed through the house; it was a dull thump, like a hammer on wood. She heard Gary letting out a roar, one she had never heard before. In an instant, she was to her feet.

The door was still open, Gary on his back on the threshold. Sarah gasped and darted towards him. She made to pick him up, then espied a deep wound to the left side of his mouth; his lip had been bust clean open.

"What the," she began, unable to finish. She looked up expecting to see the assailant, but saw nobody; only a male figure running down the street. She could not make out any features. She stood up and ran to the phone.

"That's when I rang you." Sarah concluded. She was calmer now than when she had begun the tale. Phillips turned to her.

"So, you didn't actually see the assailant then?" He asked.

"No." She sighed. Phillips made to say something, but she cut him off. "I know what you're about to say. It was Harry."

"What's your thinking?"

"He has this otherworldly propensity for violence. I mean, you take one look at his mother and you just know she should have figured out how to get down stairs without falling by now." She replied.

"That's not funny." Fiona said, sternly.

"No, I know. That's why I said it." Came the reply, mirroring what she had told them earlier. "Think about it; Harry, a violent kid with a grudge against Gary, it just makes sense."

"A grudge?" Phillips quizzed.

"The press conference. Gary more or less accused him on the spot, Harry wouldn't have taken that well." Sarah explained. Gary sighed, looked to Fiona, then back to Sarah.

"We'll go and see Harry. In the meantime, we'll send officers to have a word with your neighbours, see if they caught a look at this person." He turned to Fiona, beckoning her with a tilt of his head. She approached him silently. "We'll get this autopsy out of the way, then you get yourself to Sebastian's place." He whispered. She nodded at him.

"You going to ask her?" She asked.

"Leave it to me. Go and wait in the lobby, I'll be there in a minute" Phillips replied. With that, she turned and walked back up the hallway away from the group. Sarah moved across the corridor and sat in a chair opposite the window; it was a hard, cold plastic that besieged her with a chill. Phillips moved to sit next to her. "You must be exhausted. Have you been sleeping lately?" He asked.

"I haven't slept in days. The pills don't work."

"You must be going through hell?"

"What do you think?" He did not know how to answer that question. So, he decided to distract with one of his own.

"Sarah, I hate to ask you this, but I feel it's necessary to do so." He paused; she did not fill the silence. "Did Willow ever show signs of depression, or self-harm?" He asked, as bluntly as possible so as to avoid confusion. Sarah looked at him with a disbelief he had not seen on her yet. "I'm just trying to rule everything out that I can. Is there anything you can think of? Did you have any familial problems she might have been aware of?" He pondered.

"No," She said in an instant, then pausing. "No, nothing."

"You're sure?"

"No, of course I'm not. Jesus, how the hell does anyone just notice stuff like that?" With that, her head plunged into her hands.

"Well if you can think of anything, do let us know."

Before he had even had time to finish his sentence, the door in front of them burst open. The muffed sound of Gary screaming came from within;

"I'm fine, let me just go home!"

The nurse emerged from the door. She closed it quietly behind her, silencing the roar from within.

"There's not much we can do about his lip for the moment, but we'll try and nip the cut together and let it heal. He's got bruising to the back of his head from his fall, so we're going to keep him overnight and take a scan, just to rule anything out." She explained.

"He seems very lucid to me." Sarah said. The nurse sucked her teeth.

"That's very common, the effects could take a while to manifest. That's why we're keeping him in. We've administered some painkillers for his lip, but you're welcome to go inside now." With that, she moved away and down the hallway. Sarah stared after her as Phillips checked his watch; twenty minutes past five in the afternoon.

"You should go home and get something to eat. Gary will be fed here." He suggested.

"I think I'll stay a while. He'll be asleep before long; I'll have some time to think." She answered, standing up. "Christ," she began, "this is all I needed." On the last word, she griped the doorknob and turned it.

"In the meantime, Sarah, if you could have a think about what we discussed. I'll be on the mobile." Phillips said. She nodded without looking at him, then moved into the room; Gary was already trying to get from the bed back to the chair; he did not like a fuss. Phillips watched as the door slid quietly to a close behind her.

-18-
Cause of Death

The autopsy room was clinically perfect; it was probably wise to claim that not one single germ existed there that should not. The pale human figure atop the freezing cold metal table that was screwed to the floor was the only foreign body to be found in that room; it had seen many bodies come and go, usually those who had died of natural causes.

Three months earlier, an elderly man had died under suspicious circumstances; it was sensational news. Perhaps Heathestone had finally been the site of something more interesting than a natural death; the morbidly curious were fascinated to discern how he had died. Some blamed his wife, who had been painted as the perfect murderess. Others blamed the victim himself, such as they do. The more realistic had simply blamed old age; his heart had been failing for some time. It was alcohol poisoning; the degeneration of the liver and overall thinning of the blood was something not unusual of a man his age, but it was an indicator of a far more sinister issue at work. His poor wife was merely shocked he had died so old. Sensationalists claimed she had done it to him; perhaps spiking his lemonade with strong alcohol. The reality was far more mundane; he simply enjoyed his drink.

Willow lay in surprising grace upon the operating table; about her were scattered a variety of other anaemic surfaces, strewn with metallic instruments of nondescript purpose; scalpels, tweezers, a tense set of bone cutters. Her face was finally resting largely as it had in life, save for a pale tone to her skin, quite normal for a person who had been deceased for some time. But her face was somehow fuller, her cheeks substantial. Her hair had been cleansed of contaminants and combed clean, purely out of necessity, not out of need for aesthetic value. Upon her transference from the hospital to the mortuary, samples had been cut from her hair; her skin analysed for any sign of disturbance; anything that could be cleaned without disturbing potential evidence had been. She was a specimen in the truest sense of the word.

Mark snapped a face mask over his mouth; it settled

instantaneously upon his face. His hair had been tucked into the hairnet upon his head, and his pale green overalls kept the contaminants of his body from getting into the air. His assistant, Janine, was similarly dressed; her own hair was tucked into a tight bun within her hairnet. She stood by Willow's head, close to the selection of instruments, ready to hand one to him at a moment's notice. Phillips, in similar regalia, moved near the body, peering at her. Fiona followed; Grisham stood behind a window on the far side of the room, not daring to approach the body; he was superstitious, and never liked to be near corpses.

Phillips, on the other hand, was only too happy to be in close proximity; whilst he trusted Mark as a mortician implicitly, there was a distinction in his mind that differentiated understanding *what* an injury was, it's biological cause and its effect on the body and *how* it had come about. Mark was no detective; he could tell you all about the human body, just not how one body can affect another.

"Right," Mark said, his voice muffled by the mask, "let's begin. Are you recording this?" He said, directing his voice towards a fifth person at the far side of the room; she was young, and clutched a tablet computer in her arms. She was responsible for marking bodily features on a three-dimensional diagram crudely rendered on the screen; it was arbitrary, impersonal, *not Willow*. She nodded, somewhat nonchalantly, and motioned her fingers above the screen, as though to demonstrate that she was alert. "Let's start with a physical examination of the exterior." He continued – he was ruthlessly efficient. He took the sheet by the corners near her shoulders and slid the edge down her body.

Her form was surprisingly intact; at least as far as Phillips could see, she looked in surprisingly good shape; she had the vaguest hint of abdominal muscles and her thighs and calves were firm; her keenness for physical education was readily apparent, as her body was one of an athlete. "Some sub-epidermal bleeding to the crural, patellar, and left mammary. Left mammary bruising extending into the pectoral. Clearly evidence of trauma. Whether or not related to the death, unknown at this time." It was Phillips' analysis of the report and the investigation that would decide that.

Mark moved to her feet; he probed her toes, then her tarsals and up her legs with the tips of his fingers. He slid them firmly up to her knees. "Tendons consistent; no sign of tears or slices." All the while, the young girl made notes and labelled her body on the crude diagram. "There appears to be little external damage to the body." He moved back to her head. He gently prized open her mouth and procured a mirrored stick and a pointer from Janine, who handed him them with an expert dexterity. He held her lips apart with the mirrored stick and counted her teeth rhythmically with the pointer; "Top, left; one, two, three, four, five, six, seven, eight. Top, right, one two, three, four, five, six, seven, eight. Bottom left; one, two, three, four, five, six, seven, eight. Bottom, right; one, two, five, six, seven. Lower right, first molar, second premolar, both cracked and chipped. Central incisor missing altogether; root appears intact, possibly snapped." He said. Fiona winced – she had never been much good with hearing about tooth damage. Phillips looked over and espied the diagram on the tablet had been switched out for a plan view of an upper and lower jaw; she filled in the analysis with dexterity. Mark handed the instruments back to Janine, who put them straight into a disinfectant gel.

"We're not going to get very far if all we have is that she wasn't much good at looking after her teeth." Grisham hissed to his assistant, who paid him little enough mind not to care about his ignorance.

"I'll now check her neck for any mysterious lumps and bumps." Mark muttered, probing the soft portions of Willow's neck with his fingers; dentists were used to doing this gently so as not to injure their patients; but Mark knew that this particular patient would not mind the mishandling. He probed the area near her lymph nodes; they were not inflamed. Nothing else leapt to his attention that was unusual, other than a mysterious bruising around her throat. "Amendment to the previous sub-epidermal bleeding analysis; some fine and concentrated bruising to the throat portion of the neck." He said, frowning. Phillips moved over, sensing his confusion.

"What is it?" He asked, standing opposite him.

"This is highly inconsistent with anything I've seen before. It isn't consistent with strangulation." Mark replied.

"So what is it consistent with?" Fiona interrupted. Mark looked to her.

"It isn't consistent with *anything*. Perhaps a puncture wound to the sub-epidermal tissue of the neck, which isn't really possible." He continued, gesturing at the strange pockmarks in her skin.

"Well, why not?" Fiona quizzed.

"Because you can't *puncture* tissue without damaging the exterior, but it's perfectly intact. This puncture happened from the inside." Mark replied.

"That is unusual. Does that mean there could be something beneath the skin causing this?" Phillips asked, pointing at the concentration of injuries.

"Possibly." Mark confirmed, probing and rubbing her throat firmly in ever decreasing circles before finally pinching in a location that was seemingly arbitrary; something felt unusual to him. "Resistance. She's got something lodged in her windpipe. Between the thyroid cartilage and glands. Hand me that scalpel." He said, gesturing to it; Janine was prepared already, and had picked it up ready for him. She handed it across the table to him and he took it with a determined grip.

Phillips approached the table. The fifth person kept her distance, yet continued to mark down injuries, catching up with Mark's frantic voiceover. But for a few minutes, nobody said a word.

Mark moved the scalpel blade to her neck; the tissue was very thin, and it scythed through in an instant. Somehow, Fiona expected gore; none came. He made about a three-inch incision parallel to her trachea; without a word, he moved to the instrument desk and fished up a small pair of scissor-like retractors and secured the sides to each wall of the incision. Squeezing down on the handles, the scissors opened, prizing the edges of the incision apart. Now the group had a good look at the inside of her neck; most of it was as it should be. The trachea was ribbed with protective cartilage, interspersed, ever and again, with an exposed ribbon of muscle to allow for flex.

He reached for a fresh scalpel, this one with a much larger blade, designed for slicing through surfaces thicker and more resistant than skin and sinew. Fiona started, her throat itching, as he drew the blade across the tracheal tissue. It gave way cleanly, and as it did, some form of pressure was released; her lungs did not deflate, for they had already drained their contents. Instead, something found its way into the new opening and it was pushed through; a sharp, white tip with a smattering of blood settled on its smooth surface. Mark, startled, nearly dropped the scalpel. His trained hand quickly caught it again, but he nonetheless decided to place it on the desk. He handed it to Janine.

"What *is* that?" That was Grisham, peering closely.

"What is *that*?" Phillips echoed.

"*That* isn't meant to be there." Mark answered. "Tweezers." Janine handed them to him. With dexterity, he positioned the tweezers over the foreign object and tried to grip the thing, but the metal tips merely slid clean off of it; it was a smooth surface. *Even the surface of the eye isn't smooth – nothing in the human body is.* Mark pondered. Mystified, he moved his grip towards the pincer of the tweezers and used this leverage to achieve a firmer grip on the object. That did it; it resisted his efforts to remove it, but it began to work clear.

The object was about two centimetres across – a curved surface that simultaneously described a triangular shape. Phillips realised something before anyone else did;

"Oh my *God*." He hissed. Fiona looked at him, then back at the object. Then she too realised.

Mark glanced to her for a fraction of a second, then back to the incision. The tracheal tissue flexed as the two invisible corners of the object worked free, then finally it emerged in its entirety. Somewhat horrified, for it was not the sort of thing he usually encountered, Mark muttered an expletive, then held the thing aloft; the beams of the ceiling lights shone brilliantly through the translucent glass, blocked ever and again by the occasional smudge of blood.

"That explains where the lightbulb went at her house." Phillips said.

"Jesus. She's swallowed a lightbulb?" Fiona quizzed.

"Technically she's inhaled it, this wasn't in her oesophagus; it came from her windpipe." Mark interrupted.

"Phillips, does this fit our scenario? Could she have done this to herself, self-inflicted?" Fiona asked, quietly.

"It's highly unusual, but possible." He said, sternly.

"Maybe we should keep our hypothesis to ourselves for now?" Fiona suggested. Phillips nodded.

"I agree. Until we have proof, I don't think that's something they need to be thinking about right now." Phillips responded. Janine approached Mark with a metallic bowl, into which he placed the glass shard – it rattled about for a moment, but settled as she replaced the bowl. "Go to Sebastian, Fiona." He continued. She nodded, though her face remained one of sickness.

"Things just got interesting." Grisham hissed, lowering the handkerchief from his face.

-19-
Bloody Knuckles

Phillips knocked on the door, hard. Probably too hard. The other officers standing behind him started slightly, then peered at one another with concerned faces. Phillips did not consider that he had knocked too drastically; it worked; it only took a few moments for the sound of rushing feet to come from within, followed by the click of the lock. Louise opened the door, her face panicked and flustered, even in the instant in which Phillips had his first impression of her. She smiled, even though her face did not wrinkle around her left eye, as it should when being genuine. Her hair came down across her right eye, concealing it completely. She did not even get to say help;

"Louise, I need to speak to Harry, immediately." He said, swiftly. He tried to enter, but she blocked him with her body. She scoffed with a nervous smile.

"You're all out of luck, Phillips. He's not in." She said, her voice cracking.

"Louise, this is important. Don't lie to me, because I can tell you don't do it well." He replied.

"I already told you, he's very rarely in. I haven't seen him yet today." She said, quietly.

"Well I think he's in more than you let on, I think you're protecting him. I need you to let me in and talk to him." He hissed. At that, her only visible eye bloomed into a glistening, crimson red and a tear spilled from her eyelid. She smiled, but it faltered.

"He really is a good boy, you know?" She said, almost as a whisper.

"So I keep being told." Phillips answered, pushing on the door. Despite her insistence that he could not enter, she put up virtually no fight, even to the point that she practically opened it for him. Resigned to his presence, she turned, sighing loudly.

"I'll just get him." That was to herself.

"Wait here." Phillips said to the other officers as they made to enter. Then, he stood in the hallway and followed her with his eyes as she walked to the kitchen. She staggered on her right leg.

"May I ask how you got that limp, Louise?" He called. She grumbled something incoherently, then turned to him; she feigned a smile.

"Oh, nothing really. I just fell down the stairs this morning." She explained; Phillips saw little reality in this tale.

"You live in a bungalow, Louise?" He pointed out. She nearly fell.

"Oh, yes. That's right. Uh, it wasn't here. I was out and did it, the steps in the town square, you know the ones?" She said, her smile consistent, yet flippant.

"Right." Phillips said, unsure. He moved through the hallway towards her; he could tell she had been cooking; the smell of sausages and fat was in the air, almost to the point that he could actually take chunks out of the atmosphere. Louise stepped into the kitchen and peered in, not venturing through the door. She tapped her fingers on the door, as if deep in thought – then, she turned back to Phillips.

"Look, I really don't want to disturb him whilst he's having his dinner." She whispered, almost to avoid being heard by her son. Phillips stood erect and clenched his fists; he was an officer of the law and wouldn't be threatened by an unruly kid.

"Really? Well I would." With that, he strode across the space, almost barging past Louise, who made a hearty effort to block him.

"Look, just wait in the lounge!" She attempted to say, but by then, Phillips was already past her and in the kitchen; Harry sat with his back to the door. He was munching on a rasher of bacon when Phillips burst in.

"There's never a cop when you need one." Harry said, his mouth full. "Then when you don't, you can't get rid of them." His sarcasm was palpable. "What can I do for you?" He hissed, turning his head; Phillips could tell he had no intention of being cooperative.

"Tell me, Harry; your meals, do they all consist of the same thing? Bacon, eggs, sausages?" Phillips noted the anomaly when he noticed that thus far, he had eaten the same meal for his breakfast *and* dinner. "It's just that I haven't seen you eat anything else." He continued.

"Creature of habit. I like a good meaty meal." Harry mumbled in reply. Phillips took that as his cue.

"Excellent, then you won't miss a sausage." Phillips replied; he plunged his hand into the pile of meat and plucked out a sausage. Harry's face contorted, and he gripped Phillips' wrist with a firm, clenching tangle of fingers. Anticipating it, Phillips did not drop the food, but for a moment, there was silence.

"Harry, I'm here to investigate an accusation of assault made against you. I could have your Mother done for obstructing police; what the hell makes you think I won't add assaulting a police officer to the pile?" Phillips said, sternly; Harry pondered for a moment, for long enough that Phillips began to doubt his tactic was working. The threat had had the desired effect, however, as Phillips felt his wrist come free of Harry's grip; his enraged eyes never left the officer, however, the same vice versa.

With that, Phillips lifted the sausage to his face and took a bite; it was well-cooked and still warm. "Let me ask you this, Harry. If I were to say that I think you've been out of this house this afternoon, would I be right?" By now, he had moved around the table and was opposite him. Louise stood in the background with her arms crossed across her chest; she leaned against the counter. Harry did not reply. "Alright. Louise? Has Harry been out of the house this afternoon?" Harry closed his eyes and clenched his fists around the knife and fork. She did not move a muscle to utter or gesture a response. He looked back to Harry. "Let me explain the situation we have here, Harry. I've got a complaint made against you regarding an incident that happened at twenty-two minutes past three. So, I'll ask you once more. Were you out of this house at that time?" He hissed sternly. Harry merely grimaced with frustration.

"No, I wasn't." He replied, at last. Louise looked away and sighed, quietly. Phillips smiled.

"You know what, Harry? I don't think you're going to win this. What you fail to realise is your reaction to my nicking a sausage just now told me two things. One, you've got quite the temper, which I sort of knew already, and two, you've been punching things." He pointed to Harry's hands, which were gripping the knife and fork with such intensity that previously closing wounds on his knuckles were splitting open again, spilling droplets of blood onto the table. "So, if you haven't been out assaulting the citizens of this town as you claim you haven't, you've been assaulting someone closer to home." He moved his pointing finger from Harry's hand to his mother, who stood erect, gasping. "In any case, you're coming to the station with me."

Harry surprised both people by rising to his feet; he dropped the knife and fork down by the plate of food and placed his now free hands down in the pool of blood his wounds had oozed; little else happened, but in his haste, he alarmed Louise;

she started and gasped at the sound. Phillips moved his head.

Wordlessly, Harry stared at Phillips; the eye contact with the boy was unnerving, but Phillips held his stance with confidence. Then, Harry smiled; it was a wry, false smile that meant that something...

Crash!

His plate of food was thrown from the table; it exploded into shards of material on the cupboards opposite. Louise screamed and held her hands to her mouth, whilst Phillips started. Harry stood still; his arm extended from swiping the plate from the table.

At that, Phillips heard the front door open, followed by running feet. In a moment, the two police officers were stood in the doorway, their eyes wide with alarm. They looked at Harry with stern, menacing looks.

"It's alright, Daniels." Phillips said, gesturing to the pair with his hands. They both stopped their slow advance. "Harry is coming quietly, right?" That was aimed at the aforementioned. Harry nodded slowly, after a pause.

"That's right. I'm coming quietly." Harry replied. His eyes were locked to Phillips' for just a moment longer, before he shoved the chair from behind him, nearly striking his mother with it. It clattered across the floor. It was nowhere near her, but Louise staggered out of the way anyway.

Phillips watched as the female officer moved Harry, almost supernaturally, with a hovering hand behind his back. He looked at her with a face that read like a bad joke, then to her outstretched arm. She lowered it, but that was when the male officer, Daniels, moved between them. He extended an arm in the direction of the door; Harry looked at him with a cocked head, then followed his direction. Phillips watched as he vanished around the door.

With Harry gone, Phillips strode over to Louise, who was now sobbing quietly, leaning a hand against the cupboard. He cocked his head, then raised his hand to draw the curtain of hair from her eye; perhaps unsurprisingly, her eye was a bloodshot core to the bruised cloud that surrounded it. He sighed, as Louise rolled her head, dragging her hair free of his hand.

"Louise, there are things we can do for people in your situation. Why didn't you come to us sooner?" He asked, stepping back.

"Look, Phillips. I know you mean well and I understand how this must look, but..." She began.

"Louise, you're going to tell me that 'he's not a bad boy at heart', and I'm not going to listen to that again. You need help." He interrupted.

"*I'm* not the one who needs help." She said, cutting him off at the last syllable. "I'm his mother. It's my job to keep him out of trouble; I don't see any of this as trouble," she said, gesturing the wound on her face, "this is him *not* doing this to anyone out there. As long as he's doing this to me and nobody else, what's the harm?" Phillips was amazed at her calmness; he pitied the mother.

"Louise, you can't live the rest of your life as a punching bag. The fact that you're accepting of this tells me you *do* need help, this isn't normal." He argued back.

"Phillips, nothing about this world is *normal*. Stop pretending anything can be."

-20-
The Rendezvous

It was the middle of the evening; the sun was dipping just below the horizon, and the sky was draining of its orange majesty and descending into an inky blue of night. All over town, lights were coming on, the dazzling cluster of illumination almost insignificant against the overpowering black.

The hospital was quiet. Food was being distributed to the patients, after which the staff changeover would commence.

Gary's food lay on the folding table that was stretched over his body, slowly going cold, practically untouched; it was not that he was not hungry, it was that he was not awake. The painkillers had sedated him to the point of exhaustion, and he settled for sleep instead of consciousness. Sarah had left him for the evening; she would return in the morning.

On her way through the reception, she contemplated the journey home; Heathestone was about twenty minutes' drive away. She decided that a coffee would be required before she set off.

Sifting through the options on the antiquated coffee machine, having spent the last of her change, she uncharacteristically chose not to select the 'decaf' option. She would need all of the caffeine she could drink. It had been a long day, and her eyes were heavy, exacerbated by her continual crying that left them puffy and bloodshot.

Coffee beans were ground; water was slowly boiled, and all was mixed together. The coffee was sprayed haphazardly into the paper cup Sarah had placed beneath the nozzle; a large percentage of it ended up spraying onto the floor or down the side of the cup, but she did not care. She could have another when she got home.

She fished out a wooden stick to stir her brew; the futility of that struck her. How had coffee become so elaborate, so intricate, yet the most useless of appliances was supplied to stir it? Splintery wood was no good for putting in a drink.

The receptionist dropped a pen on the floor behind her; Sarah turned about but thought nothing of it. Disposing of the stirrer in a nearby waste bin, she took a sip of the coffee; she did not add milk or sugar; it was a strong, black coffee that wakened her almost immediately. She imagined that Gary would appreciate such a pick-me-up. It was still hot, but that did not matter.

She moved through the reception and slipped through the automatic doors; the crisp air struck her in a moment, the chill like a wall separated by a temperature difference that was instant. She bundled her shoulders up near her cheeks so as to warm up and gripped the cup firmly.

The car park was scarcely big enough for two dozen cars; barely seven or eight spaces were filled that night. Sarah's own car was closest to the hospital, parked as close as possible without occupying a disabled or ambulance bay. It did not take her long to reach her car, but something was unusual about it; it was not alone. A figure stood by the front passenger door on the other side from her; the car had been reversed into the space. She just about made out the figure, which was heavy set and had a large coat around it. In the vague lamplight from a nearby streetlight, she could see a veil of cigarette smoke rising into the air. She sighed.

"I never did like you smoking." She said; the figure turned around – he had been leaning against the door – and surveyed her, his breath wafting the smoke clear.

"It's tradition, Sarah." Howard said. She extended the key towards the car, then pressed the lock button once, to ensure that the only door unlocked was the driver's side. He flicked the cigarette away and gripped the door handle, which did not open as he pulled it.

"I'm not letting you in my car, Howard." She replied to his confused expression.

"You always used to let me in." He replied; Sarah's heart jumped. "We've had some good times in this car." He said, running a hand along the roof.

"Yes, Howard, if you say so, we did. But that isn't happening anymore, I told you that months ago." She replied, shaking her head.

"Come on, Sarah, Gary isn't going to know, right?" He implored.

"Howard, have a word with yourself. I just lost a daughter. My husband is in hospital." Howard made to protest, but she interrupted him. "Do you understand what you did to me? What our affair did to me? I hated myself every time I set eyes on you, every time I had to go into that school. So if you think for one minute I'm going to run back into your arms because of what's going on, you've got another thing coming." With that, she pulled the door of her car open and dove inside.

Within a few moments, she had the key in the ignition, the door closed and her seatbelt on. The coffee was stowed in a cupholder on the dashboard.

She breathed heavily, her eyes welling up once again; she was tired of crying, but she found herself doing so at every possible opportunity, against her best intentions. She turned to the passenger door at the sound of a gloved hand tapping the window. She did not roll the window down, for fear that he would dive for the child lock and allow himself in. "What the fuck do you want?" She hissed, leaning over.

"You think me and Willow hated each other? You think she'd have let you taker her away from me? *You* have a word with yourself." With that, he slammed a fist on the roof of the car; the metallic ring reverberated around the vehicle, and she shook in her seat, her tears flowing freely now. She saw the figure turn and disappear from the window, fading into invisibility by the distance.

Sarah shook with fear and anger, interrupted ever and again by a moment of controlled stillness she could not maintain. Finally, she let out a guttural, primal scream that dragged in her throat until her lips were stretched and strained into painful wideness. She slammed a fist into the dashboard, which splintered into a narrow crack – mere superficial damage. She forced her hands to her face and sobbed loudly, relenting to the emotion she had thus far been unable to contain anyway.

She did not care that it attracted the attention of a nearby nurse, who was leaving for the evening; she came silently and invisibly to the car and rapped slightly on the window. Sarah started and peered through the foggy window at the young lady beyond. For a moment, she thought it was her daughter; a cruel joke, brought back from the dead somehow. The mist on the windows and the overall darkness exaggerated her belief, and for a brief instant her misery was lifted; but then it returned when the nurse spoke.

"Is everything alright, madam?" Her voice was high and firm; far from the tones her daughter spoke with. Her joy dissipated. "Madam?" The nurse repeated. With that, Sarah dove for the ignition button on the dashboard and the car came to life. Without putting the lights on, she depressed the clutch which lifted the electronic handbrake. She then floored the accelerator, flicked on the headlights and sped away into the night; perhaps she imagined that in her haste, she would crash into Howard, who could not thus far have gotten too distant from the hospital. But the further she drove, the more her hope dissipated; she knew that by the time she got to the dual carriageway a few miles from there, he would be inaccessible to her.

-21-
Muddied Waters

It was a little after half past seven by the time Fiona arrived at the little street labelled *Oscar Terrace*. It was off of the main street and terminated in a small cul-de-sac; it was comprised of about five houses, each disconnected from one another. They were modest abodes, scarcely larger than bungalows; their deceptively low roofs gave way to the inky blackness of the night, against which the shining moon was sliding silently.

Fiona chose to come with assistance; a male police officer, who was a little older than she was, but not by much; he was stoic and quiet, his short beard resting against his bulky chest. He was half asleep.

"Stuart," Fiona said, abruptly; she turned the key in the ignition and the car wound down to silence. Suddenly, her voice was loud and booming; "We're here." With that, he started into alertness. He grunted something in the affirmative, then donned his cap. The pair of them undid their seatbelts, then moved for the door handles.

Once alighted, the pair felt the crisp chill of the night air of their skin; the car had been heated, but out here they were rid of such comforts. Stuart's breath collated into a thin mist before him, and he exhaled a voluminous burst that dissipated in a moment. "Get a grip, man, this is England. You should be used to cold like this?" She asked, turning to him.

"This *is* England; so you should know that it's not acceptable to call anyone 'man' anymore." He said, sarcastically. "It's not in the official vocab guidelines, you know?" He smiled. She scoffed and turned.

"Unbelievable." She muttered with a chuckle. She made for the house; number six was the home of Sebastian. At least, according to the case file, it was. Stuart made to follow. She heard the shuffling of his feet approach her. "Right, I want you to cover the front door. I'll radio if I need you." She said, turning her head slightly; even a little eye-contact was important.

"Right you are, Ma'am." He replied. He watched as she opened the rusting gate cautiously.

"I don't know that you're allowed to call me that." She joked.

He chuckled.

Fiona rapped on the front door; the houses here were older than the ones on the main street; they had a grey pebbledash, like microscopic defences, on the walls, and the windows were single pane. Across the cul-de-sac, a garden was so overgrown that she was unsure if it had been abandoned or simply the victim of laziness. It must have been the former; three of the four visible windows were broken and boarded.

Sebastian's house was strangely tidy; save for the gate, which was in urgent need of repair, it was not all that shabby. The garden was trimmed, but not perfect, and the fences looked as though they had been repainted only a week ago. The paint of the door was a chipped, dark blue, and running down the centre was a frosted glass pane that had been smashed in a corner. The wire mesh inside kept it together, though.

At first, nobody responded to the knock Fiona gave; so, she did so again. This time, she saw a curtain move in the window to her left; it was not a subtle ripple, as one would expect from someone trying badly to conceal themselves, but a more deliberate one, as though something had been prodded through it; somebody was getting up from a chair near the window. Then on came the porch light; it was a feeble yellow glow that was barely strong enough to permeate through the glass. It was, however, vibrant enough to cast the shadow of an approaching figure. It drew nearer, until it obscured the light completely; then the click of a lock, and the door pulled open. A wizened face appeared in the small crack it cleared.

"Sebastian?" Fiona said.

"Yes?" Came the hoarse reply.

"I wondered if I could come in?"

"And who are you?" He quizzed, his voice louder.

"I'm Detective Inspector Fiona Clements. I just want to ask you some questions." She said, standing her ground; she was not one to be threatened.

"What sort of questions? Who sent you? It was that Sarah, wasn't it? What's she said about me now?" He asked with increasing frustration; Fiona did not know which question to answer first.

"Just calm down, Sebastian." She said, calmly. "Please let me in for a minute, and we'll talk in the warm, yeah?" She said. Sebastian paused for a second; in the darkness, she could see a little point of light on each eye; it moved as he looked around.

"It *is* a little cold out." He said softly; he pulled the door open a little more. "Forgive me, I didn't mean to raise my voice." The inflection of his voice was different than her own; he sounded more like a Yorkshireman than anything she had heard recently. It had a strange, European tang to it that she could not quite pinpoint. "Won't you come in?" He opened the door fully now and stepped aside. He raised an arm into the hallway. She obliged. "Oh, and your friend, too?" He gestured to Stuart, who looked eager to get out of the chill of the night. Fiona smiled, as did Stuart when he realised he was to be let in.

The inside of the house was scarcely warmer than the outside. Still shivering, but convinced she would get used to the temperature, Fiona looked about; the feeble glow had come from a halogen bulb that dangled from the ceiling without a shade; a pile of papers, about three feet high, stood on the verge of toppling over atop an ornate yet very likely cheap desk against the stair case, itself a mess of discarded clothes. "Won't you go through to the lounge? It's just on your right." Sebastian said, closing the door. Fiona espied it and headed in; Stuart followed suit.

"It's cold in here, Sebastian, is there a window open somewhere?" Stuart said, disappointed at the lack of heat.

"The house is very old. There are more holes in the roof than there are tiles; I did have a permanent ladder installed at the back, so I could go up and do repairs, but I'm too old for that stunt-man malarkey nowadays." He replied with a pained hatred of whoever had built the house so poorly.

The living room was even more an exhibition of dereliction. A single armchair sat against the window; it looked to have collapsed on one side, for it sat with one foot slightly in the air. The atmosphere was damp and thick and in each corner of the room, a sludge-like mould was growing, almost visibly as she watched. "Please, take a seat," Sebastian said as Fiona was taking these things in. She started, for his voice was louder now; he shuffled past her, his back hunching slightly. "Here, take my seat." He said, gesturing the armchair.

"Oh no, it looks to me that you need to sit down more than me." She protested; he shushed her with a wave of his weary arm.

"I won't hear of it, please sit here." He beckoned her over, and she reluctantly allowed herself to follow his instruction. "It's an old chair, this." He said. She had guessed. "Do you know, my father built this for my Grandmother when she was unwell? She didn't live to sit in it for too long." He said. Fiona grimaced. "My father was German, you know? Oh yes, I lived there until I was about twelve years old. We fled just as the Wall went up. I can't remember how he got that chair out here." He pointed at the chair. "He called it the *Krankensessel*. Sick-chair." He chuckled an insane sounding chortle and turned about. There was Stuart, who smiled; it was too dark to see his mouth, though.

Fiona sat on the chair carefully; it toppled slightly more as she did so, but eventually, she found a position that was comfortable; it was warm where he had been sat in it. She could now see, as her eyes adjusted to the gloom, that Sebastian was across the room and fishing something from a cupboard. It was a flimsy looking chair with a ceramic bowl beneath it. Fiona sighed with pity; then she remembered why she was there. "Would you like a seat, young man, there's a dining chair just through there?" Sebastian asked.

"No, I'll stand, but thank you." He smiled. In truth, he thought Sebastian was going to offer him the commode, so he had already made up his mind before he answered. With that, Sebastian put the chair down near the fireplace, which was unlit, yet had clearly been used recently, and sat in it.

"So, how can I be of help to you then?" He asked, reclining in the seat. Fiona leaned out of the armchair, which was undeniably comfortable despite its dilapidation.

"I just want to preface this by saying you're not to worry about your safety, we are simply gathering information at this stage. With that in mind, I wonder if you could tell me, in your own words, anything you remember about Willow Greene?" She said, confidently; she had been rehearsing it in her mind for some time now.

Sebastian made no reply. As her eyes adjusted to the gloom, she could see his own wander minutely, up into the air; his pupils dilated and his head raised itself, almost imperceptibly. "Sebastian?" Fiona asked. On the final syllable, he spoke suddenly.

"The only thing I remember about Willow is the joy she brought to my life." He smiled as he spoke. Fiona made to ask him another question, but he continued; his voice was clear now, much louder and more confident than before. "She was very helpful to me, especially in my wife's declining years. I enjoyed her company and I like to think she enjoyed mine, bless her." He smiled a wide grin and then turned back to Fiona. She did not say anything for a moment, then leapt into the next question when it became apparent that he was not going to continue talking.

"When did your wife pass away, Sebastian?"

"Three years ago, last Tuesday." He said softly, pointing behind him with a thumb; the universal symbol of the past.

"What did Willow think about the incident involving Stacey? About your dismissal from the school?" She asked. His reaction was much different, less soft and understanding.

"I was forbidden from seeing her. She from me." His chin quivered as he answered. Now he sat erect in the chair; Fiona started back. "It was a load of bullshit, that entire show. I was accused of something I never did, something I never would have or will ever do!" He pointed with a firm finger. Stuart moved closer. "I had that job because I wanted it; I loved kids, I loved to see them enjoying themselves, to see them happy. Now mothers pull their children clear of me, they move away on the bus. It's humiliating!" He protested; the two dots of light became three as a tear emerged. "I've tried to repair my reputation; God alone knows I have. I stay out of everyone's way, hide myself away in this shithole. I try to be nice to *you people*, despite what you did to me two years ago. But it isn't enough, apparently." His voice broke in as many places as a car crash would damage a body; Fiona looked to Stuart who did not appear to be looking anywhere in particular. "My life has been ruined by somebody else's despicable actions." He hissed, breathing heavily.

"You think you were framed?" Fiona asked.

"I *know* I was. Because I know in my heart of hearts that I did nothing to that poor girl; I did *not* do anything to her then leave her lying dead in a ditch." He cried, with an impassioned voice that rang around the empty walls. "I was denied my wife and Willow when I needed them most. I was all alone, nobody wanted to know me. You don't understand what that does to a person, how can you? I had to throw away all of my sharp objects, my cleaning products and bleach, their lure was too tempting." He said, miming himself clawing at his wrists and throat. Fiona understood.

"I can't imagine." She muttered; he probably did not hear her.

"Out of all of the people of this town, only Reverend Daryll saw in me something more; he risked his reputation to take me in and help. God is in me now; I try to be at peace. I just wish *others* would leave me to be in peace. I try to build bridges, to extend my apologies to the Greene's and they send me *you*. He said, pointing to Fiona. She frowned. "I'm sorry." He said. "I don't mean to vilify you." He mused, softly.

"That's alright. You've had a bad time of it, by the sounds of things. So you found solace in the church?" Fiona asked.

"They couldn't stop me from seeing her there. It's a place of worship, they can't stop me from going, unless the Church itself dismisses me. I don't go now, of course."

"Why not?" That was Stuart.

"Because Daryll kept insisting I confess to him. He said to me one day 'Sebastian, please know that if you wish to confess anonymously, you will not be judged,' all that rap. Even after all of the help he gave me, after everything he did for me, and me for him in return, he still did not believe I was innocent." He said, his voice more irate now.

"Did you ever go back?" Fiona asked.

"Never since that day. How could I confess anonymously, even if I *did* do it? He'd recognise my voice straight away. He was trying to trap me!" He shouted. Then he began to weep; it was a hearty, impassioned sob that rang out hauntingly, like a ghoul. Fiona spoke again.

"Sebastian, please..." She was interrupted.

"I implore you; I *implore you*, find this killer of women. They could be roaming the streets now; here you sit, talking to me, who has no information to offer. Take to the streets and find them." He cried. Fiona glanced at Stuart, who she could see had now found a way to peer through the darkness in her direction.

"Where were you last Thursday night, between three fifteen in the afternoon and six in the evening?" She asked, looking back to Sebastian; he sat, breathing heavily with his forehead sandwiched between the tips of two fingers. He sat for a few seconds like that, almost whimpering to himself. Fiona tilted her head. "Sebastian?"

"*I can't remember!*" He hissed, his voice breaking. Fiona sat back in her seat. "I struggle to remember sometimes." He continued.

"You can't remember? Is there anyone who might be able to account for you?" She replied. Another pause ensued.

"Do I look like I have neighbours?" He was right, she thought. "Just leave me in peace. Go and do your job." He hissed, sternly. Fiona's face turned to one of annoyance; she had been sympathetic thus far. She simply pondered about how convenient his memory was; perhaps it was selective? As Sebastian lowered his head into his hand once again, she turned to Stuart and spoke.

"Well, on that note, I suppose we'd better leave you in

peace, Sebastian." She mumbled, leaning forward in the chair; it toppled forward as she moved. Sebastian did not say a word, even as she rose from the chair and swept across the room.

Stuart made for the door and was into the hallway when Sebastian finally moved; it was as Fiona passed him, he reached out with a swiftness he had not yet displayed. His hand, as a claw would, gripped her wrist with a firmness she did not expect, nor did she believe him capable of. She gasped slightly at his grasp and turned to face him; his face was still gazing at the floor.

"Sebastian, I advise you let go of me or I shall have you prosecuted for assault of a police officer." She said, sternly, all semblance of pity and respect she had for him had been diminished. He pulled her hand towards his face and ran his nostrils along the back of her fingers. He inhaled deeply;

"You surprise me, officer. She was just like you. Eager to help, pretty. You even smell like her. It's a bad combination in this town." He said monotonously. She wrenched her hand clear of his grasp, turned and fled the room. Her face was not one of fear but contorted into a determined grimace that was not settled even as she passed Stuart, who was clueless having not seen any of their interaction.

"What's wrong?" He asked, seeing her expression.

"Nothing." She snapped, yanking the front door open. "I need to see Phillips, take the car back to dispatch." She ordered.

"Well, won't you want a lift?" He replied, confusion overtaking his stoic face.

"No. Just take the car. I need time to think. Things have changed."

-22-
The Night Owls

Willow and Stacey were lain against a heather bush, their shoes muddy from the trek through the field to the crest of the hill. All about them danced a hundred tiny flies, each one emanating a tiny, almost inaudible buzz, such that it sounded as if power lines were humming above them. Down below them, the town was glowing with an amber light, that ended almost with an invisible wall at the edges, and in the thick, humid air, the threat of thunder lingered.

But Willow and Stacey did not care.

"Fuck him." Willow said, at last breaking her silence. Her voice carried far and away over the grass as it swayed gently in the soft breeze.

"That's the trouble, Willow. I don't want to." Stacey answered, her brow furrowed with concentration; she fumbled with a small square of paper between her fingers, minute curls of material spilling from the edges. Stacey cursed. At that, Willow started and rolled over to face her friend.

"Wait, you have already, right?" She asked with disbelief. For a time, Stacey was still, as though contemplating something. She concluded rolling the thick cigarette, another on her leg ready to be rolled. She pondered for a few seconds more, then turned her head towards Willow. Willow recognised that face; it was the sort of embarrassed look one wears when they do not want to admit the obvious. Willow scoffed, then turned her gaze back towards the sky. "Come on Stace, you've been with Scott for eleven months now. I thought you'd be getting it non-stop." She said with a wry chuckle. Stacey did not find it funny; the dirty look she threw her confirmed it.

"I don't know, Willow." She said at last, glossing over the comment and handing her the rollie. Willow took it gently, then moved it to her face, even though she did not know exactly what was in it. "Something just doesn't feel right with him." She continued. Willow furrowed her brow and turned her head sharply, lighting the joint. With it lit, she passed a curious eye over Stacey, who remained motionless, save for the ponderous look on her face which dissolved into one of relative normality.

"How d'you mean?" Willow asked by way of voicing her concern – though, it was primarily in an effort to prize more information from her. With that, she inhaled a long drag. She could not put her finger on the flavour; it was something sweet and thick.

"Well," Stacey began, the ponderous look returning, "the sex is good. Fun. But it just doesn't do anything for me. I don't enjoy it, really." She continued, rolling her entire body to face Willow. As she spoke, her eyes transitioned between a curious look to one of concern, then finally to one of resigned irritation; Willow thought that it was because the admission revealed an annoyance. Sensing a tension, Willow joked;

"Is he not kinky enough?" That was misjudged.

"I'm serious, Willow." Stacey snapped. Willow turned back to look at the sky again. "It would just be my luck, score the Dirk Diggler progeny and I hate it." She explained, a light-heartedness returning to her voice. Willow chuckled, then guffawed, as she processed what had been said to her. Stacey did not think it was all that funny; she was known for her dry wit, though it tired at times. She finished rolling her own joint.

"I love that you know I'd get that reference." Willow said at last, her voice returning from the jovial quiver it had digressed to. "What is this, by the way?" She continued, exhaling another drag, still unable to detect the taste. Stacey shrugged, putting her own to her lips. She inhaled, closed her eyes and then exhaled.

"I don't know." She admitted, her voice croaky. She coughed, the smoke strong in her throat. "He said it was good, and I didn't argue. I'm just glad to be taking some off his hands, less for him the cocky shit." She hissed with venom before smoking it once more.

"Pun intended?"

"You know it."

Then a pause. A few moments of calm between the pair, and that was unusual. Normally, they had plenty to talk about, but there was something not right this time. Stacey had been like that all day, aloof somehow. It was not the weed; she had not had any all day up until now. Willow thought she knew what the problem was;

"Tim said he'd overheard someone call you 'Scott-Sucker', what's that about?" She said suddenly, almost startling Stacey. It took a few seconds for her to register the question; the joint was beginning to have an effect.

"Yeah, Harry mentioned it to me earlier. I don't know where

he got that from." She admitted, seemingly unconcerned; Willow had expected some form of indignation from her, but she disregarded the issue seemingly at ease with it. But Willow took something else from the answer; never mind the casual disregarding of the statement, she seemed to deny the deed altogether.

"You mean you haven't done *that* yet?" She asked by way of saying so.

"*No*, I haven't. It's disgusting enough to look at, much less do that to it." Stacey said, indignant at last. That was a better response; at the very least, it reassured Willow.

"So why is he saying it? Shouldn't you talk to him about it?" She asked, still somewhat surprised that Stacey seemed this unconcerned that a rumour was spreading that was scarcely true. Even at the suggestion she do something, Stacey was unmoved.

"Nah, s'all good really." She said, casually. Willow's concern became palpable, and Stacey could sense it. To confirm her suspicion, she turned to face her friend, who wore a face of disbelief. "Honestly, it's fine." She insisted, her voice louder, forceful. Still, Willow was not satiated.

"You don't seem overly concerned?" She hissed, perhaps in an effort to coerce Stacey into realising.

"Why should I be? It's just a laugh." She answered, Willow's attempt ineffective. Resigned to a failure on this occasion, she rolled her head back.

"If you say so." She whispered. Staring upwards, back into the sky, she espied the rolling clouds clearing briefly, allowing a blanket of stars to shine through for a few moments before disappearing again. She sighed, though did not say anything, then lifted the joint back to her lips. If her parents were to find her, they would not be terribly happy with her. Though, she always had suspicions that they knew what she was up to. She filled her lungs with the thick flavour, in her biggest drag yet, then lowered the thing. Holding her breath for a few moments, her eyes began to water. Realising she could not hold for much longer, she exhaled, then coughed. Out poured the smoke again, wasted into the air. She brought a balled fist to her face and coughed heavily into it. A couple more exertions and her chest settled. She lowered her fist, then lifted the other hand with the joint between her fingers. She stared at it for a moment;

"So, where does Scott get..." She began. In all of a second, Stacey was upon her. She forced her lips to Willow's and gripped the back of her head. Startled, Willow dropped the joint and pressed her hand into Stacey's chest, pushing her away. After a few moments of struggling, she managed to free herself from Stacey's grip. She rolled away, her hand still on her to keep her away. "The fuck are you doing?" She asked, indignantly. Stacey did not say anything; her face bore a look that could be described as amazed, yet her brow was furrowed into a regretful confusion. Stacey stared for a moment, glanced about, then spoke;

"Well, dunno really." She whispered, anticlimactically.

"The hell, Stacey?" Willow cried, louder this time. She moved her hand away and crawled backwards as though to escape from her. Stacey sighed and sat up, pushing yourself away from the ground.

"Okay, I was just trying something out. Maybe it's why I don't feel it with Scott?" She admitted; Willow's heart gave a bound, and she scoffed. It jumped again as her look of disbelief morphed into something else; something she did not notice, nor intend; somehow, her mood lightened.

"Well, how did that feel?" She asked, her voice gentler.

"Good." Stacey said, shrugging, her voice little more than a whisper. Willow felt her breath become heavy and rhythmic. "Can I make sure?" She asked, her voice barely audible. Now, Willow's breath quivered. Stacey's lips unsealed and a shallow breath emerged from behind them.

Willow imagined for a moment that this was all down to the weed; Stacey was not thinking herself. There again, Willow knew she was completely lucid, and it was with that part of her brain that she made her determined reply;

"Go for it."

With that, Stacey smiled and inched closer, her movements more deliberate and less animated than they had been before. She moved her face to within inches of Willow's, their eyes locking ever and again, before they paused. Finally, Stacey cupped Willow's cheek, stroking her skin softly; it was Willow who engaged the kiss this time, lifting her own hand to Stacey's face. Much less of a small peck, as Stacey had given her previously, this kiss was more involved, sensual and deliberate.

It seemed to go on for longer than it did; those few moments crawled by as hours in Willow's head, her heart floating with a nervousness she expected, mixed with the thought that it felt *right*. She was not revulsed, as she thought she may have been; she was enjoying herself. Her eyes rolled into her head, and she thought that Stacey's would have done too, though she could not see through her closed eyelids.

As the friends kissed, Willow felt a hand on her waist; she recoiled, then settled into it, before realising that she had lifted her other hand to Stacey's chin, now cupping her face with both hands, so as to keep her as close as possible.

Eventually, and though Willow did not want it to happen, the kiss seemed to come to a conclusion; Stacey moved her face away from Willow's, then opened her eyes, slowly, drinking in her friend, who simply sat as she had been, stunned. Both of them panted heavily, their breath short from their smoking. Willow's wide eyes looked Stacey up and down and she nodded knowingly.

"So?" She asked, tentatively; her voice was scarcely more than a whisper, her throat tight. Stacey nodded, almost imperceptibly.

"Yeah. It feels good." She said between puffs of breath. It took Willow a few moments to realise that she enjoyed it too; though she knew it did not feel wrong, she only now came to accept that not only was it right, it was *good*.

With as much of a conversation, Stacey dove forward and their lips met again. *This feels the best yet*, Willow thought as a tongue probed her mouth before she returned the favour. She lifted her hand back to Stacey's waist, this time ensuring that her palm went beneath her loose top so as to touch her skin. Once more, her eyes closed and rolled, and she toppled backwards as Stacey crawled on top of her, stroking her fringe from her forehead.

If only they had chanced to look up for a moment before continuing, they would have seen, in the distance, a sharp glimmer of light bouncing off of a distorted disc. Their noises were enough to mask the brief clicks of a camera shutter being pressed, and the evil chuckles of a voyeur who knew exactly what he was doing.

-23-
Circumstantial Evidence

"How did your little *tête-à-tête* go with Sebastian?" Phillips asked, having immediately answered the phone to Fiona. He could hear panting through the earpiece. "You walking somewhere?" He asked, voicing his thought.

"I needed some air. Look, I know we haven't got anything on this guy yet, but I think he had something to do with this." She panted. Phillips folded his free arm into the crook of his elbow.

"Why, what happened?" He knitted his brow into a frown. More panting from Fiona.

"I've never seen anything like it; he was completely lucid, but at the same time he just seemed to look right through both of us. I didn't learn anything. It was like he knew every trick in the book; deflecting questions, getting irritated, pity cards, all sorts. I didn't even probe him that hard." She continued. Phillips detected a shiver in her voice that was subtle enough that you may be forgiven for having missed it.

"So, you think he's hiding something?"

"Well, the guy's got form, remember. Or even if he didn't murder Stacey…" She began.

"Which was left inconclusive?" Phillips interrupted as a reminder.

"It wouldn't surprise me if he did Willow. It makes too much sense. He had this, sort of, obsession with her; I think maybe once Stacey was out of the picture, he must have fixated on someone else." She theorised. Phillips saw her reasoning.

"Yes, I see what you're getting at; but we still don't know enough to guess just yet. Once we get the blood samples back from Mark, we should have a better idea of what we're dealing with." He said, pacing the corridor; another officer walked past him and nodded his head politely. Phillips returned the greeting.

"When are those due?" She asked as Phillips returned his attention to her.

"By the end of the day. Damned Forensics. You'd think it would be a faster process by now?" He said, moving towards the door behind him; he turned and peered through the eye hole; Harry sat with folded arms at the desk in the middle of the concrete room beyond. "Still, they're giving me time to have a word with Harry properly." He confessed, turning back around.

"You brought him in?" She replied.

"Oh yes. I'm going to see if I can break through his tough exterior. The only problem is, his mother isn't pressing charges against him, so if we can't build a case around him, our only lead right now is Sebastian." He said, sighing. Fiona replied with the same sound. "Look, I'm going to go in and interview him, where are you?" he said, glancing at his watch.

"I'm about twenty minutes from the station." Came the half-exasperated reply.

"Want me to send you a car?" He offered, sensing her exhaustion.

"No, I'll be fine. I'll be there soon." She replied.

"Right-o, I'll see you then. Bye." he lowered the phone, just about hearing her 'goodbye' before he hung up with a slide of his finger across the phone. With that, he pocketed it, turned about and tapped his key fob against the door; it sensed who he was, buzzed and unlocked, all instantaneously. He pushed the door by the metal plate and strode in. "Harry, sorry about that; urgent call." Harry barely even looked up.

"He hasn't said anything yet, Sir." Said Superintendent Grisham, who was sat across from Harry beside a vacant seat Phillips soon occupied. As he settled into the chair, Phillips fished up a folder from within his bag which was sat by the leg of his seat.

"That's okay, he's saving himself for when we start the recording." Phillips said with a condescending smile, knowing full well that Harry did not intend to say a word. With that, he raised a finger and pointed to a control panel vaguely resembling a mixing desk to his left. Harry glanced at it in time to see Phillips' fingertip press down on a tactile switch further away from him. "Recording commenced at eight thirty-seven in the evening on Tuesday the twenty-third of September, police case 19092019/019. Interview subject is Harry Baines, also present at the interview is Superintendent Grisham and I am DCI Anthony Phillips." He recited, having used the same formula for countless interviews in the past.

"May the record also show that Harry has waived his right to an appointed lawyer and has opted to conduct this interview without one or in the presence of a parent or guardian." Grisham added. Phillips nodded; Harry glanced between the two. "Harry, have you been offered food and water or otherwise a drink of your choice?" He continued. Harry nodded.

"Please answer all questions verbally, for the record." Phillips said, looking down to his papers. Harry sneered.

"Yes, I have." He said at last, tapping his foot rhythmically on the concrete floor.

"Good. If you wish to stop this interview at any time, please say so and we will have a break. You are happy with all of this? Is there anything you wish to add?" Grisham said, finally getting to the end of their speech. Harry sneered again.

"No."

"Then let's begin." That was Philips. "So, Harry, I just want to go over a few things with you, there's some bits we need to get to the bottom of. On the nineteenth of this month, you were walking home from school at around a quarter to four in the afternoon. You saw Willow approaching her house, is that correct?" He asked with autonomous precision, sifting through a few sheets of paper in the folder. Harry's foot began tapping faster.

"That's right, aye." Harry replied with monotony.

"Was she alone, or with friends, anyone like that?" Phillips continued.

A pause.

"I didn't see anyone with her." Harry muttered, unconvincingly.

"Nobody at all? Nobody who could corroborate this account?" Grisham asked, lifting his head from his documents. He was scarcely reading them, merely scanning them for a discrepancy.

"You heard me right, Copper." Harry hissed, leaning forward.

"May I say for the record that I haven't been a *Cop* for more years than I care to mention." Grisham said, sarcastically. Phillips grinned. Harry merely sighed.

"Willow didn't have too many friends." Harry continued; his bemusement was evident.

"Is that right? Because I have statements from more or less everyone we've spoken to so far saying she was '*immensely popular with a group of friends many of her classmates were in pure envy of*'. That's from the statement of Howard Worth." Phillips said, frowning. Harry merely sat back in his chair, then turned his head. Phillips sensed something, a fear he could not quite explain coming from the boy. "No, you're right, let's go with what you think, Harry. It's your statement, after all." He continued, nodding his head and discarding the statements back into his bag. "So after you see Willow near her home, do you engage with her at all, do you talk with her?"

"I did not say a word to her." Harry said with a forced inflection somewhat mocking of their own officious tone. He tilted his head back so that he faced them again.

"That's funny, because one of Willow's friends says here that you had a *'demeaning and insulting conversation'* with her." Grisham said. "Whoops, sorry, my mistake; that wasn't Willow's friend at all, because of course, she doesn't have any. No, that was *your* friend, Mustafa, who says he was with you at the time."

The fucking sneak! Harry thought, cursing his supposed friend. He had been backed into a corner; time to worm his way out of it.

"I just wanted to talk to her, that's all. Why is that such a crime?" Harry retorted.

"It isn't. But telling us you never spoke to her, then saying you did is lying to the police." Phillips snapped back. Harry grimaced. Grisham sighed.

"So you have this *demeaning and offensive* conversation?" He said, diverting attention back to the story.

"She fucking insulted *me*! In front of Mustafa!" Then it hit him... "That's what he means in his statement! *She* was demeaning and offensive to *me*! Not me to her." He protested. *Maybe he isn't a fucking sneak, after all*?

"So according to you, Willow is a popular girl with no friends, with whom you didn't talk but by whom you were insulted and demeaned in the conversation you may or may not have had, do I have that right?" Phillips said, making notes on his piece of paper. Harry screwed his face up. "Let's move on, swiftly I think, to what happened next. After the conversation you didn't have, she went to her front door. What did you do then?" He asked. Harry did not answer. He sat back in his chair such that the front two legs left the floor.

Grisham leaned in and rested his head contemplatively on his balled fist. Harry said nothing. Even Phillips sat with curiosity now, both adults desperate to hear what the youth would say next. He continued to sit in silence.

"We have statements from neighbours telling us what

happened next, but according to you the statements are all wrong. So, what's your take on it?" Grisham prompted. Still, Harry sat in silence. "Because if you say nothing, we have to assume that whatever all of *these* people are saying," he continued, brandishing a number of sheets of paper, "are all true. So why don't we get your side of the story?"

"I didn't see much more of her after that." Harry relented, at last, speaking at the last syllable Grisham offered. "She went around the back of her house, I don't know why, maybe she was trying to get away from me, maybe she didn't have a front door key, I don't know, alright?" He hissed, slamming his fists loudly down onto the desk; doubtless the sound would have caused havoc with the recording equipment, but he didn't much care.

"You followed her, didn't you, Harry?" Phillips said with a sigh.

"No."

"Well somebody did." Quipped Grisham.

"You think you know everything, or that you can make me say things that didn't happen. But what *did* happen was that I watched her house." He said with a wry smile. Grisham leaned forward.

"Oh yes? Well, if that's true, you probably saw who sneaked around the back of her house, right Harry?" He suggested. Harry paused. "*Did you see something*, Harry?" He continued, sweetly.

"I didn't see anything." Harry snapped. Grisham sat back. "I didn't see anyone or anything, nothing happened after that." He said, quickly, then he sighed. Phillips frowned.

"Anyone would think you're defending someone, Harry, is that right?"

"No."

"So you just like watching women's houses?" Phillips said, crossing his fingers in front of him. "You clearly thought a lot of Willow, so I suppose it isn't too unusual for you to be staring at her house." He resumed, hoping to illicit a response. His plan seemed to work.

"What does that mean?" Harry snapped. Grisham turned to Phillips.

"Phillips, the scrapbook, if you would." He asked. Harry started as Phillips reached into his bag.

He fished out a thick book, like a journal, brimming with print copies of photographs, the corners of which stuck out at odd angles; Harry recognised every one of them.

"How the fuck did you get that?" He hissed, leaning against the table with his hands.

"For the recording, we have introduced a scrapbook of photographs seized from Harry Baines' property and will be filed as item number double-oh nine." Phillips said, placing the book down on the table; Harry jumped from his seat; Phillips and Grisham remained as they were, expecting such a reaction.

"*You're* the bastard who took that from me?! Who gave you the right to take that?" Harry cried, slamming his fists down every second or so. Phillips and Grisham remained calm, despite their alarm.

"We are the police, we seize what is pertinent. Kindly sit down." Grisham said, assuredly. Harry made to protest. "*Sit down.*" He continued, taking a stern tone at last; Harry ceased his restlessness for a moment.

"Harry, I should sit yourself down, or you will be restrained by officers." Phillips said, adopting a similar tone of annoyance. Harry stood for a moment, peering ever now and again at the scrapbook. "Harry, sit down!" Phillips urged. In a few moments more, they would be required to restrain him. Harry breathed heavily and eventually sat back down in almost perfect rhythm with his breaths. Grisham sighed heavily.

"Good boy." Grisham said.

"Shut the fuck up." Harry retorted.

"Quite the temper, right, Harry?" Phillips interrupted. "But then again, that's nothing new, right?" Harry did not look up.

"Is it too late to say 'no comment'?" Then he laughed.

"You're allowed to say what you like." That was Grisham.

"Then I choose to say 'no comment'." Harry said with a snap.

"Not a problem." Phillips. "Just let me ask you this." He paused, then inhaled. "Did you have any desire to kill Willow Greene?" He said, sitting back in the metal chair and folding his arms. Harry raised his head and peered at the single fluorescent strip that hung menacingly from the ceiling. "You had your eye on her for a while." He continued, gesturing to the book on the table. "We've had a flick through, there's some pretty disturbing things in there, Harry. Supposing any of these got out? Maybe Willow knew about them and threatened to leak them? You'd do anything to stop that, right? *Anything*?" He continued, threateningly.

"I never wanted to kill her." Harry hissed at last, contorting his face into one of pure hatred. "She might have been a *bitch*. But I would never want to kill her. But then again, hasn't everyone had *someone* they've wanted to kill? Even you two?" Harry replied, pointing his forehead at the pair. "I bet you wouldn't mind killing me right now?" He continued, closing his hands together in front of him and gesturing at Phillips with a finger.

Phillips mirrored his appearance, then smiled a wry grin that gave nothing away, but did not waylay his feelings. Harry scoffed.

"You never *wanted* to kill Willow. Did you?" Grisham interrupted. Phillips turned to him, then back to Harry who sank into the chair a little more purposefully now.

"No comment." Harry replied with a dramatic pause in between the two words. Both interviewers sat back in their chairs and sighed.

"If that's it then?" Grisham said, opening his fingers in a conjoined shrug.

"That's it. This interview is concluded at eight fifty-three in the evening." With that, Phillips pressed the same record button that had started the session and in an instant, the recording light dimmed into darkness.

"Thank fuck, I get to go home now?" Harry sighed, unclasping his hands and sitting back in his chair again; once more, the legs left the floor. Phillips fished up the book and tossed it nonchalantly back into his bag, which he picked up by the over-the-shoulder strap.

"Ha!" He exclaimed. "Not a chance. You're staying in the cells for the night. We're not done with you." He chuckled, slinging the bag to his side. Grisham drew up his own documents to his side, then turned to Phillips.

"I'm not staying *here*!" Harry cried in protest.

"Sorry, but you're going nowhere." Grisham continued. He then gestured with a hand and a turn to the door, which signalled a pair of guards beyond the door to enter; they were menacing, burly men with dark hair and smoky skin.

"How long can you keep me for?" Harry asked, lunging for the two interviewers; the burly men stepped into his way to prevent him from getting to the pair.

"Legally we have twenty-four hours. You've been here for two, so let's say twenty-two for luck." Phillips said, moving for the door but stopping before he got to it. Grisham was now in front of him, between the guards and the DCI. Harry tried to make for the two, but the sheer wall of muscle that flanked him prevented him from doing so.

"Bastards!" Harry cried, pointing at the pair.

"We never asked that you liked us, Harry, just that you work with and respect us." Phillips retorted. "Lucky for you, you're not the only lead we have. Otherwise we'd be crawling all over you." Phillips hissed; Harry made to protest but was silenced by the guards. Grisham gripped Phillips' arm as the pair made for the door.

"Why did you bring up Sebastian?" He asked, in near silence.

"I didn't, you just did. I'm trying to bluff him. Let's see if he calls it." Phillips replied, leaning close and closing the heavy door behind him.

"But we *are* pursuing Sebastian, right?" Grisham retorted.

"Yep. But Harry doesn't know who we're pursuing. But we can get a good squeeze on him if he thinks we're pursuing *somebody*." Phillips said, brandishing a document of vague contents for little reason other than theatricality. "He'll start trying to incriminate that somebody, which we know will be a lie, then we've got him." He continued. Grisham frowned.

"This is a bit one-sided, right? You're trying to pin this on Harry when it *could* be Sebastian we're after."

"In that case, we pull the same bluff on Sebastian. It'll trip somebody up eventually." Phillips said with a sigh.

"This is very complicated, Phillips, I don't like it." Grisham said gravely.

"That's why you're not the DCI, Grisham. I know what I'm doing." Phillips replied with a wry smile.

-24-
Forgive Me, Father

Light streamed through the stained-glass window at the far end of the church, casting a multicoloured display of beams slicing through the thick, dusty air. Particularly orange was the sunrise that morning; far away in the distance, the clouds were illuminated by a blazing glow that brought a relaxing warmth to the otherwise cold town.

The place of worship, despite the beauty of the colourful air, was empty and quiet; the thick walls blocked out even the loudest birdsong, and the nearby gaggle of children on their way to their lessons was rendered completely inaudible. Only Daryll occupied the place; he had awoken early, for reasons even he could not elaborate upon. He had made and consumed his morning coffee, read the paper, whose headline still clung to the sensational story that had gripped the town, and had gone to the church to prepare it for the day.

He had just laid out the floral arrangements, even more vibrant and colourful than the rays of light throughout the building. He was not required to do so on a daily basis, but the quietness of the hour gave his mind time to be in action; he liked to be busy and found anything he could do to be occupied.

How much of human life is wasted in being alone? That was what he always thought as he looked at the floral arrangement in the vestibule. An explosion of purple and red flowers backed on a green bed of leaves and stalks. *How much of floral life is wasted in not being seen*? He thought next, considering that he had adorned every room with blooms, even though most would be invisible for the rest of the day. He did not concern himself with these thoughts for too long. *So long as I appreciate them, their presence is worth it*. He smiled at his handiwork, then espied Mrs Jones, an elderly lady from whom he had acquired the flowers. He waved to her, partially in an effort to catch her eye and so as to engage in a conversation.

"Mrs Jones, the very best of mornings to you!" He called to her. She started at his sudden salutation and turned to face him;

then she chuckled.

"Oh, Reverend Daryll, good morning to you too." She smiled. By now, Daryll was halfway towards her, his trousers clinging to his legs in the heavy wind that met him.

"Terrible gusts today, aren't there?" He said, stepping closer to her; his voice mingled with the tumultuous roar of the wind in the trees such that as he approached and lessened the volume of his voice, she struggled to hear him.

"What? Oh yes, very windy indeed. You ought to keep those doors closed, or your flowers will be all over the place before you know it." She said, gesturing to them. He turned his head to face them momentarily.

"It's a good vestibule, it rarely catches the wind. Just seems to rush right past, the air is as still as a statue in there." He grinned. He turned back to her, but as he did, he could swear he saw somebody approach from the gate at the end of the path. It looked almost like -

"Oh, Reverend, I meant to ask you. How were your Peonies?" Mrs Jones said, distracting him. He swung about again.

"Sorry?"

"Your Peonies? My supplier got in touch yesterday and mentioned that they had had a bit of a pest problem that affected the quality of the petals." She continued, making pinching motions with her fingertips. Daryll was confused; certainly, he had not noticed any issue. There again, this was probably the biggest issue in her profession; *not everyone shares your life, nor your problems. She probably does not lose sleep that I nearly ran out of communion wine at the last sermon, it isn't her care to.*

"I'm sorry to hear that, I didn't notice anything." He said, half-heartedly. Mrs Jones pulled a confused face.

"I'll have to look into it, then." She continued. Daryll saw the conversation drawing to an end, so he swung about again to look in the direction of the mysterious person he imagined was Willow; Some glimmer of hope manifesting itself in his imagination. She was not there. Perhaps a vision? He turned back around; Mrs Jones was still rambling. "Perhaps it has something to do with insects growing resistant to pesticides? Not that I use flowers that have been drowned in pesticides, Reverend..." she laughed, trailing off. Daryll was not paying much attention.

"Very probably." He said, nonchalantly. Mrs Jones' laughter ceased almost immediately; he half realised that he was being obvious. "I'm sorry, I've a lot on my mind, would you excuse me?" He said, gently tapping her elbow with the tips of three fingers. He smiled a reassuring smile; it was not enough to assuage her doubts, for her face did not mirror his own. His own expression was resolute, though, and he maintained it as he swept past her to head back to the Church.

He did not stop to look back at her once he had arrived there, but he was certain she was already leaving; she was, in fact, still perturbed at his abruptness. He moved through the vestibule, taking a moment to pause and check a sample of petals on some select flowers. He did not see any defects and disregarded the concerns of his supplier as insignificant.

He pushed aside the monolithic wooden door with such a quietness as to surprise even himself; it had recently been oiled and lubricated, perhaps that was it? He was unsure.

Now that the Sun had risen beyond the horizon, the orange through the windows was more of a bright white; it filtered through the stained-glass in all sorts of vibrant colours, but even so, it was dark and gloomy, especially in contrast to the brightness of the outside that his eyes had adjusted to. He was convinced, as he moved between the pews towards the altar that he could hear a female voice talking; who was this mysterious person haunting him? Was it still his imagination playing tricks on him? For what purpose?

It seems he was not being paranoid.

A lone figure sat at the front of the room, staring out towards the cavernous far end of the Church. He could tell, even at this distance, that it was a woman; long, straight hair and a slender silhouette against the light through the window told him so. He was about to call out to the figure to identify them, but then he heard their voice again; he had lost it previously to the clutter of his mind as he used clearer thoughts to try to identify them. The soft voice spoke quietly, such that it was almost inaudible; it was not even echoed by the cathedral-like space above them.

"I can't pretend to know what I'm supposed to say, because I don't, really. Perhaps if Willow was here, she would be helping me." The voice said, gently; Daryll took a moment to see if he could tell who it was; he moved himself quietly into one of the rows of pews and seated himself; his hands became clasped in his lap and he exhaled in near silence.

"Well done, Sarah, seeking solace in the Lord, you've been listening to my sermons." He rejoiced to himself. He listened carefully to her words;

"Willow always knew just what to say. She loved it here. In fact, I'm sure she loved the service Reverend Daryll led the other day; I know a lot of people did. It's strange, you know, but I was hoping that something good could come of all this. I thought that this whole damned affair..." she brought herself up. "Sorry. I'm still getting used to this." In near silence, Daryll chuckled to himself. "I was just wanting to hope that even though I can't think of anything worse that could happen, I could come out of this with some sense that things will get better. That somehow, things would improve. But all it's done is bring the bad dreams out of the woodwork. All I do is argue with Gary. Phillips' investigation hasn't gotten anywhere yet, so I'm no closer to closure. What's worse is that Howard is making his moves again." Daryll sat forward in stark amazement; *making his moves*?

He listened in, closer now. His concentration magnified her voice to something of a shout in his ears, but he was convinced there could be no actual elevation to her amplitude. "All I want is to be at peace. Not have to face the mistakes I've made in the past. These things are meant to stay there, right? Everything that happened between me and Howard are bygones, things that, even though me and Gary aren't happy anymore, haven't affected our relationship in any way. So why does he insist on coming back? I know he liked Willow, and she him, but it's not fair for him to just come into our lives now that she's..." she stopped again. He could hear her voice breaking at the last few words and knew where she was going with that though because of it. He brought his hand to his face to conceal his amazement, or at least to prevent it from audibly manifesting itself.

He could have interrupted her; stopped her from continuing. How would she react when she knew that he had been eavesdropping; probably not well. But she was confiding in the Lord; He could not interrupt her, for it was not his place. He was in a moral quandary; one he had not needed to consider before. So, with the best of intentions, he allowed her to continue. Even so, he could not hear her voice anymore; all had gone quiet. Had he been noticed? Had she turned around and espied him? The soft crying he could hear at the head of the room was now all the sound that permeated that space; it was quiet and subdued, but through it she soon resumed.

"I'm sorry, Father. I've done things I'm not proud of, and I fear I've jeopardised my life with Gary. But even that isn't the worst thing, the thing that bothers me the most. I just worry that Willow found out about me and what I've done." At that, Daryll's heart sank; he didn't need her to continue to figure out what she was about to say next, but she did anyway; "What if she's done this to herself? What if this is all my fault?"

-25-
The Rumour Mill

Harry leaned against the wall; Mustafa stood to his right, laughing heartily in the way only boisterous students know how to do. Another friend was positioned opposite, his hands plunged into the deep pockets of his long coat, his head hunched over as though he was looking at something on the floor.

Harry surveyed the smaller students as they milled about in a large crowd through the corridor; many of them were scared of him, and did not acknowledge his presence, despite their knowing he was there. He peered at many but focussed on only a few.

"Boys, to class!" Came the cry of a teacher at the far end of the corridor; she was a tall lady, holding her hand beside her mouth to project her voice; all three of the boys peered after the sound, spotted her stern face and in true miscreant style, ignored her. When they looked back again, she had gone.

"Harry, a word?" Came a voice to his left; he turned, expecting another teacher, then locked eyes with Willow, whose face was one of thunder. He stifled laughter, then spoke in between chuckles.

"Lucky me." He said, turning to his friends, both of whom were also trying to stop laughs from leaving their lips; Willow was decidedly unimpressed;

"Shut up." She hissed, viciously, at them. Then, turning her attention back to Harry; "Come here." She said, gripping his arm and dragging him away from his cohorts. In her other hand, she held a piece of paper which was wrinkled and torn in places but nonetheless in one piece. Harry knew what it was immediately. She hauled him from the corridor and out into the open air of the courtyard outside, which was packed with cars belonging to teachers and senior students.

Finally, she pushed him up against a wall in a small, enclosed space with a locked cage at one end between the main building and the toilet block. "Look, I know it was you." She said, crossing her arms and stepping away from him; his breath was repugnant enough to validate distance between them.

"What was me?" He asked with feigned innocence. She

scoffed, then held out her hand, brandishing the piece of paper it held at him; upon it was a photograph, crudely framed, of two female figures, one recognisable as Willow and the other was Stacey. Both figures were captured from the waist up, naked, wrapped in an embrace, their faces together. "Oh, that." He said, taking the sheet from her and admiring his photography work. *Yes, that, you ignorant fuck*, thought Willow, who could barely contain the rage she knew would cause him injury if it was unleashed. He and his friends had put a number of copies up in the female toilets before the school day had started; Willow had found this copy mere minutes before her approaching him.

Willow tore the sheet from his hand, ripping it clean down the middle.

"Why would you do this to me, Harry. Why the fuck would you do that?" She asked, not quite crying but with an incensed tone that startled even him.

"You're right, maybe I didn't get your nose quite right." He replied, not quite aware of how angry she really was, despite the palpable annoyance in her words.

"I'm not talking about your artistic abilities, you dick, I'm talking about what you're saying about me. About *Stacey*." She retorted, almost screaming at him; though it made no difference to her, it was fortuitous that the space had largely been vacated of people. Harry scoffed, and raised his hands in protest.

"What's wrong with it, if it's true?" He defended. Willow let out a laugh, one of disbelief, but it was enough to confuse him. She paused after her outburst had trailed off, then sighed, shaking her head. The rage began to burn in her, but it was one that she knew she had to supress before she made any reply. That was a hard task; she wanted to throttle him, then and there, and she did not care that anyone would know it was her. She bit her bottom lip and that seemed to satiate her frustration such that she felt she could finally address his point.

"You don't get it, do you?" She began, locking eyes with him. "I don't care what people think of me; I loved Stacey, that's true, and nobody can take that away from me. But you don't understand what this kind of thing does to girls in school, to girls anywhere. You'll never understand, because this kind of thing just doesn't happen to people like you. The bullies, the ones everyone is scared of." Her apparent calmness surprised even her, but not as much as the fact that Harry actually seemed to be listening to her. "You *do* remember Stacey, right? Do you actually know any women by name, or just by how they look?" She asked as a rhetorical question. "Can you remember what they used to say about her? What everyone, even her boyfriend, called her?" She paused for just enough time for him to think, then answered the question for him. "They called her Scott-Sucker. I've seen people come up to her in the street, people I've never met before, people I'm sure *she'd* never met before, and call her that to her face. All because Scott told somebody a lie *once*. I know it was a lie because she told me it was. She didn't do *anything* with him because she thought he was disgusting, and she didn't even like men, but she knew he would destroy her because *that's what men can do to women*. Guess what, she was right to be worried, because he did destroy her. It was a rumour that *he* started. Everyone believed it, nobody would listen to her even when she could prove it wasn't true. That's what this kind of thing does, Harry, it sticks. You might think it's little more than a joke, a little schoolboy laugh with your mates, but you've never had it happen to you and it never will."

For a moment, all was still; Willow's lips tingled, and her ears were ringing; her heart pounded out of her chest. She had wanted to say something for so long, and now that she had said it, she felt a release, a catharsis that she struggled to contain; but the more she thought about it, the more she simply allowed floods of tears to spill from her eyes, but she did not sob. Harry simply stood before her, his face unchanged, neutral in its composition. He was completely still, as if he was made from wax.

"I'm sure Scott didn't mean for her to top herself." He said after a few moments of musing. As soon as his face moved to form words, Willow almost started in shock; the audacity of him! She soaked in his words, finding them ridiculous. *How would he know what Scott intended? Did Stacey even take her own life?* Willow did not know, but the fact remained the same; the situation was the same;

"Go and tell that to her fucking headstone." She said aloud.

-26-
Reviewing the Evidence

"Sarah was having a fucking affair with Howard Worth." Phillips shouted, slamming the phone down into the cradle. He more or less destroyed both, but he was too annoyed to care. He strode out of his office and into the other room, about which were scattered a collection of Investigators, Detectives, police officers and the Superintendent. Fiona waited for him at his door and followed him out.

"Phillips, calm down." She warned him. He swished past her and she turned to follow him. All eyes peered across the room at his stride, which commanded the room with an annoyed stoicism. Grisham, who was sat on a desk with one of his feet propped up on the chair set at it, furrowed his brow and flexed his fingers.

"Where does that put things?" The Superintendent quizzed. He brought a hand to his face as to await a reply.

"If she's been keeping that from us, who knows what else she's been secret about." Phillips replied, his voice calmer. "Quite aside from that, what do we think would have happened if Willow found out about it?" He suggested. Fiona sighed.

"Are we still pursuing the suicide theory?" She asked eventually.

"I think Phillips is right. It strengthens the theory, and in any case, we should pursue every avenue." Grisham said, continuing the thought Phillips had established. "Where are we on other suspects, what have we got?" He asked, gesturing to a nearby whiteboard, replete with photographs, names and hastily drawn lines. Phillips sighed and moved towards the board, snatching a Sharpie from an unsuspecting Detective who had been chewing it for the duration of the conversation. He plucked off the lid with his teeth – momentarily forgetting that it was being consumed by someone else moments earlier – and began to scribble on the board.

"Harry Baines. What do we know about him?" He began as a rhetorical question. "History of violence and abusive behaviour. His mother, Louise, is one of his main victims, but she has never yet pressed charges. Father unknown." He recited, stabbing the board with the nib of his pen.

"What motive would he have?" Grisham asked.

"The photo album. Tim, their friend at school, told us that Willow discovered the existence of it after Harry photographed her and Stacey before her own suicide, though that's going back about two years ago now." Fiona answered instantly. "Harry kept up his charade, because the book is filled with photos of women, mostly classmates." She said. Phillips fished the aforementioned from the evidentiary container that sat on the floor between the castors of the board stand; it was in a plastic evidence bag, sealed with a zipper to contain it; he passed it across to Grisham along with black and white photocopies of all of the pages. Grisham took them and began to pore over the contents.

"Most guys just have a folder on their phone or something." He hissed, dryly.

"Sir?" That was Phillips, his face one of concern.

"What does this tell us?" Grisham asked, putting the images down and removing is glasses.

"Stalker. It's obvious that these pictures were taken without the subject's knowledge. So we know he's violent, has a problem with women and has is a stalker, so in the best possible terms, he's showing signs of insecurity. Combine that with the fact that he was the last person to see Willow alive, the fact that his statements are inconsistent with his friends' means he's got something to hide." Phillips continued. "We need to consider Harry as suspect number one."

"Any physical evidence linking him?" Grisham retorted, handing the book and papers back to Phillips.

"Where are we on forensics, Mark?" Fiona asked, turning to the aforementioned person. Mark was stood in the doorway sifting through a selection of papers he had authored with the forensic assistance of Jacqueline. He started at the sound of his name coming across the room to him.

"No prints on the body." He said, closing the stapled booklet.

"Did we expect that?" Phillips asked.

"Yes. She was submerged for at least twelve hours, so she's been cleaned of them." Mark confessed.

"What about the blood found at the scene?" Fiona quizzed.

"Still waiting on the results from the lab." He replied. Phillips sighed and slammed a fist onto the table.

"It's been nearly a week, now, how does it take this long?" He shouted, alarming Fiona. He had not been so angry before.

"These things take time, you know that." Mark said, defending himself. "People think this kind of thing can be done in minutes, but this isn't the movies." He continued. Phillips held his hands up.

"Okay, fine, please ignore me." He said, calmly. "I would like those results expedited, they're of great importance. If the blood isn't Willows, it clears the suicide theory and we might be able to run a check." He said. Mark nodded his head in agreement.

"Who else?" Grisham asked. "What about this Sebastian character?" Phillips moved to an old photograph of Sebastian that hung on the board; it had been taken from the previous case file.

"Sebastian has a history. He was the prime suspect in the murder case of a young girl a few years back." Phillips said.

"He was never convicted, let's remember that." Fiona protested.

"But at the same time, other suspects were cleared, and he wasn't, for one simple reason; he didn't have an alibi. He didn't have one then, and he doesn't have one now." Phillips began. Fiona interrupted him again.

"I think Sebastian is a bit of a red herring."

"How so?" That was Grisham.

"I don't think he's a vicious killer at all; he seems to just be a lonely old man, really. His public image has been destroyed by the apparent preconception that he's done this before when it was never proved, so I think people see him as an easy target." She said, raising her hands and gesticulating wildly.

"That's as maybe, Fiona, but we need to seriously consider that he's using that as a mask." Grisham countered, causing her to sigh.

"A double bluff? Fiona scoffed. "I suppose there's evidence linking him?"

"Not yet." Phillips admitted.

"Think about it, it looks as though the Greene household was broken into, and I don't think Sebastian, in his frailty, is capable of knocking a door in." Fiona said. Phillips considered for a moment; perhaps she was right.

"Okay, he's not high on our list." He said at last.

"I see Daryll is also on your board there?" Grisham pointed out.

"Yes, he found the body. No motive, it seems he and Willow were good friends. But still, he doesn't have a watertight alibi so we're just keeping an eye on him." Phillips admitted.

"So he isn't a serious consideration?" Grisham asked.

"No, but we're *considering* every angle." Fiona interrupted.

"Even frail old men." Grisham interrupted. Before Fiona had time to respond, he continued: "Okay, so run me through your scenario, what's the current angle we're following here?" Grisham asked.

"Fiona?" Phillips said, moving towards her and handing her the Sharpie. She moved across the room, essentially swapping places with her colleague. She ensured the board was immobile and then flipped it around using a knob situated on the side of the frame. The other side was completely blank.

"So, we have Willow leaving school at three twenty-five in the afternoon with two friends, Tim and Amy. At three thirty-seven, she arrives home where Harry exchanges words with her, according to him 'for seconds', but his friend Mustafa said they talked for at least five minutes." As she spoke, she wrote a timeline with the relevant times followed by what was going on at that moment.

"This is when there's some inconsistencies with the narrative, right?" Grisham asked.

"Correct. What we do seem to agree on is that Harry insists that once Willow stopped talking to him, she went around the back of the house, but he did not follow her." Fiona said, catching her writing up with her speech.

"All the while, her parents, Gary and Sarah are out for an anniversary meal. They don't get back to the house until shortly after seven o'clock, at which point they discover her missing." Phillips added.

"Yes, so unfortunately, we haven't got anything between around quarter to four and seven o'clock, which we haven't been able to fill." Fiona resumed.

"But you know what happened to her, right?" Grisham asked. "You must have *something* concrete for me?" He pleaded.

"We have theories." Phillips interrupted as Fiona was about to explain.

"There was a rock with a high concentration of blood across a small area." Mark said, surprising everyone.

"Yes, if we can ascertain that that blood is Willow's, we have the murder weapon." Phillips added.

"Now, even that did not have any fingerprints on, it was analysed in the lab. So it was either cleaned by the attacker or it was cleaned by the rain. Only problem is, the night was dry that day." Mark pointed out. "But, the autopsy revealed that her skull was damaged as a result of impact with an object, so we're confident we have the murder weapon." He continued.

"Here's the rub, she was also found with shards of glass in her throat, so it seems she was fed a lightbulb. One was missing from an appliance at her home. All of this combined negates the whole suicide thing." Mark confessed.

"That aside, she either jumped or was thrown from the cliff with heavy stones in her pockets to help keep her beneath the surface." Fiona added. "So Mark is right, it's highly unlikely she would have been able to fill her pockets with stones, swallow a light bulb, clout herself in the back of the head with a rock and then jump from a cliff. Framing the whole thing as a kidnapping, by breaking her own door down, is quite elaborate and very unlikely." She continued.

"Explain this suicide theory to me, where did that spring from?" Grisham asked. Phillips sighed.

"So, Stacey, who was found murdered, apparently by Sebastian, but that was never proved," Phillips said, satiating the annoyed face Fiona had just thrown him. "She and Willow were very good friends. From what Tim told us, they were actually *more* than good friends. We found alarming messages on her laptop talking about how 'she wanted to join her', so it seemed to us that she wanted to take her life because she thought that would lead to her and Stacey being reunited."

"That seems a bit far-fetched, she likely just missed her friend." Grisham protested. Fiona quickly shot him down.

"We think the death traumatised her more than others. But that's just a theory." She explained. Grisham nodded his head.

"That's why I believe that if she had found out about her Mothers infidelity, it may have tipped her over the edge. Her parents don't exactly have the best relationship, from what I've seen." Phillips said. Fiona nodded too.

"I get that vibe. I don't think it's a happy house." She agreed.

"So, what's the next step?" Grisham asked.

"We need to get those DNA test results from the lab, Mark, I want you to get in touch with Jacqueline, see what she can arrange. Give her all of the samples she needs. I want them no later than tomorrow evening, so you've got sixteen hours to get on to the lab and get them through the system." Phil said, pointing at him. Mark nodded.

"I'll get on it now." He said; he turned about and stepped

back through the door, vanishing into the machinery that was the bustling floor of the station.

"We also need to strengthen the case against Harry, we'll need a full rundown on his activities between those missing hours." Fiona said, pointing at the timeline with her Sharpie.

"Good, get on that, I want those hours watertight." Grisham said, standing up and buttoning his suit jacked tightly shut. "Have someone check with Sarah and Gary, I want to know their movements on the night of her disappearance, where their cards were used, where they were."

"Yes, sir." Phillips said. At that moment, Fiona moved across the room, and forced the Sharpie back into the mouth of the Detective from whom it had been snatched.

"There's something else, as well." Grisham said, just as he got to the door.

"What's that?" Phillips asked.

"It's an unenviable task, but I want you to look into Howard. If he was having an affair with Sarah, that means he's had access to the house. So I want you to go to Sarah's and ask her about the situation." Grisham said.

"You want us to go and basically tell them we know she's had an affair? What if Gary is there?" Fiona hissed. It was a valid concern.

"We can't let personal issues get in the way of the investigation. Phillips is right, this muddies the water more than I'd like it to. We need to know everything. If that means breaking up the family, we don't have much choice." Phillips stood up.

"With all due respect, sir, you can't break this family up, not after what they've been through." He said, threateningly.

"And until you come up with some answers, Phillips, we're going to run this investigation my way. Your evidence is scarce, and I'm becoming restless." Grisham retorted.

"Sir?" Phillips said, his heart beating a little faster.

"You *are* going to ask Sarah. And don't even think about coming back here until you've got an answer." With that, he turned about and dove through the door, slamming his hand against the frame as he went. Fiona stared after him, then back to Phillips, who had by now half-turned towards her; his face was one of shame and a nervous complacency she had not seen on him in all the time she had known him.

She didn't like it at all.

-27-
Broken

"I don't like this." Fiona said as Phillips knocked on the door. He merely sighed; she was not the person who was going to have to ask the question. He voiced that thought sternly, surprising her;

"Well this isn't going to be a walk in the park for me. Just be glad it's not you having to ask them if their daughter was ever suicidal." He turned to her as he spoke, then realised that he hadn't actually considered how he would word the enquiry. Did he explain the situation first, or ask questions and explain later? *Dammit*, he thought. "Please, just be quiet and let me think for a moment." He immediately regretted his curt tone but made no apology for it. He meant the words he had used.

She made no effort to protest his annoyance; in a way, he was right, so it did not matter what he said, simply how he did. She stood firmly, straightened up and sighed under her breath, so inaudibly that even she was not aware that she had done it.

Both officers then returned their attention to the door; in fact, they rather had their attention drawn to it by the sudden clunk of a twisted knob and a whoosh of air as it swung open. Fiona started, but Phillips' stoicism remained absolute. Gary, stood in the middle of the open doorway, did not say a word to them even as Phillips raised a slight smile.

"Gary, good afternoon. Sorry to disturb you again," he began. His sombre tone was masked somewhat by the cheeriness of his smile, even though it was feigned.

"Who is it?" Came Sarah's voice. Hearing it even at a distance gave cause for Phillips' heart to jump slightly; even in distress, her sweet tones seemed too innocent to soil. Gary turned around and brandished a hand, beckoning them inside; in his grip was held a half-filled scotch glass, one which threatened to spill as the liquid within sloshed up the side walls of the glass.

"Police." Gary said, replying to her. The single word was enough to convince the pair that he was drunk; he slurred it so much that it barely came out as the intended word. He swayed as he moved, and his head was slouched. He barely managed to make it through the living room door without crashing headlong through it. Fiona closed the front door behind her, then came to realise that there were, scattered around, several papers, belongings and other such paraphernalia that though similar, did not seem to create a semblance of relation. Perhaps nobody had concerned themselves with cleaning anymore, leading to such disorder.

Phillips entered the living room after Gary, though his entrance was much more dignified and deliberate. As he moved into the room, Sarah came to her feet; she was much more graceful and seemed to be completely sober.

"Phillips, Fiona, good evening." She said with surprise. She looked from one to the other and Fiona smiled, somewhat reluctantly; she knew what they were there for. "What can we do for you? Is there any word on what happened?" She asked, gesturing to Gary. Fiona grumbled.

"We're just here on a bit of an info gathering mission. We need to ask you some questions about Willow, Sarah, I wonder if we could have a few moments in private?" Phillips said. His voice was gentle, yet it bore an undertone of firmness, a subtle hint to Sarah that their presence there was not going to be for a positive purpose. Sarah sighed and turned to Gary, who did not get up out of the chair he had become ensconced in.

"Fuck that." Gary slurred. Everyone turned to him, startled. "Anything you've gotta say to her you can say to me." He pointed at his chest with a thumb, prodding it in his direction.

"Gary, I don't think you're in any fit state to..." Sarah began. Phillips interrupted her, somewhat unintentionally.

"We're being very lenient with you, Gary, given your current situation, but any more bad language and I'll have to caution you." He said, authoritatively. Gary merely chuckled.

"You cops, you think you can just go about waving cautions and threats around, you're so cliché." He said, somewhat lucid. "You're gonna be askin' my wife questions and I want to know what you guys are sayin'." He continued, barely intelligibly this time. Sarah made a move towards him to rid him of another sip of scotch, but he took another swig from the glass regardless, nearly halving the contents. She should have hidden the bottles.

"Gary, I think you've had enough. How about you come with me and we get a coffee?" Fiona asked, gently tapping her hand against his shoulders. *Nice thinking, Fiona.* Phillips thought. But still, Gary would not move.

"Nah, you talk to us both or you don't talk at all." He protested angrily. Sarah sighed, Fiona looked to Phillips and Phillips spoke, his voice towering above the others.

"Sarah, I'm sorry to ask you this and please forgive me, but would Willow have any reason to know about your affair?" Then silence.

He had spoken so quickly that he feared he may have had to repeat himself to be understood; yet, his assuredness ensured that the message was perfectly clear.

Sarah started and nearly collapsed back into her chair in amazement. Gary pulled an exaggeratedly bemused face whilst Fiona turned around in despair.

"The fuck?" That was Gary.

"How did you find...?" Sarah began, but stopped herself in a fluster before she could finish. Phillips paused.

"I'm afraid I can't tell you how this came to our attention, and as far as we're concerned, that isn't important. It possibly bears relevance to the investigation, so we have to ask you; *is there any way Willow could have found out about your affair?*" He spoke with a slower intonation this time so that he was clearly understood. Sarah dropped her head upon her chest and began to quietly sob; *perhaps Gary will be too pissed to figure out what's going on*, she hoped to herself. It was a vain hope.

"Sarah, what is he talking about?" Gary whimpered with a combination of anger and surprise. Rather than respond, her sob became a full-on weep, until soon, nothing could be heard but the rise and fall of her cries. "You'd better fuckin' answer me, or I swear to God!" He hissed, standing up. Fiona stood in his way as Phillips kept his eyes on Sarah.

"When we first found out, Sarah, we really weren't sure if it was true, but your response to the question confirms it. We're not here to judge you, just to find out if it's something we need to keep considering." He asked, calmly. Behind him, Gary had broken free of Fiona's interference, dodging her skilfully and pushing past Phillips such that he nearly fell over. Sarah recoiled into the chair and let out a yelp of alarm as Gary raised his free hand into the air.

Phillips intercepted the intended blow by gripping his wrist; Fiona dove for the glass which had fallen from between his fingers and was tumbling to the ground.

"*Gary*! Gary, stop!" Phillips protested, wrestling the surprisingly pliable man away. In a move not particularly appreciated in the Police force, he used all of his weight and threw Gary across the room. His off-balance sent him careering into the armchair he had previously leapt from. Panting, Phillips turned to Fiona, who was presently occupying herself with finding a place other than Gary's hand for the scotch glass, which had by now spilled its contents onto the floor. "You alright?" He said. He meant it as a question for both her and Sarah, but neither replied. Gary sat panting in his chair. "I should have you arrested for attempted assault. Now here's what's going to happen; you're going to sit there quietly and behave like the good little boy you are." Phillips hissed, pointing with a stern finger.

Calming his breath with controlled inhales, he turned back to Sarah, who had relaxed somewhat; perhaps by the authority displayed which reassured her that Gary would not get to her. "Sarah, I'm going to ask again. Willow, could she have found out?" He asked, shortening the query down for the sake of saving time. At first, she did not reply; it took her a moment to gather her thoughts. When she did speak, it was in tones barely audible to her audience;

"There's not many chances she'd have had to ever have caught us." A sigh. "We were always so careful to avoid being found out. Usually we waited until he'd gone out," she gestured to Gary. "Then we would meet. The closest we ever came to being discovered was one night years ago when me and Gary had had an argument. She came down from her room, I think for a glass of water, or something. Me and *him* were sat in here, and she came in. I don't think she knew what was going on, really. She probably just thought it was me and Gary." She explained.

"And that's the only time?" Fiona queried.

"That's the only time. She was probably too young to ever have any idea what we were up to."

"Sarah?" Gary interrupted in a surprisingly generous tone. Everyone turned to him, Phillips on alert. "I'm a grown man and even I didn't know what you were doing." He slurred. "Who was it?" He asked, burping halfway through the question. Sarah did not answer; then, a pause; "Who the *fuck* was it?" He yelled, Phillips throwing him a stern look. At that, Sarah took issue;

"Oh shut up, just *shut up*! You think I'm the only one to have had an affair? Don't think I don't know about you and your little meet-ups. People half your age texting you at three in the morning. The difference with me, Gary, is that *I regret what I did*, I cut him off completely. So it doesn't matter who it was. Isn't it bad enough that it happened?" She yelled the tirade, such that Phillips' ears began to ring. He did not stop her; someone had to say it. Gary recoiled into his chair, panting, his brows knitted together, angrily. He peered out of the window eventually, deciding not to look at anyone in the room.

All of this confirmed Phillips' suspicions; clearly, Willow had had a brief glimpse of their rendezvous', but Phillips could not yet decide if this was enough to warrant it being something to do with her death. He did not have much time to contemplate this thought, for from behind him;

"The bastard!" Gary hissed; Phillips swung around, expecting him to leap across and attack Sarah again; but before he could jump to stop him, Gary was to his feet and had darted behind the chair and out of the lounge door; the sound of slamming feet came from the hallway and the front door clattered open. Gary and Fiona gave chase, whilst Sarah, in surprise, turned and peered out of the window; an old man in a grey overcoat stood at their garden wall, peering in through their window.

Outside, Gary staggered from the door and made his way up to the path towards Sebastian, who did not even notice that he was on his way.

"You!" Gary cried, pointing an unsure finger. Sebastian turned slowly towards him.

"Gary, what are you doing?" Phillips cried, trying to stop him. He had not yet broken into a run, for he wanted some indication of intent; he soon had it as Gary rolled up his sleeves and cracked his knuckles; a somewhat cliché method of conveying that he was about to land a punch on the man; sensing it, Phillips hastened his approach.

"Gary, no!" That was as he came upon him, grabbing him in a headlock, which was easier said than done. Fiona bypassed them both, rounded the end of the wall where it met the garden path and gently gripped Sebastian by the shoulders. Sebastian was surprised by the fuss being caused.

"Who'sere?" He hissed in alarm; Fiona reassured him.

"It's Fiona, Sebastian, we met a few days ago?" She spoke in gentle tones. Sebastian barely responded with the hint of an unsure nod.

"Let go of me, let me at him!" Gary cried, chomping at the bit. Phillips was not about to let go.

"Gary, calm down, come back inside, you don't want to cause a scene!" He said, hissing into his ear; by now, a small crowd had begun to gather across the road; a dog began to bark, soon to be hushed by the angered owner.

"I'm not gonna calm down, let me at that bastard! He killed my... he killed Willow!" He began to blink away tears, but soon he was unable to stop them. His pathetic wailing was completely incongruous with his demeanour, and Phillips at first imagined it was a forced act designed to make him lower his guard. If that was the case, it did not work.

"I'm sorry!" Sebastian called from behind Fiona's guard. Both Phillips and Gary turned to face him. "I didn't mean for any of this to happen." At that, Fiona turned to him, surprised. Immediately, Gary's tear dried up and his face returned to the scornful grimace he had been wearing prior. Mere crocodile tears. As his fury returned, Gary wrestled him backwards, against a tide of protests that tried to escape his clutches.

"Gary, I'm gonna take Sebastian home! I'll see you back at the station." Fiona called, gripping Sebastian gently by the shoulders. She espied a subtle thumbs up from her cohort, who by now was dragging Gary over the doorstep and into the porch. "Okay, come on, Sebastian, let's get you home." She said, gently.

"I'm really sorry, I didn't mean to make all this fuss." He said, his voice but a quivering whisper.

"That's alright, let's just get you back and a nice cup of tea." She continued. She noticed the crowd again and turned to face them. "Show's over folks. Off you go." She called. Even then, the crowd failed to disperse. She turned about and looked back at the house, finding that the door had been closed. She did not know what conversation was going on there now as she guided Sebastian up the hill towards his home, but she expected it to be a stern one.

Gary was thrown into his living room, which the pair now found empty. Sarah was nowhere to be found; perhaps she had gone upstairs? Phillips was certain he could hear footsteps on loose floorboards signalling her presence.

"Gary, I'm not going to warn you again. You seriously need to reconsider your attitude. We're here to help *you*, but we can't if we're having to deal with your misbehaviour all the time." He warned, sternly. Gary was surprisingly quick to respond.

"You heard him, Phillips, you heard what he said, 'I didn't mean for any of this to happen', what do you think he meant by that?" His voice was loud and piercing. "He's basically confessed."

"I would hardly call it conclusive. Now, we're investigating Sebastian but we need evidence to support theories, not the other way around." Phillips retorted.

"Oh yeah, and what 'evidence' have you managed to find in this whole investigation? How close are you actually to solving this?" Gary fired back, squaring off against Phillips.

It was then that Phillips realised they had very little in the way of solid evidence thus far; though even if there was, he could not simply expel this information to anyone outside the force, so he simply said nothing, which gave Gary all the information he needed.

Without a word, Gary walked calmly past Phillips to the front door, which he walked quietly through. Phillips turned and peered through the window at him. He noticed him walking to the left, away from the direction Fiona had gone. Phillips sighed and shook his head. He would let himself out of the house, but clearly more thorough investigation was needed.

-28-
The Tin Man

"That was very nearly a big scrape you got yourself into back there, eh, Sebastian? Fiona asked with a slight chuckle.

"I'm very sorry, officer, I didn't mean to waste your time." He said in a friendly fashion. Fiona chortled heartily, opening his front door, which she was surprised to find unlocked.

"You haven't wasted any time, we need to make sure you're safe, erm, Sebastian, your front door is unlocked, why don't you lock it when you go out?" They were both paused in the doorway. He merely laughed, nervously; Fiona imagined he was concerned she was reprimanding him. She was about to remind him that leaving a door unlocked was not illegal, but he spoke before she had the chance;

"Eh, I see no point. What do I have worth stealing?"

"I don't mean stealing stuff, I mean what if someone breaks in when you're home? Would you be able to defend yourself?" She asked, bringing her face near to him so he could hear. He just chuckled again.

"Ah, that's what you're here for, to protect." He laughed.

"We can't be there for everyone, unfortunately. Please remember to lock your doors from now on, there's lots of unkind people out there." She pushed him gently through the door. He crossed the threshold and moved into the darkness of his porch. He staggered into the gloom until he was virtually invisible; she sighed and called after him. "Sebastian, you've left your door open!" But he did not reply. "Christ." She hissed before diving after him into the house. She closed the door behind her and found herself in almost complete blackness; "It's very dark in here, Sebastian, should I turn a light on?" He heard that.

"The bulb in that light popped yesterday and I don't have any spares." He called back. At that moment, she stumbled over a new stack of papers that had not been there at her last visit. She yelped as she struggled to catch her footing, plunging her boot straight into another soggy stack of papers. "Can I get you a cup of tea?" Sebastian called, unaware of the chaos behind him.

"No, you're fine. You get yourself sat down, I'll make you one." She shouted back, moving the papers aside so that she could move again and wiping her boot clean of mouldy paper.

"Don't worry yourself, I'll just have this one I made earlier." With that, he appeared, or at least his silhouette did, in the doorway and moved through into his living room; as her eyes became accustomed to the darkness, she espied the glimmering form of a mug in his hand, inside of which was the residue of a cold drink of tea. She followed him through the door, using his footsteps as a guide.

"Sebastian, can I ask you a question?" She asked finding her way into the room as Sebastian sat down in his favourite armchair.

"Ask away, dear." He replied, his voice coming from invisibility.

"What did you mean, 'I'm sorry, I didn't mean for any of this to happen'? Didn't mean for what to happen?" Her voice was a low whisper; she feared any degree of volume would bring the house down upon their heads. Sebastian sighed.

"I went over to their house, and I probably shouldn't have because I know we haven't got the best of relationships, me and them. I didn't mean for him to get so angry, so I did what I do best; I apologised." He explained. Fiona sighed.

"So you didn't mean to get him annoyed, that's what you meant?" She asked. He became indignant;

"What did you think I'd meant?" He asked her. She merely sighed and rubbed the back of her head. Then, he realised. "Ah, you thought I didn't mean to have killed their daughter, right?" He asked with a scoff.

"Well, not quite." Fiona said in a feeble effort to defend herself.

"Have a word with yourself, you're the copper here. I haven't once resisted your efforts, you're very welcome to take me in if you believe you have something against me." He retorted.

"No, I'm sure that won't be necessary." She protested.

"Let me tell you this; others may be in cahoots with their loved ones for alibis, but my alibi is dead. *Both* of my alibis are dead. Remember that when you start throwing around accusations." He said in the clearest voice he had used yet.

Fiona merely stood in the darkness, mulling over his words. Now that she could see clearer, she noticed that the house had indeed become messier, as though some universal rubbish bin was being emptied into his living room with every new visit.

"Did your alibis also help you clean up?" She chuckled in a veiled attempt to lighten the mood. He scoffed quietly to himself, such that Fiona heard nothing.

"I never was much for order. That's funny coming from an old headmaster, right?" He said with a smile she could barely see. "Ever since wifey died, I just let these things build up around me until Willow came to me and helped out. Even then, it just kept building and building. I think it will continue until eventually, it just fills the place and bursts free." He said, whimsically.

"What do you mean by that?" Fiona asked, with a concerned tone that was not lost on him.

"I can't keep relying on people to help clear my burdens for me, I need to learn to do it myself. Everyone I ever relied on has failed me in some way or another, be it their fault or mine." Fiona merely smiled and approached him so that she could talk quietly; already, she could feel the house shaking at their words.

"It's okay to ask for a little help now and again. It's not a sign of weakness." With that, she gripped his hand. He turned to her and smiled, resting his own hand on hers such that their grips were intertwined in an impossibly assembled puzzle. "Now how about I make you a fresh tea?" She asked, gesturing at the cold cup he had set upon the windowsill.

He said nothing, though confirmed the favour with a wordless nod.

-29-
The New Headmaster

"He's a bit weird, isn't he?" Willow said, her friends lagging somewhat behind. She did not have the same skip that usually embellished her step.

"I've always found Mr Worth a bit weird, Willow." Said Timmy, his bag overflowing with schoolwork. "Now he's the Headmaster, we'll be seeing more of him, so we'll just have to find him not-weird." He continued. Willow realised that Timmy was right.

"I just can't believe what happened. Poor Stacey." Said Gemma.

"I know. It's horrible. I heard he suffocated her with a fire extinguisher nozzle." Replied Timmy, his excitedness somewhat facetious. Willow scoffed.

"We don't know that *he* did anything, Timmy. Mr Shaw has denied it all." Willow replied, dejectedly.

"Of course he has. You don't admit to that kind of thing." Timmy replied, jumping about, childishly.

"I don't think he would have done it, though." Willow said.

"Yeah well, he's been sacked now anyway, so none of it really matters." Gemma said, pushing Timmy such that a few carefully organised documents came tumbling from his partly closed rucksack. He cried out as he moved to catch them before they struck the damp floor.

"Oi!" He cried.

"Oh, get a grip, I'm just trying to lighten the mood." Gemma replied, woefully defending herself.

"What does that mean?" Willow hissed, spinning around, stopping the approaching Gemma in her tracks. A few of the straggling students around them paused to look, but they did not concern themselves with this for very long. "Why do you need to lighten the mood? Stacey is dead!" She continued, not giving Gemma a chance to reply to any of the questions she posed. Gemma started backwards.

"Do you think I don't care?" She finally managed to say. Stumbling on her words, she continued; "Stacey was my friend too, Willow. I know you're different, but you don't get to have Stacey all to yourself." She said, louder now; Willow approached, her face thunder.

"*Different*? What do you mean?" Willow replied, indignantly. Gemma recoiled, stumbling as she feigned ignorance;

"What does *what* mean?" She said, with little conviction.

"You know what I mean. *Different*? What's so different about me?" Willow replied, approaching a now worried Gemma. By now, several the students who had passed by had returned, drawn by the sound of scandal; a group of boys now approached, but they kept their distance as the argument unfolded.

"Well, you know. You always did like Stacey in a different way to the rest of us, it was more than just friendship." Gemma said, defending herself at last.

"Not being funny, Willow, but she's right." Timmy interjected, finally finishing the arrangement of his documents. Willow was about to reply, but before her voice came, the boys shouted after her.

"Wahey!" One of them called. Another pulled out his phone and pointed the camera at her. He laughed, boisterously, as the other goaded the shouter. Willow pulled a face, shook her head, then turned to face the group. She then marched across the road towards them; as she approached, their faces steadily dropped; first, she raised a hand and swiped the phone out of the grasp of the boy who was using it to record the encounter, sending it tumbling to the ground. The screen flew off with a crash, much to the protests of the group.

"What are you doing?" The recorder yelled, his face becoming one of rage. Willow pointed a stern finger at him.

"Get *fucked*." She would have struck him, but she was above that. In any case, she had other concerns. She turned about and espied Gemma trying to make a sly escape. "Where do you think *you're* going?" She cried, marching back towards her, leaving the boys to salvage the broken components of the phone.

"Come on, Willow, I didn't mean anything by it." Gemma said, turning around and realising she was not going to get away. "I was just making a point that you obviously feel for Stacey in ways I don't, but that doesn't mean the rest of us don't feel for her at all." She continued; by now, Timmy had recovered his documents and was catching up.

"I don't give a shit what you think, or anybody else. What does it matter what I do or don't do behind closed doors? Yes, I maybe had something more for Stacey than anyone else did, but why does that make me different? What does it matter to you? You don't get to decide how I react to what happened. I don't get to decide how *you* do! So maybe stop screwing with my life and let me just work this out on my own. I don't need you or anybody else." As she spoke, her face contorted and a vein appeared, pulsating, on her neck. Gemma appeared to recoil as she spoke, becoming ever more shrunken with every word. Willow pointed with a straight finger that almost made contact.

Timmy moved towards the pair in an effort to break them apart;

"Look guys, come on now. Willow, you know Gemma didn't mean it, right?" He said, turning to the pair of them as he mentioned them.

"Right," Gemma said, "I was just making a point."

"Don't even bother. I don't want to hear it. You want to be all righteous and shit? Go find someone else who's *different*." Willow replied, moving away from the pair, yet continuing to shout. She never wavered and not one tear came to her eye; yet her annoyance and frustration was palpable, such that as she turned to storm off, neither of her friends tried to stop her. They realised that no matter what they tried to say, no matter the sincerity, they would not be able to sway her. Timmy turned to Gemma.

"Nicely done, Gemma." He said.

"What? I didn't realise she was going to flip like that, I didn't mean it!" She protested. "*They* didn't help either." She continued, pointing at the group of boys across the road, who were busy looking at the remains of the phone. They busied themselves with conversation.

"I can't believe it, this is brand new!" One of them said.

"Forget that, I can't believe what just happened!" Another boy said. "Mustafa, get your phone. We've got to tell Harry about this." He said, chortling evilly. They turned and watched as Willow disappeared around the corner of her garden path, imagining just what Harry's reaction would be.

-30-
Cracking the Bottle

Night descended on the town almost as quickly as it had vanished that morning. A thin ribbon of light kissed the horizon above the hills in the distance where the sun was at its lowest ebb. The sky was clear of clouds and stars, such that the brightest body was the disc of the moon moving silently across the inky blackness.

The streets below were just as clear; not a soul dared to venture out late anymore. It was a classic case of hysteria; nobody thought to point out that Willow had not gone missing during the night, but in broad daylight – yet the town continued as normal during the daylight hours, oblivious to the dangers it posed.

One person, however, did find the wherewithal to be seen out and about during these hours. He walked in such an ungainly fashion that if he were to be seen by a passer-by, they would think him strange. Curious a sight as he was, he did not pay any heed to the strangeness of his appearance; his hair was bedraggled, and his shirt torn from a fight he had had not half an hour earlier. His drunkenness was the cause of all of this disarray, and his vacuous, staggered walk was only just about taking him in the direction of his home.

He fought his way through the gate at the end of the garden path and drove headlong towards the front door; his arrival was not a dignified one, for he missed the keyhole with his key several times until he finally managed to get his hand-eye coordination together. He had not even turned the key when the door fell away from him and he fell through it into the darkness of the porch. He let out a grunt of annoyance, though he was hardly taken by surprise due to his almost complete unawareness. He careered to the floor and lay in a heap for a few moments until the sound of a voice met his ears;

"You're back, at last."

Gary let out a grunt; the floor was surprisingly comfortable. "Where have you been?" It was Sarah, who was tying a dressing-gown belt around her waist. "Get up and close the door." She ordered, turning about and switching on the porch light. His eyes were instantly aflame with searing brightness that felt as though his retinas would be scorched. He yelped.

"Urgh. What time is it?" He murmured, speaking his most comprehensible word in hours.

"Twenty to two in the morning. I said get up." She repeated. With that, Gary made efforts to struggle to his feet, though he was unsteady in his attempt. He used the wall to support himself, then bounced along it to follow Sarah who had now disappeared into the living room.

The world around him was a swirling whirlpool of bright white, punctuated ever and again with a shadow-like detail his eyes could barely identify. His balance bounced from right to left then back again and his direction went with it until he staggered through the door towards the kitchen. "Where do you think you're going?" Sarah yelled, emerging from the lounge door. She got there just in time to see Gary rest against the worktop and wrestle with the fridge door until it swung ajar. From it, he fished a brown bottle with some German name on the label. She sighed loudly, though it failed to get his attention. "You've got to be kidding! Don't you think you've had enough?" She asked, rounding the doorframe and approaching the kitchen.

"One more is never too much." He slurred. The bright white of the lights was enough to stir him slightly, such that his stance was more stable now than it had been; he still, however, was unable to remove the metal twist-off cap from the bottle for he could not get sufficient grip on the sharp edges. He fought with it for a few moments.

"I can't keep doing this." She said, unfolding her arms and striding across the room in annoyance.

"Can't keep doing what, Sarah?" Came the half-thought reply.

"This, you. You're not the same as you were." She said with a loud tone that was not quite a shout. She had pulled out a chair from beneath the dining table and was now sitting in it.

"Well it's obviously been a long time coming if you're already back on the market, love." He said, sarcastically. "So go on then, how long have you and fancy man been on the go?" He continued, becoming visibly frustrated at his inability to unseal the beer. She sighed as her response. "Stop fucking sighing, you're starting to sound like a knackered engine."

"Smooth." She said. "I don't know why I bother trying to talk to you sometimes, nobody listens to a drunk." She shot.

"Really? That's funny, I think I'm the only one who's talking any degree of sense around here." He retorted, dropping the bottle to waist height in frustration. "Who is this guy anyway?" He asked in a surprisingly calm tone.

"It's pointless arguing with you. I'm going back to bed." She said, evading the question.

"No, here's what's going to happen, you're going to tell me who this guy is. I've got some words to say to him." That was enough to convince Sarah that he was not in a fit state to talk to her properly; she wanted a mature attitude from her husband, but none was forthcoming. Without a word, she stood up, nearly casting the chair across the room. She made for the door, but in a moment was prevented...

Smash!

The bottle was whacked against the edge of the worktop, which cracked and splintered as the bottle exploded into a raining mass of liquid and curved shards that glimmered and rolled towards her. In an instant, he was upon her, forcing her against the wall with his other hand at her neck. He lifted the remainder of the bottle and pressed the broken rim to her face – not enough to pierce her skin, but just enough to make her think he would.

She screamed; his heart gave a bound. He didn't know why he was doing this; suddenly his mind was clear as a rush of ill-deserved adrenaline began to course through his body. He didn't like what he was doing.

"Worth, Howard Worth! It was Howard!" She screamed, mortified that he was going to do worse if she did not talk. In an instant, Gary's rage subsided. He stepped away, dropping the bottle to the floor. It chipped a little on the tiling, but it retained its form as it rolled away. He continued to back away, still amazed at himself for what he had done; not proud, but disgusted. He barely registered the name she called out, or if she was telling the truth.

The name!

Howard Worth; how could she prefer *Howard Worth* over himself? It didn't seem real. His drunken state exacerbated his ever-decreasing mood which threatened once more to boil over.

Sarah slid down the cupboards down to the ground, sitting down in a puddle of beer and broken glass; her despair was such that she could not feel the glass in her skin as she sat upon it; instead, she let out an inaudible sob as tears streamed down her face. The cry quickly morphed into a scream of agony that rang through the house as Gary dove through the hallway and back out of the front door.

His resolve had become absolute – *that bastard*, he thought; a thousand scenarios ran through his mind, like a crazed and angry madman runs through the streets. *I bet they slept in my bed*. He suddenly became very defensive; the idea that his wife was sharing herself drove him into a jealousy he had scarcely experienced before. It surprised even he, that he should be driving headlong to someone else's home to confront them over such a matter.

By now, his drunkenness was subdued and he was more aware of his functions, lucid; his steps were made with purpose and conviction, his resolve stronger than before.

He came upon the Worth household shortly after, having had his journey interrupted by not a single soul. He doubted anybody would have stopped him anyway, for his appearance was one of frustration, annoyance and anger that would have deterred even the most steadfast of assailants.

The house was a semi-detached Victorian house in one of the older parts of the town. Trees lined the road and a number of swish vehicles sat idle along the pavements. The rumbling of the first trains of the day making their way to the station three streets away drifted gently over the rooftops, silencing Gary's violent approach. He vaulted the wall, intentionally knocking aside several expensive looking plant pots cascading with green tendrils and blue heads. This should have been the first indication to the occupants that something was wrong, and already a number of lights in nearby windows were illuminating with interest.

He pounded on the blue wooden door, which nearly smashed through as his fist struck it – it was either that or his own fingers would smash themselves to smithereens on the surface. Had the door fallen apart in front of him, he would certainly have used it as an excuse to let himself in. However, for the duration of his wait for the call to be answered, the door remained resolute in its resistance.

The face of a woman appeared in an upstairs window; her sleep enlivened by the sounds from below. By now, a minute or so had passed, and Gary was becoming increasingly fatuous and incensed that his presence was being ignored.

His fingers bleeding, though he could not feel it, he stepped back to see if his actions had achieved attention; he stepped down from the porch and back into the garden, peering around at the house. Nobody was in the living room window, nor the bathroom one above the door. But in the front bedroom window, he espied the face.

"Sandy!" He cried up to her with an enraged tone. "Open this door!" He continued, as her face suddenly vanished as a flurry of white curtain material filled in the space she had previously occupied. By then, he knew she would not come to the door; she would not risk herself by confronting him during his current spell in an incandescent rage. Nor, did he suspect, would Howard. There was only one thing for it.

He darted back to the door, gripping the brass knob with one hand and throwing himself against the panel with his other shoulder. He struck against it once, then twice, and as he watched he espied the door split down the grain; slightly at first, growing greater and deeper with every impact. He did not consider it, but he should be lucky bone is more resilient than wood, or he would most certainly have split his shoulder blade instead.

He continued to pound against the door, not pausing to consider that he would fall straight through it. He would not have stopped even if he did realise that as a possibility; he would not stop until he was in the house.

It took a number of impacts against the door before he finally scythed his way through, his arm a somewhat blunt blade against the splintering wood. He careered through the void amidst a clattering and a cloud of fine wood dust that filled his nose and mouth to the point that he ended up lying in a pile of debris almost completely unable to breathe. He struggled to his feet and peered into the gloom; the porch opened up into a wide, long sitting room, tastefully adorned with wooden furnishings; a sideboard, a rocking chair facing the bay window, and on the floor, a standing mirror, that in the dark appeared to be reflecting a void. Above him, at the top of the stairs, a landing that more resembled a mezzanine or balcony clung spider-like to the wall, leading to the bedrooms that sat above the right-hand wall. The room directly below the bedrooms, he thought, must have been a kitchen, which was closed behind a door.

"Howard! Where are you, Howard?" He called out into the gloom, crazed. A faint glow around the bedroom door gave him the idea that somebody had turned a light on in there. His suspicions were confirmed a moment later as the door came ajar, a shadow moving beyond it; the shadow manifested itself as Howard Worth a moment later, as he flipped a master switch that filled the house with a warm glow. It was so bright to Gary that he could not see for a moment as his irises reduced their dilation to compensate. He groaned as he rubbed his closed eyes.

"What are you doing in my house, Gary? And why, for the love of God did you knock that door down, it was an original panel?" He protested sarcastically. Gary moved slowly across the room towards the foot of the stairs. "That's close enough, one more step and I'll call the police." Gary stopped.

"Yeah?"

"Yeah."

"You wouldn't, we're friends." Gary said, innocently.

"Maybe, but it stopped you, didn't it?" He told, rather than asked. Gary scoffed. "Why are you in my house, Gary?" He asked again. This time, Gary answered.

"You know why I'm here." He said. Howard shook his head and gestured as if to ask for an explanation. "Don't play stupid, you can't pull it off." Howard bowed his head, almost burying his chin into the folds of his dressing-gown.

"Has Sarah finally told you?" He asked. Gary scoffed again. "Has she finally admitted that she doesn't need you anymore?"

"No, no, no. This isn't how this happens. You don't get to dictate to me what you think my wife wants." He said, wagging a finger, a scowl creeping onto his face.

"Who *is* going to dictate, then, you? You didn't even know any of this was going on, what makes you think you understand your wife?" Howard retorted. "I'm not ashamed to have had an affair, Gary. She came to me, she wanted out from you. I'm more ashamed for Sandy, who I have told about this before you ask, apologised to her and have moved on with. She's forgiven me." He said, as though he had been planning this for months. In a way, he had. "Now, would you have forgiven Sarah? Did she even tell you, or did you find out somehow?" He asked. It was then that Gary remembered his own reaction to the news had not been as stoic as he imagined Howard would have reacted.

"I didn't have to come here and defend her, but I did." He argued back. "So, you look me in the eyes and tell me I don't care for her." He said. Howard smiled.

"But you do have to wonder if she was happy with you to begin with. Trust me, she was only too happy when she was with me. I made sure of it."

That did it.

Gary launched himself across the room, knocking over a table with an expensive-looking vase in the middle of it as he went. He was at the stairs and up them in a moment, so fast that Howard did not have time to react. A guttural roar accompanied his movement, and as Howard made for the safety of his bedroom, he was accosted.

Gary pulled on the loose tails of Howard's dressing gown and dragged the man towards him. In an instant, Howard was defensive; he raised his arms in protest as Gary swung him around until they were facing one another. The bleeding fingers Gary had used to destroy the door were soon upon Howard's throat, gripping his soft neck until he was convinced the man could not breathe. His suspicions were confirmed, as his face quickly became red; Howard's pitiful grunts and groans as he struggled for air were music to Gary's ears, and he relished in the sound of his suffering.

Howard's lips began to turn blue, and with his the last of his strength, he grappled with Gary's face with his free hand, pushing him backwards against the balcony rail. It nearly gave way, for it was made of wooden pillars and railing, but for a time it held; Gary was forced back over it, but his clinging to Howard prevented him from going over. For a period, Gary pulled against Howard to the point that he would almost certainly have broken his neck; Howard's vision became a blur, and his body came to stop resisting. By that point, Sandy had appeared in the doorway, having heard the sound of a struggle; she moved to protest, but stopped as she espied Gary's enraged face. In the same instant, Gary relaxed his grip as he felt Howard's own loosen upon his face.

It was a clever trick.

Howard immediately tensed back up as his lungs captured another grasp of air. He made to land a punch on his assailant, but in one expert dodge, it missed; Gary toppled aside in his avoidance, such that Howard put all of his weight over the edge of the balcony, crashing through the railing and plunging through the air.

"Howard!" Sandy cried, darting over. Gary stood in surprised disbelief; he was unsure if he intended to kill Howard, but now that he was plunging through the air to the living room below, he wondered if he had succeeded.

The sound of his body hitting the ground rang through the house; a number of loose decorations shook as the hollow floor rippled with the impact. Sandy peered over the edge after him, amazed that he had missed the furniture completely; perhaps he would have fared better had he landed on the sofa; he may have crashed through it or it may have softened his fall. It was a game of *What If?* that was not worth playing.

Sandy forced her way past Gary, who was still shocked with amazement at what had happened. He merely followed her with his gaze as she darted down the stairs, gasping and exclaiming as she went.

She was upon her husband in a moment, resting her hands on his body; it heaved and moved with ragged breaths in and out. He had survived, somehow. Gary moved slowly down the stairs, unsure if he should apologise or simply leave; he merely existed in a limbo between the two, standing in near silence save for a few barely recognisable utterances of apology.

"Sandy, I... I mean, I, what I want to, erm..." He mumbled.

"Don't just stand there, phone an ambulance! Howard, stay with me..." She cried, then whispered. Her terse tone, though understandable to most, was surprising to Gary, who had never heard her scream at anyone like that before. He started back in surprise then blinked twice, as though to photograph the scene.

With that, he believed he was finished. He had done all he could, which was nothing at all to the normal observer. In any case, he knew the police would be coming for him soon; he had nothing left. So, he turned about and made for the door, or what remained of it. He stepped through the empty frame and out into the street, where he espied a number of neighbours converging across the road, most in their pyjamas. Far and away, a dog barked somewhere as the sky began to brighten with the first dawn of a new day.

It was a new day in this strange new world Gary had been born into. He did not believe it could get any stranger from here.

-31-
Love Thy Neighbour

The sun outside the window was bright and searing; it was to be another scorching day, Fiona thought, and there she was spending it indoors. Typical.

She sat with her back to the door; there, a smart looking man in a grey turtleneck stood with his arms behind him, his stoicism like a presence beside him. He sniffled once, and that was enough to draw her attention to him; she glanced up at him, then back down to her papers. Big letters spelled out *Affidavit* on the header, followed by a number of official stamps, signatures and dates, some of which she thought were probably redundant.

She sighed as she read through the statement the affidavit contained; she probed the words she saw written there for holes but found none. She then looked up at the clock; ten fifteen and, she estimated, about twenty-two seconds.

"So, Daryll. I'm just reading your little tome, here." She began, putting the papers down onto the desk; now, she had an unobstructed view of Daryll, who was sat across from her. "Can I just say, it is a bit strange seeing you in that get up and not your usual gear." She said with a friendly tone; she gestured to his sweatpants and t-shirt.

"I'm only human, sometimes I dress like one, just for kicks." He said, smiling and glancing down at his clothing. She chuckled.

"It suits you. So, I just have a couple of questions about your statement, you were aware that when you made this it was being entered into a record and that you signed this as being the truth, to the best of your recollection?" She said, pressing down on the sheets with extended fingers. She leaned across the table to him. His smile faded minutely.

"Yes, that's right, I did." He confirmed.

"So you're still saying this statement is the truth, correct?" She asked. He nodded. "Verbally, for the record, please." She requested; he sighed with the curl of his lips signalling a begrudging amazement.

"Yes, the statement you're referring to is the correct statement as best as I can recall." He exaggerated his response to minimise the number of repeats he would need to make.

"Good, now," She gulped. "There's just something I need to ask because I want everything to be watertight. I'm not asking you this out of suspicion, it's just to plug a leak."

"Of course." He replied. She took a copy of the affidavit from her bag, which sat against her chair leg. This was an annotated version and was covered in red scribbles and highlighted sections. She turned it around and slid it across the table towards Daryll, who sat up and gripped it with his own fingers.

"For the record, I have passed Daryll *Document #15.b*, an annotated copy of his statement. Daryll, could you please read paragraph B, the highlighted section." With that, she pulled her own copy towards her and read along as Daryll spoke the words he had written.

"*Soon after, I started to work on the top of the cliffs opposite. I noticed a considerable degree more litter than I was accustomed to. I started to clear...*" He was cut off.

"Please read as it is written, don't paraphrase." Fiona warned.

"Sorry. Erm, *soon after, I started to work on the top of the cliffs opposite. I noticed a considerable degree more litter than I was accustomed to and I set about the task of clearing it. It was dark and I did not see anything unusual up there.*" He said. Fiona once again interrupted him.

"Thank you, just a couple of points." Daryll lowered the sheets and raised his eyes to meet Fiona's gaze. "Why did you feel it was important to bring up that it was dark so you could not see anything unusual? Were you looking for something unusual, or were you using hindsight?" She quizzed. It was a strange and, in his mind unnecessary, question.

"I'm not sure I follow?" He confessed, shrugging his shoulders.

"I don't see why you would mention that you couldn't see anything unusual unless you were looking for something unusual. Or, as I said, with hindsight you now know something unusual was there and you were meaning that you didn't notice anything at that time. Which is it?" She explained. Her clarification did little in the way of succeeding, but Daryll believed he understood.

"I guess I was using hindsight, yeah. Now that I know that was a crime scene, I was explaining that I didn't notice anything out of the ordinary." He said.

"So you weren't looking for anything, then?"

"No."

"Okay, good. Something else that is bothering me, why had you decided to go and do this little clear up so late at night? I know the days tend to be lighter at this time of year, but I have to ask what you were doing in a crime scene around that late hour?"

"You think I killed her?"

"That's not the question I asked." The mood had changed, Fiona had sensed it. For a moment, Daryll paused, then chuckled. Fiona smiled in response, knowing that they were playing a game of wits.

"You've heard of the sermon 'Love Thy Neighbour', haven't you, Fiona?" He asked in a tone that was more telling than querying. He was *telling* her that she was aware of it. She nodded. "*Jesus said unto him, Thou shalt love the Lord, thy God, with all thy heart, and with all thy soul, and with all thy mind. This is the first and great commandment. And the second is like unto it, Thou shalt love thy neighbour as thyself. On these two commandments hang all the law and the prophets.* Matthew twenty-two, thirty-seven to forty." He recited with expert intonation and recollection.

"You have a better memory than me, Daryll, I'll give you that." Fiona joked in a thinly veiled effort to lighten the mood.

"One of the questions I always get asked is 'who is *thy neighbour*?', do you know what the answer is?" He asked. She made no reply, expecting to be educated. "Thy neighbour is everyone; not one single person is to be excluded. Thy neighbour is your neighbour, but it is also their neighbour, and their neighbour beyond, and every neighbour. You begin to see? Well, let me explain my problem. I loved Willow, of course." He explained. Fiona interrupted him again.

"It's amazing how many people say they loved her, yet her family insist she had very few friends." She pointed out. Daryll ignored that comment.

"She was one of my favourites, you know. She turned to God in a time of need, and that is what God is for. He's there to help, he's there to be a pillar for people who lack one. So in a way, I hate to see new people join the congregation, I always wonder what emotional baggage they're bringing with them, they have to have a reason to have turned to God, usually it's not a good one. With Willow, I knew she was struggling, I always knew something really terrible had happened in her life.

The same with Sebastian. I had only a little idea of his history when he came to us. The more I learned about him, the worse my impression of him got. He is a man with a sordid past, and I'm not *meant* to judge. Seeing Willow become more and more involved with him disturbed me, knowing what he did and seeing it happen again before my eyes." He said, his impassioned voice belying a rage that had begun to surge within him.

"Why didn't you express concern to the police, as you did with Sarah and Howard?" She said, perhaps against protocol. His breath heaved.

"Because there was never anything that would have proved what I believed. I prayed for the strength to face him, but the more I saw Willow being drawn in by him, the more he was winning against my belief in God. My pillar was crumbling, and it still is for all the time Sebastian has been part of my flock. It's killing me to know that there is one neighbour I cannot love." He confessed, his voice wavering now. "The only way I can stay sane is to occupy my mind; it rebels at stagnation, I need work, something to think about. If that involves writing a sermon, or rewriting it, or even going out into the early hours to clean up other people's shit, then so be it. Anything to stop thinking about him and what he's doing to my mind. A flimsy excuse, I know, but that's the truth." He finally concluded. Fiona did not speak for a few moments.

"So you have some kind of a dislike for Sebastian, is that right? You do understand how that could create something of a conflict of interest?" She quizzed at last. He did not reply. Then she remembered her own giving Sebastian help; that was a conflict of interest if ever there was one. She would not mention that here.

"Can I answer no comment, will that make your paperwork easier?" Daryll said, nonchalant. "I didn't kill Willow, Fiona. As much as I rejected her decision to befriend Sebastian, it wasn't my decision to make and I had to respect her choice. Besides, seeing her family fall apart at that time was enough to make me realise she had nothing." That was that. Fiona shuffled some more papers and then looked back to Daryll with a smile.

"Thank you, Daryll, that will be all. Interview concluded at, ooh, what time do we call it? Ten-nineteen a.m., unless anyone has anything else to add? No?" Daryll shook his head. "Okay, interview concluded." She pressed the red record button, ceasing the interview.

"May I go, now?" Daryll said, gesturing with his hands. Fiona sighed.

"Yes, you can. Cartwright will see you out." She said, gesturing to the door. Daryll stood up, pushing the chair away with his feet. He had barely reached the door when he was stopped.

"Daryll?" Fiona called. He turned with his hand holding the door ajar.

"Mhmm?" He muttered.

"I'm sorry. I really am." She said, her voice but a whisper. Daryll smiled.

"Don't worry, I understand. I'll see you soon." He concluded, leaving the room completely. He nearly crashed into Phillips in the narrow frame of the door, but through some skilful manoeuvring, they managed to avoid contact. Daryll smiled, Phillips returned the greeting, then they passed one another completely. Phillips closed the door behind him.

"How did that go?" He said, darting across the room; he took seat where Daryll had been, then folded his arms across the table. Fiona sighed.

"Urgh, a complete waste of time." She hissed. Phillips was surprised.

"Wait, you didn't get anything?"

"Nothing of any relevance. If anything, he seemed to have lessened my suspicions of him."

"Don't tell me; your hunch that his alibi was too good didn't pan out?"

"Yep. He's got this thing about Sebastian, and it isn't a good thing. He seems under the impression that his faith is being diminished because of some perceived hatred of the guy, when I don't really see why he has one."

"You've been to see Sebastian twice now, right?" He said. She nodded. "You need to be careful around him, Fiona. Once he knows he's in, he'll play you like a fiddle." She made to protest. "I'm not saying he's got to you. I just don't want you to be lured in only to be dropped at the last minute. It could jeopardise the entire investigation." She looked downtrodden; she lowered her head, knowing that she had already let Sebastian into her heart more than she should have done; it was one thing to interact with a suspect, it was quite another to feel sorry for him.

Phillips, however, remained strangely jovial. "I do have good news. Well, as good as it can possibly be." He produced a file. "I've got the swab results from the rock we found at the scene of the accident. There was blood found on it, as you know and we've decided it was the murder weapon, right?" She nodded in a half-hearted reply. "Well, I had the blood DNA tested, Jacqueline handed me this on my way over." He said, brandishing the folder. "There were two DNA profiles found in the blood, one of them was from Willow with, they say, a ninety-six percent certainty." He said, peering at the arrangement of numbers in the pages of the folder. "The other doesn't match anyone we have on record. Which means Harry never touched that rock or had his blood on it." He said, closing the folder.

"Hold on, when did we take a DNA sample from Harry?" She asked, quite rightly.

"We already have some, to a point. Without wanting to get too crude, he left plenty of DNA on that scrapbook of his we found. Seems it was a personal collection for his," he coughed, "private use." He said. Fiona was nearly sick on the spot; she sat coughing and retching. "Feel for me, I handled the damn book." He said.

"So Harry wasn't involved?"

"No, surprisingly, we can rule him out for now. But whether he was involved in this doesn't matter, what matters now is that we have a killer out there who isn't in our system. Which doesn't rule many people out, as we haven't got profiles on most of the people in this town."

"No shit?"

"That's the problem of having such a low crime rate, you've got to put in so much more effort when something big does come along." He quipped. Fiona's mood brightened.

"So, in theory, all we need to do now is run tests on all of our suspects, and we've got our guy?" Phillips shot her a look. "I mean, we've got our person?" She corrected herself.

"This is the first piece of solid evidence we have in this case; if we can positively identify who that profile belongs to, we've got a solid prosecution. I've got Jacqueline isolating the profiles so we can be one hundred percent on Willow, then in theory, whatever is left is the person we're looking for." He said. Fiona's mood lightened in a moment, and a smile appeared across her face.

"We're *this* close to blowing this thing wide open. I can feel it." She said.

-32-
The Second Service

Light left the town with surprising speed; as the sun descended below the horizon, it set the sky to a bloom of orange fire that stretched far and away above the heads of the gathered masses. Ever and again, clouds would dance and swirl in the ever-darkening quagmire until eventually, it was twilight and the smooth body of an overcast sky took over everything.

The congregation moved with an almost pilgrim-like reverence, not speaking, never deviating from their path; the stream of people stretched far and away, the darkness seeming to increase the numbers; spots of light here and there signalled the presence of a candle or a torch, casting a feeble glow onto the grass below.

The sound of mass footfalls was all that could be heard in the soft grass; nobody stumbled on the mottled, muddy field as they went. At the crest of the hill, in the lengthening shadow of the town castle, stood a circle of a hundred people or more, gently swaying in the night. Below them spread the town; an endless sea of slate roofs and labyrinthine streets, lit by orange streetlamps and the occasional car. The ring of people was wide and tumultuous, a babble of folk surrounding a large sheet of fabric held in place in each corner by heavy, grey rocks. Upon it was printed a school photograph of Willow, ten feet wide by as many tall. Her smile beamed out at the crowd, rippling in the gentle breeze such that she resembled a living photograph, brought to life from beyond the grave.

Beside her, stretching out towards the opposite wall of people, was her name, constructed from vibrant floral arrangements, speared here and there with hundreds of plastic stems, each flowering in a piece of paper bearing some message written by the gathered masses. The circle moved around the creation in a slow anti-clockwise flow, though Sarah, positioned within the circle, remained stationary; as somebody new passed her, they would offer a word of encouragement, or gently touch her on the shoulder; other signals of condolences were forthcoming in whatever form they took.

Daryll approached sometime during the first hour of the

vigil; he moved so inconspicuously and made himself known so unobtrusively that she barely noticed he was there.

"Sarah." He said eventually, before he was pulled away by the crowd. She jumped as he spoke.

"Oh, Daryll, you startled me." She said with a nervous chuckle.

"I think this is a wonderful thing that's been organised for you here. I don't think I've ever seen such a fine display of community spirit." He said, looking around at the living mass; a passer-by smiled at him and nodded; he returned the gesture.

"Yes, it's wonderful." She whispered with a trembling voice. "It's just a shame it's come at the expense of the life of my little girl." She continued, dabbing her eye with a tissue.

"Unfortunately so, Sarah. But you must remember that sometimes from darkness emerges the most beautiful light; a divine light that works to unite us all." He explained. Sarah scoffed.

"I'm sorry, Daryll, I always have to chuckle at your words of wisdom. No matter how comforting they are." She replied, immediately realising how she must have sounded. "I didn't mean that." She said almost immediately.

"You did, and it's fine. Sometimes what I say is what I know people need to hear." He explained. She smiled again, then a silence. Daryll filled it in a moment; "Where is Gary, is he organising the lanterns?" He asked. He could tell instantly that he had touched a nerve. Sarah dipped her head, and her sad sniffles stopped. "Sorry, did I say something?"

"Gary has been arrested. This morning, for assaulting Howard Worth, who's currently in hospital with cracked ribs. All because somebody told the police that I was having an affair with him." She said, quickly. A guilty feeling of dread blossomed inside him, growing until eventually he could only contain it with wavering words.

"I'm sorry to hear that, Sarah. Your honesty and bravery are amazing, I must say." He said, making vague efforts to change the subject. Sarah smiled a facetious grin, then turned to him.

"Actually, Daryll, I'm not just putting on a brave face. I've figured out that there's something I need to do, something that's become more and more real to me over these past few days." She said, confidence brimming. Daryll, seemingly unconcerned, smiled and tilted his head.

"Really?" He said, wryly. "What would that be?" He asked, knowing full well she would tell him anyway.

"It's not something palpable or sane, anything your teachings would tell me is a good idea. But you say that God gives us the support we need? Well for a while now, I've prayed to God for the strength to find the bastard who got my daughter. I will find him, Daryll. They're gonna wish I don't, because if, no, *when* I do, I am going to kill him. I don't care what they do with me. They can do what they like." He assumed that *they* referred in some manner to the police; he didn't imagine she was about to let the person responsible do anything to her. "Is that the kind of strength I'm meant to be praying for?" She said, a monologue that Daryll recognised as her most stoic moment yet. But he was startled; in a way, he found his faith close to rekindled. Clearly, she had gained strength from somewhere.

"Faith is a powerful healer, Sarah, and it gives strength to us all. But you're looking for something else, I can tell." He said. Sarah scoffed.

"Ever the one for understatements, Daryll."

"Now I understand the way you're feeling." He said, ignoring her. "But the strength you've sought is not what He would give. I want you to realise the strength of forgiveness. To put aside your hatred and learn to live with your sadness. Because every moment of grief, of suffering, is an opportunity to learn peace. Find *that* strength, Sarah. Use it well." He said, placing a gentle hand upon her shoulder. She made no reply; she instead bowed her head. She did not see him smile as he considered that she was listening to his advice.

Suddenly around them, the light grew brighter, as though some mysterious force had pushed the sun back overhead. They remained chilled, however, as though its heat had remarkably been extinguished. Startled, both she and Daryll looked up, realising immediately that the steady flow of people had ended; instead, they stood still in a static mass that had swelled considerably during their discussion.

All about them, sounds of amazement were made as the air became filled with hundreds of points of flame, each held aloft by a tall balloon filled with warm air. Instantly, the sky was concealed from view as the lanterns caught the breeze in the air and were carried upwards above the heads of the group, then over the castle, until eventually the entire town was illuminated by the tiny dots. Beneath each, a length of string gripping a rolled scroll written by whomever had released the lantern; some bore messages of commiseration, others of encouragement. Whatever they said, it was up to the writer. Such was Daryll's amazement at the sight as they floated ever closer to the heavens, he let out an airy laugh that startled her. "It's beautiful, isn't it?" He asked, not looking back to her. Her smile, however, remained unmanifested, absent from her face.

"Yeah, great. Just wait 'til morning when they've all burst, and people are complaining about how they have to clean up." She said, sarcastically; he knew she meant it. "All because of some girl people will have forgotten about this time next month." She continued, with a more serious tone.

"You know that isn't true." He retorted, still not looking at her.

"Isn't it? She asked. Now Daryll did look at her, his face a vision of amazement crossed with anger. His emotion was less complex; frustration. He could not conceive of someone less grateful of the outpouring of support she had received; someone so singular in their purpose that they refused to see beyond their veil of ignorance.

With that, he realised that she had not listened to a word he had spoken to her. So he spoke some more.

"Sarah, I can't pretend to understand how you feel. But the sooner you realise cynicism prevents acceptance, the longer you're going to suffer. You can't see beyond your own hatred, and it's made you cruel. Nobody can change that, it's something you have to do yourself. For all the time you spend not doing that, you just make people hate you. Nobody will remember Willow if you stop them from having a reason to care." With that, he turned around before she had chance to reply. She turned in an effort to stop him, but by the time she had rotated to face him, he was already elbowing his way to the crowd, back to the town below.

She turned back, and peered across the empty centre of the mass, only to lay eyes immediately upon the figure of an elderly man; Sebastian had once again wormed his way into her life. Immediately, she was incensed; what would it take to rid herself of the living nuisance? She hoped, to herself, that Sebastian was responsible; it was a cruel thing to wish on anybody, but she was adamant in her want for it to be him. She would see to his demise herself, if she had to.

As she considered these things, she was accosted by the unwelcome presence of a man to her right. She became aware of him by virtue of his nearly careering into her, forced over, perhaps, by the crowd. She nearly collapsed under his weight and went to complain; she swung about and faced him, only to be greeted by another unwelcome sight.

"Urgh." She groaned. "What makes you think I want to see you?"

"You never complained before." Howard said, his voice hoarse.

"I thought you were in hospital?" She said, ignoring his apparent ailment.

"You mean you hoped I was?" He asked; she did not clarify. He chuckled a facetious chuckle. "Well, I was. Now I'm not." He muttered mysteriously.

"Did you self-discharge, or are you out 'officially'?" She asked. He laughed, louder this time.

"It doesn't matter *how* I'm out, just know that I come in peace. I'm not trying to get up your nightie this time." He said, rubbing his gloved hands together; once more, he was not without them. "I'm here to rescue you from your own mind." He said.

"You always did like talking in riddles."

"I know, aren't they fun?" He asked. This time, her reply was a sigh; no coherent response here. "He bothers you, doesn't he?" He said, nodding his head gently towards Sebastian, who even now was driving the surrounding group away by his appearance. He immediately regretted doing so, for a pain shot up his neck such that he groaned loudly. Sarah ignored his outcry.

"All of the men in this town bother me. Especially you; thanks to you, my husband is in a cell for the next twenty-four hours."

"It takes two to tango, babe. Don't lay the blame entirely at my feet." He then drew his lips close to her ear in what she thought was a thinly veiled effort to kiss her; he stopped about an inch from her face, then whispered. "How long do you think it will take the people of this town to hate you when they realise that the grieving mother was out with another man whilst her husband was at home looking after their daughter? I know you've never cared what people think of you, but I can turn you from revered symbol of strength to vilified cheat faster than you can lower your drawbridge. Now believe it or not, I still have respect for you, so I don't want to do this without your say so; you let me go and speak to Sebastian on your behalf, and I swear I'll keep my trap shut and I'll never bother you again." He said; the intensity in his hushed voice troubled her more than his threats. It gave them palpability, they became real by virtue of the manner in which he spoke; with every word, her heart sank lower and faster until eventually she believed she would look down and find it lying, barely beating in the grass. She turned to him, her voice a quivering whisper.

"It takes two to tango, *babe*. You try to ruin me, you ruin yourself." She hissed.

"I'm leaving this town, Sarah." Her heart gave another bound, such that it nearly dragged her over. "I'm transferring to the city in a month. These people can think what they like about me, by the time I'm gone, nobody will care to remember me. Sure, I'll have a legacy, but nobody will remember who left it. They'll just remember you." He said. He had covered all bases; she did not know if his revelation was true, but she was not willing to call his bluff. "Just know this, Sarah, you're the one tying a noose around your neck. All I'm here to do is kick away the chair. So, the way we resolve this is you let me go over there, right now, and talk to Sebastian. Will you let me?"

"What will you say to him?"

"That doesn't matter."

"It matters to me if it's on my behalf. What are you going to say?"

"Nothing as bad as if you don't say *yes* to my next question. Are you going to let me talk to him?"

She paused.

She said nothing.

She considered.

"Talk to him."

The voice in his head screamed.

"Good choice." He instantly began to move away. She let out a relieved sigh. He soon became lost in the tangle of people, but she knew he was moving around to get to Sebastian; her eyes followed where she estimated him to be, until he re-emerged from the throng just a few yards away; he clung to the interior ring of people, for it was faster, and soon he was directly opposite.

He gripped Sebastian silently by the arm and whispered something in his ear; the elder of the two was immediately alert, leaping almost into the air with surprise; he turned to face his assailant, then relaxed as he espied it was Howard. As Howard spoke, Sarah made efforts to lip read what was being said; *Hi... come away*, or was it *come with me*? She had never been much good at the practise.

As Howard spoke, he made a gesture; *follow me*, she assumed, made with his hand and a tilt of his head; somebody passed in front of her, and by the time she could see around them again, the pair had been enveloped by the crowd; *dammit,* she thought. She could just make out the glimmering bald flesh on top of Sebastian's head as they battled their way through, vanishing almost immediately after as the last of the lanterns was either extinguished or had vanished from view.

In the distance, she could just about make out the thin sliver of sunlight slowly fading on the horizon, and soon, the throng was dispersing; already, the interest in the entire thing appeared to wane, as conversation around her turned to more arbitrary and localised discussion. The dispersion was less organised than their arrival, as people fanned out in all directions, back to their homes, back to their lives.

Back to what they actually cared about.

-33-
Into Her Own Hands

Louise sat at the kitchen table with the newspaper in her hand. Headline after headline for the last week all said the same thing, or to the effect of the same. Compassionate beginnings alerted to *devastated family loses daughter*, to more recent entries of *Police ineffective, investigation gets nowhere*. It amazed her as she read such attention-grabbing titles that the investigation was still in relative infancy; when she was younger, things like this could take months.

She sat in near darkness, with nothing but a single lamp to illuminate her. She rolled her arm over and peered at her watch; a quarter to twelve. Harry was still not home yet. She scanned the watch face for a moment longer, then turned her head towards the stairwell through the door; three suitcases full of belongings sat there.

She turned her attention back to the paper, opening it to the second page. No sooner had she done that, however, than a key began to rattle in the lock; it eventually succeeded in its function and the door swung open with a slam. Louise did not need to look to recognise Harry's signature entrance.

"Hello, Harry." She said, friendlily. He did not reply; somewhat startled, for she had never greeted him home so quickly; normally there was a sickly welcome laid out for him, many words said; but this time was different. This time, she barely said a thing.

"I'm hungry. Tea ready?" He said with a gruff voice, walking quickly towards the kitchen; the front door had not even been closed.

"I haven't made you any food." She said with the same tone as before; she gently closed and folded the paper, sliding it onto the table to concentrate on Harry. "I made something for myself, but I knew you didn't care much for risotto." She continued, her heart beginning to race. Harry's face began to contort and frown.

"Why would you make something I don't like?" He said, not quite in a shout, but certainly loudly.

"I'd like you to sit down." She said. He did not want to sit down, so he did not; he told her as much.

"I'm not sitting down, and if you don't explain yourself, you won't be in that chair for much longer." He said, pointing a firm finger at her and drawing close. She smiled and let out a nervous laugh.

"You sound just like your father when you're angry." She said, looking away from him. Before he had chance to reply, she continued; "In fact, you're exactly like your father when you're angry. And, just like your father, I can't stand the sight of you anymore and I'm ending this now." She said, her voice becoming more confident by the moment. He began to breathe heavily with a welling anger that he was barely able to contain.

"You fucking bitch." He said, just about the only words he could manifest.

"I can't stand to be in the same house as you anymore, Harry. I'm not going to take any more of your abuse. Ever since your father left, I've had you at your worst and I'm *tired* of it." She shook her head. "You passed the bags I've packed when you came in. If you ever pay attention to what's going on around you, you would have figured this out by now."

"So what?" He said, breathlessly. "You're going to run away, just like he did?" He continued. She laughed, to his surprise; she *actually* laughed at him. He continued; "You always blame dad for everything that's gone wrong in your life, but it's you, you, you... it's always been *you*! Ever since you forced him out, you've treated me like a fuckin' kid, and you say you can't stand *me* anymore? You've been suffocating me for years, so what did you expect? That I would just live in your little box of love forever, not rebel? I've been telling you for years now that *I don't want to be loved anymore*! Why can you not just treat me like a man?" He shouted, drawing closer and closer with every word.

"Because you'll never be a man, Harry. You'll always be a pathetic little coward who takes his anger out on the nearest victim you can find. I'm afraid you learned from the worst, having your father in the house is enough to turn anyone crazy. The only way you'll learn not to strike out is to have a sudden change. So as much as I'm sure you'd love to have this house for yourself, I'm not the one who's leaving." She said, calmly. Harry's face dissolved into confusion. "Come on! You really think everything I own could fit into three suitcases? By the morning, you'll be gone, all your furniture will have been taken away by the skip I've put them in, and I won't have to think about you ever again."

"Wha...?" He began.

"I got a phone call this afternoon, from the police. They say they're dropping you from the investigation. It seems forensics has cleared you." She said, calmly. Before he had chance to contemplate how they acquired his DNA, she continued. "They said you were free to go where you like from now on. After I told them it didn't matter that he wasn't supposed to go anywhere anyway because you *never listen*, I called your father. I told him what was going on, and I told him you were going to live with him. After a great stream of abuse I simply ignored, he decided it was a good idea. 'Anything to get him away from a selfish, haggard old cow like you', he said." Her voice wavered. Harry once again made to protest, but she stopped him. "I've always told the police that you're just a misunderstood boy, and I've never filed charges against you. You might be innocent when it comes to the Willow situation, but the police won't spare you when I tell them about the things you've done to me. So you *will* leave this house, now, and go to the city, or I *will* take you to the police. I'll drag you there with my bare hands if I have to." She said, enunciating each word. All the while, Harry's demeanour changed from one of anger to intense worry.

"You're sending me to the city? To be with dad?" His own voice began to falter. Her threats were working.

"You know as well as I that your father won't take your shit like I do. If I can't teach you, maybe it's time he did." He fell to his knees, then crawled over to her.

"Please, you can't send me there, you *can't*." He pleaded. She stood up before he reached her and moved across the room.

"You'll find some money in the front pocket of the brown suitcase. It should be enough for food for you tonight, a train ticket and the first month's rent at your father's. After that, you're on your own." She moved to the window and folded her arms. She espied a number of lanterns floating away into the distance, then watched as they vanished from view.

In an instant, Harry was upon her, clouting her over the head with a purple vase that sat in the middle of the table. The flowers flew from the shattered vase as water enveloped her head; she felt as though she had been shot and drowned at once, and she collapsed to the floor, lying in a pool of blood, water and shattered pottery. As she lay almost numb to the pain, her bleary eyes recognised the shape of Harry moving down to the front door. "Harry?" She called, tears leaping to her eyes. He stopped, gripping two of the suitcases by the handles.

"The fuck do you want?" He said, throwing them down

again.

"I want you to know something; something I should have told you a long time ago." She said, her first round of tears fading as her confidence returned.

"Yeah? What?" He said. She smiled.

"I sincerely wish you'd never been born. I genuinely never want to see you again for as long as I live." She said, chuckling. Harry considered her words, turned to the left, then back at her. He marched across the hall, into the kitchen where he was illuminated again; she saw his angered features as he approached. He gripped her hair close to the scalp and raised her head off the ground; still, the pain did not register with her; perhaps she was used to it by now, or so much adrenaline was coursing through her veins that she did not recognise the feeling anymore. Either case was awful.

"I can't help being born. But I love the fact that I have this effect on you. You'll always be scared of me, no matter how big you think your balls are, and you'll never, ever be happy." He then released her hair, without slamming her head into the ground, which she expected. In an instant, he was across the room and back into the hall. She espied him check each suitcase pocket for the money, finding it in the second brown one she had packed. He rezipped the pocket, picked up the single suitcase, leaving the other two, and heading for the door. She called after him again.

"You're wrong, you know." He turned back to her as he yanked the door open, almost clean off of its hinges. "I can honestly say that this is the happiest I've been in seventeen years, and it's only going to get better now. I've won. You were never going to." She said, smiling. In an instant, he twisted his face, flung the door open such that he smashed the mirror on the wall, marched through it and slammed it behind him.

In that instant, the house was silent, and Louise realised that for the first time in as long as she could remember, she was truly alone. She raised a hand to the back of her head and wiped her scalp clear of blood; of course, it was a futile effort, but as she raised herself with the aid of a nearby chair, she felt the light-headedness she had expected to feel vanish from her thoughts; instead, she was confidently to her feet, chuckling. Because for the first time, she was not only alone and happy, she was content.

She would not need to concern herself with the thing she once called a son again. She kicked aside the wreckage the vase had left; she would clean it up later. Sitting back down in her chair, she fished up the newspaper, opened it back up to page two and smiled. Then chuckled, then burst into almost hysterical laughter. Blood trickled down her hair and onto the floor, but she did not care. She had spent most of her recent existence bleeding; a little more was a mere contrivance. Existing in bliss and happiness was a new concept, and one which she hoped she could get used to.

She would throw the remainder of Harry's belongings away in the morning. Then, all remnant of him would be gone. That was a nice thought.

-34-
Incriminated

"So, Gary. Why don't we start from the beginning?" Phillips said, leaning across the table. Gary scowled at him from across the empty space between them. Phillips smiled.

"Can I ask something, first?" Gary said, interrupting Phillips who was about to leaf through some papers. He looked up, confused.

"Of course, what is it?" He said with a friendly tone.

"Why in the name of God did you bring me here now?" He said. Phillips' confusion deepened. "I've been here for nearly twelve hours, why am I only just being seen now?" He asked. Phillips chuckled.

"Because when we picked you up this morning, you weren't in any fit state to lie down, let alone assist us with our enquiries. After having a skinful, people tend to be very difficult to talk to." Phillips explained. "Now, luckily for you, Superintendent Grisham has signed an extension on your custody for a further twelve hours whilst we conduct our investigation." He continued, returning to his papers.

"You can't do that!" Gary protested.

"Actually, we can. Otherwise, we wouldn't have done it." Fiona interrupted. Gary looked to her, then almost immediately back to Phillips.

"So I'm stuck here for thirty-six hours?" Gary hissed.

"Well, seventeen more hours. Which is why we need to do this interview quickly." Phillips said. Gary turned to the suited man beside him; he was in the midst of cleaning a speck of muck from the lens of his glasses.

"They can't do this, right?" Gary said to him, pointing to the pair across the table. The lawyer looked at him, and with a calm voice said;

"There's legal precedent, they're entitled to seek extension where they believe it's warranted."

"So if I were you, I'd let us get on with this, otherwise we'll apply to the Magistrate's and keep you here up to ninety-six hours. I can't be bothered with the paperwork, and I'm sure you'd rather be anywhere but here?" Fiona interrupted. Gary could not believe it; he turned once again to his lawyer, who nodded. Gary scoffed.

"I don't believe this. I don't even know what you're charging me with?" He nearly shouted.

"We did tell you when you were booked, but it's no surprise, really, that you can't remember." That was Fiona.

"My client is not here to be ridiculed, so if you'd, as you say, like to get to the point?" The lawyer said, gesturing sternly with his hand. Phillips smiled.

"Yes, time runs quickly, right?" Phillips said. "So, Gary. Let's start at the beginning." He repeated. "At three o'clock this morning, you broke into thirteen King's Avenue, correct?"

"You don't have to answer, remember." The lawyer said. Gary spoke before he had finished the sentence.

"Well, yes, I did!" He said, with indignance, almost as if the crime should have been broadcast from the highest point in the town already. The lawyer sighed.

"You also threatened and then put a Mr Howard Worth in a situation where he fell from a second story balcony to the ground below, causing him considerable injury and damage to his personal property?" Fiona added. Gary stumbled for a moment before speaking.

"Well yes, I did, but the bastard was having an affair with my Sarah!" He protested, becoming incensed.

"Legally, cheating does not constitute a criminal offence. However, breaking into someone's house and throwing them from a balcony is a bit more serious." Fiona insisted. The lawyer scoffed.

"He didn't admit to throwing him from the balcony, he said, as you worded it, 'put him in a position where he fell'." He protested.

"That's as maybe, but there's no indication he would have fallen had Gary not have been there and performed the actions he did." Fiona retorted.

"What actions would they be?" Gary hissed.

"Well, seeing as we're being pedantic, you; 'ran up the stairs and fought with my husband for a brief period, at one point causing my husband, in an act of self-defence, to throw a punch that put him over the balcony rail. He then fell…' etc, etc. 'An act of self-defence', you caused his injury, indirectly." Fiona read from Sandy's statement, being aware of Gary's frustration growing, even though he could not see it happening.

"Okay, I admit that I *may* have done… all of what you just said," he began.

"We don't need an admission, we have CCTV of you

breaking into the house, that's a criminal offence as it is. The rest is just academic. In fact, you're lucky. Howard has decided to drop all charges against you." She said. Gary exhaled with relief, but the lawyer almost choked.

"Wh- so, wait a minute. There are no charges against him, so why is he here? You realise you have no right to hold my client without charge?" He said, hurriedly. Phillips chuckled.

"Of course we do. We wouldn't be any good at our jobs if we didn't. You're here for something that interests me, and I just want to ask you a couple of questions." Phillips said, starting with a chuckle.

"Well would you care to tell us so we can get this over with?" The lawyer asked. Phillips put down his papers and crossed his arms. Fiona picked out a number of shiny photographs from the folder in front of her, sliding them across the table. "Take a look at those."

All three of the photographs showed some variant of the same subject; a busted latch lock from the front, back and side; wooden splinters were bursting from the split portion where it connected to the door and scratches and chips covered the metal surface. Gary scanned the photos, looking at each with bleary eyes.

"Well, these are a door lock." He said at last, putting the photographs down.

"Correction, they're *your* door lock. More specifically, they're photos of the door lock that was busted by whoever took Willow when they broke down the door." Fiona said, drawing the photographs back towards her.

"So?" Gary said, shaking his head. "What does this have to do with me?" Phillips leaned further across the table.

"Suppose Willow found out about your Mum and Howard Worth." He said. Gary, confused, turned to his lawyer, who he was surprised to find listening more intently than he. He looked back to Phillips. "Maybe, just maybe, you noticed that she was starting to behave differently around you and Howard. You noticed that most at the parents evening last month. You started putting two and two together, maybe you noticed how Sarah was being overly friendly with Howard." He continued.

"This is all pure conjecture." The lawyer said.

"Hear us out." Fiona replied.

"You came to the conclusion that maybe Sarah was having an affair with Howard and Willow knew. She'd already figured it out." That was Phillips.

"Don't." Gary said, shaking his head.

"You realised that you'd not been the best father to Willow, or the best husband. After all, why would she have an affair if you had been?" Phillips continued.

"I know where you're going with this, and I'm asking you to stop." Gary said, louder this time.

"They have nothing incriminating you, so calm down." Said the lawyer with a reassuring gesture of his hand.

"Doesn't stop us making a point." Fiona said.

"What point would that be?" The lawyer said.

"Your door was broken down before Willow was taken. What a shame we don't know anyone who can knock down doors." Phillips said.

"Wait, Phillips, we do!" Fiona said, exaggeratedly.

"Oh, yeah. We do." Phillips said, flatly.

"So, let me get this straight, you're saying I somehow found out about Sarah's affair, got worried that Willow was going to like being with Howard more than me, so I burst down my own door to kidnap her when I was out on my own anniversary dinner?" Gary said, trying to understand.

"We also found a used paternity test in Willow's bedroom, and an interesting search history on her laptop." Said Fiona. Gary turned to her, dumbstruck.

"Eh?"

"It looks like Willow knew that something was amiss with her parents. So despite Sarah's insistence that she can't have known, she clearly had suspicions." She continued, ignoring his enquiry.

"Willow thought someone else was her Father?" Gary whispered to himself. "She thought it was *Howard*?" He grumbled.

"Now, we don't know the results of this test, but it doesn't matter. The point is, if Willow knew, it isn't much of a stretch to think that you did in some capacity, too." That was Phillips.

"Now, come on, this is ridiculous. You've got nothing to back any of this up, it's *all conjecture*." Hissed the lawyer, who up until now had been listening quite intently.

"Okay. That's fine. We'll file that idea and go back to the night in question. Your anniversary dinner, was it nice?" Fiona asked, filing her paperwork away. Gary frowned, his face blooming into red.

"Wh- what?" He quizzed, confused; he was still processing

the latest development.

"Except your anniversary isn't for a while, is it Gary?" Fiona resumed. Gary paused, his heart giving a bound. "Daryll married you and Sarah, right? Now he tells us you got married in December. So, that means you had either a very early or late dinner. Which was it?"

"Remember, you don't have to answer any of their questions, Gary." The lawyer said.

"Shut it, Dan." Gary retorted. The lawyer was silent immediately. "Okay. It wasn't an anniversary dinner. We'd had another argument. We decided we would go out and try and sort things out together, but it didn't work out. We didn't go for dinner, but we kept fooling ourselves. I guess we thought that if we kept telling people the same thing, it would somehow be real, you know?" He continued, with more remorse than the police had seen from him yet. "That if we told people what we were doing, even if it wasn't true, we would somehow get closer together. Sarah is very careful about how people see her, and we've known for a while that things were falling apart. I certainly didn't have a clue she was already with another man." He said.

"So you didn't go out together at all that night? You just told everyone, including us, that you were to keep up appearances?" Fiona said, her brow knitting.

"I guess." Gary replied.

"Where were you both?" Fiona asked.

"I don't know where Sarah was. Well, I think I can guess where she was in hindsight, but at the time I didn't have a clue. I'd got a train into the city, and before you ask, I can't remember most of the night. If you want my full itinerary, I suggest you go 'round all of the bars and ask if anyone saw me. I'd be interested to know myself." Gary said. Fiona made to say something, but he continued. "I shouldn't have lied, but I was ashamed of what you would think if I told you the truth." Gary defended. "But that doesn't mean I kidnapped Willow."

"You can't even call her your *daughter*, Gary. Not once in this interview have you called Sarah your *wife*." Phillips said.

"This has nothing to do with anything, it's pure *conjecture*." Dan repeated.

"His breaking down of the door isn't." Phillips said.

"Why would I break down my own door?" Gary asked, almost in a shout. Phillips was fast on the answer.

"Deflection of blame. Who else would break down a door

than someone with no need to? So, they could say at interview 'why would I be so stupid?'" He said. Dan scoffed.

"This is ridiculous, there is no evidence to back any of this up, this is all purely circumstantial. If you have evidence, use it!" He said, angrily. Gary spun his head around to face the pair again.

"Yeah, and besides, you were there when you asked Samy *wife* about the affair, you remember, I didn't have a clue about any of it." He pointed out.

"Another diversion technique. Gives you plausible deniability. It was the first thing you said, 'even I didn't know, Sarah'. That's a really convenient thing for you to have said." Fiona explained. Gary looked from her, to Phillips, then back again, scoffing with every twist of his neck.

"This is absolutely fucking insane, you're seriously telling me you think I broke down my own door and kidnapped my daughter, then threw her into the lake? All because I'd found out that my wife was having an affair with the headmaster?" Gary scoffed."

"Did you?" Fiona said immediately.

"You do realise how stupid all of this sounds?" Gary asked, silencing his lawyer who he knew was about to try and interrupt.

"Doesn't stop us from checking." Phillips said, calmly. Gary paused, then looked to Dan, who was silent, probably because his words were falling on deaf ears anyway. He turned back to the pair.

"*No comment.*" He said, quietly.

-35-
The Confession Tape

The following morning came just as quickly as the previous night had left. This time, the sun rose behind a backdrop of an overcast sky that was not congruent with the time of year.

Phillips had not been home; he spent most of the night at the crime scene, which was still sealed off from the public. The forensics team had long since packed up and gone, leaving nothing but the bagging team to remain and take away all pieces of interest, naming them carefully against the numbered flags that had been used to mark them. He helped here and there, but most of his time was spent watching, observing. Wondering what Willow was thinking as she choked on a lightbulb, reeling from a wound to the head from a heavy, sharp, jagged rock. He thought, in a way, that he would rather she was already dead by the time she was thrown from the cliff.

It was the early morning when Phillips returned to the Police station. Fiona joined him in the car park, nearly crashing into him with her car, having not quite seen him.

"No need for that, Fiona." He said, with a wry smile he could barely muster up the strength to bring to his face.

"You shouldn't be walking in the middle of the road. Heavy death torpedoes use roads, not people." She pointed out, pulling her coat out of the car as she exited.

Fiona signed in, as usual, at the desk; it was not unusual for Phillips not to do so, but she was too well aware that it meant he had not signed out from the night before.

"You've been here all night, haven't you?" She asked, handing him the case file which she had previously kept in her messenger bag.

"I've been here. I also went up to Vicarage Cliffs, spent some time with the bagging team. Got a bit wistful. Tried to figure out her final movements." He said with a sigh that soon became a yawn.

"Anyone would think you loved this job." She chuckled sarcastically. "You find anything useful?" She asked as Phillips opened the door to the stairs. They left the empty waiting area behind them.

"No, not really. I didn't expect to; it's been too long for anything to have survived." He replied, dejectedly. Fiona sighed. "I also spent a bit of time outside Gary's cell. Thought I might have heard him say something in his sleep, I got desperate. He slept well enough, but no midnight mutterings." He confessed; Fiona sighed too as she pushed the corridor door open at the top of the stairs. They entered the space and walked alongside a surplus department office, then moved to the far end.

"What did you expect? You're not psychic." She said. Then, she spun around in a move that startled him. "Oi, you didn't talk to him, did you?" She asked, alarmed. Phillips groaned and forced the door to his department open.

"I'm not stupid. Most of the time." He replied with a deadly serious tone.

"That's true, but you do have your moments. Hi, Jane." Fiona said, smiling to the officer they found in the office; she was wrestling with the coffee machine, prodding it yet ignoring the high-pitched beeping that protested her efforts. "Plus, I doubt Dan would have been too pleased to have found you talking to his client without his presence. Phillips became incensed almost immediately.

"That lawyer knows his job too well." Philips said, slamming the case file down onto a table. He did not know to whom it belonged, but he also did not care. The thud of the heavy document resounded around the office, startling Jane, who had finally managed to get the machine; she nearly threw her cup across the room. Fiona sighed.

"He wouldn't be a very good lawyer if he didn't, let's be honest." She said, picking up the case file; it needed taking care of; nobody had produced a copy yet.

"Yes, but why can't these public defender types be on our side? Next time, we need one from Corruption Secondary, or at least sort out launching a course on helping the police." Phillips continued, sarcastically. "Isn't that what people are told to do?"

"The problem isn't that he's good at his job, Phillips, it's just that we've been ridiculously bad at ours." Fiona retorted in a semi-serious tone he did not expect.

"You've got a point there." Phillips said, opening the door to his office. A light on the ceiling turned on as the door swung into the space; Phillips followed it, then did Fiona. "I've never known a case like it. Not a single shred of forensic evidence, well, other than the blood and the stitch. Remind me to check on Jacqueline's progress later." He continued, moving over towards his bookshelf. He picked up the carafe that was there, finding it empty. "Remind me to top this up, too." Fiona chuckled as a reply.

"Do you really think we're going to find anything on Gary? Do you actually believe he did this?" She asked. Phillips rested the carafe back down and eyed her suspiciously.

"You don't?" Asked he.

"Dan's right, it's a bit flimsy." She shot back.

"It's our job to think the unthinkable. But we've got about twenty-four more hours to crack this thing." Phillips said, moving across to his desk; he became aware of a beige shape in the centre of his desk. He turned his desk lamp on, illuminating the shape, which he came to recognise as a parcel, almost in a spotlight.

"We'll see what we can come up with." Fiona said, eyeing the package as Phillips gripped it with his hand. "What's that?" She asked.

"It's a parcel."

"I can see that."

"Why ask, then?"

"Piss off, Phillips."

A pause.

"I don't know what it is."

"You just said it was a parcel?"

"Piss off, Fiona."

She chuckled.

"Nice to see we can both still have a laugh. We need one, these days." She said. Phillips turned the beige package over in his hands; the loose paper of the wrapping shuffled beneath his fingertips. "What do you suppose it is?" She asked, leaning forward. Phillips sat down across the desk from her.

"Well, how do you figure out what's in a parcel?" He said, sarcastically.

"Well, normally you know already, because you've ordered it." She said, even more sarcastically.

"I suppose I should open it." He said, shrugging.

"Yes, do."

"Even I'm getting tired of this, let's just see what it is." He said, a serious tone coming over him. Fiona did not reply.

He tore open the wrapping; piercing the paper with his fingernails, he ripped it open, like a madman pierces flesh. The paper fell away easily, revealing a white cardboard box within. "Did

Santa Clause send this?" Phillips said with frustration.

"I thought you didn't want to carry on with the sarcasm?" Fiona pointed out.

"I didn't. Can you find out who this was delivered by, please?" He replied, looking up to her for an instant. Immediately, she was to her feet, and she bolted across the room. She pulled open the door and called out to the officer who was clearing up the coffee before it stained.

"Jane, get on the phone to Lloyd downstairs, I want to know who delivered this parcel and when it happened." Fiona said through the gap in the ajar door. She went to move back into the office but was stopped.

"What about this spillage?" Jane protested.

"Doesn't matter, it was our fault anyway. Get downstairs!" She ordered. Jane, not one to argue when she knew she couldn't, immediately dropped the rag she was wiping the carpet with, came unsteadily to her feet and moved swiftly and with purpose out of the room. Her footsteps echoed on the hard floor beyond the carpeted room, softening into the distance. The room fell into silence; only Fiona and Phillips remained.

Fiona turned, closing the door. Phillips was stood across from her, his fingers breaking open the box; it was a short, wide thing with a flap at the top which Phillips was tugging at.

"Dammit, come on!" He called out in frustration. He would end up tearing the lid, saving his calmness for another time. The lid, now in two halves, came apart effortlessly, the loose end falling to the ground atop the heap of brown paper it had one been encased In.

Phillips peered inside. Bubble wrap covered a black shape, which was ensconced in the soft protective material. He could not make out what it was at first.

"What is it?" Fiona asked, moving slowly but surely around the desk.

"Let me…" Phillips began, sliding a hand into the box; he tugged at the edge of the wrap, lifting it slightly so that he could see within more clearly. Details of the shape came to him clearer now; he saw that it was made of plastic, moulded into two halves and sandwiched together. A clear plastic strip down the middle of the flat edge revealed an intricate assembly of two black discs, one larger in diameter than the other. Phillips examined it closely, his hands probing the surface until he realised what he was prodding.

"It's a cassette tape." He said, lifting it clear of the box. He put the container down on his desk, more or less exactly where it had been left before their arrival.

"A cassette tape?" Fiona asked, surprised. "I didn't realise people still used those?" She said, scoffing.

"They don't, usually. But I bet we know somebody who *would* have a tape recorder and a surplus of empty tapes." He replied, holding it towards the light; written hastily, it would appear, in pen on the label, were the words 'Play Me'. Fiona's heart gave a bound.

"Who do you mean?" Fiona asked.

"Until we've played it, we'll assume it's Jigsaw. We must have a tape recorder in the department somewhere, let's check George's desk." Phillips said. He was across the room in a moment, so fast, in fact, that he was through his office door before Fiona even had chance to register the movement. She followed him out, pausing in the doorway; she watched as Phillips moved.

He darted across the empty room, shuffling his feet to slow himself as he arrived at the ordinary looking desk belonging to George.

"Why would George have a tape player?" Fiona asked, surprised at the speed with which Phillips had gotten into the locked top drawer of his desk.

"Are you joking? The guy has been here since the late eighties. If anyone is going to have a tape recorder, it's George." He said; this time, despite what Fiona recognised as a jovial statement, it was delivered with a seriousness that she was alarmed by. She did not enjoy it when Phillips was completely serious. "Aha!" He yelled, fishing a black box from the detritus within the drawer. Papers fluttered hither and thither, but Phillips did not care; he would sort it later.

As Phillips raced back into his office, almost knocking Fiona aside as he went, he failed to notice the power plug dangling from a long wire behind him. Fiona retrieved it, almost tripping in her attempt, and pursued him into his office. He slammed the box down upon the desk, such that it was nearly dashed into smithereens. Fiona ran around the other side, where she knew there was a socket; the power strip was cable-tied haphazardly to the leg of his desk, but it was replete with free sockets. She slammed the plug into one of them, then pressed the switch; a faint hum of electricity filled her ears. "Yes! Bless you, George." Phillips said, alerted by the red light beside the cassette door which flickered unsurely.

He slid open the player door and it sprang away from the body. Into the cavity, he slid the tape, being careful not to touch it with his bare fingers to smudge any prints; he tucked them within his sleeve and used it as a makeshift glove. Then, he slammed the door closed and clicked the *Play* button. The room filled with silence. Then a little fuzzy hiss.

Then a voice.

"Hello, whoever is listening to this." Came the elderly voice from the tinny speakers, Fiona finding it vaguely familiar. It was too distorted to make out, but the voice continued. "I am recording this message because I cannot live with my mistake anymore, and I have not told you directly because of my forgetfulness." Then Fiona recognised it.

"Oh my God." She said, under her breath.

"What?" Phillips replied as the voice continued in the background. Fiona raised a hand and shushed him so that she could hear.

"I'm confessing to the kidnap and murder of Willow, erm, Greene. I forced my way into her house, kidnapped her, then threw her into the lake behind the Church. I think she died on impact." Phillips' heart gave a bound.

"Get Grisham, *now*!" He said, pushing Fiona with a forceful hand. She nodded, then stood up and ran for the door. "And bring Jacqueline! This thing might have fingerprints we can use!" He continued, calling out to her. He hoped he had been heard, for she had already fled the room. He would find out soon enough. The tape continued.

"Erm, I regret the actions I mention, and. Er… *I regret the actions I*; I regret the actions I mentioned and wish to be brought to justice. You know where I live. Sebastian." Concluded the message. The sound of a click on the tape signified a complete recording, but the reels continued to spin. Evidently it was a long play tape.

Phillips sat back in his chair, though he did not pause the tape. The sound of distant feet drawing nearer met his ears, and he sighed a long sigh, then rubbed his face, for he was tired. He peered over at the clock; a quarter past seven.

"Fuck." He whispered in the emptiness, as he realised that the day was only just beginning.

-36-
He Had a Heart

The car screeched, almost sideways, around the corner. A passer-by, not expecting such stunt driving, prepared to dive out of the way, for fear that the car would mount the kerb and run him over. He considered that he should call the Police; such wanton mayhem on the quiet streets of Heathestone deserved being dealt with. But then, through the haze of rubber smoke and debris kicked up by the rapidly spinning wheels, he espied a flash of high-visibility green on a dark grey body. To his surprise, and slight annoyance, it *was* the Police.

"Phillips, slow down." Fiona urged over the sound of the screaming engine. She was nearly across the centre console and sitting in his lap, such was the forces at work against her. She gripped the ceiling-mounted handle to prevent herself from snapping the handbrake lever with her hips as she attempted to right herself.

"There's no time." Phillips replied, a surprising air of calm about him, despite the fact that his foot was practically welded to the accelerator pedal.

"Sebastian will still be there when we arrive!" She continued, louder this time to be heard above the roar of a gear change. He sounded the horn as he veered around some dithering driver in front of him; he made the quickest of glances around to ensure they were not going to be involved in a head-on collision with anything sharing the lane; after a few moments, during which they were not killed, he swerved back into the correct lane. Fiona genuinely feared for her life.

"You know Sebastian better than any of us, Fiona. If he's going to talk, it'll be to you." He said, in between almost careering off of the road as he manoeuvred a tight corner. "We need to get to him first before anybody else does." He said.

Fiona was quiet after that. In fact, she was quiet for the remainder of the fraught journey, in which she estimated he had nearly killed both of them and anybody else unfortunate to get in his way a dozen times, at least. By now, she was very pleased his carafe had been empty; goodness knows what would have happened if he had taken to the roads drunk. But in the corners of her mind, she could not help but realise that he was right. Sebastian seemed easily confused, but he recognised her; he would be receptive to her questioning, or at least, less hostile than to anyone else.

"There!" She said at last, pointing to the junction that formed the entrance to Sebastian's street. This abrupt warning came as a surprise to Phillips, who almost missed the turn. He was forced to act quickly; he hooked the wheel full to the right, and once more the car was sideways. He yanked on the handbrake lever, and a scream of tyre squeal filled the air; Fiona was nearly flung from the car had the door not been there. A look of effort crossed somewhat with pain befell Phillips' face as he struggled to maintain the manoeuvre.

Eventually, though, he found himself pointing in the right direction; he espied the dilapidated dwelling at the head of the cul-de-sac. He straightened the wheels, released the brake and floored it. The car moved with such a pace that Fiona thought they would plough straight into the house, but Phillips was prepared. He slammed his foot on the brake, came into neutral and screeched to a halt. Had Fiona not been wearing a seatbelt, she would almost certainly have been cast headlong through the windscreen. She cried out in alarm.

"*Christ!*" She yelled, though Phillips did not notice. "What the hell are you doing, Phillips?" She continued. Phillips ignored her. It was only as he alighted the car that she realised he was never wearing a seatbelt; that made her even more annoyed at his recklessness. He dove clear of the door and approached Grisham, who, despite Phillips' swift arrival, had arrived first with a squad of others; about a dozen police had descended on the house, and Phillips, as well as Fiona, knew that Sebastian would likely be spooked.

"That was a bit of an unnecessarily dramatic arrival, Phillips." Grisham said, dryly.

"I knew I shouldn't have stayed to brief Jacqueline." Phillips replied; Fiona emerged, swaying, from the car behind them.

"Why, what do you know that we don't?" Grisham asked, menacingly. Phillips, now alongside him, looked at him, panting.

"What makes you think I know something? Look, Fiona knows this guy better than any of us, if anyone should talk to him, it's her. All you're going to do with all these people is confuse him, or worse yet, terrify the living daylights out of him." Phillips replied, angrily. Grisham turned his body to face him.

"We could maybe have done with knowing that before we got here." He replied in a pathetic effort at self-defence. There again, he did have a point; "Why *did* you stay and brief Jacqueline, Phillips?" He continued. Phillips started back and grunted.

"Lis- "

"Grisham, look!" Fiona shouted, pointing at something in the air.

"Wha...?" Grisham began, swivelling around. All around him, hurried chatter and orders were shouted between the assembled officers. All eyes were at the roof of the house; a scrabbling, stick-like figure emerged from the far side, clambering and gripping with desperate, claw-like hands.

"Is that Sebastian?" Phillips asked, confused.

"There's a ladder on the other side, I'm going around!" Fiona hissed, remembering what Sebastian had told her. She bolted through the crowd and made for the side of the house, where she was certain she would find a garden gate.

"Fiona, wait!" Phillips shouted, running after her. Grisham watched the figure rise unsteadily to his feet; he was wearing little more than a dressing gown, which fluttered and lifted in the breeze.

"Now what the hell are you doing up there?" Grisham muttered before moving towards the officers to dispense responsibilities for the ensuing operation.

Fiona crashed into the fence, for she did not manage to stop herself in time. It was so flimsy a construct that she nearly fell through it. Phillips followed close behind, steadying her so that she could proceed. She darted for the metal gate that she espied at the end of the fence, again slamming into it; this time, it was intentional. She had hoped it would open as she forced herself onto it, but it was stoic and resilient in its defence of her. She let out a cry as her body crushed up against the metal bars, exacerbated by Phillips who immediately clattered into the back of her.

"You okay?" He asked, stepping back. She strained an answer.

"Yeah, yeah, I'm fine. Get me over this thing, would you?" She said, clutching her torso, such that the stabbing pain began to subside. With her free hand, she gripped a metal bar, being careful to avoid the numerous rusty patches that plagued the surface where the black pint had chipped away. Phillips cupped his hands below her; in an instant, her foot was upon the makeshift platform, and he raised himself to full height, sending her high into the air.

She rolled expertly over the top of the gate, manoeuvring herself such that she landed upright as soon as she released her grip from the bars.

She landed quite neatly on her feet, sent a hurried 'thanks' through the gate, then darted further down the path until she rounded the corner of the house and out of view. "There's a ladder, I'll try and talk him down!" Came her voice. Phillips grimaced at the idea but was nonetheless indebted to her efforts. He turned and ran back to the front of the house to get a better view of the situation; the relief as he espied Sebastian still atop the house was palpable, as was his worry that he was up there in the first place.

Fiona moved to the foot of the ladder; a rickety thing it was. One rubber foot was missing, and the other was worn away to near nothingness. "Shit." She said slowly, gripping the vertical metal bars. She put her left foot on the first rung, but the ladder nearly slid backwards, almost sweeping her off her feet. She steadied the thing and pushed it closer to the wall; it scraped on the concrete slab upon which it was stood. She could see now that the screws holding it to the wall had rusted to near nothingness, and it was no longer fixed.

She stood back and peered around her; a few feet from her began a green lawn of surprisingly well-kept grass, which she resented by virtue of it not being closer so that she could stand the ladder upon it to steady it.

In the distance, on the far side of the lawn, stood a dilapidated shed that was little more than a rotting husk of a building. A shattered window on one side allowed a tangle of vegetation to spill in from a nearby hedge that formed the far boundary of the garden. She espied a stack of loose, grey concrete stood at the door to the thing and she reasoned that he had used it as a makeshift step; they would be perfect, she thought.

She started across the lawn, peering back ever and again to ensure she still had time to reach Sebastian. He was facing away from her, staring out across the front garden space. He steadied himself in the stiff breeze with outstretched arms. She then looked back to the shed, which she was upon a moment later. She almost fell to her knees, but as her hands fell upon the edge of the top-most slab, she steadied herself, half-hovering above the ground. Anticipating a heavy load, she heaved backwards, bringing the slab with her in a hail of mud and insects that flew hither and thither. Using the same momentum, she spun around and launched herself back across the lawn; the thing was not as heavy as she had anticipated, but she hoped that it would be enough to keep the ladder stationary.

She darted back onto the concrete patio, finding grip in an instant. She threw the concrete to the ground, cracking it across the middle; a web of lines criss-crossed the surface, but it did not matter. She pushed the slab towards the feet of the ladder with her foot, and it retained its form, such that she was confident the ladder would not move. She tested it by pulling on the vertical bars, which remained steadfast and unmoving. She muttered something to herself as she began to clamber up the rungs; each one was flimsy and unnerving, but she did not remain on each one long enough for her feet to go straight through it.

By now, she was aware of a voice calling out from around the front of the house;

"Sebastian, please try not to move. We want to help you, please stay where you are." She recognised the sound as that of Grisham, through a loudhailer that amplified his voice to extraordinary levels. *Leave it alone, Grisham, I've got this!* Fiona thought. *Leave it to Grisham to interfere.*

"You bastards just want to take me in, I never liked a one of yas!" Came Sebastian's enraged response, in a tone she had not heard from him yet. It frightened her to hear that he was capable of such viciousness. She awaited the reply from Grisham, but none came; evidently Phillips had deterred him from interfering.

"Sebastian?" Fiona shouted, nearing the top of the ladder. She peered across the roof at him, clinging onto the gutter to steady herself against the steadily blowing wind; it was stronger here than it was at ground level.

"Who's that?" Sebastian replied, in a quieter voice. "You trying to ambush me?" He cried, almost spinning around. Fiona scrabbled across the loose tiles, picking her route carefully to avoid the perilously dangerous ones. Now she could see that he had adopted a stance that caused his feet to bend across the angled ridge of the roof. As she watched, one foot slipped, but he caught himself just in time.

"Sebastian, it's me!" She shouted, just quietly enough not to startle him. "I'm behind you, don't turn around." She continued as an extra measure.

"Who?" He asked, confused.

"It's me, Fiona!" She shouted over the howl of the steadily worsening wind. "We've talked before, I helped you home a couple of days ago, remember?" She explained, helping to jog his memory.

"I don't, I don't remember you." He muttered, spinning his head around.

"I want to help you, Sebastian, let m- aargh!" She began before losing her footing on an erroneous tile that split and gave way as she trod on it. She dove forward and gripped the gable with strained fingers. Sebastian looked at her but made no effort to help. She breathed heavily for a moment and puffed her cheeks out, as though psyching herself up. She hauled herself up using the peak as a handhold, then found sturdier ground with her feet. "Please, come down, we can talk about this rationally." She continued, pulling herself to her feet.

"There's Fiona, let her talk to him." That was Phillips' distant voice.

"No! No, you're just like the rest of 'em, you want to bring me in and lock me away!" Sebastian yelled. Fiona stopped approaching him, though she extended a hand towards him.

"Just come down, Sebastian. Please." She said, ignoring his concerns. She threw a sideways glance to the assembled group below, then espied a small crowd approach, only to be kept away by the officers.

"No, no, no! How many times?" Came his resistant reply. "All you people have done to me is vilify me, abuse me and treat me like the *shit* you pretend not to be!" He growled, staring at Fiona; she winced with fear, not knowing from where this abuse towards her was coming. But as she began to draw nearer, she realised he was not staring at her, but somewhere in the distance. She did not even know if he knew she was there.

"What are you talking about, Sebastian?" She queried quietly.

"You all, all of you, you all down there!" He pointed at the rapidly expanding crowd. "All you've done is treat me like I'm some big Mr Bad, but it's all bullshit! You think you're so much better than me? You think that just because you think I did something awful that it's true? Well I can't stand it, not again." His last words were tearful, though the aggression and frustration were as clear as ever. "You did this to me once, I'm not going to let you do it again. Not again." That was muttered to himself. "This is on you! Now *you're* all gonna have blood on your hands!"

"Sebast- "

"I'm gonna jump!" He cried, bending his knees. A great cry of *no* rang out from the assembled crowd, and from Fiona, who dashed forwards, using the movement as an excuse to gain ground quickly. A scream from below as Sebastian steadied himself, swaying his arms.

"Sebastian, let me... let me, I want you to tell me something." Fiona said, changing tack. Sebastian froze, almost physically, as she spoke.

"Wha, what?" He said, shivering.

"You recorded us a message. You recorded us a message on a cassette tape? Telling us that you killed Willow?" She asked, taking slow, steady steps towards him. Sebastian muttered something to himself, then began to cry again.

"Somebody was at my house, wi- with a tape recorder." He said, turning to face her properly. Fiona moved closer.

"Who, Sebastian, who?" She replied. She eyed Phillips, whose eyes met hers at exactly that moment. Sebastian was silent, though he looked around. "A man, a woman, who, Sebastian?" She prompted.

"A woman, I, I think." He replied, almost cutting her off.

"A woman?" Fiona repeated loudly, for the benefit of the officers below. "And, what did this woman say, Sebastian, what did she want?" Sebastian's eyes darted back and forth, over to the countryside behind his house, then to the town in front. By now, his tears were like an amniotic fluid around the foetus of his eyes. Some were swept away in the breeze, cast into the air where they became lost into the rain that was quickly filling the air.

"Sh- they, they told me that Willow needed peace, that her family needed peace, and that they could get that if I just admitted to killing her, so I..." He began. Fiona understood.

"You admitted to killing her so that her family could have closure." She explained, finding that that perfectly encapsulated what Sebastian was trying to say. He nodded, as did she. "Who was this woman, Sebastian, who came to your house?" She whispered, now scarcely more than a yard from him. Now, he simply dissolved into hysterics, loud outcries filling the air.

"I don't *know*, I can't remember his name, or who they were." He sobbed, tilting his body into the breeze. *His name?* Fiona thought. Had she misheard him? She made to ask but realised that it would be futile; something in her mind clicked.

"You've got dementia, haven't you, Sebastian?" She said as a statement rather than a question. She already knew the answer and his silence confirmed it. "That's why you can't remember?" She continued. Sebastian staggered backwards and gripped the metal bar of the aerial that was screwed to the gable tiles. Fina breathed a silent sigh of relief; she did not have to worry about him falling now, unless the tiles or the screws gave way.

"I prayed for so long, Fiona." He began, finally remembering who she was. Her friendliness came flooding over him, like the tears he was expelling. "I prayed to God for the strength to forget everything. To forget about Stacey, to forget about the way the people of this town stared at me with terrified eyes, with looks that could have killed me on the spot. Nobody but me knows what that's like, *nobody but me knows*." His mouth squirmed and wriggled as he gulped.

"I can't imagine what that must have been like, truly, I can't." She said, perhaps foolishly.

"No, nobody does. But nobody thinks what it's like to be me, to suffer like that. But do you know the worst part? About begging to forget?" He asked. Fiona shook her head. "It's that God fights tooth and nail against the Devil, and sometimes he loses. I forgot, alright. All of the good bits. I lost my wife, everything that's left of her memory that lived in me, gone. The hatred, the suffering, the sheer *fucking* misery of my existence stayed. Everything I didn't want.

I would never kill Willow. She was the only beautiful, happy thing I had left. Now she's gone too. Just like everything else. But do you want to know the funny thing?" He asked. He did not wait for a reply. "No matter what I did, ever since Stacey, my life has been leading up to this moment. I was always meant to end up here, on this roof, right now. Maybe not talking to you, maybe not with so much attention, but I would always end up here and I know what's going to happen next, so I've made peace with myself. No matter how badly I've been treated by these *people*," he continued, gesturing the crowd below him, "I vowed I would continue to love them. I would be better than them and I am. I've forgiven everybody who ever wronged me, and do you know what? That's how I will be judged at the Gates." He said, in perhaps the most eloquent monologue she had heard from him yet. But she did not have chance to muse his words, for no sooner had he stopped than he leaned away from the aerial, tilting sideways over the edge of the roof.

Fiona realised what he was doing before he had chance to do it, but she was not fast enough. His fingers released the metal bar.

He toppled sideways.

Almost instantly, his limp body was hurtling through the air, over the edge of the gutter. A gasp of alarm from the crowd below, all eyes following his trajectory. Fiona lost sight of him, and she dropped to her knees, but she had to use her hands to steady herself, for she nearly inadvertently followed him over the edge.

"No!" Came Phillips' voice. Sebastian was silent.

Then, for a moment, the air was still; the rain stopped, silence fell. The world seemed frozen, or at least in slow-motion.

It all ended with a final, sickening thud, as Sebastian's body hit the concrete of his garden path. A foot to the left or right would have landed him on the grass; he may have been horribly injured, but he could have survived. It was as he said; his life was always meant to end where it did.

Fiona was stunned; she looked down at the crowd, which was recoiling in horror at the no doubt gruesome sight she could not see; one woman collapsed, whilst a man nearby threw up beige liquid into a nearby drain. Grisham whispered something to Phillips, then turned and returned to his car as the other officers began ushering the crowd away. A small number of officers approached what remained of Sebastian in an attempt to conceal him. In a way, Fiona was happy that she could not see him, yet in the back of her mind, she wondered if she could have done more. She glanced down at Phillips but found him missing; he had vanished into the crowd somewhere, perhaps aiding in the escorting of them away.

Then she found him again a moment later; he extricated himself from the bustling group and approached a lone straggler, who up until then had defied notice. The man was staring straight up at her, his face one of stony resilience. Phillips gripped his shoulder and turned him.

"Come on, Howard." She heard him say. "The show's over." With that, she was left alone, but Phillips turned back once Howard had been lumbered with a generic police escort. He stood and stared at her, in much the same way Howard had. "You need a hand down?" He said, calmly. Fiona nodded.

-37-
The Devil Among Us

"There was nothing else you could have done." Phillips said, pulling the seatbelt across him. Fiona sat beside him, her head down in guilty solitude. "You did very well. We have information now, another lead." He reassured.

"But Phillips, that isn't the point!" She said, loud enough to startle him. He sat back in alarm. "A man died today, because I couldn't assure him enough. Hell, the guy had dementia, that would have made his confession inadmissible as evidence. He wasn't stable of mind." She said, turning back. Her face reddened, perhaps in anger, or it could have been to block the swell of tears she sensed coming through.

"You're right, I'm not denying that. He was troubled, we should have seen that from the beginning." Phillips said, sternly. "But he died because somebody lured him, used his weakness as an advantage. You said a woman came to his house?" He began. Fiona interrupted him.

"Yeah, but he then said 'he', or 'his', I can't remember exactly. So how can we know any of what he said was true?" She argued back, cutting him off.

"He seemed pretty lucid towards the end, all that talk of God. Look, you knew him better than any of us, what did you think?" He asked.

"You really want to know?" She replied, nodding uncertainly.

"Mhmm." Phillips mumbled.

"I think the whole thing is fucked. We've got zero forensic evidence worth anything, all of our leads have dried up, the only guy who could identify a suspect couldn't remember anything about them and is now dead, we've got parents of the victim who hated each other and she probably knew it and no end in sight to this fucking case." She said, becoming ever more incensed as she spoke. Phillips nodded, but did not say anything. "No one ever said it would be so hard." She continued.

"*Then let's go back to the start.*" Phillips sung. He then turned to her and let out a chuckle. Fiona looked at him sternly.

"You're an asshole, you know that?" She said.

"Yeah, I know." He admitted. "We *will* get to the bottom of this. We owe it to Willow, and Sebastian." He said, resting an assuring hand on her shoulder.

"How do you do it, Phillips?" She asked, looking at him with shallow eyes. He was unsure what this 'it' was, but he made an answer based on an assumption.

"It's part of the job. You just have to not care sometimes. Get over the emotion, don't form attachments. Trust me, it makes it easier." He said, removing his hand.

"That's what I mean. How do you do *it*? How do you not care?" She asked, her voice firm and determined. He sat back and sighed.

"Nobody has ever asked me that before. Now that I think about it, I don't really know. I guess I've seen too much. I'm cynical. If this whole thing has taught me anything, or at least reaffirmed anything, it's that nobody is perfect, everyone is terrible in some way. Sometimes the people you're meant to care about and pity turn out to be as monstrous as the so-called villains." He said, gesturing ever and again with his hands.

"You mean like Gary and Sarah?" She asked, sensing that she already knew the answer. He smiled, then turned to her. She knitted her brows, as if commanding him to answer her.

"*Everyone is terrible*, Fiona. Some a little," he gestured at her, "some a lot."

"What about you?" She said, nodding at him. He breathed once. "How monstrous are you?" Then he turned away.

"There's a devil among us, Fiona. It's our job to find them. Nobody has to like us, they can hate us, it won't concern me." He said, somewhat deflecting the question.

"What if the devil just threw himself from a roof? You don't think it was Sebastian?" She asked. He scoffed. "Huh, don't tell me. *It's our job to suspect everyone*. Of course it could have been Sebastian, right?" She mused. Phillips chuckled. "What?" She asked.

"I said there *is* a devil among us. It's still out there somewhere." He muttered quietly; he knew she had a point; nothing so far had excluded Sebastian.

"Yeah?"

"Yeah. He might be able to climb a ladder, but do you really think he was capable of busting a door down?" He asked. She smiled as she realised that Phillips harboured no ill-will against him. "It's not over yet. We've still got the cassette. It's down to what Jacqueline can find." He said, reaching for the ignition button.

Before he had chance to, however, a vibration in his pocket, accompanied by a chirpy ringtone, drew his attention.

"That's the phone." Fiona said, sarcastically.

"Yep, got it." He replied, fishing his mobile phone from his pocket. He briefly scanned the screen and identified the caller as Grisham. He tapped the green button to accept the call, then lifted the device to his ear. "Go ahead." He said, forgoing his usual 'hello'.

"Phillips, it's Grisham. Came the tinny reply.

"Yep, saw that." Phillips sighed. "What's up?" He asked.

"We're sending a clean-up team for Sebastian. Are you still at the scene?" Grisham asked. Phillips grimaced at the insensitivity. Through a sigh, he replied;

"Yes, we're both still here. You want us to wait for the clean-up team?" He asked. Grisham muttered a reply in the affirmative.

"Yes, remain there until Jacqueline arrives."

"Wait, wait, wait, you're sending Forensics in?" Phillips asked. Fiona made a confused sound; her face reflected the feeling.

"No stone left unturned. I'm sure you understand, look, as soon as they arrive, I want you back here. I need a word with you." He continued, unflinchingly.

"Why do you need to, look, Fiona did the best she could, she doesn't need…" Phillips began in protest.

"Wait, what have I done?" Fiona asked, worriedly, though her voice was tinged with an indignant tone. Phillips silenced her with a hand.

"Not Fiona, she acted admirably. I'd like her to come and be seen, she's probably a bit shaken. She needs someone to talk to. I'd like to talk to *you*." Grisham explained. Phillips moved his hand to the mouthpiece to silence his words.

"You're okay, he wants to see me." He said to Fiona, before removing his hand and talking back into the phone. "Yes, no worries, I'll be there ASAP." He assured. Grisham grunted positively.

"Good man, thanks. Tootilly-bye." He said cheerfully; then, an electronic, descending tone filled Phillips' ears, signifying the call had been dropped. *Great*, Phillips thought, *just what I need*.

-38-
Scaling Back

Jacqueline arrived at the scene of the accident with Mark shortly after. Their appearance was one of little fanfare; so little, in fact, that Phillips did not realise she had turned up with her team until she was already upon the body. It was Fiona who saw her first; she pointed her out to Phillips, who urged his DI to remain where she was. It was only when he was talking to Jacqueline that he finally saw the corpse; it was little more than a twisted mass of flesh and broken bones; little remained of the head. Phillips almost recoiled at the sight, but Mark was more accustomed to the grit and viscera that usually accompanied these scenes.

Phillips drew a line when Mark prodded a protruding portion of putrid brain matter; he bid Jacqueline a farewell and returned to the car, at which point he decided to hurry back to the station to see what Grisham could possibly want. The journey was one far quieter and safer than their previous cruise. Evidently downtrodden, Fiona said very little; in fact, Phillips noticed that she said nothing at all. Whatever the case, Phillips said even less; he focussed on the road. At times, Fiona could sense that Phillips' driving was intentionally laid back, as though he was wishing to delay their arrival.

But soon, arrive they did. With some reluctance, Phillips parked the car in an unusually swift time; in most cases, he would be forced to search for a space, as the car park was filled to the virtual brim with vehicles. *So much for walking or carpools*, Phillips would think on some days. But this time, the locating of a space was the work of little more than a moment.

"Funny, it's usually busier than this." Fiona pointed out, somewhat redundantly. Phillips was already out of the car.

"You read my mind, Fiona." Phillips agreed, zipping up his coat, which up until then had hung about him like a form-fitting tent.

"You don't suppose Grisham has fired everyone, do you?" She asked in jest, though Phillips was bracing himself from discovering that the very idea was one with traces of verisimilitude.

Once inside and in their department, their hunch manifested itself quickly; the office was unusually quiet; gone was the usual bustling activity Phillips was used to during daylight hours; many of the assembled persons were quietly typing away on laptops emblazoned with personal decorations or writing furiously on loose pieces of paper. The rest appeared to be doing little more than chatting to one another in idle fashion. Fiona did not notice the lack of activity at first; instead, she was aware of the vacant seats and desks.

"What's going on here, then?" Phillips said, voicing his concern and irritation. He peered around at the assembled party, who immediately silenced and looked back at him. "Where is everyone?" He continued. Fiona drew up beside him, surveying the scene with stern eyes.

At that moment, a door to his right opened. The click of the latch drew his attention, and her turned to face the sound. He espied Grisham stood in the door on the long length of the office wall. Fiona peered too and saw him; his face was one of grim knowing that did not sit well with her.

"This can only mean good news." She whispered to Phillips; Grisham beckoned him with his free left hand; Phillips became aware that Grisham was holding a thick pile of papers with one arm, sandwiching them between it and his body. Phillips sighed, blowing out his cheeks, then started forward, with Fiona following quickly behind. All eyes were upon them as they moved, and the uniformity of the staring alarmed both of them; Fiona visibly began to shake.

"No, no." Grisham said, shaking a finger. "Just Phillips." He continued, pointing at last at the aforementioned. Fiona stopped in her tracks, and Phillips turned his body half towards her. "Fiona, I want you to get yourself down to medical, have a chat. Let off some steam, yeah?" He urged. Fiona stumbled on her words, but her efforts to protest were ignored.

Phillips turned back around and stepped through the door, which Grisham closed behind him. *Just go, Fiona*, Phillips thought. His musings, however, were interrupted. "Sit yourself down, Phillips." Grisham said, passing him; it was only now that Phillips realised, he had stopped in his way. He started, then looked around at the room, details of which came bounding at him with vivid abundance; a certificate of commendation hanging in an old frame on the wall, the green blotting paper of the desk, stained here and there with coffee rings and leaked pens. A chair on the closer side of the desk, in which Phillips was expected to sit.

He moved towards it, withdrew it, though he did not have

to, then sat in it. Across from him, Grisham did the same.

"Er, yes sir, what is it?" Phillips asked, somewhat in a daze. Grisham smiled.

"Don't look so worried, Phillips. I've got good news, but unfortunately, some bad news, too." Grisham said, his smile fading for a brief instant at the end of his sentence. Phillips sighed.

"There's a surprise. I'll take the bad news, first." He said, reluctantly, expecting the worst.

"No, I'll give you the good news first." Grisham said, his tone completely different; terse, stern. Curt. "I'm retiring. I've been offered early retirement; I finish this December." He said, leaning his arms upon the desk, squashing the blotting paper. Phillips knitted his brow. This was good news?

"Sorry sir, I thought you said you would give me the good news first?" He said, voicing his confusion. Grisham chuckled.

"Oh, you're too kind." His spirit lifted, as did his tone. "This *is* the good news, trust me." Phillips' confusion deepened. "Look, I've worked here for nearly thirty years, this desk has been my second home for eleven. Now I know this is hardly the Naked City, but I can't do this job forever." He explained. Phillips listened, though with half an interest; the idea of *bad news* preyed on his mind. "Now, Central are yet to assign my replacement, but I want to nominate you." He said. Phillips nearly fell off his chair.

"Wh, sir? Are you sure?" He began. Confusion befell Grisham, his face confirming it. "I mean, you've always called me a bit of a loose cannon, a, err, a risk? Only yesterday, you were talking about how inept we were being." He explained. Grisham sat back in his chair.

"Nobody's perfect, Phillips. Not even you, even though you like to think you are." He said, half-jokingly.

"Well, actually…"

"But believe it or not, I think you're capable. If nothing else, you're unorthodox. Now I stick my neck out for you, and I have done more times than I care to mention. Now I know you've been drinking on the job. I don't know for how long, and I don't particularly care. Anybody else would fire you on the spot, but as long as you get the job done, that's fine by me. That being said, I'm sticking my neck out for you one more time. I'm willing to disavow any evidence found against you or this department in this investigation." He explained, somewhat confusing Phillips.

"Evidence, what evidence?" He asked.

"I don't know. Anything that comes up regarding your *habit* and I'm even throwing in a Get Out of Jail Free card for Fiona." He said.

"Why would Fiona have anything to do with this?" Phillips quizzed.

"Oh, come on. Don't play stupid, you can't pull it off. I know as well as you do that Fiona had a personal interest in Sebastian. You think she would be able to keep her visits to him off the books? She couldn't do that, she isn't you. Our little incident this morning all but confirms that she had a platonic attachment to him, now that wouldn't hold up very well at trial. If nothing else, it's a serious conflict of interest. So, in the interest of keeping the peace, I'll make sure none of that ever goes public. If it does, it's on me." He continued.

"But sir, that's..., you can't do that?" Phillips exclaimed.

"I can. It's because I like you, and I want to give you a chance." He smiled. Phillips replied in kind. "That being said." He continued. The smile faded from both men's faces.

"This is the bad news?" Phillips asked. Grisham nodded, subtly but surely.

"How *is* the investigation going? I want you to tell me, because I don't want to make assumptions." He continued. Phillips sighed and leaned back, hard, into his chair.

"It's going, well, I guess. We're still pursuing leads..." He was interrupted.

"What leads? Tell me, Phillips." Urged Grisham.

"I thought you weren't making assumptions?" Phillips said in a vague effort at distraction. It did not work.

"I'm not. I'm also not an idiot, so don't treat me like one. I'm going to ask again, and please answer honestly. *How is the investigation going*?" Grisham repeated, urgently. Phillips groaned.

"To be honest, things are starting to dry up. All our suspects are being eliminated from the investigation; we've got a distinct lack of evidence." He began, bluntly.

"What about forensics, what does Jacqueline have?"

"Very little. There's no fingerprints on the murder weapon, the body. All we have is a contaminated DNA profile she's struggling to isolate and possible, *possible*, fingerprints on the cassette tape." Phillips admitted.

"No boot prints in the soil?"

"The rain washed them away before we got there."

"What about transfer on the door that was smashed in?"

"Nothing. Even if DNA transfer was admissible in court,

there's nothing usable. We did find clothing fibres in the wood, but there's nothing unique that would lead to a match. They're completely generic." Phillips said, his words riding on a sigh.

"So let me get this right. There's no leads, no evidence, nothing? This is a bit of a shitshow, Phillips, wouldn't you agree?" Grisham replied, bluntly. Phillips nodded his head, then gulped deeply.

"Yep, that's right. There's just the tape left and whatever Jacqueline can pull from the DNA profile on the rock. We've got Gary in custody for another twelve hours, but all we have is a hunch and circumstantial evidence." Phillips replied.

"And that's it?"

"That's it."

The pair paused. Grisham inhaled, then sighed out loudly.

"Well, unless we get a full confession, that's not good enough, is it?" Grisham said, tersely, at last. Phillips nodded, like a schoolboy called before the headmaster. He sighed and spun his head at the sound of a loud crash outside; it appeared to be nothing, perhaps a chair being pulled across the floor. He turned back around to face Grisham, who was now regarding his papers closely, running down them with a pen.

"What's that, sir?" He asked. Grisham, expecting the question, answered without looking up.

"This, Phillips, is a list of our expenses so far. This whole tome." He said, lifting up the stack, which Phillips estimated to be over an inch or so thick. "This is just for this department, for this investigation." He slammed the stack onto the desk, which nearly keeled over under the weight. Phillips jumped slightly in his chair. "Now, I get it. These kinds of things are incredibly rare in Heathestone. I'm not saying this is your fault, but we can't afford to keep haemorrhaging money like this." He explained. Phillips made to protest, but Grisham waved a hand. "Listen. I'm going to cut you a deal, here. I want this to be solved just as much as you do, but we're going to have to make some cuts. Now I've taken half of the officers off the case and I'm scaling back your forensic allowance." He said, flipping the pages of his document. Phillips scoffed.

"By how much?" He asked, incredulously.

"Half."

"*Half?*" Phillips protested.

"You're also one of the personnel I'm cutting from the investigation. I'm taking over your role." That was even worse news.

"But sir, I've been on this from the start, with all due respect, you've been out of the loop for a lot of this." Phillips protested, leaning across the desk.

"I've read the case file. I'm sure I'll get the gist. I'll retain Fiona, but only for as long as she's up to it, she can take leave whenever she wants." Grisham explained, seemingly under a guise;

"Are you bribing me?" Phillips asked, his voice one of trembling anger.

"I'm sorry?"

"The promotion, compassionate leave for Fiona, protection from the public, you'll give us all of that, but only if I step down?" He asked, clarifying a point he thought was already clear enough.

"I'm not asking you to step down, I'm reassigning you." Grisham then rested his fingers lightly on a small pile of transfer papers; many were already signed. *That's why they're clearing out their desks out there. Grisham has reassigned them already.* "I've yet to sign yours." He continued, cupping his hands in front of him and leaning across the desk.

"With all due respect, sir, I haven't finished the case yet. You can't reassign me." He said, sternly, his brow folded almost in on itself. Though he was pleading more than anything, he attempted to convince Grisham to change his mind. Grisham chuckled.

"Phillips, I'll say it again." Grisham explained, smiling once again. "I *haven't* signed yours yet." He said, nodding as though telepathically giving Phillips a clue; it took a moment for the thought to bridge the gap, but eventually, Phillips understood. He'd been given a lifeline.

"Give me twenty-four hours." He said, by way of acknowledging the hint. "Twenty-four hours, I'll do everything I can and if I haven't solved this, you can reassign me." Phillips knew it was an impossible task. There was no way a change in their fortunes would land the villain in their hands within a day, but Phillips had to acknowledge that though it was a broad hope, it was a hope nonetheless.

-39-
The Smoking Gun...

Phillips burst from the office, slamming the door against the wall. The window nearly shattered as he did so, and the metal blinds flew and billowed in the tumultuous air. Phillips emerged through the door, then drew it closed behind him in a similarly dramatic fashion, sending a loud thud echoing through the room. Once more, all eyes were on him, quite understandably. He made no apology, instead, he immediately darted between the desks, most of which were now abandoned, and made for his office.

Fiona, spotting him, stood up from the chair she was sat in; she had not gone to medical, instead relying on her own self-proclaimed resilience.

"Phillips? What happened?" She asked, drawing nearer to him. He hastened his step and was soon upon his office door; he gripped the knob, pushed the door open and entered. The lights came on in a moment, and he made to close the door behind him, but Fiona stopped it from closing in her face with an outstretched arm. "Don't you fucking dare shut me out, Phillips." She said, sternly. Phillips ignored her again. He made for his bookshelf, inside of which his carafe stood empty. Apparently, this did not matter, for he pulled open a small set of double doors close to the bottom. Fiona could not see what was behind those doors, but a light turned on within as soon as a secondary door was pulled ajar. "Really, Phillips, a fridge? What's in there this time, lemonade? Orange juice?" She said sarcastically, shrugging. Phillips rummaged around within; the sound of glass on glass clinking and chinking came from inside.

"Nope." He pulled out a bottle; it was a tall, wide thing with a narrow neck. "You remember that case of ciders you bought me for my birthday last month? Still getting through them." He explained, twisting off the metal cap. Fiona scoffed as he lifted the bottle to his lips.

"Phillips, this is ridiculous. What's going on, why did Grisham want to see you?" She urged as Phillips rounded his desk and sat in his chair. Fiona approached, resting her hands on the desk. Philips sighed.

"Don't get used to talking to me as your superior, that's about to change." He explained, cryptically. Fiona frowned and stumbled on her words as she made to enquire what he was talking about. "I'm being reassigned, Grisham is taking over. We're over-budget and we've got no evidence to show for it." He said, taking another enormous swig from the bottle. Fiona sighed.

"So, what happens now?"

"Everyone who used to be in there but has now cleared their desk has been reassigned. I asked for twenty-four hours to solve this before he takes over and he's given me that twenty-four hours but we've only got half our forensic allowance into the bargain." He said. Fiona sat down and let out a long, heaving sigh.

"Twenty-four hours. Did you tell him our progress?" She asked. Phillips laughed.

"He has an unusually good way of getting information from you. Maybe he should have been in charge of questioning all along."

"So 'yes', then." Fiona said, leaning back in her chair. Phillips lifted the bottle to his lips once again, then consumed the last of the dry, bubbling drink; Fiona scoffed. Phillips stood to his feet and moved back towards the bookshelf to get another bottle. Fiona, however, was having none of it; she stood up quickly and moved to block Phillips from doing so.

"Excuse me, you're in my way." Phillips said, somewhat jokingly.

"How long is this going to go on for, Phillips? We've got twenty-four hours and the way I see it we can't spend any of it getting wasted. You won't find any answers at the bottom of a bottle." She explained, forcefully.

"There's no answers anywhere else, so I think it's worth a try."

Fiona swiped her hand down, sending the bottle tumbling out of his grip and onto the floor. It was carpeted, but the wooden structure below caused it to smash into a thousand rain-like shards in a crash that echoed throughout the room.

"The fuck?" Phillips cried, jumping clear of the shower of glass at his feet. Fiona remained where she was.

"This ends, Phillips. Now. It ends now, or I quit, how about that?" She said, almost sobbing.

"Eh?"

"End it now, or I quit, how about that? You'll never see me again." She continued, actually crying now. Phillips peered at her with suspicious eyes.

"Did you go to medical?" He asked, stepping back towards her.

"Sebastian doesn't bother me. *You* bother me, Phillips. You bother me because you say you don't care, but I think you do. You care too much to let this go, that's why you asked for twenty-four hours." She said, almost in a yell. Phillips stared in stoic determination to hear her out. "You can't stand the idea that someone else will solve this. You want to do it, not for the glory or the gratitude it'll get you, but because you want justice. You want to give the Greene's closure, no matter how monstrous their actions have been. So stop fucking around and let's do this. Twenty-four hours is an eternity when you put your mind to it." Her words rang inside his head. Possibly in a funny order; words became letters, became sounds, became thoughts he could understand and imagine on his own. His mind became clear and he thought for a moment; the thoughts became sounds, became letters, became words, became sentences that became a resolve.

"You're right." That was all she needed to hear, but she continued to hear; "I've been an idiot." He sighed. "I've just been so caught up in making this work by the books that I'd forgotten. I'd forgotten about the girl at the centre of all this." Fiona smiled. "Let's get the son of a bitch."

"That's what I like to hear. What's our first move?" She asked, gripping his arms and shaking him. His smile vanished.

"Oh, I don't know." He groaned. "Where *do* we start?" He said, sitting back down in his chair. Fiona's heart sank.

"Gary? What do we have on him?" She asked, sitting opposite him.

"The fibres on the shirt he said he was wearing that night don't match the fibres in the door, surprisingly. I mean, they're so generic and unremarkable that I'm pretty sure my shirt fibres would match." He said, despondently.

"Okay then, how likely is it to be Gary?"

"I don't know anymore. I've had officers trying to dig up anything they can, but his card was used to buy a train ticket that morning, and he has payments in bars that afternoon, so he was in the city. We should have released him by now, I suppose." He continued.

"So we're counting Gary out?" She enquired, already knowing the answer.

"We're counting Gary out. Harry has been cleared,

Sebastian is out of the picture now, I mean, I don't know that we've even got anyone else. Other than the suicide theory, but even that's a bit flimsy." The phone rang. Fiona started in her seat and both people turned to stare at the phone, as if it were some kind of alien contraption neither of them had seen before.

Phillips stood up and moved over to the bookshelf, whilst Fiona stared after him to ensure he was not going for the fridge again. "This can only be good news." He said, rubbing the back of his head.

"Never mind good news, we need a miracle." Fiona called back. The phone rang again, then a third and a fourth time before Phillips got to it. He lifted up the receiver from the cradle and it stopped ringing immediately. He did not even check who the caller was this time, a bizarre anomaly in his character.

"Hello, Phillips." He said. For a moment, no reply came to him; he imagined at first it was connecting to a tele-sale company and that was the source of the delay; but things were not that bad yet; it was connecting to someone in the same building.

"Phillips, it's Jacqueline." Came the soft reply. Phillips' heart gave a bound. This could be the news they'd been waiting for.

"Jacqueline, great! How are you?" He asked, suddenly rejuvenated.

"I'm good, thanks, look, I've got the print test results back on the cassette tape you had sent down." She said, her voice fading in and out of clarity. He pressed his hand against the mouthpiece and turned to Fiona.

"It's Jacqueline. She's got the fingerprint results back from the tape. She sounds positive, could be good news." Fiona sat forward in her seat and smiled. "Go ahead, Jacqueline, please tell me we have something, or that could be the last forensic test you do in this investigation." He cryptically muttered down the phone, clenching his fist beside his face.

"Sorry?" She asked, as Phillips realised she probably had not been told yet about *the news*.

"Never mind," he deflected, "just, er, what's the story on the fingerprints?" He asked. The time in between his asking and her reply seemed an eternity; he was unsure if it was his own mind playing tricks on him or if she was, in fact, pausing for dramatic effect.

The reply was depressingly predictable.

"Nothing. It's like it's been scrubbed clean, but there's no scrub marks. This thing has never been touched, at least by bare hands." She explained. Phillips nearly collapsed.

"God-fucking-*dammit*!" He screamed, throwing the phone. It flew through the air, straight and sure, almost striking Fiona. It crashed onto the desk and practically exploded on the hard wood. Fiona winced, raising her arms to protect her face from the plastic shards and tiny screws that now found themselves as miniature projectiles that arched through the air. "This is impossible, how in the name of God can there be *no forensic evidence*?" He gripped the edge of the desk, his knuckles whitening as his grip tightened. "I'm not imagining this, am I? Nothing about this case makes any sense." He cried, moving back across the room.

"No, you're not imagining it. It's the worst case I've ever been involved in. You're right, there's never been a situation where we have no forensic evidence anywhere, it's as if somebody with no fingerprints has been at work." She replied, rubbing her face with frustrated hands.

Phillips paused, hovering in his seat, in a state somewhere between annoyance and sudden realisation.

"Wait a minute, wait a minute, say that again." He urged, standing up straight. Fiona shook her head, her eyes wide with surprise.

"Er, what? Somebody with no fingerprints?" She said, unsurely.

"Yes, exactly! We've been so preoccupied with finding evidence and making things fit that we haven't seen that the lack of evidence is exactly what we needed, don't you see?" He said, opening his arms as if to celebrate; Fiona sat, confused for a moment, before her eyes met his as though she had realised something; she smiled, knowingly and stood up, gripping Phillips' arms.

"No." She said, smiling. Phillips sighed.

"Oh for... listen, there's a reason there's been no fingerprints on anything we've found. It's because someone has hidden their fingers from everything they come in contact with, right? Someone has intentionally hidden their identity from us. *What a shame we don't know anyone like that.*" He said, urging her to figure out who he was talking about.

Then she did.

Her eyes lit up; as soon as she thought of the name, the pieces of the grisly scenario came flooding to her; suddenly, everything made sense.

"You don't seriously think...?" She began.

"Who else?"

"But, there's never been precedent for this, has there, how will it stand up in court?"

"Let's hope for a confession." Phillips hissed, smiling. He turned and moved for the door.

"Phillips?" Fiona stopped him. He turned to face her again. "If we're wrong, we don't drink the bleach. We go back to the drawing board." She urged. Phillips opened the door halfway.

"No more drawing boards, we can't afford to be wrong. We're *not* wrong. I've got a good feeling about this." With that, he turned away and swept through the door again. He signalled the three remaining officers in the room beyond to follow him. They complied in a moment, and they followed him out of the room, filing through the door with Fiona bringing up the rear.

"Where are you all going?" That was Grisham. He saw the commotion through the window of his office door, and now was stood framed in the space. Fiona turned back, peering across the now empty room.

"We might not need twenty-four hours, Grisham." She said with a smile.

-40-
...and the Hand That Holds It

"Wait here. Nobody goes in or out." Phillips said to the officers at the gate. They all nodded in near unison, then moved to station themselves close by; one at either side of the gate, others scattered here and there to waylay anybody who tried to flee or enter. Phillips turned and followed Fiona, who had not stopped at the gate. He hastened his step and soon was upon her again. "You want to do the talking or shall I?" He asked. Fiona marched at pace, and despite numerous eyes upon her, she made no apology for her frustrated appearance.

"You can do the talking, Phillips. I'll be the cavalry." She said. Phillips smiled, wryly.

"Great news." He said. He sidestepped past a group of students who were huddled around a central figure clutching a football, who watched in dispirited disbelief as the officers moved with such a purpose as to command a space with their presence. The school building loomed; suddenly, it resembled a prison, not a place of education.

"Into the Gulag." Fiona said. Phillips chuckled, then pushed open the front door. The receptionist situated behind her desk perpendicular to the door looked up, then smiled at the officers. They did not stop and return the greeting; her fleeting smile vanished, then her face turned to one of surprise.

"Excuse me, you have to sign in!" Her voice became a shout as the pair moved further from her voice. They marched around a corner, forcing a student clear of their path. The receptionist jumped up from her position; "Beth, just watch the desk, will you?" She said to a nearby colleague, who was equally as confused. "*Excuse me*, officers!" The receptionist cried, not stopping to make sure Beth had heard her. She scooped up the registration documents necessary for authorised entry, then bolted after them. Fiona heard her protests, then turned.

"This is an urgent police mater, please don't intervene." She said, extending an arm as the receptionist approached; the latter stopped almost immediately, then scoffed.

"I don't care who you are, you don't get into this school without signing in. *It's policy.*" She urged, with an unfriendly tone. Fiona lowered her hand, then approached as Phillips continued on down the corridor.

"I don't care about policy right now. We have a legal right to be here, with or without your say-so. So I suggest you go and do your job and leave us to do ours." She said with a surprisingly menacing voice. Fiona made no apology for it; the receptionist started.

"Huh." She scoffed. "Well, we'll just see what Mr Hendricks has to say about this!" Her indignation manifested itself as a peacock-like posture, a dramatic turn of her head, then a march away from Fiona, who was left on her own; Phillips had not waited for her. She turned, unperturbed by the threat, and followed Phillips; she just about saw him vanish around the next right-hand turn. Her step was a quick one, for it was necessary to catch up to him. *Show him the athletics track*, she thought, *he'll trounce even the best student.* That was a surplus thought, she realised in a moment, for as she rounded the corner after him, she realised they had reached their destination; all along the corridor, brightly lit classrooms hummed quietly with stay-behind students who were revising, working on homework, or socialising.

At one point, Harry would have been in one of those rooms. But they weren't here for him. They were there for the person behind the final door. Phillips pushed it open with a smile.

"Mr Howard Worth!" He said, beaming. In the instant before Howard moved, Phillips saw him bent over, examining something in a low cupboard. As soon as his name was called, however, Howard leapt, almost into the air, surprised. Spinning around, he called out some expletive that was masked by his breathless amazement. "Surprised to see us?" Phillips asked. Seeing who was in his office, Howard seemed to relax.

"Oh, Phillips. Sorry, you rather startled me there!" He said, his chest heaving. His voice was barely audible, for his ribs were still healing from his tete-a-tete with Gary. Phillips did not care for this detail; instead, his eyes fell upon the very thing he had wanted to see from the beginning; Howard had, unconsciously or not, put both of his arms behind him; perhaps his hands were clenched together, but Phillips suspected that stance was intentional.

"I can tell. You weren't expecting us?" Phillips said. Howard's smile dropped in a moment, replaced by a look of confusion that Phillips recognised immediately as somewhat disingenuous. Clarifying his point, he pointed at Howard's desk; amongst the clutter of papers, stationary and other school-type detritus, sat a pair of brown leather gloves atop Howard's mobile phone. Howard's eyes moved to them, and after a brief moment in which Phillips imagined Howard was thinking *oh, shit*, Howard looked back to him, then to Fiona, who had at last filed into the room. He chuckled, nervously.

"Oh yes, my gloves, thanks for reminding me." He began to move for the desk, but Phillips stopped him.

"Woah, woah, wait right there a minute." Howard complied surprisingly easily. "I do hope you've disinfected everything in here." Phillips continued, as Fiona started moving around the room; she picked up a few loose items and ran her fingers across school photographs. Howard visibly winced. "I mean, a germaphobe like you shouldn't be going about with gloves on if nothing's been disinfected. At least, that's what I'd do." He continued. Howard let out another laboured chuckle.

"That's why I'd like to put them back on. I simply removed them to handle my, erm, lunch. I store it in there during the day." He gestured to the cupboard with his head, still not using his hands.

"Oh yes, I can understand that. They must be expensive gloves, right? Genuine leather? Be a shame to spoil them with grease and crumbs." Phillips sarcastically remarked. "Don't you have a spare pair somewhere?"

"Erm, they were damaged a while ago. I had to get rid of them and haven't replaced them, look, Phillips, what can I help you with? I'm a very busy man." Howard protested with a frown.

"Show me your hands." Phillips said. Fiona, now, was close to the far-left side of the room and was still teasing Howard by touching everything she could lay her hands on. Howard glanced at her, then back at Phillips.

"Sorry? What is this?" He asked, somewhat unconvincingly.

"Show me your hands."

"Some nice trophies here, Howard." Fiona said, handling the shiniest cup she had ever set eyes on; her fingerprints smudged the pristine surface. Phillips could have sworn that Howard was beginning to sweat.

"Can she not do that?" He asked Phillips by way of asking him to make her stop.

"She can do what she likes. Besides, I daren't tell her to stop, she doesn't like me bossing her about, why don't you not think about it and show me your hands instead." Phillips continued, extending a friendly arm out towards him. Howard once again did nothing but look concerned.

"Look, Flora, Fiona? Please can you not do that?" He asked in a surprisingly friendly way.

"Get my name right, I might consider it." She said, putting the golden cup back on the shelf. She hoisted another into the air and peered at the shiny surface as it caught the sunlight in a dancing seam of light along one side.

"Look will you just *fuck-* put the damn trophy down?" He asked, his confused tone being replaced with a more aggressive one.

"Do you not like being in control, Howard? Of not being able to tell us what to do?" Phillips muttered, drawing nearer.

"Eh?" Howard retorted.

"Show him your hands."

"Show me your hands."

"I don't want to show you my hands, what's the point? I've got nothing to hide."

"Apart from your hands."

"Show him your hands.

"Show me your hands."

"No, I won't show you my hands, and put the *fucking thing down*! He yelled, diving towards her. She was ready in an instant, for she threw the trophy to the ground; the cup cracked, and three long, thick curves split from it, bounced into the air, then back down. Howard, his arms outstretched, made to strangle her, or so it would appear; his fingers arched from white knuckles and she bounced out of his way. He clattered into the shelf, nearly sending the trophies held there tumbling after the first. Fiona stood erect, gripping Howard's right wrist and kicking him in the popliteal fossa; his leg buckled, and he was brought to his knees, with an agonised sound and an equally pained expression. She held his hand by the wrist up to the light that streamed through the window; peering at his palm, into which his fingers were trying to curl to hide the injury she espied; his palm was a mass of knotted and knurled skin which was still healing in places; great rises and pits, as though his palm had been torn and ripped with some force.

"That's quite the injury you've got here, Howard. How did you get it? Sporting injury?" She asked. Phillips stepped forward into the silence Howard insisted on continuing.

"Or maybe you've been building a rockery?" Phillips eyed the open cupboard door about which Howard had been busying.

He marched over to it, and amidst protests from Howard, he examined the contents carefully. Sure enough, within, there was a plastic container containing a half-eaten lunch, and beside it, an old, circular tin which rattled with the sound of coins. However, it felt dense; not heavy by itself, but as though something else was within. So, Phillips stood erect with the thing in his hands, then prized off the lid; it was badly rusted, but nonetheless easy to open. He threw the lid down, then peered inside. Sure enough, a collection of old and foreign coins, and at one 'side', a black slab of glass with a white rear; the screen as cracked in places, but Phillips recognised it immediately.

Phillips' heart lightened gloriously at the sight; his hunch was correct;

"Bingo." He muttered.

"Really?" Fiona replied. "I thought we were above clichés?"

"Strange that you'd need *two phones*, Howard?" He said, gesturing to the phone on the desk with the tin; as he did, he watched as Howard grimaced under another painful pinch from Fiona. Then, he was momentarily distracted by the sound of the door opening behind him.

"Sorry, what's going on here?" Said the man as he surveyed the scene. The receptionist was behind him, peering in through the open door; this must be Mr Hendricks.

As his voice sounded, suddenly all eyes were upon him; Fiona turned, Phillips turned, and in the moment in which her eyes were drawn away, Howard seized his opportunity. With his free arm, he aimed his elbow at her thigh, then thrust back with it, cracking her leg with the sharp point. Fiona let out a cry of pain, in which time Howard wrenched his arm free, then dove for the sliver of trophy that had split from the cup. He swung around on his knees, punched her in the waist with his right hand, and with his left, plunged the shard hard into the other side of her; blood sprayed onto Howard's face as she staggered backwards, almost crashing into his desk. Her scream was almost silent, but her face became one of a panic, not pain.

Phillips cried out and rushed to her. She slowly lowered herself onto the desk to prevent blood from flowing down from the wound; Phillips was upon her in a moment, and in his negligence, did nothing to prevent Howard from scrabbling to his feet, then barging past Mr Hendricks and the receptionist, whose face was one of horror. Mr Hendricks did not know what to think of the episode; he merely stood in stunned silence and made no effort to prevent his superior from fleeing.

Phillips pressed his hand onto Fiona's wound, but a yelp from her, and a pain in his hand, signalled that the penetrating metal was still present. That was good news; it would stem the flow of blood, and somewhat maintain pressure. Removing it could make things worse. Fiona knew this in an instant, and she panted a few words with the only strength she was able to muster.

"Phillips, don't worry about me." She rested a hand on his cheek, smearing him with a bloody handprint. He steadied himself, and in that moment of relative calm, she spoke again; "Go get the son of a bitch." She smiled a resilient grin, which he mirrored. Then, a hand on his shoulder. It was Mr Hendricks; Phillips turned and looked at the man in his round face.

"We'll take care of her. He went right, towards the car park." Mr Hendricks said. Phillips nodded, as did Mr Hendricks. Phillips then eyed Fiona for a moment, then finally turned and bolted for the door; he tore past the receptionist, who by now had managed to locate a first aid kit. A number of inquisitive students were now huddled around the door, clearly fully disinterested in their studies. Nonetheless, they parted to allow the officer through. He slammed against the opposite wall, and an audible gasp filled the air.

Unperturbed, he regained his footing, bolted through the crowded corridor, then around the corner. His eyes scanned over the heads of the students, many of whom were looking in the same direction; in the distance, he espied a teacher helping up a student from the ground. Incoherent mutters of 'did you see him?' and 'he just shoved her over!' met his ears; it did not take him long to piece together what had happened.

"Out of the way, move!" He called, battling his way through the crowd. He pushed on, thrusting students aside and sliding between those who actually listened and got out of his way. "Which way did he go?" He called as he met a crossroads; right would have taken him back outside, going left appeared to lead to another exit further down the corridor. A student pointed left. Trusting them, he bolted in that direction, which was mercifully clearer than the bustling hub of the reception area.

He darted along the corridor, occasionally brushing against the wall of lockers to his left to avoid crashing headlong into an errant student here and there. He sidestepped to the right-hand side of the corridor, then forced open the door to the outside world. He vaulted over a railing that ran alongside a ramp from the tarmac to door level.

As he landed, he peered through the space, which he found was filled with cars; red ones, blue ones, white ones that needed cleaning – as helpfully pointed out by pranksters writing in the filth – and black ones. Here and there were staff and older students moving between the cars, with occasional backward glances of bewilderment to a certain vehicle. Phillips did not need a telescope to look at the driver of the black hatchback; Howard was sat in the driver's seat, apparently desperately fighting with the ignition key, which buzzed as the engine struggled to start. Phillips seized his opportunity;

"Get out of the car *now*!" He cried; the stragglers immediately scattered, darting clear of the sea of vehicles the fastest way they could. Howard continued to wrestle with the key, but sensing fate was against him, he gave up. In an instant, he had forced the door open, then dove clear of it. Rather than stand up immediately, he used his wits; he remained ducked, so that Phillips could not see him. "Shit." Phillips said under his breath. He entered the labyrinth with a low stance and headed straight for Howard's vehicle. He sidestepped to a different aisle here and there, brushing against the bodywork; his jacket rustled, jeopardising his secrecy so for a moment he paused and abandoned it. He did not care if he left it completely, somebody else cou-

Crack!

A foot slammed across his face; his jaw cracked. He fell backwards, dazed; for a moment, all he could see was white. His other senses spoke to him; he smelled blood, then heard footsteps retreating away from him. Whether or not the blood was his own was inconsequential, it could well have been Fiona's, but he doubted that.

His vision returned a moment later, and though his brain was rattling, he tried to get to his feet; he closed his eyes, shook his head, then opened them again, just in time to see Howard darting left at the end of the row of cars. *Dammit*, Phillips thought, *I'm not sure he's got cracked ribs after all*. He struggled to his feet, then followed the path Howard had taken.

He rounded a corner at the end of the car park, then found himself running down a narrow strip of tarmac around the side of the main building; ahead of him, he espied Howard going at full tilt; beyond, the main yard, about which the greatest concentration of students were congregated. To the left, he saw the main gate, which was still being closely monitored by the officers he had the foresight to have stationed there earlier. His heart gave a bound at the sight of them, and he called out as loud as he could.

"Stop him, get on him!" Phillips yelled, his voice barely audible over the rabble of the schoolkids in the yard. A dozen or so eyes followed the sound, including those of the officers; by now, those on the interior side of the gate had gone to the other side, so their advance was delayed by their efforts to traverse it. But it did not matter; Howard was cornered; he saw the officers at the gate, stopped dead, then turned the other way, back towards the school entrance. That too was blocked, so Howard carried on straight ahead, hoping to lose Phillips on stamina alone. "Out of the way, *out of the way*!" Phillips called out, trying to avoid shoving students aside if he could.

His efforts were halted ever and again by stubborn students who either could not get out of the way or simply did not do so in time. "Oh, for the love of..." he began, unholstering his pistol; the cold metal of the grip scalded his fingers as they wrapped around it as tight as he ever could; should he drop it, it would be a disaster. He aimed the barrel into the air, then squeezed the trigger; a deafening bang rang out that could be heard, doubtless, all across the school. Phillips was used to the sound, but the students, less accustomed to such action and adventure, all immediately threw themselves to the ground; screams, thuds, the sounds of bodies crashing into one another.

Anybody close to a door or a way out of the yard went that way; about two dozen students vaulted the gate, forcing the officers there backwards and impeding their advance on the escaping villain. Phillips' way, however, was clear, and he darted forward, his ever-present carefulness ensuring he did not tread on anyone beneath his feet.

"Don't come any closer!" Howard cried; at last, Phillips could see him properly. He had turned around and was now facing the officer. Phillips raised his gun-wielding hand but froze in an instant; he espied, before Howard, a male student, a sixth-former so far as he could discern. He was being held close to him by his vice-like grip clutching an arm in a lock hold; Howard's other free hand gripped another of the shards of trophy; he must have picked it up in his escape for just such an eventuality. He held it level with the student's neck, pressing the sharp point into his skin, though not quite forcefully enough to split it. Phillips pointed the pistol directly at the headmaster, who by now had no hope of declaring himself innocent.

"Drop it, Howard. The game's up!" Phillips yelled,

maintaining the distance he had established. By now, it did not matter that nobody had secured an arrest warrant against Howard; it was an oversight Phillips had been trying to think his way out of up until then.

"I said don't come any closer! I'll do him!" He yelled back, twisting the student's arm further, such that he cried out in pain. All about them, the sea of fallen school kids sobbed and exclaimed ever and again in horror, waiting for something terrible to happen. Phillips trained his aim on Howard, whose face was just visible beside the boy's head. *Dammit, stop moving!*

"Howard, don't make this worse than it already is! Let the kid go and come quietly!"

"Do you think I'm stupid? Drop the gun, or the kid gets it!" Howard pressed the shard harder against the skin of the student's neck, until a burst of crimson blood ejected from the rapidly slicing skin. The boy yelled and writhed to break free, but that only served to exacerbate his injury.

"Okay, okay!" Phillips said, sensing that he could not get a shot that would not kill both of the men. He raised his hands, surrendered his gun by placing it in a clearing on the ground and standing back up. "Okay, no weapons. Now let the kid go!" He continued, stepping over his firearm – casting a warning glance to the students on the floor there that they immediately recognised as *do not pick that thing up*. Howard chuckled.

"And if I don't?"

"It's over, Howard. We've got you, time to come quietly."

"You haven't got shit! If I can make you disarm yourself, what else can I make you do, I wonder?" Howard chuckled.

Then, out of the corner of his eye, Phillips espied a rapidly moving shape; darting between the students on the ground, he recognised Fiona, moving with such a speed as he could not have foreseen for somebody so recently injured. She jumped the final couple of yards between herself and her folly. Phillips grinned proudly, but Howard turned at the last moment and spotted her. He growled as she tackled him, launching the student forwards. In an instant, she and Howard were practically airborne; Phillips watched, almost in slow motion, as both of them fell to the floor, Howard plunging the metal deep into her back, sides, or anywhere he could land a blow. Her screams were not of pain, however, but of determination and grit, such that Phillips wondered if she was even feeling any of the stabs. In one motion, he spun, around, ducked, gripped his firearm with light fingers and swung back to face forward again, aiming it in the general direction of the fight; his eyes struck the pair right at the moment Howard struck the ground, the back of his head slamming into the; a grunt and he was silenced; Fiona's body flopped atop him, practically lifeless.

"Get on them, get on them!" Phillips called, gesturing to his cohorts, who by now were able to make their way unimpeded into the yard. For all the time he spent approaching the scene, his pistol was trained steadily on Howard, who by now he could see was still breathing – either fortunately or unfortunately. Moments later, he was upon them; "Fiona, can you hear me?" He asked, gingerly; she too was breathing, her back rising and falling in steady rhythm; but her exhalations were ragged and rough, as though her throat had been lined with sandpaper, and as he watched, a steadily expanding pool of blood extended towards him. He called out for an ambulance, but his outcries were silenced and lost against the backdrop of a hundred students rising at once to their feet and fleeing as quickly as they could.

-41-
The Victim

The afternoon air was alive with the music of birdsong; a light breeze kept the kaleidoscopic shimmer of plant life that flanked a ribbon of road and pavement in continuous, lackadaisical motion.

Another vestige of civilisation that the otherwise undisturbed countryside had allowed to reside in it was a busy secondary school; a typical place, with black fences around the otherwise miniature perimeter to keep the unwanted strays of civilisation from getting inside, and indeed to keep the renegade amongst the students within its confines. But now home time was here and the gates of the school had been swung open, and a great outpouring of students was on the way home.

One student, particularly fond of that wandering home at that time of the evening, was on her merry way with her body of friends, each savouring the afternoon air in their own, subtle way; though one thing they could all agree on, the four of them, was that this was the perfect time to wind down after a difficult day of student life.

Willow never once considered that she would ever become someone different to who she was at that present moment; two years had passed since Stacey had died, and she had begun to move on. She was able to enjoy life, her outlook forever changed by the idea that life could be cut short in an instant. She laughed, more so than she had been able to until recently, as one of her friends made an off-handed joke that meant nothing in the grand scheme of her existence, but that was amusing to how she felt in that current moment; in an hour or so, she may feel different; maybe, she thought, she would not have laughed at that joke had it been made sometime later.

Nonetheless, Willow, and her clique of friends, were carefree and in full enjoyment of that fact that one life was ending and their evening selves were emerging; soon they would be free of their school wear, their formal shells, and into more casual attire, in reflection of their less systematised inclinations. No doubt their parents would be waiting at home, a plate full of food ready for them to demolish, and then they would be away, onto activities unknown; certainly, the young ladies would not tell their parents what they were up to; some degree of independence was all they craved, and any less than that was regarded as a vicious invasion of their personal privacy.

It is no accident that their peaceful regard for their evening was shattered by the unwelcome arrival of a somewhat irksome distraction; a rough type they had encountered before, Willow certainly recognised him; he was sat with his legs hanging casually into the cool air, he regarded the group with the sort of assured calculatedness that one scarcely finds amongst even the most confident of males; and certainly, Harry was one of those teenagers who was most confident in his exuberance; he knew that Willow thought so; she had been fooled by it before. But now she knew better; and despite his confidence and his physical presence upon the very precipice of her own home, she did her very best to ignore him, but he was to have none of it.

"Where are you going?" He called out to her as she split off from her group to go into her home; she made some vague effort to ignore him despite his hurried voice; he repeated the question, somewhat more urgently this time, but once again she failed to initiate a conversation; the remainder of her friends continued onwards in an effort to vacate the situation; however, they were so friendly, or perhaps so nosey, that they paused behind the tall hedge that separated Willow's garden and the neighbouring one in order to see where their prospective conversation went.

By now, Willow had gotten to the end of her path; if she could just ignore Harry for another few moments, she thought, she would be free of him for another day; she was fully aware that her entourage were regarding her from the safe and passive distance of the next garden along, but she was not concerned; she would do as she had done almost every night for the last month; simply pretend Harry did not exist until the lie became true.

"Yo, Willow!" he called to her, his voice lower. "Where are you going? It's not like you to ignore me!" He continued, somewhat more exaggerated now; she was aware that he was trying to draw attention to the situation. 'Just open the door, then you'll be rid of him' she considered, before realising that her front door was locked. "Oi, Willow!" Harry continued again, swiping his muddy blonde hair from his forehead. "Do you only get with lasses because you ignore blokes?" He called with a chortle; it was a surprisingly articulate sentence for him.

After struggling with the door for a few moments and

realising that she had not brought her front door key, Willow realised an inconvenient truth; whilst she couldn't get in the house, she was not able to deflect his advances convincingly; she would have to get rid of him.

At a distance, Harry's own group of comrades engaged in a childish throng of chuckling at his words. Though he thought to himself that Willow was not one to retaliate, he would soon realise that he was wrong about that. Nonetheless, he watched with glee as she swung about and approached, marching with confident strides up her garden path. He hopped from his pedestal upon the wall and approached her with a rictus grin. Her face gave no evident sign of emotion as she drew up near him; she regarded him with an intelligence, as though some calculating thoughts were marching about her mind, waiting for a way to be expressed by her lips. Eventually, she did not even think about her words; they just emerged as perhaps a reflection of her innermost thoughts; she was a talking Freudian slip.

"Harry, when are you going to realise that even if you were the last man on earth, I still wouldn't be getting with you. In fact, if you're the best example of male-kind, consider me disappointed." She hissed, drawing him near so he could hear every syllable with only a modicum of doubt as to what she had said. He began to scramble for a reply. She interrupted him before he could say a word; "Oh, and just pray I never meet your next future ex. I'll tell her exactly what you're like with women. It'll save her the bruises." She said, and with as much of a warning, she strode back up the way she had come, back towards the school; Harry merely followed her with his gaze as she walked, something of a brooding annoyance brewing in his subconscious; he simply hoped that it did not bubble onto the surface and prove her last statement right.

He peered as she reached the edge of the garden and took a sharp left down the side of her neighbouring house. Harry knew that the pathway led to an alleyway at the back of the little street; he knew that her back garden was one of many that backed onto the little, overgrown stretch of path.

By the time she was out of sight, concealed behind the magnificent bushes her father was so very proud of maintaining, the crowd had dispersed. As he realised this, Harry reasoned that she would be in her kitchen which overlooked such a spectacular dreamscape over the hills beyond; brilliant colours danced in the orange haze of the evening. But Harry could not abandon his pursuit of her now; his friends would find him cowardly, a defeatist who gave up at the very sight of menace; so he decided to wait a while.

Ever and again, as he watched the house, a light would go on; sometimes in the bathroom, sometimes the kitchen. But never did a room remain illuminated for more than a few moments, as though a regular inspection was being carried out. He was transfixed by the regularity of the illumination.

After a moment or two more, the streetlamps began to light, too; suddenly, Harry was bathed in the orange glow of the artificial light. He watched as the one opposite him lit; then the next one, and the one after that. *Wait, who is that?* A figure became illuminated in one of the nearer columns of streetlamp light; ghastly shadows cascaded down what he recognised as the face of the figure, such that they masked his appearance. Harry moved forward, out of the light of the lamp that hung above him in an effort not to be recognised, but it was too late; the figure had seen him.

"Go home, Harry." The figure said, menacingly; Harry started backwards. The voice was familiar to him.

"H-Howard? Mr Wor-"

The figure raised a finger briskly to its face; a silent shush bridged the gap between them, and Harry fell as silent as the exchange had become. After a moment, in which an eternity seemed to pass, the finger lowered, then was joined by its three comrades, who all pointed to the ground; they flicked backwards and forwards a few times; a reverse beckon.

Somewhat reluctantly, but nonetheless driven to do so, Harry started backwards, then turned and walked away. He imagined that the instant his eyes left the figure, it would be upon him, but nobody came; he was as alone as Willow was. But what amazed him most was how he found the entire situation so strange yet so forgettable, until not half an hour later, he wondered why he was power walking away at all.

-42-
Open Wounds

Blackness. That was all he could see; a penetrating darkness that seemed to press on him from all angles. He felt that his eyes would be squashed, burst, by it, such that the last thing he would feel was the dribbling, slithering feeling of their juices trickling like tears down his face.

He forced them open.

White. That was all he could see; a searing brightness that burned his retinas, and he raised his arms to bring his hands to his eyes, as if to pop them out himself. One hand came easily; his fingers prodded and rubbed at his face. He was not sure why that soothed him, but it did. Now, if only he could get to the other eye. What was wrong with his right hand? It had not gone dead, he could feel it well enough; stuck.

He wrestled his wrist about for a moment, wiggling it violently here and there; ever and again, he could feel a tight metallic grip that slipped over the radius and ulna of his wrist, and it pained him such that he had to stop. He sighed, then grunted and tried to sit up; now he became aware that he was lying down in loose clothing; gone was his suit jacket, trousers, tie and shirt. His legs were naked, and there was a loose gown draped about him. Beneath him, a soft bed, constructed, he thought, out of feathers, or clouds. It was a comfort he did not expect; was that why his slumber was so deep?

As he blinked, light spilled once more into his eyes. As they learned to be used to the searing bright, details emerged from it. He saw a window to his right; thin, metal venetian blinds filtered the light that streamed in from the countryside beyond. He peered closer to him and saw that he was handcuffed to the minimal metal frame of a bed, and all about him, he espied equipment he did not understand; medical, he assumed.

He was right.

At the foot of his bed, he espied a nurse scribbling something on a clipboard. She was young; maybe in her mid-twenties, with silver-white hair that came halfway to her shoulders. Her face was one of focus and concentration; he looked her up and down, then sat up further. As he watched, his head began to pulse, almost physically in and out; with every inch his head moved upward, the feeling became worse, and he instinctively raised his free hand to his forehead. What his hand fell upon was a soft surface, one which he could move independently of his skull. He was sure he had hair before, had he been shaved? He tugged at the surface for a moment before determining that he had been bandaged; his injury was causing a headache he wished would just finish him then and there.

The nurse saw that he was awake. She watched him moving, almost worm-like, in the bed, then lowered the clipboard expertly into the slot at the foot of the bed. With that, she turned and moved off to his left, towards a door he was just now noticing.

"Hey! What's goin' on, where am I?" He slurred before she had chance to leave the room. She either did not hear him or pretended not to, as she continued towards the exit. Hey! I'm talking to... come back here!" But by then, she was out. He was alone again, only this time he was fully awake to his solitude. The five other beds, two beside him, and three mirrored on the opposite side of the room, were unoccupied. They may not have been before his arrival, but they certainly had been vacated now.

Where was he before he was brought here? *Why* had he been brought here?

Then, he remembered.

He recalled that he was Howard Worth, that he had fled the police. Why was he fleeing the police again? *Oh yeah, I remember... shit*.

Suddenly, the door flew open; this time, a nurse was not responsible. Five burly men entered the room, each dressed from head to toe in police gear; high visibility strips caught the light; they were somewhat superfluous, Howard thought. One officer was portly, bald, but had a bushy black beard. Another was younger and clearly an investor of sorts in gym equipment. Nonetheless, he did not recognise any of these policemen; no doubt he had encountered during in one of their many visits, but they were not recognisable individuals. He thought they were the kind of people action figures were modelled after; individual in their own way, but they resembled such clichés that they did not look real at all.

Ah, now, I recognise you he thought as Phillips strode into the room; he was silent, un-flinching and he did not look at Howard at all in all the time he was in motion; he seemed more interested in ensuring the camera tripod he was holding did not catch on the floor.

This was to be a videoed session.

The tripod was set up at the foot of the bed, the camera lens pointed straight at Howard's face. He smiled and waved with his free hand whilst one of the burlier policemen busied himself with its operation. "Make sure to get me in critical focus, won't you?" Howard chuckled. The policeman gave a sideways glance at him, then looked back at the buttons and knobs he was adjusting.

Phillips dragged a nearby chair over to the bed and slammed the raised front legs onto the floor; the resounding thud overcame Howard, who jumped slightly.

"The fearless Howard. I expect nobody ever calls you that?" Phillips said, sitting down in the chair. He adjusted his posture, but the back was too low to support him.

"Keep trying, it might catch on." Howard replied, groaning as he sat up properly too.

"I don't think I'll bother." Phillips muttered. "How's the head?"

"Probably broken enough for me to sue you."

"Sure, I'll put you in touch with our legal team, just as soon as you pay Fiona's for all the damage you did to her."

"Ah, the blushing Fiona. How is she?" Howard, gunning for a reaction.

"By the time we got her to the hospital, she'd lost thirty seven percent of her blood volume. If she's doing anything, it isn't blushing." Phillips said, a vein on his temple pulsating. Howard chuckled. "That thing on?" Phillips said, turning to the cameraman.

"Almost got it. I just need a minute."

"You can't have it. Is it rolling?" Phillips, flustered. The policeman sighed, then prodded the red 'REC' button; it clicked loudly, a red tally light began blinking then became solid as information started to be written. Beside him, another policeman, who was clutching a small audio recorder, gestured with a thumbs-up to indicate that a separate audio recording was being made. Phillips cleared his throat. "For the record, I'm DCI Anthony Phillips of the Heathestone CID, interview subject is Howard Worth, in regard to case 24062019/019. Interview beginning at three twenty-five on the tenth of July 2019." Phillips said, taking a handful of sheets from another policeman.

"Do I get a lawyer?" Howard asked, shrugging. Phillips looked up; he knew he had a right to one.

"Do you want one?" He said, knowing that if he said 'yes', it would only be a delay, not an issue. Howard smiled; he sensed that he was not fazing Phillips.

"No. I can handle this." He said. Phillips sighed too.

"Okay, for the record, the subject has decided to conduct this interview without the presence of a lawyer. So, Howard. Let's start from the beginning. You really are a germophobe, aren't you? It nicely explains why we've never had your fingerprints on file, until now. They match unidentified prints in a cold case from before I worked at the CID." Howard's smile disappeared. "You murdered Stacey Galloway, didn't you?" Phillips quizzed. Howard slipped back down the bed, until he was virtually lying down.

"Phillips, this is going to be really painful for me, listening to your witticisms and your roundabout ways, so do you mind if I take over?" He said, with a hefty sigh. Phillips shrugged.

"Be my guest." He replied, gesturing flamboyantly with his arm. In an instant, Howard was sitting up straight again.

"Great. Let me start, as you say, from the beginning. Three years ago, I got a job at that school. I enjoyed it at first, being looked up to, respected. That first year as deputy head was a great period of my career. But then, the cracks began to show. When my old man kicked the bucket and left me nothing in his will but a smelly pair of shitty gloves, well. That was me. A reminder that I was little more than a failure with nothing to show for it. So I started to put on weight. I started going bald, luckily that stopped. But the students started to notice, started saying things I didn't appreciate. It was like I was back in the schoolyard, a source of ridicule.

Then, one day, I had enough. I discovered the ringleader, that Galloway girl. She'd been stirring the pot, corralling her peers to gang up on me, rip me apart on this stupid social media thing."

"So you killed Stacey because she was mean to you?" Phillips asked, disbelieving him; it was scarcely an excuse for murder, he thought.

"I killed her because she was awful. Kids like that, they don't listen, they don't respond to change, they just let this awfulness grow inside them until they're nothing but awful in a human-shaped shell."

"She was a teenager who was taking the mick out of their deputy head, everyone does that. Hell, I did it when I was younger."

"No, Phillips, you're missing my point. I was the *deputy* head. Not the headmaster, that was Sebastian. The students loved him; he could do no wrong. Which is unusual because kids usually hate the headteacher. So, they weren't attacking me because I had power, they were attacking me because I had let myself go. Badly. This was a personal attack."

"That's still no reason to murder a teenage girl."

"Why do I need a reason? Not everything is like you see on the TV, not everything is so complicated."

"What do you mean?"

"I killed Stacey Galloway. You can put that one to rest now. I guess, though, you're right. When they found fingerprints on that girls' body, it made me realise just how close I had been to being found out; I would have been dead in the water. If you'll pardon the pun."

Phillips did not look amused.

"Go on." He said, wanting to move on from that point as soon as possible. What astounded him most was the swiftness with which Howard had glossed over the affair, as though it was routine.

"It got to me, being that close to being found out. So, I adopted the gloves, paranoid that I would leave some signature on anything. Then, when you lot homed in on Sebastian, it made my day. Not only did you guys frame him, but it got him out of the way and I got a cushy promotion. Now *I* was in the position of power.

The only problem with power, is that you have to listen to people. I didn't really know Willow until long into my tenure. She came to me distraught one morning, much earlier than school hours. It seems she'd run away from her parents because they had been fighting again. It only occurred to me as she was describing them that I realised who her parents were."

"You didn't know who Willow's parents were?"

"Fuck no! They look nothing alike. I didn't put two and two together until she told me their names. It was only then that I realised I'd been sleeping with her mother for years."

"How many years?"

"Well, I moved to Heathestone in about 2003, so it will have been around then." Phillips paused and did a mental calculation. When he realised, his heart sank.

"The year Willow was born?" Phillips asked. Howard nodded. Phillips scoffed. He knew from interviews that Gary had been with her since at least 2002, which begged the question; "So, you could be...?" He asked.

"I haven't got a clue. But she looks nothing like either of them, so I'd hazard a guess and say *yes*." That would not be a welcome detail at trial. "So, anyway, Willow was concerned. She had seen what a marital breakdown had done to Harry's family. She didn't like it. Of course, I couldn't admit that she could be my bastard love child. That would have crucified her."

Phillips realised; it was something he had missed, something that seemed so painfully obvious to him now, that he was kicking himself for not thinking of it sooner.

"The paternity test."

"What? She was getting a paternity test?" Howard snapped; he stared at Phillips with eyes that were almost completely buried beneath furrowed brows. He sensed from Phillips' silence that he was closer than he thought to being found out. "Well, she's smarter than I thought. Anyhow, over time, I watched the family. I saw them slowly destroy each other over the whole thing because like Stacey, they were awful too."

"But that was your fault? Would they have destroyed each other if you had never got involved?"

"Phillips, you have to remember, Sarah came to *me*. I was young, and handsome and irresistible." He said, sarcastically and flicking his non-existent hair. Phillips scoffed at that. "I was the new guy, and she wanted a bit of rough, so I gave it to her."

"So why *did* you kill Willow?"

"You're a DCI, Phillips, you have people working under you, inferiors? You know what it's like to have power?"

"Not really. In fact, we're a very collaborative group."

"Ah. That's the difference between you and me. You rule softly, I go with the *iron fist* approach. As you can gather, I wasn't very popular with the school kids, so I didn't like collaboration that much. My experience left me cynical and resentful. It's a hateful thing, trust me."

"Go on then, Mr No-Motive. Why did you kill her?" Phillips leaned in, hoping that he would eventually answer the question.

"I killed her because she was getting wise to me. She was closing in. She had slowly started to warm to me, I became a good friend of hers. I treated her well, and she treated me well. We became close. We had, almost a father and daughter bond going, I suppose, because that's we were. But she's clever; she knew something, she started to see the similarities. Eventually she began asking questions; *why do I not like my parents? Why do I not look like them? Why do my parents not love each other?* I knew eventually she would discover the truth."

"The truth that she was actually your daughter, or that you were the reason their marriage was falling apart?"

"A little of both" Howard said, snidely.

"It still doesn't seem like the kind of thing to murder her

over."

"It isn't, I guess. But there again, I think that's where our differences lie." Before Phillips could reply, Howard continued. "It's people like you, Phillips; people who sit on a throne of power, authority, that really scares the people. You see, everyone is capable of murder. All it takes is a little strength and fingers around someone's throat. That's it, right? Even you must concede that?"

Phillips shrugged to assert his belief in the affirmative; it was an invisible gesture that the camera would not pick up. "So, what stops people? Morality? Some misguided belief that you're better than those people who hide in the shadows. No. It's simpler than that; it's guilt."

"How so?" Phillips leaned in.

"Take someone you really hate; someone you absolutely hate more than anything in the world, who you want nothing more than to strangle them to death. Where's your morality then? Your irrational brain kicks in." He tapped the side of his head with his free hand. "All that stops you from killing that person is this idea of guilt. It's a great defence mechanism; if you never had to face a consequence for your actions, you'd never stop. Take this, for example; if you killed me, here, in this bed. Suffocated me with a pillow, not as a policeman, but as a person, you'd go to prison. But if there were no prisons, police, no justice system or stigma, no consequences whatsoever, nothing could stop you."

"That's why we have all of those things; it's people like you that mean we have to control everyone else." Phillips interjected, worried that Howard's monologue would continue; frankly, he found his words dreary.

"After Stacey, I learned to lose the feeling of guilt; I knew the tricks, I wore gloves to hide my fingerprints. You know, we're all born with fingerprints, like a biological calling card. They're used against us whether we like it or not."

"So you decided not to leave *any*."

"Correct. Crime isn't all forensics and evidence. Sometimes you have to get into the head of your enemy. You have to think like them. It can destroy you, or it can make you see. Either way, the old you does not remain."

"It's good. It's very good. You sound like a smart guy, Howard."

"I try."

"So I want you to walk me through what happened on the night Willow was killed. We have evidence, but it's… patchy."

"Of course it is, I'm just that good." Howard chuckled; Phillips did not. "She came to me that day, not a lot seemed to be wrong; she was her usual confident self, but I knew she'd been upset. She told me that her parents were fighting every day, and that she suspected her mum was having an affair. Turns out she'd found Sarah's phone, there were some texts from an unknown number."

"Yours?"

"Exactly."

"What did you recommend?"

"I told her not to think too much about it. I told her it was probably spam, or something like that. But she's clever, I never gave her credit for that. She told me she was going to wait until her phone was free, write down the number, then do a search for it."

"Then she would have found out it was you." Phillips interrupted, nodding.

"She could never know. I was her confidante; I was the one she came to in need. You don't let that go, Phillips; you do *not* let that go. But at the same time, I knew that whilst she was alive, I was never going to be able to keep the secret." Howard sighed.

"So did you do it that night?"

"I had to! As far as I knew, she was going to find out that night so I had to get to her first. So, I waited until she'd gone home, because I couldn't do it in my office. You'd have caught me immediately."

"I didn't think you felt guilty?"

"I don't. But if I can get away with it, I will."

"So, you go to her house. Harry was there, he insists he never saw you, but I think he did." Phillips said, pulling out Harry's statement and regarding it; "*SP Grisham; Did you see something, Harry? Harry Baines; I didn't see anything. I didn't see anyone or anything, nothing happened after that. DCI Phillips; Anyone would think you're defending someone, Harry, is that right? Harry Baines; No.*" Was he threatened by you? Was he defending you?"

"Let me tell you this. Harry is the kind of kid who fears men. His father left years ago, and he's resentful; that's why he targets women. I'm not blind to it, I saw it happening." Howard explained, sharply.

"You mean men like you?" Phillips interrupted. Howard paused; a silence for a moment, that was soon filled by Phillips' words. "Seems father figures are a bit of a sore spot for you, and you said it yourself; your own father wasn't exactly a bright part of your history." Howard ignored him.

"So maybe Harry feared me that night." He continued after an extended pause. "Maybe this shadowy figure who was bigger and more imposing gave him a fright. He fled pretty sharpish."

"So now you're alone with Willow's house. How long since your interaction with Harry did you go to the house?"

"Almost immediately. I made sure I was alone. I'd seen Sarah and Gary go out; separately, then I went to the back door." Howard explained. "It was locked, but I soon saw to that." He continued, rubbing his right shoulder with his free hand. "I think she was upstairs, but she soon came down. She was shouting 'Dad, dad?', thinking it was Gary. But, I guess she was calling out for the right person." He continued, shrugging. "Anyway, I waited for her to come downstairs; I took a bulb from their lamp because I thought she might scream. A damn good thing I did; as soon as she was in the kitchen, I jumped out from behind the door and went for her."

"When did you make her eat the bulb?" Phillips asked.

"Did that bit make you squirm?" Phillips did not answer. "That went in as soon as she opened her mouth. It worked quite well, in that it shut her up. She stopped struggling after that. Shock, most probably. But she was still alive by then."

"So why did you then take her to the cliffs by the vicarage?" Phillips quizzed. Howard chuckled.

"I wanted it to be a little bit poetic, you know. As most good tales are, there was some thought that went into it. I thought her final resting place should be within a stone's throw of the church, so I buried her nearby." He said. Phillips furrowed his brow.

"You dragged her across the fields behind her house. Sniffer dogs led us from the Vicarage to her estate." Philips interjected. Howard smiled; his work was being recognised and he was pleased.

"So, we arrive at the cliffs and she comes to. That was a surprise; I thought the blood loss would have finished her off, but no such joy." Howard continued. *Joy.* Phillips began to suspect Howard was secretly revelling in the excruciating detail of his recollection.

"She's a fighter." Phillips said.

"That she is. She put up a helluva fight, I'll give her that. She's her father's daughter, alright." He said with a smirk. "It didn't take long for me to get the upper hand, though. That rock did most of the heavy lifting."

"It did betray you in the end." Phillips interrupted.

"Oh yeah, I should have just brought a hammer." He began, raising his palms to eye level – as best as he could being handcuffed to the bed – and pored over the knurled and knotted scarring the rock had carved into his skin. "Well, I didn't realise until after I'd thrown it away, but by then it was too late. It *did* do the trick, I suppose." He said.

"All you had to do was load her pockets with rocks and toss her over the edge. Make good your escape. No evidence; no forensics, or so you thought. You played everyone quite well, here; you knew eventually the Greene's would blame Harry and Sebastian." Phillips said, crossing his arms; a sense of finality came over him, and he relaxed.

"I just let them destroy each other and sat back. If someone else got to take the blame for it, no worries on my part."

"But you made sure we would investigate everyone else; we looked into your expenses whilst you've been out. Four days ago, you bought a tape recorder and a five-pack of tapes. You went to all that effort to making Sebastian confess. You exploited his illness to get you off the hook." He continued, leaning closer. Howard did nothing but chuckle, maniacally. "I'm glad you've found this so funny; I hope you're proud. Because you've destroyed this town. Two people are dead, you've ruined your own relationship, there's a detective inspector in critical condition, students are scarred, you've destroyed two families, I mean, how much damage have you done to the people of this town?" Phillips said, becoming more incensed as he realised that nothing in Heathestone would ever be the same.

"They were doing it to themselves, Phillips. I was just the catalyst."

"Howard, if all of what you have said is the truth, we'll need to perform pre-trial investigations to corroborate your claims. That will take time. If what you've said is not true, please tell us now. If this confession *is* true…"

"All of what I have said is the complete truth, the whole truth and nothing but the truth, I hereby confess to the murder of Willow Greene and Stacey Galloway." Howard interrupted and said eccentrically. Phillips stood up, pushing the chair back.

"Then Howard Worth, I hereby arrest you for the murder of Willow Greene. Also, for the murder of Stacey Galloway." Then he paused; Howard grinned. "Also, for the manslaughter of Sebastian and the assault of an officer of the law with the intent to cause bodily harm. You do not have to say anything, though it may harm your defence if you do not say anything that you later rely on in court. Anything you do say may be given in evidence." Howards smile became more subdued as more and *more* charges were thrown at him. "This interview is concluded at three forty-five." With that, the other policeman concluded the recording.

"So, is that it?" Howard asked as Phillips turned to leave. The other policemen continued through the empty room and exited, leaving the two men alone. "Will I get to see you before I'm put in the stocks at midday?" He quizzed. Phillips turned and faced him.

"You surprise me, Howard. As a headmaster, I'd have thought you were all for conformity and playing by the rules. Have you always been like this?" He asked.

"No." Came the blunt reply. "I've spent a lifetime playing by the rules. In school, through University, then all my training. If everyone played by the rules, great things can't happen; it isn't allowed. You have to break the rules every now and again, it's the only way to stay sane."

"Huh, you're sane, is that right?" Phillips said, scoffing.

"I'd have to be. Otherwise, that entire confession is no good, right? You should know that, Phillips." Howard retorted. Phillips' heart sank; was this just another attempt to destroy hopes further?

"So why are you confessing? You got away with Stacey's murder, why not try and deny this?" Asked an admittedly confused Phillips. Howard smiled again.

"Two reasons; first, I've hurt that family enough; they can do the rest themselves."

"The rest?"

"Gary and Sarah won't survive each other now. But I'm also doing this because I simply don't *care* anymore. I've got nothing left to lose. What would you do, nearing retirement, realising your life is nearly over?" Phillips' mouth trembled with frustration.

"I'll tell you what I wouldn't do."

"What's that?"

"I wouldn't take the life of a young girl just because mine was ending. Not everyone is as monstrous as you." Phillips hissed. He then fished a silver shape out of his pocket, then prodded what Howard recognised as a screen; it was a phone. After a moment of dextrous manipulation of the icons on the screen, prodding at numbers, he spun the phone around and threw it onto the bed.

"What's this?"

"If you don't care, then you can do the most unpleasant part of my job. You're going to tell the person at the other end of that phone what you've just told me and I'm not going to leave until you're done."

Confused, Howard picked up the phone; he did not recognise the number. He held the device up to his ear and listened for the fuzzy echo of a voice; none was forthcoming. Instead, the loud buzzes of a line still ringing met his ears.

Phillips was not surprised he did not recognise the number; it was not the recipient's normal phone; he had given it to her to communicate directly with him. Phillips sat down.

Howard recognised the voice when it finally came through the earpiece; hearing the voice, Howard's heart collapsed.

"Hello?" Sarah asked.

-43-
Bravery in the Field

The heart rate monitor beeped softly, steadily. That was a good sign; it meant Fiona was still alive. Grisham sat beside the hospital bed, peering at her face. He had never seen it like this; it had lost everything that had once made it alive; the colour, the fullness of her cheeks. His heart sank lower and lower at the sight of her, such that he decided eventually to avert his gaze. Her soft breathing, almost in perfect synchronicity with the heart rate monitor, ensured his worry over her condition was unfounded

The door behind him opened softly; he turned about in his seat, half-heartedly. He expected a medical professional, perhaps someone checking her notes. Instead, he found Phillips, closing the door behind him. Grisham sighed.

"Has he talked?" Grisham asked, despondently, his voice masked by his hand half-covering his mouth. Phillips raised his hands behind his neck and stretched.

"Oh yeah." He groaned with a cheerful tone. "He made a full confession. Monologued for quite a while, I didn't take all of it in." He continued, moving slowly into the room. "I'll send you the recording once it's offloaded." He said, sitting down beside Grisham. He furrowed his brow and rubbed his nose with a thumb.

"How was he?" Asked Grisham, sitting back in his chair.

"Surprisingly lucid for someone who's been unconscious for twenty-four hours. I'll have the psychiatrists take a look, make sure he's sound of mind. Otherwise it might not be valid." Phillips explained, sighing loudly at the final word. Grisham nodded.

"Good idea. This needs to be airtight." Grisham concurred, nodding. By then, he was simply pleased that they had a confession; all of the details could be confirmed later. He turned to Phillips, who he saw was leaning across the empty space between himself and the hospital bed. He surveyed Fiona with a silence that screamed louder than a shout; Grisham leaned over and rested a hand on his shoulder. "You've done a great job, Phillips. Both of you." He continued, darting his eyes from Fiona to him. "This hasn't been easy on any of us, none more so than you. I don't think any of us could have expected anything like this to happen, I think the entire department did a great job under the circumstances." He continued, removing his hand. Phillips scoffed.

"Is it really right that we get treated like heroes on the back of tragedy?" Phillips mused. Grisham chuckled in disbelief.

"Come on, Phillips; yes, it's a tragedy, but you know the game. You can't get attached, you have to be completely impartial and indifferent." Grisham defended.

"It's not that simple anymore, Grisham, it isn't black and white anymore. The people you're meant to treat as the victims are just as bad as the villains." Phillips snapped, his voice crisp in the small room. Grisham started back.

"Well, if it's any difference to you, I've been on the phone with my superiors. They've considered my proposal and given the situation they've decided if anyone deserves to be my replacement, it should be you." Grisham said, slowly so that Phillips could absorb his statement. He sighed.

"Well, that sure puts me in a tricky position." He chuckled. "I'm sorry, Grisham, I didn't mean to be so blunt. Thank you, I appreciate the offer. I think I need a bit of time to think about it." Phillips said, smiling and leaning across the space between the two men with his hand, offering it up for Grisham to shake. Grisham peered at it, as though he had been handed a handful of snails.

"It's no problem, Phillips." He said, standing up. Phillips clenched his open palm closed, then drew it back to himself. "For the record, I think it's good you care. Shows you've got a soul." Grisham by now was behind him, almost at the door.

"Oh please, you don't really believe in all that hocus pocus stuff?" Phillips said, laughing heartily.

"Not really. But it sounded cool." Grisham replied.

"Things aren't 'cool' anymore. Not at your age, anyway."

"Piss off, Phillips. I'll see you tomorrow." Grisham, laughing. He walked through the door, allowing it to close behind him. Phillips' smile slowly faded. *I'll see you tomorrow*. Things would always be the same; *everything has changed but nothing has changed*. After pondering for a moment, he quickly turned his attention back to his loyal subordinate.

"Come on, Fiona. You're not gonna let a little thing like death get in the way of your job." He chuckled, standing up and gripping her practically lifeless hand. He was careful to avoid the drip that interfaced with her via a needle; he wasn't sure what good it was doing, but removing it probably would not help matters. "We got him, Fiona. *You* got him." He said, correcting himself in an instant. "Let's hope he didn't get you." Then he sighed. "What do I do, Fiona? Grisham's giving me this job, but I don't know if I can do it. What would you have me do, you always were my voice of reason?" He hissed, sliding the chair towards him with a flick of his foot; he sat down, but remained precariously on the edge of the seat. "You were right; I do care too much. Probably to my detriment. You always had the more rational head; so whilst you're letting yourself knit back together, have a think for me, won't you?" He said, stroking her head. "Let me know what you think I should do. Do I go for it?"

He must have sat with her for several hours after that. In all that time, he maybe said three or four more words, no sentences; likely just disjointed ramblings, manifestations of the conversation he was having with himself; he did not even realise he was saying these things; *forget*, *fool*, *regret* and *humble*.

Whatever sense anyone could make from them was entirely made of their own volition; perhaps some interpretation could be made, but Phillips certainly did not intend to; perhaps he was subconsciously thinking of Sebastian, Harry, Howard and himself when he said each of those words.

By the time he left later that night, he had no recollection of his thoughts; they were but fleeting glimpses of his psyche, manifestations of an internal struggle only he could understand.

-44-
No Going Back

Sarah peered out of the window, clutching a large, bulbous glass. A clear, golden liquid stood, almost completely still inside, rippling ever and again with the force of her fingertips rubbing against the curved side of the glass. The sun was low in the sky, now, but it was late. She knew colder days were coming, though she doubted it would make a difference, to her mood. She lifted the glass to her lips and consumed a little of the liquid; the wine within danced on her tongue with an acidic hit that she was used to by now, then, as she closed her mouth, lowering the glass, a warmth on the roof of her mouth.

Over the Sancerre, she thought to herself, quietly. She thought, considered, rolled over in her mind her opinions. Somehow, Howard's confession made perfect sense; of course, she was involved in many of his machinations, probably a cause for many of them. She did not blame herself, or consider that she was in some way responsible for her daughter's death; she liked to think she was on the right side of good and evil; that put in the same position, she would not do the same.

Despite her involvement, she knew that Howard had ruined her. Gary too, for that matter; all would come out in the trial; she would be scorned, elbowed into insignificance by her peers. *Well screw them all. They can pretend they're better than me all they want.*

"Sarah?" Gary said, moving into the room. She did not reply; instead, her breath became deeper, more controlled in order to prevent the suddenly rising anger from spilling over. She put down her wine glass.

"What makes me think I want to talk to you?" She said, still staring out at the garden.

"Because we need to talk; we can't just keep pretending we don't know each other." He said, moving towards her; his tone of voice was one pleading with her to see reason, but she was having none of it;

"But we really *don't* know each other, do we? We never did." She snapped, spinning around; the belt of her undone dressing-gown flicked out and swung behind her, nearly swiping her glass of wine from the windowsill. She saw Gary's face, one of confusion and distress; it did nothing to satiate her annoyance. "How long have we been pretending?" She pointed out. He struggled to get his words out.

"But it was Howard, though; he's inveigled his way into our life and made us unhappy, it's not because we hate each other." He tried to protest, struggling to puzzle together a reasonable argument. He would just keep talking until she believed him.

"No, no, no, no, no." She said rapidly, such that each word was masked by the next. "We've always been fooling ourselves. We've tried to love each other before, and maybe there was something there at the beginning, but Gary, there just isn't anything between us anymore; nothing but hatred and lies and a despairing feeling that we're forever going to push one another apart." She approached him slowly and looked up at him as she drew nearer; "We were never going to have a happy ending together."

"But..." He began. She gripped his face with a hand.

"I don't blame you. All these years, I've been thinking it's you, because you never had the bond with Willow, and now I understand." Gary started backwards, gasping. "We've both known for a while now that Willow isn't yours."

"I never wanted to find out one way or the other, though." Gary interrupted, his eyes growing shiny with tears. "I maybe didn't have a bond, but she was still my daughter!" He protested in between sobs.

"No, she wasn't though; as soon as I sullied our relationship by going to Howard, I doomed all of us. Willow was never your daughter, no more than I've been your wife." She said, speaking loudly ever and again over the sound of his rapid inhalations; by now, his eyes were puffing and red, saturated like small sponges.

"No, no, it's *my* fault, I should never have given up on the pair of you so easily. I've done horrible, terrible things to you both." He sobbed, as she nodded her head. "You never deserved any of that, and I know it's gonna take work, but I want you to forgive me; I want you to realise that I never imagined I would hurt you. I want us to try again." He said, gripping her arms softly. She smiled, a hollow one that appeared more like a grimace.

"Do you want to know something? I have known..." she paused. "...true happiness with you. We've had some good times, and some bad times. I don't think we can pretend we're unique, I'm sure everyone has bad times." She said, her smile wavering.

"*For better and for worse.*" He said, a smile slowly coming not his own face. She laughed through her tears; he chuckled, too. She wrenched her arms from his grip and placed both of her palms on his chest.

"Exactly." She said, his heart giving a bound. "That's exactly why we can't be together." His smile faded and his heart sank.

"Wha-" He could not even finish the word. He shook his head, confused.

"I don't think we're ever going to have any more 'for better' days. If we stay together, we're just going to be living 'for worse'. We can't live like that, Gary. I'm sorry, we just can't." She removed her hands from his chest, then turned away and headed back for the window; she picked up the glass of wine. "We both have our medication, right?" She gestured by holding up the glass, her medicine within. "We can't go on like this, Gary. And we can't use Willow's death as an excuse to try." She said. Gary forced a soft groan out, one for which he could not find a source.

"So, there's no chance? You can't change your mind?" He asked, haltingly, slowly, painfully. She scoffed.

"Come on, Gary. We had to fight for one another a long time ago. We saw the signs, but we just carried on regardless. I'm afraid that by staying together, we're just going to keep hurting each other. Let's not destroy ourselves; let's just agree to quit whilst we can, yeah?" She said; Gary remained silent, motionless; he was still frozen with shock. "It's for the best." She concluded, reluctantly raising the glass in a 'cheers' that was somewhat facetious, but nonetheless a gesture of finality. Gary, unable to stand on legs that were as jelly, flopped into the chair behind him; he did so with such force, that it actually slid on its casters backwards across the carpet. He scoffed loudly.

"All this time I've been kidding myself. I thought we could get over this, I thought we would struggle on." He said, his voice singing with amazement. Sarah shook her head. "That's it? Howard's won." He said, throwing his hands into the air, allowing them to land loudly on the arms of the chair. He threw himself up from the seat, turning as soon as he was of the correct posture, then sandwiched his nose between his thumb and index finger. She sighed loudly.

"No, he hasn't. If he'd *really* won, we'd stay together. We'd destroy each other. But that isn't going to happen. We're saving ourselves. That's a win for us in my book." She concluded, taking a final sip from the wine glass. She placed the empty thing down on the coffee table, then rubbed the thumb and index finger of her right hand across the warm, gold ring on her left ring finger; she observed it for a moment, considering; then, deciding, that it was the right thing to do, she slipped it over her the joins of her finger; her skin did not drag, for she had become so thin from the ordeal of the last month or so that it was amazing that her wedding ring had not slipped off already. "I'm going to pack some bags. Ashley has said she'll put me up for as long as I need." Ashley, her sister in the city. Gary did not turn; she gave him opportunity to do so.

With as much conversation, she moved back towards the coffee table and dropped the ring into the bowl of the glass. The resounding clink of it settling against the glass rang out and met Gary's ears uncomfortably; he knew exactly what she had done.

She paused, looked at the ring sitting sadly in the residue left in the glass for a moment, then raised her head; by now, she had stopped crying; her resolve was strong enough to give her the confidence to stop. She moved slowly across the room to Gary, who still had not moved. She placed her now naked hand upon his shoulder, held it for a moment, expecting him to make a remark or do something, but he did not.

With that, she turned away and walked slowly through the door to the hallway. Gary listened for the sound of her receding steps as she marched up the stairs; he sighed heavily, then raised his head and turned around; he finally saw the ring at the bottom of the glass. He moved over to it, his feet falling silently on the plush carpet; he gripped the glass by the narrow stalk and lifted it so that the base of the bowl was level with his eyes; he peered at the ring, which was distorted and wavy from the spherical shape of the glass.

He breathed in, then out again. Finally, and with one last explosion of rage that lasted but a millisecond, he threw the glass at the wall; it exploded into a million pieces, becoming a dangerous mist of tiny particles; the ring bounced away somewhere, he did not see where, and a small trickle of residual wine slithered like a snail trail down the wallpaper, soiling the once vivid colour.

He cried out with frustration, slamming his fists upon the headrest of the armchair, sending the cushions bouncing from it and onto the floor. Upstairs, Sarah heard the commotion and decided to herself that she had made the right decision.

-45-
The Other Half

Sandy pushed the wooden door open; it was old and creaky, but nonetheless functional. The room beyond was dark and gloomy; the curtains across the room were drawn and no lights were switched on; a false, clinical light spilled in from the corridor to the inside, illuminating ghostly shapes within; a double bed, a desk and a mirror leapt out to her immediately.

As her eyes became accustomed to the gloom, she espied the purple carpet, cheerful welcome signs on everything and the cheapest-looking hairdryer she had ever set eyes on hanging limply from a plastic holder on the wall; the room did not scream quality.

"So this is home." She said, sighing her words; the officer to her left, who was stood with her hands clenched in front of her and her arms crossing her body, replied after a moment.

"I'm sorry, this is the best we can do for you right now. We're going to look at moving you somewhere more permanent by the end of the week." She said, professionally; Sandy scoffed loudly.

"I have a home. I don't want to be relocated. Especially seeing as you've seized most of my belongings." She said, sternly; she gripped the suitcase by the extended handle and stepped into the room. The officer followed her, flipping the switch that illuminated the hotel suite in a flood of bright, pale yellow light. The suitcase rolled silently across the carpet, and as she could now see more of her surroundings, Sandy warmed to the space. "It's not too bad, I suppose." She released the handle, allowing the suitcase to stand on its own in the middle of the room; she spun about once, then twice; with each rotation, she became aware of more amenities; she saw the door to her en-suite bathroom; a desk with a single chair, both in front of another mirror by the window, with a multitude of condiments and coffees scattered on the table.

"As I say, we'll have sorted out a more permanent location for you by the end of the week." The officer repeated, also stepping into the now occupied home; Sandy sat down onto the bed, testing the comfort the mattress supplied. "I'm sorry we have to move you like this; we'll be releasing your belongings to you when they've been cleared. We're not sure how long that will take." The officer resumed. Sandy sighed loudly; the officer smiled and chuckled. "I'm sorry. You're not a robot, we need to stop treating folks like one." She said. Sandy smiled a somewhat reluctant grin.

"It's alright, it's your job. I get it. Howard was always playing a part with people. He was always so eloquent, so well-spoken. But get him in private, he was just like everyone else." Sandy mused. The officer chuckled. Sandy then jumped to her feet and clapped her hands together. "I hope you don't mind if I get unpacked?" She said, rubbing her clasped hands together. The officer gestured with her hand in the affirmative; with that, Sandy began to busy herself with the suitcase; she hoisted the heavy-looking thing onto the bed, allowed it to bounce, then unzipped the front panel.

"Well if there's nothing else I can help you with, I just need to go through a few housekeeping things with you." The officer said, moving further into the room; she perched herself on the end of the bed and remarked aloud at how comfortable it was.

"Could be a bit firmer for me." Sandy replied.

"If that's how you like it." The officer chuckled. "Erm, yes, so I just need to explain the next steps to you. So, as I say, you'll be here 'til the end of the week, then we'll move you. We're looking at getting you a nice little cottage for rent outside the city. By then, we should have your belongings cleared for release, but we'll keep you up-to-date with any and all holds we have to keep in place on things we need." She began, reeling off a mental list she had tried her best to memorise.

Sandy moved over to the cupboard with a handful of clothes; it was more or less all she could pick up in the hurry she had been taken from her home in.

"What about the rest of my clothes? I know I won't be going out to parties anytime soon, but I could do with a few more bits than what I managed to bring." She asked, sweetly. The officer glanced up at her.

"Your clothes should be fine for release already. I'll be in touch with our investigators and have them deliver any items you want, either here or wherever you end up next. You have, of course, our direct number should you need anything in the meantime. Just in case, here's a full information card, I'll just put it here." The officer said, fishing a crisp white card from her breast pocket; with it, she moved across the room and slipped it carefully between two mugs, securely enough that it would not fall over but obvious enough that it would be noticed whenever Sandy passed it. "Now,

Willow | Sam Bateson

I think that's it. Feel free to go for breakfast and dinner daily, the hotel will be reimbursed by our program loan, so don't worry about that expenditure. If there's anything else you need, ring either us or have the hotel staff get in touch. We're available twenty-four, seven."

"Thank you." Sandy, returning to her suitcase, which was perhaps a little oversized for the number of items within it. "I'm sorry to be blunt, but I'm a little tired after everything. I'm sure I'll be in touch if I have any questions." Sandy sounded stern but did not mean to be; the officer nodded, perhaps somewhat despondently.

"Yes. Yes, sorry, I'll get out of your hair." Said the officer, who looked about then jumped from the bed to her feet. "If there's anything you need, any support or any questions, call us. We'll be happy to help." She explained, backing past the corridor that the en-suite bathroom formed against the opposite wall. Sandy smiled sweetly, though a little exhaustedly. The officer responded in kind, before turning and leaving the room entirely, closing the door with a tactile.

Finally, and for the first time in many years, Sandy was completely alone. She did not have Howard, his stories of conquest over his student subordinates; no more police swarming around her or her home; her life was now a hotel room and seven sets of clothes. Never in her wildest dreams did she expect any of what had happened to her; how could Howard have done it to her? Not just what he had done to Willow, but also to herself. She fumbled with some socks for a moment, before resting a hand inside the suitcase to support her, as she covered her eyes with her free hand; she clenched her face forcefully so as to waylay the forthcoming tears, but it was no use. They came thick and fast.

You bastard. What made things worse was that the police could not give her all of the details of his confession; she knew she was about to learn things she could not imagine him doing. That was somehow worse; the feeling of the unknown she was about to be wise to.

She gathered her thoughts and regained her composure; that was all in the future. If things were about to get worse, she needed to enjoy the now. She dried her eyes with a half-hearted wipe with her fingers, then peered at the lights above her; *damn artificial light*. She moved around the bed, manoeuvring between it and the desk to get to the window, which was obscured completely by a long set of drapes. She approached them with extended arms and grabbed the sheets with a firm grip. Pulling them aside, she allowed natural light to cascade in, filling the room with a warmth that she suddenly realised had been missing from her life. She looked out on a world that was new; she was five stories up, looking out on a sea of grey buildings, each well-constructed, but the same as all of the others; it was a far cry from the life she had lived on the affluent street that she only just now realised was probably a front; a façade Howard had been corralling for longer than she could remember.

It was a new world out there. It was a new world she could not wait to live in.

-46-
Case Closed

Phillips sat alone. It was a rare moment of solitude for him and was substantially different from the hustle and bustle of police work. It was the middle of the day, and the sun was high in the sky; he was not even disturbed by shadows and the world about him was quiet and still, disturbed here and there by a contemplative twittering from the plethora of birds in the trees that shuffled and waved in the light breeze. He peered at the houses opposite the park, which was behind the bench he was sat upon.

His view was disturbed ever and again by a number of vehicles which passed him, oblivious to him even being there. He was in his own little world, taking in the environment in a shower of peace and calmness he had missed for the last several weeks.

A bird flew close to his face, in a sweeping arc he did not see the beginning of; he watched it flit here and there, before it settled upon the chimney stacks of the houses opposite, twittering and bouncing its head, surveying the surroundings it so commanded.

The rumble of a slowing engine caught his ear; Phillips barely noticed it at first until it was so loud that he could hear little else; he turned his head a few degrees to see the approaching vehicle; it was dressed in a high visibility jacket, and was emblazoned with the word *POLICE* down the side and written in reverse on the nearly level bonnet. He chuckled. He could not see the occupants due to the harsh shadow cast by the roof of the car disguising everybody within.

The first face he recognised was Grisham, who left the car first; he stood erect, closing the door behind him. He smiled cheerfully, then started towards him along the long, winding path from the pavement to the park bench; Phillips had plenty of time to enjoy his alone time just a little more, though he nonetheless returned a smile and continued to look around. He closed his eyes; his sunglasses were not doing much good.

"They suit you." Grisham said, pointing and arriving before him at last.

"They're shite." Phillips replied, prodding them with a lean finger. "What can I do for you, Grisham?" He looked up, shielding his eyes with the dark shade his raised hand provided.

"Nothing. You've lost weight." Chuckled the Superintendent.

"I've lost it, you've found it." Phillips chuckled, pointing.

"You cheeky bastard." Grisham, with faux indignance. He chuckled too, sitting down on the bench beside Phillips. "I haven't heard from you for a while. Thought you'd fallen out with me." Came the sarcastic continuation of the conversation. Phillips guffawed, and removed his shades.

"I've liked the solitude. It doesn't work if you go about talking to people." Grisham laughed at that. "Besides, I needed time to think about your proposal." Phillips continued; Grisham suddenly became serious.

"That's why I wanted to see you. And?" He quizzed, staring directly at him. Phillips sighed deeply.

"I can't, Grisham. I know you think I'm the man for the job, but I'm not, I'm sorry."

"I thought you might say that." Grisham sighed loudly too, then continued; "I can't tell you I'm not disappointed. You've proven your worth in the few years I had the pleasure of having you work under me. You'd have made a fine Superintendent." He turned back to Phillips, who he now saw was contemplating something. "You alright? Oh, I'm sorry. I've ruined your little relaxation session." He laughed. "I'll leave you to it."

"No, no, I'm enjoying the company. Look, I'd love to take the promotion. I'm just not ready. I don't think I'll ever be ready; I guess, I keep fooling myself, I keep… thinking I can be impartial, but I'm just pretending." Phillips pressed with his fist to enunciate his point.

"It's okay, Phillips. You don't have to explain yourself. Look, the work we do, it saves lives every day; we just got unlucky with this one. You mustn't feel you've failed." Grisham said; Phillips furrowed his brow.

"I don't?" Confusion filled his answer. Grisham gripped his shoulder;

"I've been there. I know that you're feeling guilty, that you've been humbled by this whole thing. It's perfectly normal; embrace it! How can we better ourselves if we bury our heads in the sand, eh?" Phillips looked deep into Grisham's eyes, considering his words; he came to the realisation that they made sense; they resolved the conflict he had been battling with.

"Thanks, boss." He whispered by way of acknowledging as much. Grisham patted his shoulder, releasing it at last.

"Don't mention it. Look, I've got a meeting, I'll leave you to it. If you can think of anyone to replace me, give me a shout. Otherwise some pencil-pusher city-type will get in." Grisham stood up and glanced at his watch; it was a little after half-twelve. He swung around and swiped Phillips' glasses from his face, quite expertly, between two dextrous digits. In one motion, they were on his own face, and through them, Grisham peered around. "You're right, these are shit." He said, laughing.

"They suit you, actually." Phillips replied, not concerned at all at the theft; on the contrary, it saved him a job of throwing them away. He watched as Grisham moved at pace away from him, back towards the car. "Hey, Grisham!" He called; Grisham turned on his heels, backing away with small steps.

"What?" He called back.

"They're very slimming!" He joked, pointing. Grisham chuckled, silently by the distance. He turned away, slowly, and hastened his step towards the car. The passenger door opened, but Phillips did not notice. Instead, he averted his gaze, peering once more at the houses.

Somebody was stood directly opposite him, frozen, almost in time, on the pavement; she was somewhat incongruously dressed, with tight grey jeans, a black tank top and a long, purple cardigan that was perhaps three sizes too big; the woman gripped the end of the sleeves with clenching fingers. She must have been warm, but evidently, she did not mind the weather. Phillips recognised her immediately.

He nodded, acknowledging Louise's presence. She looked better; her skin was no longer a mottled mess of bruises and scars; a faint flutter of a smile flickered across her face, which he recognised as her signature facial expression, but this time it was somewhat different; it was one genuinely constructed from her emotions, and they were obviously more positive than the last time he had seen her. He smiled back at her, his grin more confident and expressive than her own half-hearted effort; but seeing his face convinced her to try her own confident smile. It was difficult, even painful, to force muscles to contort into shapes they had not taken the form of naturally for years; she managed something of a half-smile that was much more genuine than any he had seen before; seeing hers allowed his to beam more brightly, and he chuckled with joy. His eyes blinked, and in that instant, the smile appeared to fade completely; then, she turned slowly, haltingly, and started walking slowly down the street. She swept a few stray hairs from the side of her head so that now they sat over her ears. He watched her go, walking uncomfortably in her flat plimsolls.

As she vanished into the shade of the trees beyond the end of the street, his smile dropped; he had no reason to maintain it anymore. Then, as if on cue, a soft voice behind him.

"That seat taken?"

He recognised the voice immediately. He turned slowly and looked up at the voice; Fiona stood before him, in plain-clothes.

"Christ, what is this, *This Is Your Life*?" Phillips scoffed, quite amazed that so many people had happened upon him.

"Nice to see you too." Fiona, indignant.

"You know you're supposed to have a big red book, right?" Phillips continued as she walked past him then sat down beside him.

"Erm, I'm fine, thanks for asking." She always knew to take Phillips with a grain of salt.

"I swear to God, if you've dug up my mother and brought her along…!" He chuckled.

"Shut up, will you?" She laughed. Phillips chuckled again.

"When did they let you out?" He asked, turning to her and crossing his arms. Fiona pondered.

"What day are we on, Thursday? About a week ago. I've been convalescing at home."

"Christ, you been reading a thesaurus whilst you were there? 'Convalesce' is quite a big word."

"I can't remember you ever being so insufferable." She chortled.

"Then they must have done something with your brain as well. How did you know where I was?" Phillips asked, not annoyed that he had been found; "I only ask because if anyone else shows up, I'm gonna have to look for the little tracker I've obviously had attached." He looked around his clothing with faux worry.

"Don't be so paranoid, Grisham offered to give me a lift. He drove past here three days ago, then again, the day after and yesterday. We sort of assumed you would be here again today. Entered a little routine, have we?"

"Has he been stalking me? I never saw him!" Phillips, confused.

"Enough with the hysterics, Phillips, it's normal to have a routine."

"I didn't even realise I was being so predictable." He mused; perhaps he would part with this apparent routine and trounce everyone who expected him with regularity. He laughed to himself, but then paused, and sighed.

"Your thoughts are very loud, Phillips Fiona said, noticing his displeasure. He looked at her with a sideways glance. "What's on your mind, then?"

"They found the suit Howard was wearing when he kidnapped Willow. A blazer, with blue stitching and a torn shoulder."

"The blue stitch." Fiona said, nodding her head, knowingly.

"He's been a clever bastard. It was the same colour as the school blazer, he knew we would suspect students before him." Phillips continued. Fiona sighed.

"But we were smarter." She said, looking at him. He stared at her, then turned to face ahead. "That's not all though, is it?"

Phillips sighed again.

"Oh, I don't know, Fiona. I rang Sarah up earlier. She's moving to the city to be with her sister. She's leaving Gary."

"Well, there's some good news out of all of this." Fiona replied, with the vaguest hint of pleasure expressed at the idea.

"That's what I thought. I also apologised to her; I told her I was sorry we didn't properly investigate Stacey's death, and for allowing Howard to go about unchecked. She didn't really say much back to me." He explained. Fiona groaned apologetically.

"Oh, Phillips." She raised her hand and rubbed his cheek with her knuckles. "You've got the world on your shoulders."

"It's not just that, though."

"Oh?"

"I've been thinking about this promotion Grisham's offered me." He confessed. She scoffed at him.

"Oh, come on, Phillips! Even I knew you wouldn't take it, the instant he offered you it." He peered at her with the same suspicious glance. "It's no great surprise you couldn't say yes."

"It's not just that, though." He continued, slapping his hands upon his thighs. "I've been thinking, for a while now, that I can't cope with this kind of thing. I'm... I'm thinking of quitting the force." He said; then a pause; by now he was not looking at Fiona, but he realised almost immediately that her eyes were boring into the side of his head.

"And that's what you want? To quit the force?"

"Not particularly. But I don't think I can honestly carry on. This town is too small; it might sound weird, but I think if we were crime central, I might be used to it. But nothing prepared me for this." He said, lifting his hands to his face and rubbing his eyes with tender fingertips.

"Trust me, Phillips, this hasn't been easy on any of us. If there was another way, I'd try and convince you, but I somehow doubt you're going to change your mind." Fiona hissed, scratching her nose with her thumb. "If you're prepared to step away, then do."

"What about you?" Phillips asked, turning to her. "You going to stay?"

"Definitely. If the last month has taught me anything, it's that there's more out there; there's always another story, another crime. I doubt anything will ever be as taxing as this. I'll miss having you around, Phillips, I won't deny. I mean, you did a pretty good job of piecing this whole thing together with not much to go on."

"I can't take all of the glory, though. I lack the sympathetic touch that comes naturally to you. This was a team effort; we've all had a hand in this." Phillips sighed again. Fiona sat back in the chair; it wobbled slightly, for it was not affixed to the floor.

"I would argue everyone had a hand in what happened to Willow, somehow. So I wouldn't bet on the joys of teamwork." She hissed, seriously; Phillips turned to her, somewhat perplexed.

"I can't even think how that conclusion is supposed to cheer me up." He said, quietly, shaking his head.

"It isn't. That's the grim reality of this town. You're better off escaping from it; every punch is stronger, here, because they're more infrequent."

"You should put that to the mayor, it would make a nice town motto. It'll sound lovely in Latin." Phillips said, facetiously. Fiona did not reply at all, even with noises.

For a few moments, the pair sat in silence, each alone with their thoughts; Phillips considering his rejection of the proposal, Fiona thinking about what would happen next.

"Look, I'm gonna have to go. Got to have my dressings changed." She said, patting her torso. Phillips smiled; with that, she pushed herself up from the chair, slowly so as not to tear her stitches.

"You okay?" Phillips asked, raising a hand to steady her; she raised her own in protest.

"Fine, thanks. Look, I'll be alright. You take it easy, yeah?" She said, reassuring him; he nodded and raised his arm again to dismiss her worries.

"I will, you too." He said, as she patted his shoulder with an unwavering hand; he raised his hand to hers and gripped it in a fashion that made him believe he would never see her again, or some other drastic change.

They exchanged nods and allowed their brains to communicate with the language of their bodies. He smiled at her, then she at him, then she stepped past him and made her way back up the park path to the pavement. She did not stop to look back at him as she moved; her strong strides reassured him that she would be alright; she was a tough cookie and could take care of herself.

It was in that moment, that Phillips had a brilliant idea. His hands dove into his pocket and fished out his phone, whose screen was alive in a moment; he tapped on the 'phone' app icon and dialled a number with a superb dexterity. Once the speaker was to his ear, he listened for the muffled beeps of a ringing line; one, two, then three bleeps followed by a voice that was barely audible;

"Phillips, yeah?" Came the hollow voice.

"Grisham, you busy?" Phillips said, quickly.

"Just on the road, but I can talk. What is it?"

"About that promotion; you still looking for somebody?" Phillips continued, so fast that his words were barely understandable.

"Yeah, why, changed your mind?"

"Not changed it, no. Made it up, yes. I have a candidate for you."

"Yeah? Who? I'll put it to the board."

As Phillips conversed, he peered after Fiona, who wandered away, completely oblivious to the career Phillips was concocting for her.

So that was the end. Phillips sat on that bench for a particularly long time that day, irregularly so. Very few people who passed him even registered his presence; so innocuous was his appearance. If anyone had any idea what was going on in his little world, they would maybe have stopped and asked him;

"How are you feeling today?"

Willow | Sam Bateson

Willow

Sam Bateson

Need Help?

If you are struggling with depression, or are experiencing suicidal thoughts, there are things you can do:

Tell someone. Let your friends or family know how you are feeling. Sharing a burden allows others to support you. If you are uncomfortable talking to close friends or family, call your GP and ask for an emergency consultation or appointment. Call 111 for out of hours support.

If you do not feel like talking, coping mechanisms are important. Think about getting through today, not about the future. Find a safe place. Remember, drugs and alcohol are not solutions. Surround yourself with supportive friends, family or whoever you feel safe with and are comfortable around. If you have something you enjoy doing or experiencing, do that to distract yourself. Avoid triggers.

If you have concerns for someone who has expressed depressive or suicidal thoughts, ensure that they are not alone. Do not tell them to cheer up, as doing so may not be easy for them. Be compassionate and encourage them to talk about their feelings; understand that a problem for them might not be a problem to you, but they still need your support. If you believe someone is in immediate danger, ensure they are safely with someone or allow them to talk about their feelings with you. Compassion and reassurance are important.

The following services are available if you have any concerns, either for yourself or for someone you know:

Samaritans: 116 123
Text Shout to 85258
MindInfoline: 0300 123 3393
Campaign Against Living Miserably (CALM): 0800 58 58 58

On average, 800, 000 people a year commit suicide globally. Even one person is too many.

More from Sam Bateson

Midnight
After Dark
First Light

The Into Darkness Trilogy: The Supplements
The Into Darkness Trilogy: The Complete Trilogy

Woodland

www.sambateson.wixsite.com/sambateson

www.sambateson.wixsite.com/sambateson
Copyright © 2020, Sam Bateson

Printed in Great Britain
by Amazon

47458415R00170